DARWIN'S CHILDREN

DARWIN'S CHILDREN

GREG BEAR

BALLANTINE BOOKS

NEW YORK

A Del Rey® Book
Published by The Random House Ballantine Publishing Group

Copyright © 2003 by Greg Bear

www.delreydigital.com

Library of Congress Cataloging-in-Publication Data
Bear, Greg, 1951–
Darwin's children / by Greg Bear.
p. cm.
ISBN 0-345-44835-9
1. Mutation (Biology)—Fiction.   2. Parent and child—Fiction.   3. Social control—Fiction.   4. Children—Fiction.   5. Virginia—Fiction.   6. Viruses—Fiction.   I. Title.
PS3552.E157 D39 2003
813'.54—dc21   2002036669

Manufactured in the United States of America

First Edition: April 2003

10   9   8   7   6   5   4   3   2   1

TO MY FATHER,
DALE FRANKLIN BEAR

DARWIN'S CHILDREN

PART ONE

SHEVA + 12

"America's a cruel country. There's a whole lot of people would just as soon stomp you like an ant. Listen to talk radio. Plenty of dummies, damned few ventriloquists."

"There's a wolf snarl behind the picnics and Boy Scout badges."

"They want to kill our kids. Lord help us all."
                                        —Anonymous Postings, ALT.NEWCHILD.FAM

"Citing 'severe threats to national security,' Emergency Action this week has requested of the U.S. Justice Department the authority to hack and shut down SHEVA parent Web sites and even e-journals and newspapers guilty of spreading inaccurate information—'lies'—against EMAC and the U.S. government. Some parent advocacy groups complain this is already the norm. Mid-level Justice Department officials have passed the request along to the office of the attorney general for further legal review, according to sources who wish to remain anonymous.

"Some legal experts say that even legitimate newspaper sites could be hacked or shut down without warning should approval be granted, and the granting of such approval is likely in itself to be kept secret."
                                        —Seattle *Times-PI Online*

"God had nothing to do with making these children. I don't care what you think about creationism or evolution, we're on our own now."
                                        —Owen Withey, *Creation Science News*

1

Morning lay dark and quiet around the house. Mitch Rafelson stood with coffee cup in hand on the back porch, dopey from just three hours of sleep. Stars still pierced the sky. A few persistent moths and bugs buzzed around the porch light. Raccoons had been at the garbage can in back, but had left, whickering and scuffling, hours ago, discouraged by lengths of chain.

The world felt empty and new.

Mitch put his cup in the kitchen sink and returned to the bedroom. Kaye lay in bed, still asleep. He adjusted his tie in the mirror above the dresser. Ties never looked right on him. He grimaced at the way his suit hung on his wide shoulders, the gap around the collar of his white shirt, the length of sleeve visible beyond the cuff of his coat.

There had been a row the night before. Mitch and Kaye and Stella, their daughter, had sat up until two in the morning in the small bedroom trying to talk it through. Stella was feeling isolated. She wanted, *needed* to be with young people like her. It was a reasonable position, but they had no choice.

Not the first time, and likely not the last. Kaye always approached these events with studied calm, in contrast to Mitch's evasion and excuses. Of course they were excuses. He had no answers to Stella's questions, no real response to her arguments. They both knew she ultimately needed to be with her own kind, to find her own way.

Finally, too much, Stella had stomped off and slammed the door to her room. Kaye had started crying. Mitch had held her in bed and she had gradually slipped into twitching sleep, leaving him staring at the darkened ceiling, tracking the play of lights from a truck grumbling down the country road outside, wondering, as always, if the truck would come up their drive, come for their daughter, come to claim bounty or worse.

He hated the way he looked in what Kaye called his Mr. Smith duds—as in *Mr. Smith Goes to Washington*. He lifted one hand and rotated it, studying the palm, the long, strong fingers, wedding ring—though he and Kaye had never gotten a license. It was the hand of a hick.

He hated to drive into the capital, through all the checkpoints, using his congressional appointment pass. Slowly moving past all the army trucks full of soldiers, deployed to stop yet another desperate parent from setting off another suicide bomb. There had been three such blasts since spring.

And now, Riverside, California.

Mitch walked to the left side of the bed. "Good morning, love," he whispered. He stood for a moment, watching his woman, his wife. His eyes moved along the sleeve of her pajama top, absorbing every wrinkle in the rayon, every silken play of pre-dawn light, down to slim hands, curled fingers, nails bitten to the quick.

He bent to kiss her cheek and pulled the covers over her arm. Her eyes fluttered open. She brushed the back of his head with her fingers. "G'luck," she said.

"Back by four," he said.

"Love you." Kaye pushed into the pillow with a sigh.

Next stop was Stella's room. He never left the house without making the rounds, filling his eyes and memory with pictures of wife and daughter and house, as if, should they all be taken away, should this be the last time, he could replay the moment. Fat good it would do.

Stella's room was a neat jumble of preoccupations and busyness in lieu of having friends. She had pinned a farewell photo of their disreputable orange tabby on the wall over her bed. Tiny stuffed animals spilled from her cedar chest, beady eyes mysterious in the shadows. Old paperback books filled a small case made of pine boards that Mitch and Stella had hammered together last winter. Stella enjoyed working with her father, but Mitch had noticed the distance growing between them for a couple of years now.

Stella lay on her back in a bed that had been too short for over a year. At eleven, she was almost as tall as Kaye and beautiful in her slender, round-faced way, skin pale copper and tawny gold in the glow of the nightlight, hair dark brown with reddish tints, same texture as Kaye's and not much longer.

Their family had become a triangle, still strong, but with the three sides stretching each month. Neither Mitch nor Kaye could give Stella what she really needed.

And each other?

He looked up to see the orange line of sunrise through the filmy white curtains of Stella's window. Last night, cheeks freckling with anger, Stella had demanded to know when they would let her out of the house on her own, without makeup, to be with kids her own age. Her kind of kids. It had been two years since her last "play date."

Kaye had done wonders with home teaching, but as Stella had pointed out last night, over and over again, with rising emotion, *"I am not like you!"* For the first time, Stella had formally proclaimed: *"I am not human!"*

But of course she was. Only fools thought otherwise. Fools, and monsters, and their daughter.

Mitch kissed Stella on the forehead. Her skin was warm. She did not wake up. Stella as she slept smelled like her dreams, and now she smelled the way tears taste, tang of salt and sadness.

"Got to go," he murmured. Stella's cheeks produced waves of golden freckles. Mitch smiled.

Even asleep, his daughter could say good-bye.

2

Center for Ancient Viral Studies, United States Army
Medical Research Institute of Infectious Diseases: USAMRIID

FORT DETRICK, MARYLAND

"People died, Christopher," Marian Freedman said. "Isn't that enough to make us cautious, even a little crazy?"

Christopher Dicken walked beside her, tilting on his game leg, staring down the concrete corridor to the steel door at the end. His National Cancer Institute ID badge still poked from his jacket pocket. He clutched a large bouquet of roses and lilies. The two had been engaged in debate from the front desk through four security checkpoints.

"Nobody's diagnosed a case of Shiver for a decade," he said. "And nobody ever got sick from the children. Isolating them is politics, not biology."

Marian took his day pass and ran it through the scanner. The steel door opened to a horizontal spread of sunglass-green access tubes, suspended like a hamster maze over a two-acre basin of raw gray concrete. She held out her hand, letting him go first. "You know about Shiver firsthand."

"It went away in a couple of weeks," Dicken said.

"It lasted five weeks, and it damned near killed you. Don't bullshit *me* with your virus hunter bravado."

Dicken stepped slowly onto the catwalk, having difficulty judging depth with just one eye, and that covered by a thick lens. "The man beat his wife, Marian. She was sick with a tough pregnancy. Stress and pain."

"Right," Marian said. "Well, that certainly wasn't true with Mrs. Rhine, was it?"

"Different problem," Dicken admitted.

Freedman smiled with little humor. She sometimes revealed biting wit, but did not seem to understand the concept of humor. Duty, hard work, discovery, and dignity filled the tight circle of her life. Marian Freedman was a devout feminist and had never married, and she was one of the best and most dedicated scientists Dicken had ever met.

Together, they marched north on the aluminum catwalk. She adjusted her pace to match his. Tall steel cylinders waited at the ends of the access tubes, shaft housings for elevators to the chambers beneath the seamless concrete slab. The cylinders wore big square "hats," high-temperature gas-fired ovens that would sterilize any air escaping from the facilities below.

"Welcome to the house that Augustine built. How is Mark, anyway?"

"Not happy, last time I saw him," Dicken said.

"Why am I not surprised? Of course, I should be charitable. Mark moved me up from studying chimps to studying Mrs. Rhine."

Twelve years before, Freedman had headed a primate lab in Baltimore, during the early days when the Centers for Disease Control had launched the task force investigating Herod's plague. Mark Augustine, then director of the CDC and Dicken's boss, had hoped to secure extra funding from Congress during a fiscal dry spell. Herod's, thought to have caused thousands of hideously malformed miscarriages, had seemed like a terrific goad.

Herod's had quickly been traced to the transfer of one of thousands of Human Endogenous Retroviruses—HERV—carried by all people within their DNA. The ancient virus, newly liberated, mutated and infectious, had been promptly renamed SHEVA, for Scattered Human Endogenous Viral Activation.

In those days, viruses had been assumed to be nothing more than selfish agents of disease.

"She's been looking forward to seeing you," Freedman said. "How long since your last visit?"

"Six months," Dicken said.

"My favorite pilgrim, paying his respects to our viral Lourdes," Freedman said. "Well, she's a wonder, all right. And something of a saint, poor dear."

Freedman and Dicken passed junctions with tubes branching southwest, northeast, and northwest to other shafts. Outside, the summer morning was warming rapidly. The sun hung just above the horizon, a subdued greenish ball. Cool air pulsed around them with a breathy moan.

They came to the end of the main tube. An engraved Formica placard to the right of the elevator door read, "MRS. CARLA RHINE." Freedman punched the single white button. Dicken's ears popped as the door closed behind them.

SHEVA had turned out to be much more than a disease. Shed only by males in committed relationships, the activated retrovirus served as a genetic messenger, ferrying complicated instructions for a new kind of birth. SHEVA infected recently fertilized human eggs—in a sense, hijacked them. The Herod's miscarriages were first-stage embryos, called "interim daughters," not much more than specialized ovaries devoted to producing a new set of precisely mutated zygotes.

Without additional sexual activity, the second-stage zygotes implanted and covered themselves with a thin, protective membrane. They survived the abortion of the first embryo and started a new pregnancy.

To some, this had looked like a kind of virgin birth.

Most of the second-stage embryos had gone to term. Worldwide, in two waves separated by four years, three million new children had been born. More than two and a half million of the infants had survived. There was still controversy over exactly who and what they were—a diseased mutation, a subspecies, or a completely new species.

Most simply called them virus children.

"Carla's still cranking them out," Freedman said as the elevator reached the bottom. "She's shed seven hundred new viruses in the last four months. About a third are infectious, negative-strand RNA viruses, potentially real bastards. Fifty-two of them kill pigs within hours. Ninety-one are almost certainly lethal to humans. Another ten can probably kill both pigs and humans." Freedman glanced over her shoulder to see his reaction.

"I know," Dicken said dryly. He rubbed his hip. His leg bothered him when he stood for more than fifteen minutes. The same White House explosion that had taken his eye, twelve years ago, had left him partially disabled. Three rounds of surgery had allowed him to put aside the crutches but not the pain.

"Still in the loop, even at NCI?" Freedman asked.

"Trying to be," he said.

"Thank God there are only four like her."

"She's our fault," he said, and paused to reach down and massage his calf.

"Maybe, but Mother Nature's still a bitch," Freedman said, watching him with her hands on her hips.

A small airlock at the end of the concrete corridor cycled them through to the main floor. They were now fifty feet below ground. A guard in a crisp green uniform inspected their passes and permission papers and compared them with the duty and guest roster at her workstation.

"Please identify," she told them. Both placed their eyes in front of scanners and simultaneously pressed their thumbs onto sensitive plates. A female orderly in hospital greens escorted them to the cleanup area.

Mrs. Rhine was housed in one of ten underground residences, four of them currently occupied. The residences formed the center of the most redundantly secure research facility on Earth. Though Dicken and Freedman would never come any closer than seeing her through a four-inch-thick acrylic window, they would have to go through a whole-body scrub before and after the interview. Before entering the viewing area and staging lab, called the inner station, they would put on special hooded undergarments impregnated with slow-release antivirals, zip up in plastic isolation suits, and attach themselves to positive pressure umbilical hoses.

Mrs. Rhine and her companions at the center never saw real human beings unless they were dressed to resemble Macy's parade balloons.

On leaving, they would stand under a disinfectant shower, then strip down and shower again, scrubbing every orifice. The suits would be soaked and sterilized overnight, and the undergarments would be incinerated.

The four women interned at the facility ate well and exercised regularly. Their quarters—each roughly the size of a two-bedroom apartment—were maintained by automated servants. They had their hobbies—Mrs. Rhine was a great one for hobbies—and access to a wide selection of books, magazines, TV shows, and movies.

Of course, the women were becoming more and more eccentric.

"Any tumors?" Dicken asked.

"Official question?" Freedman asked.

"Personal," Dicken said.

"No," Freedman said. "But it's only a matter of time."

Dicken handed the flowers to the orderly. "Don't boil them," he said.

"I'll process them myself," the orderly promised with a smile. "She'll get them before you're done here." She passed them two sealed white paper bags containing their undergarments and showed them the way to the scrub stalls, then to the tall cabinets that held the isolation suits, as glossy and green as dill pickles.

Christopher Dicken was legendary even at Fort Detrick. He had tracked Mrs. Rhine to a motel in Bend, Oregon, where she had fled after the death of her husband and daughter. He had talked her into opening the door to the small, spare room, and had spent twenty minutes with her, unprotected, while Emergency Action vans gathered in the parking lot.

He had done all this, despite having already contracted Shiver from a woman in Mexico the year before. That woman, a plump female in her forties, seven months pregnant, had been severely beaten by her husband. A small, stupid, jackal-like man with a long criminal record, he had kept her alone and without medical help in a small room at the back of a shabby apartment for three months. Her baby had been born dead.

Something in the woman had produced a defensive viral response, enhanced by SHEVA, and her husband had suffered the consequences. In his darkest early morning vigils of pacing, tending phantom twitches and pains in his leg, alone and wide awake, Dicken had often thought of the husband's death as natural justice, and his own exposure and subsequent illness as accidental blow-by—an occupational hazard.

Mrs. Rhine's case was different. Her problems had been caused by an interplay of human and natural forces no one could have possibly predicted.

In the late nineties, she had suffered from end-stage renal disease and had been the recipient of an experimental xenotransplant—a pig kidney. The transplant had worked. Three years later, Mrs. Rhine had contracted SHEVA from her husband. This had stimulated an enthusiastic release of PERV—Porcine Endogenous Retrovirus—from the pig cells. Before Mrs. Rhine had been diagnosed and isolated at Fort Detrick, her pig and human retroviruses had shuffled genes—recombined—with latent herpes simplex virus and had begun to express, with diabolical creativity, a Pandora's box of long-dormant diseases, and many new ones.

Ancient viral tool kits, Mark Augustine had called them, with true prescience.

Mrs. Rhine's husband, newborn daughter, and seven relatives and friends had been infected by the first of her recombined viruses. They had all died within hours.

Of forty-one individuals who had received pig tissue transplants in the United States, and had subsequently been exposed to SHEVA, the women at the center were the only survivors. Perversely, they were immune to the viruses they produced. Isolated as they were, the four women never caught colds or flu. That made them extraordinary subjects for research—deadly but invaluable.

Mrs. Rhine was a virus hunter's dream, and whenever Dicken did dream about her, he awoke in a cold sweat.

He had never told anyone that his approach to Mrs. Rhine in that motel room in Bend had had less to do with courage than with a reckless indifference. Back then, he simply had not cared whether he lived or died. His entire world had been turned upside down, and everything he thought he knew had been subjected to a harsh and unmerciful glare.

Mrs. Rhine was special to him because they had both been through hell.

"Suit up," Freedman said. They took off their clothes in separate stalls and hung them in lockers. Small video screens mounted beside the multiple shower heads in each stall reminded them where and how to scrub.

Freedman helped Dicken pull his undergarment over his stiff leg. Together, they tugged on thick plastic gloves, then slipped their hands into the mitts of the pickle-green suits. This left them with all the manual dexterity of fur seals. Fingerless suits were tougher, more secure, and cheaper, and nobody expected visitors to the inner station to do delicate lab work. Small plastic hooks on the thumb side of each glove allowed them to pull up the other's rear zipper, then strip away a plastic cover on the inner side of a sticky seam. A special pinching tool pressed the seam over the zipper.

This took twenty minutes.

They walked through a second set of showers, then through another airlock. Confined within the almost airless hood, Dicken felt perspiration bead his face and slide down his underarms. Beyond the second airlock, each hooked the other to their umbilicals—the familiar plastic hoses suspended on clanking steel hooks from an overhead track.

Their suits plumped with pressure. The flow of fresh cool air revived him.

The last time, at the end of his visit, Dicken had emerged from his suit with a nosebleed. Freedman had saved him from weeks of quarantine by diagnosing and stanching the bleeding herself.

"You're good for the inner," the orderly told them through a bulkhead speaker.

The last hatch slid open with a silky whisper. Dicken walked ahead of Freedman into the inner station. In sync, they turned to the right and waited for the steel window blinds to ratchet up.

The few incidents of Shiver had started at least a hundred crash courses in medical and weapons-related research. If abused women, and women given xenotransplants, could all by themselves design and express thousands of killer plagues, what could a generation of virus children do?

Dicken clenched his jaw, wondering how much Carla Rhine had changed in sixth months.

Something of a saint, poor dear.

3

Office of Special Reconnaissance

L E E S B U R G ,   V I R G I N I A

Mark Augustine walked with a cane down a long underground tunnel, following a muscular red-headed woman in her late thirties. Big steam pipes lined the tunnel on both sides and the air in the tunnel was warm. Conduits of fiber optic cables and wires were bundled and cradled in long steel trays slung from the concrete ceiling, and away from the pipes.

The woman wore a dark green silk suit with a red scarf and running shoes, gray with outdoor use. Augustine's hard-soled Oxfords scuffed and tapped as he trailed several steps behind, sweating. The woman showed no consideration for his slower pace.

"Why am I here, Rachel?" he asked. "I'm tired. I've been traveling. There's work to do."

"Something's developing, Mark. I'm sure you'll love it," Browning called back over her shoulder. "We've finally located a long-lost colleague."

"Who?"

"Kaye Lang," Browning replied.

Augustine grimaced. He sometimes pictured himself as a toothless old tiger in a government filled with vipers. He was perilously close to becoming a figurehead, or worse, a clown over a drop tank. His only remaining survival tactic was a passive appearance of being outpaced by young and vicious career bureaucrats attracted to Washington by the smell of incipient tyranny.

The cane helped. He had broken his leg in a fall in the shower last year. If they thought he was weak and stupid, that gave him an advantage.

The maximum depth of Washington's soulless vacancy was the proud personal record of Rachel Browning. A specialist in law enforcement data management, married to a telecom executive in Connecticut whom she rarely saw, Browning had begun as Augustine's assistant in EMAC—Emergency Action—seven years ago, had moved into foreign corporate interdiction at the National Security Agency and had finally jumped aisle again to head the intelligence and enforcement branch of EMAC. She had started the Special Reconnaissance Office—SRO—which specialized in tracking dissidents and subversives and infiltrating radical parent groups. SRO shared its satellites and other equipment with the National Reconnaissance Office.

Once upon a time, in a different lifetime, Browning had been very useful to him.

"Kaye Lang Rafelson is not someone you just lure and bust," Augustine said. "Her daughter is not just another notch on the handle of our butterfly net. We have to be very careful with all of them."

Browning rolled her eyes. "She's not off limits according to any directive I've received. I certainly do not regard her as a sacred cow. It's been seven years since she was on Oprah."

"If you ever feel the need to learn political science, much less public relations, I know of some excellent undergraduate courses at City College," Augustine said.

Browning smiled her patent leather smile once again, bulletproof, certainly proof against a toothless tiger.

They arrived at the elevator together. The door opened. A Marine with a holstered nine millimeter greeted them with hard gray eyes.

Two minutes later, they stood in a small private office. Four plasma displays like a Japanese screen rose on steel stands beyond the central desk. The walls were bare and beige, insulated with close-packed, sound-absorbing foam panels.

Augustine hated enclosed spaces. He had come to hate everything he had accomplished in the last eleven years. His entire life was an enclosed space.

Browning took the only seat and laid her hands over a keyboard and trackball. Her fingers danced over the keyboard, and she palmed the track-ball, sucking on her teeth as she watched the monitor. "They're living about a hundred miles south of here," she murmured, focusing on her task.

"I know," Augustine said. "Spotsylvania County."

She looked up, startled, then cocked her head to one side. "How long have you known?"

"A year and a half," Augustine said.

"Why not just take them? Soft heart, or soft brain?"

Augustine dismissed that with a blink revealing neither opinion nor passion. He felt his face tighten. Soon his cheeks would begin to hurt like hell, a residual effect from the blast in the basement of the White House, the bomb that had killed the president, nearly killed Augustine, and taken the eye of Christopher Dicken. "I don't see anything."

"The network is still assembling," Browning said. "Takes a few minutes. Little Bird is talking to Deep Eye."

"Lovely toys," he commented.

"They were your idea."

"I've just come back from Riverside, Rachel."

"Oh. How was it?"

"Awful beyond belief."

"No doubt." Browning removed a Kleenex from her small black purse and delicately blew her nose, one nostril at a time. "You sound like someone who wants to be relieved of command."

"You'll be the first to know, I'm sure," Augustine said.

Rachel pointed to the monitor, snapped her fingers, and like magic, a picture formed. "Deep Eye," she said, and they looked down upon a small patch of Virginia countryside flocked with thick green trees and pierced by a winding, two-lane road. Deep Eye's lens zoomed in to show the roof of a house, a driveway with a single small truck, a large backyard surrounded by tall oaks.

"And . . . here's Little Bird," Browning's voice turned husky with an almost erotic approval.

The view switched to that of a drone swooping up beside the house like a dragonfly. It hovered near a small frame window, then adjusted exposure in the morning brightness to reveal the head and shoulders of a young girl, rubbing her face with a washcloth.

"Recognize her?" Browning asked.

"The last picture we have is from four years ago," Augustine said.

"That must be from an inexcusable lack of trying."

"You're right," Augustine admitted.

The girl left the bathroom and vanished from view. Little Bird rose to hover at an altitude of fifty feet and waited for instructions from the unseen pilot, probably in the back of a remoter truck a few miles from the house.

"I think that's Stella Nova Rafelson," Browning mused, tapping her lower lip with a long red fingernail.

"Congratulations. You're a voyeur," Augustine said.

"I prefer 'paparazzo.' "

The view on the screen veered and dropped to take in a slender female figure stepping off the front porch and onto the scattered gravel walkway. She was carrying something small and square in one hand.

"Definitely our girl," Browning said. "Tall for her age, isn't she?"

Stella walked with rigid determination toward the gate in the wire fence. Little Eye dropped and magnified to a three-quarter view. The resolution was remarkable. The girl paused at the gate, swung it halfway open, then glanced over her shoulder with a frown and a flash of freckles.

Dark freckles, Augustine thought. *She's nervous.*

"What is she up to?" Browning asked. "Looks like she's going for a walk. And not to school, I'm thinking."

Augustine watched the girl amble along the dirt path beside the old asphalt road, out in the country, as if taking a morning stroll.

"Things are moving kind of fast," Browning said. "We don't have anyone on site. I don't want to lose the opportunity, so I've alerted a stringer."

"You mean a bounty hunter. That's not wise."

Browning did not react.

"I do not want this, Rachel," Augustine said. "It's the wrong time for this kind of publicity, and certainly for these tactics."

"It's not your choice, Mark," Browning said. "I've been told to bring her in, and her parents as well."

"By whom?" Augustine knew that his authority had been sliding of late, perhaps drastically since Riverside. But he had never imagined that Riverside would lead to an even more severe crackdown.

"It's a sort of test," Browning said.

The secretary of Health and Human Services shared authority over EMAC with the president. Forces within EMAC wanted to change that and remove HHS from the loop entirely, consolidating their power. Augustine had tried the same thing himself, years ago, in a different job.

Browning took control from the remoter truck and sent Little Bird down the road, buzzing quietly a discreet distance behind Stella Nova Rafelson. "Don't you think Kaye Lang should have kept her maiden name when she married?"

"They never married," Augustine said.

"Well, well. The little bastard."

"Fuck you, Rachel," Augustine said.

Browning looked up. Her face hardened. "And fuck *you*, Mark, for making me do your job."

4

Mrs. Rhine stood in her living room, peering through the thick acrylic pane as if searching for the ghosts of another life. In her late thirties, she was of medium height, with stocky arms and legs but a thin torso, chin strong and pointed. She wore a bright yellow dress and a white blouse with a patchwork vest she had made herself. What they could see of her face between gauze bandages was red and puffy, and her left eye had swollen shut.

Her arms and legs were completely covered in Ace bandages. Mrs. Rhine's body was trying to eliminate trillions of new viruses that could craftily claim they were part of her *self*, from her genome; but the viruses were not making her sick. Her own immune response was the principle cause of her torment.

Someone, Dicken could not remember who, had likened autoimmune disease to having one's body run by House Republicans. A few years in Washington had eerily reinforced the aptness of this comparison.

"Christopher?" Mrs. Rhine called out hoarsely.

The lights in the inner station switched on with a click.

"It's me," Dicken answered, his voice sibilant within the hood.

Mrs. Rhine decorously sidestepped and curtsied, her dress swishing. Dicken saw that she had placed his flowers in a large blue vase, the same vase she had used the last time. "They're beautiful," she said. "White roses. My favorites. They still have some scent. Are you well?"

"I am. And you?"

"Itching is my life, Christopher," she said. "I'm reading *Jane Eyre*. I think, when they come here to make the movie, down here deep in the Earth, as they will, don't you know, that I will play Mr. Rochester's first wife, poor thing." Despite the swelling and the bandages, Mrs. Rhine's smile was dazzling. "Would you call it typecasting?"

"You're more the mousy, inherently lovely type who saves the rugged, half-crazed male from his darker self. You're Jane."

She pulled up a folding chair and sat. Her living room was normal enough, with a normal decor—couches, chairs, pictures on the walls, but no carpeting. Mrs. Rhine was allowed to make her own throw rugs. She also knitted and worked on a loom in another room, away from the windows. She was said to have woven a fairy-tale tapestry involving her husband and infant daughter, but she had never shown it to anyone.

"How long can you stay?" Mrs. Rhine asked.

"As long as you'll put up with me," Dicken said.

"About an hour," Marian Freedman said.

"They gave me some very nice tea," Mrs. Rhine said, her voice losing strength as she looked down at the floor. "It seems to help with my skin. Pity you can't share it with me."

"Did you get my package of DVDs?" Dicken asked.

"I did. I loved *Suddenly, Last Summer*," Mrs. Rhine said, voice rising again. "Katharine Hepburn plays mad so well."

Freedman gave him a dirty look through their hoods. "Are we on a theme here?"

"Hush, Marian," Mrs. Rhine said. "I'm fine."

"I know you are, Carla. You're more sane than I am."

"That is certainly true," Mrs. Rhine said. "But then I don't have to worry about *me*, do I? Honestly, Marian's been good to me. I wish I had known her before. Actually, I wish she'd let me fix her hair."

Freedman lifted an eyebrow, leaning in toward the window so Mrs. Rhine could see her expression. "Ha, ha," she said.

"They really aren't treating me too badly, and I'm passing all my psychological profiles." Mrs. Rhine's face dropped some of the overwrought, elfin look it assumed when she engaged in this kind of banter. "Enough about me. How are the *children* doing, Christopher?"

Dicken detected the slightest hitch in her voice.

"They're doing okay," Dicken said.

Her tone became brittle. "The ones who would have gone to school with my daughter, had she lived. Are they still kept in camps?"

"Mostly. Some are hiding out."

"What about Kaye Lang?" Mrs. Rhine asked. "I'm especially interested in her and her daughter. I read about them in the magazines. I saw her on the Katie Janeway show. Is she still raising her daughter without the government's help?"

"As far as I know," Dicken said. "We haven't kept in touch. She's kind of gone underground."

"You were good friends, I read in the magazines."

"We were."

"You shouldn't lose touch with your friends," Mrs. Rhine said.

"I agree," Dicken said. Freedman listened patiently. She understood Mrs. Rhine with more than clinical thoroughness, and she also understood the two feminine poles of Christopher Dicken's busy but lonely life: Mrs. Rhine, and Kaye Lang, who had first pinpointed and predicted the emergence of SHEVA. Both had touched him deeply.

"Any news on what they're doing inside me, all those viruses?"

"We have a lot to learn," Dicken said.

"You said some of the viruses carry messages. Are they whispering inside me? My pig viruses . . . are they still carrying pig messages?"

"I don't know, Carla."

Mrs. Rhine held out her dress and dropped down in her overstuffed chair, then brushed back her hair with one hand. "*Please,* Christopher. I killed my family. Understanding what happened is the one thing I need in this life. Tell me, even the little stuff, your guesses, your dreams . . . anything."

Freedman nodded. "Good or bad, we tell her all we know," she said. "It's the least she deserves."

In a halting voice, Dicken began to outline what had been learned since his last visit. The science was sharper, progress had been made. He left out the weapons research aspect and focused on the new children.

They were remarkable and in their own way, remarkably beautiful. And that made them a special problem to those they had been designed to replace.

5

"I hear you smell as good as a dog," the young man in the patched denim jacket said to a tall, slender girl with speckled cheeks. He reverently set a six-pack of Millers on the Formica countertop and slapped down a twenty-dollar bill. "Luckies," he told the minimart clerk.

"She doesn't smell *good as* a dog," the second male said with a dull smile. "She smells worse."

"You guys cut it out," the clerk warned, putting away the bill and getting his cigarettes. She was rail thin with pale skin and tormented blonde hair. A haze of stale cigarettes hung around her coffee-spotted uniform.

"We're just talking," the first male said. He wore his hair in a short ponytail tied with a red rubber band. His companion was younger, taller and stooped, long brown hair topped by a baseball cap.

"I'm warning you, no trouble!" the clerk said, her voice as rough as an old road. "Honey, you ignore him, he's just fooling."

Stella pocketed her change and picked up her bottle of Gatorade. She was wearing shorts and a blue tank top and tennis shoes and no makeup. She gave the two men a silent sniff. Her nostrils dimpled. They were in their mid-twenties, paunchy, with fleshy faces and rough hands. Their jeans were stained by fresh paint and they smelled sour and gamy, like unhappy puppies.

They weren't making much money and they weren't very smart. More desperate than some, and quick to suspicion and anger.

"She doesn't look *infeckshus*," the second male said.

"I mean it, guys, she's just a little girl," the clerk insisted, her face going blotchy.

"What's your name?" Stella asked the first male.

"I don't care you should know," he said, then looked to his friend with a cocky smile.

"Leave her be," the clerk warned one more time, worn down. "Honey, you just go home."

The stooped male grabbed his six-pack by its plastic sling and started for the door. "Let's go, Dave."

Dave was working himself up. "She doesn't fucking *belong* here," he said, wrinkling his face. "Why in shit should we put up with this?"

"You stop that language!" the clerk cried. "We get kids in here."

Stella drew herself up to a lanky five feet nine inches and extended her long-fingered hand. "Pleased to meet you, David. I'm Stella," she said.

Dave stared at her hand in disgust. "I wouldn't touch you for ten million dollars. Why ain't you in a *camp*?"

"Dave!" the stooped fellow snapped.

Stella felt the fever scent rise. Her ears tingled. It was cool inside the minimart and hot outside, hot and humid. She had been walking in the sun for half an hour before she had found the Texaco and pushed through the swinging glass doors to buy a drink. She wasn't wearing makeup. The others could see clearly whatever the dapples on her cheeks were doing. So be it. She stood her ground by the counter. She did not want to yield to Dave, and the clerk's halfhearted defense rankled.

Dave picked up his Luckies. Stella liked the smell of tobacco before it was lit but hated the burning stink. She knew that worried men smoked, unhappy men, nervous and under stress. Their knuckles were square and their hands looked like mummy hands from sun and work and tobacco. Stella could learn a lot about people just by a sniff and a glance. "Our little radar," Kaye called her.

"It's nice in here," Stella said, her voice small. She held a small book in front of her as if for protection. "It's cool."

"You are *something*, you know it?" Dave said with a touch of admiration. "An ugly little turd, but brave as a skunk."

Dave's friend stood by the glass doors. The sweat on the man's hand reacted with the steel of the handle and reeked like a steel spoon dipped in vanilla ice cream. Stella could not eat ice cream with a steel spoon because the odor, like fear and madness, made her ill. She used a plastic spoon instead.

"Fuck it, Dave, let's *go*! They'll come get her and maybe they'll take us, too, if we get too close."

"My people aren't really *infeckshus*," Stella said. She stepped toward the man by the counter, long neck craned, head poking forward. "But you never know, Dave."

The clerk sucked in her breath.

Stella had not meant to say that. She had not known she was so mad. She backed off a few inches, wanting to apologize and explain herself, say two things at once, speaking on both sides of her tongue, to make them hear and feel what she meant, but they would not understand; the words, doubled so, would jumble in their heads and only make them angrier.

What came out of Stella's mouth in a soothing alto murmur, her eyes focused on Dave's, was, "Don't worry. It's safe. If you want to beat me up, my blood won't hurt you. I could be your own little Jesus."

The fever-scent did its thing. The glands behind her ears began to pump defensive pheromones. Her neck felt hot.

"Shit," the clerk said, and bumped up against the tall rack of cigarettes behind her.

Dave showed the whites of his eyes like a skittish horse. He veered toward the door, giving her a wide berth, the deliberate smell of her in his nose. She had snuffed the fuse of his anger.

Dave joined his friend. "She smells like fucking *chocolate*," he said, and they kicked the glass doors open with their boots.

An old woman at the back of the store, surrounded by aisles jammed with puffed bags of potato chips, stared at Stella. Her hand shook a can of Pringles like a castanet. "Go away!"

The clerk moved in to defend the old woman. "Take your Gatorade and go home!" she barked at Stella. "Go home to your mama and don't you *never* come back here."

6

The Longworth House Office Building
WASHINGTON, D.C.

"We've been over and over this," Dick Gianelli told Mitch, dropping a stack of scientific reprints on the coffee table between them. The news was not good.

Gianelli was short and round and his usually pale face was now a dangerous red. "We've been reading everything you sent us ever since the congressman was elected. But they have twice as many experts, and they send twice as many papers. We're drowning in papers, Mitch! And the *language*." He thumped the stack. "Can't your people, all the biologists, just write to be understood? Don't they realize how important it is to get the word out to everybody?"

Mitch let his hands drop by his sides. "They're not my people, Dick. My people are archaeologists. They tend to write sparkling prose."

Gianelli laughed, stood up from the couch and shook out his arms, then tipped a finger under his tight collar, as if letting out steam. His office was part of the suite assigned to Representative Dale Wickham, D., Virginia, whom he had faithfully served as director of public science for two of the toughest terms in U.S. history. The door to Wickham's office was closed. He was on the Hill today.

"The congressman has made his views clear for years now. Your colleagues, scientists all, have hopped on the gravy train. They've joined up with NIH and CDC and Emergency Action, and they pay their visits mostly across the aisle. Wilson at FEMA and Doyle at DOJ have undercut us every step of the way, squirming like puppies to get their funding treats. Opposing them is like standing outside in a hail of cannonballs."

"So what can I take home with me?" Mitch asked. "To cheer up the missus. Any good news?"

Gianelli shrugged. Mitch liked Gianelli but doubted he would live to see fifty. Gianelli had all the markers: pear shape, excessive girth, ghostly skin, thinning black hair, creased earlobes. He knew it, too. He worked hard and cared too much and swallowed his disappointments. A good man in a bad time. "We got caught in a medical bear trap," he said. "We've never been prepared. Our best model for an epidemic was military response. So now we've had ten years of Emergency Action. We've practically signed away our country to Beltway bureaucrats with military and law enforcement training. Mark Augustine's crew, Mitch. We've given them almost absolute authority."

"I don't think I'm capable of understanding how those people think," Mitch said.

"I thought I did, once," Gianelli said. "We tried to build a coalition. The congressman roped in Christian groups, the NRA, conspiracy nuts, flag burners and flag lovers, anybody who's ever expressed a shred of suspicion about the guv'ment. We've gone hat in hand to every decent judge, every civil libertarian still above ground, literally and figuratively. We've been checked every step of the way. It was made very clear to the congressman that if he threw up any more dust, he, personally, all on his lonesome, could force the president to declare martial law."

"What's the difference, Dick?" Mitch asked. "They've suspended habeas corpus."

"For a special class, Mitch."

"My daughter," Mitch growled.

Gianelli nodded. "Civil courts still operate, though under special guidelines. Nothing much has changed for the frightened average citizen, who's kind of fuzzy about civil rights anyway. When Mark Augustine put together Emergency Action, he wove a tight little piece of legislative fabric. He made sure every agency ever involved in managing disease and preparing for natural disaster had a piece of the pie—and a very smelly pie it is. We've created a new and vulnerable underclass, with fewer civil protections than any since slavery. This sort of stuff attracts the real sharks, Mitch. The monsters."

"All they have are hatred and fear."

"In this town, that's a full house," Gianelli said. "Washington eats truth and shits spin." He stood. "We can't challenge Emergency Action. Not this session. They're stronger than ever. Maybe next year."

Mitch watched Gianelli pace a circuit of the room. "I can't wait that long. Riverside, Dick."

Gianelli folded his hands. He would not meet Mitch's eyes.

"The mob torched one of Augustine's goddamned camps," Mitch said. "They burned the children in their barracks. They poured gasoline around the pilings and lit them up. The guards just stood back and watched. Two hundred kids roasted to death. Kids just like my daughter."

Gianelli put on a mask of public sympathy, but underneath it, Mitch could see the real pain.

"There haven't even been arrests," he added.

"You can't arrest a city, Mitch. Even the *New York Times* calls them virus children now. Everyone's scared."

"There hasn't been a case of Shiver in ten years. It was a fluke, Dick. An excuse for some people to trample on everything this country has ever stood for."

Gianelli squinted at Mitch but did not challenge this appraisal. "There isn't much more the congressman can do," he said.

"I don't believe that."

Gianelli reached into his desk drawer and took out a bottle of Tums. "Everyone around here has fire in the belly. I have heartburn."

"Give me something to take home, Dick. Please. We need hope," Mitch said.

"Show me your hands, Mitch."

Mitch held up his hands. The calluses had faded, but they were still there. Gianelli held his own hands beside Mitch's. They were smooth and pink. "Want to really learn how to suck eggs, from an old hound dog? I've spent ten years with Wickham. He's the smartest hound there is, but he's up against a bad lot. The Republicans are the country's pit bulls, Mitch. Barking in the night, all night, every night, right or wrong, and savaging their enemies without mercy. They claim to represent plain folks, but they represent those who vote, when they vote at all, on pocketbooks and fear and gut instinct. They control the House and the Senate, they stacked the court the last three terms, their man is in the White House, and bless them, they speak with one voice, Mitch. The president is dug in. But you know what the congressman thinks? He thinks the president doesn't want Emergency Action to be his legacy. Eventually, maybe we can do something with that." Gianelli's voice dropped very low, as if he were about to blaspheme in the temple. "But not now. The Democrats can't even hold a bake sale without arguing. We're weak and getting weaker."

He held out his hand. "The congressman will be back any minute. Mitch, you look like you haven't slept in weeks."

Mitch shrugged. "I lie awake listening for trucks. I hate being so far from Kaye and Stella."

"How far?"

Mitch looked up from under his solid line of eyebrow and shook his head.

"Right," Gianelli said. "Sorry."

7

SPOTSYLVANIA COUNTY

The old frame house snapped and popped in the morning heat. A moist breeze blew through the small rooms in lazy swirls. Kaye walked from the bedroom to the bathroom, rubbing her eyes. She had awakened from a peculiar dream in which she was an atom slowly rising to connect with a much larger molecule, to fit in and complete something truly impressive. She felt at peace for the first time in months, despite the barbed memory of last night's fight.

Kaye massaged the fingers of her right hand, then wriggled her wedding ring over a swollen knuckle into its familiar groove. Bees droned in the oleanders outside the window, well into their day's work.

"Some dream," she told herself in the bathroom mirror. She pulled down one eyelid with a finger and stared at herself speculatively. "Under a little stress, are we?"

A few freckles remained under each eye from her pregnancy with Stella; when she was upset, they could still change from pale tan to ruddy ocher. Now, they were darker but not vivid. She splashed water on her cheeks and clipped her hair back, preparing for the hot day, ready to face more difficulties. Families were about staying together and healing.

If the bees can do it, so can I.

"Stella," she called, knocking on her daughter's bedroom door. "It's nine o'clock. We slept in."

Kaye padded into the small office in the laundry room and switched on the computer. She read the lines she had written before the squabble last night, then scrolled back through the last few pages:

"The role of SHEVA in the production of a new subspecies is but one function performed by this diverse and essential class of viruses. ERV and transposons—jumping genes—play large roles in tissue differentiation and development. Emotion and crisis and changing environments activate them, one variety at a time, or all together. They are mediators and messengers between cells, ferrying genes and coded data around many parts of the body, and even between individuals.

"Viruses and transposons most likely arose after the invention of sex, perhaps because of sex. To this day, sex brings them opportunity to move and carry information. They may have also emerged during the tumultuous genetic shuffling of our early immune system, like soldiers and cops running wild.

"Truly they are like original sin. How does sin shape our destiny?"

Kaye used a stylus to circle that last awkward, overreaching sentence. She marked it out and read some more.

"One thing we know already: We depend on retroviral and transposon activity during nearly every stage of our growth. Many are necessary partners.

"To assume that viruses and transposable elements are first and foremost causes of disease is like assuming that automobiles are first and foremost meant to kill people.

"Pathogens—disease-causing organisms—are like hormones and other signaling molecules, but their message is challenge and silence. Our own internal lions, pathogens test us. They winnow the old and weak. They sculpt life.

"Sometimes they bring down the young and the good. Nature is painful. Disease and death are part of our response to challenge. To fail, to die, is still to be part of nature, for success is built on many failures, and silence is also a signal."

Her frame of mind had become increasingly abstract. The dream, the drone of the bees . . .

You were born with a caul, my dear.

Kaye suddenly remembered the voice of her maternal grandmother, Evelyn; words from nearly four decades ago. At the age of eight, Evelyn had told her something that her mother, a practical woman, had never thought to mention. "You came into this world with your tiny head covered. You were born with a caul. I was there, in the hospital with your mother. I saw it myself. The doctor showed it to me."

Kaye remembered squirming with delicious anticipation in her grandmother's ample lap and asking what a caul was. "A cap of loose flesh," Evelyn had explained. "Some say it's a mark of extraordinary understanding, even second sight. A caul warns us that you will learn things most others will never comprehend, and you will always be frustrated trying to explain what you know, and what seems so obvious to you. It's supposed to be both a blessing and a curse." Then the older woman had added, in a soft voice, "I was born with a caul, my dear, and your grandfather has *never* understood me."

Kaye had loved Evelyn very much, but at times had thought her a little spooky. She returned her attention to the text on the monitor. She did not delete the paragraphs, but she did draw a large asterisk and exclamation point beside them. Then she saved the file and pushed the chair under the desk.

Four pages yesterday. A good day's work. Not that it would ever see the light of day in any respectable journal. For the last eight years, all of her papers had appeared on clandestine Web sites.

Kaye listened closely to the morning house, as if to measure the day ahead. A curtain pull flapped against a window frame. Cardinals whistled in the maple tree outside.

She could not hear her daughter stirring.

"Stella!" she called, louder. "Breakfast. Want some oatmeal?"

No answer.

She walked in flapping slippers down the short hallway to Stella's room. Stella's bed was made but rumpled, as if she had been lying on it, tossing and turning. A bouquet of dried flowers, tied with a rubber band, rested on the pillow. A short stack of books had been tipped over beside the bed. On the sill, three stuffed Shrooz, about the size of guinea pigs, red and green and the very rare black and gold, hung their long noses into the room. More cascaded from the cedar chest at the foot of the bed. Stella loved Shrooz because they were grumpy; they whined and squirmed and then groaned when moved.

Kaye searched the big backyard, tall brown grass faded into ivy and kudzu under the big old trees at the edge of the property. She could not afford to let her attention lapse even for a minute.

Then she returned to the house and Stella's bedroom. She got down on her knees and peered under the bed. Stella had made a scent diary, a small blank book filled with cryptic writing and dated records of her emotions, scents collected from behind her ears and dabbed on each page. Stella kept it hidden, but Kaye had found it once while cleaning and had figured it out.

Kaye pushed her hands through the balls of dust and cat toys beneath the bed and thrust her fingers deep into the shadows. The book was not there.

Peace the illusion, peace the trap, no rest, no letting down her guard. Stella was gone. Taking the book meant she was serious.

Still shod in slippers, Kaye pushed through the gate and ran up the oak-lined street. She whispered, "Don't panic, keep it together, *God damn it.*" The muscles in her neck knotted.

A quarter of a mile away, in front of the next house down the road in the rural neighborhood, she slowed to a walk, then stood in the middle of the cracked asphalt road, hugging herself, small and tense, like a mouse waiting for a hawk.

Kaye shaded her eyes against the sun and looked up at bloated gray clouds advancing shoulder to shoulder along the southern horizon. The air smelled sullen and jumpy.

If Stella had planned this, she would have run off after Mitch left for Washington. Mitch had left between six and seven. That meant her daughter had at least an hour's head start. That realization shoved an icicle down Kaye's spine.

Calling the police was not wise. Five years ago, Virginia had reluctantly acquiesced to Emergency Action and had begun rounding up the new children and sending them to camps in Iowa, Nebraska, and Ohio. Years ago, Kaye and Mitch had withdrawn from parent support groups after a rash of FBI infiltrations. Mitch had assumed that Kaye in particular was a target for surveillance and possibly even arrest.

They were on their own. They had decided that was the safest course.

Kaye took off her slippers and ran barefoot back to the house. She would have to think like Stella and that was difficult. Kaye had observed her daughter as a mother and as a scientist for eleven years, and there had always been a small but important distance between them that she could not cross. Stella deliberated with a thoroughness Kaye admired, but reached conclusions she often found mystifying.

Kaye grabbed her handbag with her wallet and ID, pulled on her garden shoes, and exited through the back door. The small primer gray Toyota truck started instantly. Mitch maintained both their vehicles. She ground the tires down the dirt driveway, then caught herself and drove slowly along the country lane.

"Please," she muttered, "no rides."

8

Walking along the dirt margin of the asphalt road, Stella swung the plastic Gatorade bottle, rationing herself to a sip every few minutes. An old farm field plowed and marked for a new strip mall stretched to her right. Stella tightrope-walked a freshly cured concrete curb, not yet out of its mold boards. The sun was climbing in the east, black clouds stacked high in the south, and the air spun hot and full of the fragrances of dogwood and sycamore. The exhaust of cars going by, and a descending tail of carbon from a diesel truck, clogged her nose.

She felt at long last that she was doing something worthwhile. There was guilt, but she pushed aside concern for what her parents would think. Somewhere on this road she might meet someone who would not argue with her instincts, who would not feel pain simply because Stella existed. Someone like herself.

All her life she had lived among one kind of human, but she was another. An old virus called SHEVA had broken loose from human DNA and rearranged human genes. Stella and a generation of children like her were the result. This was what her parents had told her.

Not a freak. Just a different kind.

Stella Nova Rafelson was eleven years old. She felt as if she had been peculiarly alone all her life.

She sometimes thought of herself as a star, a bright little point in a very big sky. Humans filled the sky by the billions and washed her out like the blinding sun.

9

Kaye swung left just beyond the courthouse, turned the corner, drove half a block, and pulled into a gas station. When she had been a child, there had been little rubber-coated trip wires that caused a bell to ding whenever a car arrived. There were no longer any wires, no bell, and nobody came out to see what Kaye needed. She parked by the bright red-and-white convenience store and wiped tears from her eyes.

She sat for a minute in the Toyota, trying to focus.

Stella had a red plastic coin purse that held ten dollars in emergency money. There was a drinking fountain in the courthouse, but Kaye thought Stella would prefer something cold, sweet, and fruity. Odors of artificial strawberry and raspberry that Kaye found repugnant, Stella would wallow in like a cat in a bed of catnip. "It's a long walk," Kaye told herself. "It's hot. She's thirsty. It's her day out, away from mom." She bit her lip.

Kaye and Mitch had protected Stella like a rare orchid throughout her short life. Kaye knew that, hated the necessity of it. It was how they had stayed together. Her daughter's freedom depended on it. The chat rooms were full of the agonized stories of parents giving up their children, watching them be sent to Emergency Action schools in another state. The camps.

Mitch, Stella, and Kaye had lived a dreamy, tense, unreal existence, no way for an energetic, outgoing young girl to grow up, no way for Mitch to stay sane. Kaye tried not to think too much about herself or what was happening between her and Mitch, she might just snap, and then where would they be? But their difficulties had obviously had an effect on Stella. She was a daddy's girl, to Kaye's pride and secret sadness—she had once been a daddy's girl, too, before both her parents had died, over twenty years ago—and Mitch had been gone a lot lately.

Kaye entered the store through the glass double doors. The clerk, a thin, tired-looking woman a little younger than Kaye, had out a mop and bucket and was grimly spraying the counter and floor with Lysol.

"Excuse me, did you see a girl, tall, about eleven?"

The clerk raised the mop like a lance and poked it at her.

10

WASHINGTON, D.C.

A tall, stooped man with thinning white hair sauntered into the office carrying a worn briefcase. Gianelli stood up. "Congressman, you remember Mitch Rafelson."

"I do, indeed," Wickham said, and held out his hand. Mitch shook it firmly. The hand was dry and hard as wood. "Does anybody know you're here, Mitch?"

"Dick snuck me in, sir."

Wickham appraised Mitch with a slight tremor of his head. "Come over to my office, Mitch," the congressman said. "You, too, Dick, and close the door behind you."

They walked across the hall. Wickham's office was covered with plaques and photos, a lifetime of politics.

"Justice Barnhall had a heart attack this morning at ten," Wickham said.

Mitch's face fell. Barnhall had consistently championed civil rights, even for SHEVA children and their parents.

"He's in Bethesda," Wickham said. "They don't hold out much hope. The man is ninety years old. I've just been speaking with the Senate minority leader. We're going to the White House tomorrow morning." Wickham laid his briefcase down on a couch and stuck his hands in the pockets of his chocolate brown slacks. "Justice Barnhall was one of the good guys. Now the president wants Olsen, and he's a corker, Mitch. We haven't seen his like since Roger B. Taney. A lifelong bachelor, face like a stoat, mind like a steel trap. Wants to undo eighty years of so-called judicial activism, thinks he'll have the country by the balls, six to three. And he probably will. We're not going to win this round, but we can land a few punches. Then, they'll lash us on the votes. We're going to get creamed." Wickham stared sadly at Mitch. "I do love a fair fight."

The secretary knocked on the door jamb. "Congressman, is Mr. Rafelson here?" She looked right at Mitch, one eyebrow cocked.

Gianelli asked, "Who wants to know?"

"Won't use her name and sounds upset. System board says she's on a disposable cell phone using an offshore line. That's no longer legal, sir."

"You don't say," Wickham said, looking out the window.

"My wife knows I'm here. No one else," Mitch said.

"Get her number and call her back, Connie," Wickham said. "Put it on the puzzler, and route it through, oh, Tom Haney's office in Boca Raton."

"Yes, sir."

Wickham gestured toward his desk phone. "We can link her line to a special scrambler for congressional office communications," he said, but tapped his wristwatch. "Starts and ends with garbage, and unless you know the key, it all sounds like garbage. We change the key every call. Takes NSA about a minute or so to break it, so keep it short."

The secretary made the connection. Mitch stared between the two men, his heart sinking, and picked up the receiver on the desk.

11

Stella sat in the shade of an old wooden bus shelter, clutching her book to her chest. She had been sitting there for an hour and a half. The Gatorade bottle was long since empty and she was thirsty. The morning heat was stifling and the sky was clouding over. The air had thickened with that spooky electric dampness that meant a big storm was brewing. All of her emotions had flip-flopped. "I've been really stupid," she told herself. "Kaye will be so mad."

Kaye seldom showed her anger. Mitch, when he was home, was the one who paced and shook his head and clenched his fists when things got tense. But Stella could tell when Kaye was angry. Her mother could get just as angry as Mitch, though in a quiet way.

Stella hated anger in the house. It smelled like old cockroaches.

Kaye and Mitch never took it out on Stella. Both treated her with patient tenderness, even when they clearly did not want to, and that made Stella feel what she called *steepy,* odd and different and apart.

Stella had made up that word, *steepy,* and lots of others, most of which she kept to herself.

It was tough to be responsible for a lot, and maybe all, of their anger.

Hard to know she was to blame for Mitch not being able to go dig up pottery and middens, old garbage dumps, and for Kaye not being able to work in a lab or teach or do anything but write articles and books that somehow never got published or even finished.

Stella knit her long fingers and raised her knee, filling the hollow of the fingers and tugging her arms straight. She heard a vehicle and pushed back into the shadow of the enclosure, lifting her feet into the gloom. A red Ford pickup drove slowly by, clean, new, with a smooth white plastic camper on the back. The camper had a square shiny little door made of smoky plastic in the rear. It looked expensive, much nicer than the little Toyota truck or Mitch's old Dodge Intrepid.

The red truck slowed, stopped, shifted smoothly into reverse, and backed up. Stella tried to squeeze into the corner, her back pressed against splintery wood. She suddenly just wanted to go home. She could find her way back, she was sure of it; she could find it by the smell of the trees. But car exhaust and pretty soon rain would make that harder. The rain would make it much harder.

The truck stopped and the engine switched off. The driver opened his door and got out on the side away from Stella. She could only see a little bit of him through the truck's tinted windows. He had gray hair and a beard. He walked slowly around the truck bed and camper, the shadows of his legs visible under the frame.

"Hello, Miss," he said, stopping a respectful four or five yards from where she was trying to hide. He put his hands in the pockets of his khaki shorts. In his mouth he clenched an unlit pipe. He adjusted the pipe with one hand, removed it, pointed it at her. "You live around here?"

Stella nodded in the shadow.

His goatee was all gray and neatly trimmed. He was potbellied but dressed neatly, and his calf-high socks and running shoes were clean and white. He smelled confident, what she could smell behind thick swipes of deodorant and the rum-and-cherry-scented tobacco tamped into the pipe.

"You should be with your family and friends," he said.

"I'm heading home," Stella said.

"Bus won't come by again until this evening. Only two stops a day here."

"I'm walking."

"Well, that's fine. You shouldn't take rides with strangers."

"I know."

"Can I help? Make a phone call to your folks?"

Stella said nothing. They had one secure phone at home, strictly for emergencies, and they bought disposable cell phones for occasional use. They always used a kind of family code when they talked, even with the disposables, but Mitch said they could identify your voice no matter how much you tried to change it.

She wanted the man in shorts to go away.

"Are your folks at home, Miss?"

Stella looked up at the sun peeking through the clouds.

"If you're alone, I know some people who can help," he said. "Special friends. Listen. I made a recording of them." He dug in his back pocket and pulled out a small recorder. He pressed a button and held out the machine for her to listen.

She had heard such songs and whistles before, on TV and on the radio. When she had been three, she had heard a boy sing songs like that, too. And a few years ago, in the house in Richmond, the big brick house with the iron gate and the guard dogs and four couples, nervous, thin people who seemed to have a lot of money, bringing their children together to play around an indoor swimming pool. She vividly remembered listening to their singing and being too shy to join in. Sweet interweaves of tunes, like meadowlarks singing their hearts out in a berry patch, as Mitch had said.

That was what she heard coming from the recorder.

Voices like hers.

Big drops of rain left crayon-jabs of wetness on the road and in the dirt. The sky and trees behind the man with the goatee flared icy white against the charcoal gray of the sky.

"It's going to get wet," the man said. "Miss, it isn't good to be out here by yourself. Heck, this shelter could even attract lightning, who knows?" He pulled a cell phone from his back pocket. "Can I call someone for you? Your mom or dad?"

He didn't smell bad. In fact, he did not smell of much at all except for the rum-and-cherry tobacco. She had to learn how to judge people and even take chances. It was the only way to get along. She made a decision. "Could you call?" Stella asked.

"Sure," he said. "Just tell me their number."

12

Mark Augustine placed his hand on the back of Rachel Browning's chair. The room was quiet except for the hum of equipment fans and a faint clicking noise.

They were watching the plump man in khaki shorts, the red truck, the lanky, awkward girl that was Kaye Lang Rafelson's daughter.

A virus child.

"Is that your stringer, Rachel?"

"I don't know," Browning said.

"A good Samaritan, maybe?" Augustine asked. Internally, he was furious, but would not give Browning the satisfaction of showing it. "He could be a child molester."

For the first time, Browning revealed uncertainty. "Any suggestions?" she asked.

Augustine felt no relief that she was asking his advice. This would simply involve him in her chain of decisions, and that was the last thing he wanted. Let her hang herself, all by herself.

"If things are going wrong, I need to make some calls," he said.

"We should wait," Browning said. "It's probably okay."

The Little Bird hovered about thirty feet above the red truck and the bus stop, the paunchy middle-aged man and the young girl.

Augustine's hand tightened on the back of the chair.

13

The rain fell heavily and the air got darker as they climbed into the truck. Too late Stella noticed that the man had stuffed waxed cotton up his nose. He sat on the bench seat behind the wheel and offered her a mint Tic-Tac, but she hated mint. He popped two into his mouth and gestured with the phone. "Nobody answers," he said. "Daddy at work?"

She turned away.

"I can drop you at your house, but maybe, if it's okay with you, I know some people would like to meet you," he said.

She was going against everything her parents had ever told her, to give him the house number, to sit in his truck. But she had to do something, and it looked as if today was the day.

She had never walked so far from home. The rain would change everything about the air and the smells. "What's your name?" she asked.

"Fred," the man answered. "Fred Trinket. I know you'd like to meet them, and they surely would like to meet you."

"Stop talking that way," Stella said.

"What way?"

"I'm not an idiot."

Fred Trinket had clogged his nose with cotton and his mouth sang with shrill mint.

"Of course," he said reasonably. "I know that, honey. I have a shelter. A place for kids in trouble. Would you like to see some pictures?" Trinket asked. "They're in the glove box." He watched her, still smiling. He had a kind enough face, she decided. A little sad. He seemed concerned about how she felt. "Pictures of my kids, the ones on the recorder."

Stella felt intensely curious. "Like me?" she asked.

"Just like you," Fred said. "You're sparking real pretty, you know that? The others spark the same way when they're curious. Something to see."

"What's sparking?"

"Your freckles," Fred said, pointing. "They spread out on your cheeks like butterfly wings. I'm used to seeing that at my shelter. I could call your house again, see if somebody's home, tell your daddy or mama to meet us. Should I?"

He was getting nervous. She could smell that much, not that it meant anything. Everybody was nervous these days. He did not want to hurt her, she was pretty sure; there was nothing horny about his scent or his manner, and he did not smell of cigarettes or alcohol.

He did not smell anything like the young men in the convenience store.

She told herself again she would have to take chances if she wanted to get anywhere, if she wanted anything to change. "Yes," she said.

Fred pushed redial. The cell phone beeped the tune of the house number. Still no answer. Her mother was probably out looking for her.

"Let's go to my house," Fred said. "It's not far and there are cold drinks in the ice chest. Strawberry soda. Genuine Nehi in long-necked bottles. I'll call your mama again when we get there."

She swallowed hard, opened the glove box, and pulled out a packet of color photos, five by sevens. The kids in the first photo, seven of them, were having a party, a birthday party, with a bright red cake. Fred stood in the background beside a plump older woman with a blank look. Other than Fred and the older woman, the kids at the party were all about her age. One boy might have been older, but he was standing in the background.

All like her. SHEVA children.

"Jesus," Stella said.

"Easy on that," Fred said amiably. "Jesus is Lord."

The bumper sticker on Fred's truck said that. On the tailgate was glued a golden plastic fish. The fish, labeled "Truth," was eating another fish with legs, labeled "Darwin."

Fred turned on the motor and put the truck in gear. The rain was falling in big hard drops, tapping on the roof and the hood like a million bored fingers.

"Battle of the Wilderness took place not far from here," Fred said as he drove. He turned right carefully, as if worried about jostling precious cargo. "Civil War. Holy place in its way. Real quiet. I love it out this way. Less traffic, fewer condo-minimums, right?"

Stella leafed through the pictures again, found some more stuck in a plastic pocket. Seven different kids, mugging for the camera or staring at it seriously, some sitting in big chairs in a big house.

One boy had no expression at all. "Who's this?" she asked Fred.

Fred spared a quick look. "That is Will. Strong Will, Mother calls him. He lived off snakes and squirrels before he came to our shelter." Fred Trinket smiled and shook his head at the thought. "You'll like him. And the others, too."

14

The red truck pulled up to a two-story house with tall white columns. Two long brick planters filled with scrawny, dripping oleanders bordered the white steps. Fred Trinket had done nothing overt to upset Stella, but now they were at his house.

"It's about lunchtime," Trinket said. "The others will be eating. Mother feeds them about now. I eat later. It's my digestion. None too good."

"You eat oatmeal," Stella said.

Trinket beamed. "That is right, young lady. I eat oatmeal for breakfast. Sometimes a single slice of bacon. What else?"

"You like garlic."

"For dinner, I have spaghetti with garlic, that's right." Trinket shook his head happily. "Marvelous. You smell all that."

He opened his door and came around. Stella got out and he pointed up the porch steps to the house. A big white door stood there, solid and patient, flanked by two tall, skinny windows. The paint was new. The doorknob reeked of Brasso, a smell she did not like. She did not touch the door. Trinket opened it for her. The door was not locked.

"We trust people," Trinket said. "Mother!" he called. "We have a guest."

15

Mitch pulled into the dirt driveway beneath a sodden gray sky. Kaye was not in the house when he arrived. She honked at him from the road as he came out after searching the empty house. His long legs took him in five quick strides to the old truck.

"How long?" Mitch asked, leaning in. He touched her wet cheeks through the driver's side window.

"Three or four hours," Kaye said. "I took a nap and she was gone."

He got in beside her. Just as she put the truck in gear, Mitch held up his hand. "Phone," he said. She cut the engine and they both listened. From the house came a faint ringing.

Mitch ran to the house. The screen door slammed behind him and he picked up on the fourth ring.

"Hello?"

"Is this Mr. Bailey?" a man asked.

That was the name they had told Stella to use.

"Yeah," Mitch said, wiping rain from his brow and eyes. "Who's this?"

"My name is Fred Trinket. I did not know you were living so near, Mr. Bailey."

"I'm in a hurry, Mr. Trinket. Where's my daughter?"

"Please don't be upset. She's in my house right now, and she's very worried about you."

"We're worried about her. Where are you?"

"She's fine, Mr. *Rafelson*. We'd like you to come and see something we think is interesting and important. Something you may very well find fascinating." The man who called himself Trinket gave directions.

Mitch rejoined Kaye in the truck. "Someone has Stella," he said.

"Emergency Action?"

"A teacher, a crank, somebody," Mitch said. No time now to mention the man knew his real name. He did not think Stella would have told anyone that. "About ten miles from here."

Kaye was already spinning the truck around on the road.

16

"There," Trinket said, putting away the phone and drying his short hair with a towel. "Have you ever met with more than one or two of the children at a time?"

Stella did not answer for a moment, it was such an odd question. She wanted to think it over, even though she knew what he meant. She looked around the living room of the big house. The furniture was *colonial*, she knew from reading catalogs and magazines: maple with antique print fabric—butter churns, horse tack, plows. It was really ugly. The wallpaper was dark green flocked velvet with floral patterns that looked like sad faces. The entire room smelled of a citronella candle burning on a small side table, too sweet even for Stella's tastes. There had been chicken cooking in the past hour, and broccoli.

"No," she finally said.

"That is *sad*, isn't it?"

The old woman, the same as in the photos, entered the room and looked at Stella with little interest. She walked in rubber-soled slippers with hardly any sound and held out a long-necked bottle of Nehi strawberry soda, brilliant red in the room's warm glow.

Trinket was at least fifty. Stella guessed his mother might be seventy, plump, with strong-looking, corded arms, peach-colored skin with only a few wrinkles, and thin white hair arranged neatly on a pallid, taut scalp, like the worn head of a much-loved doll.

Stella was thirsty, but she did not take the bottle.

"Mother," Trinket said, "I've called Stella's parents."

"No need," the woman said, her tone flat. "We have groceries."

Trinket winked at Stella. "We do indeed," he said. "And chicken for lunch. What else, Stella?" he asked.

"Huh?"

"What else do we have to eat?"

"It's not a game," Stella said huffily.

"Broccoli, I'd guess," Trinket answered for her, his lips forming a little bow. "Mother is a good cook, but predictable. Still, she helps me with the children."

"I do," the woman said.

"Where are they?" Stella asked.

"Mother does her best, but my wife was a better cook."

"She died," the old woman said, touching her hair with her free hand.

Stella looked at the floor in frustration. She heard someone talking, far off in the back.

"Is that them?" she asked, fascinated despite herself. She made a move toward the long, picture-lined hall on the right, following the sound of voices.

"Yes," Trinket said. He shot a quick glance at the book in her hands. "Your parents kept you secluded, didn't they? How selfish. Don't we know, Mother, how selfish that would be for someone like Stella?"

"Alone," his mother said, and abruptly turned and set the bottle down on the small table beside the candle. She rubbed her hands on her apron and waddled down the hallway. The combined sweetness of candle and Nehi threatened to make Stella dizzy. She had seen dogs whining to be with other dogs, to sniff them and exchange doggy greetings. That memory brought her up short.

She thought of the two men in the Texaco minimart.

You smell as good as a dog.

She shivered.

"Your parents were protecting you, but it was still cruel," Trinket said, watching her. Stella kept her eyes on the hallway. The wish that had haunted her for weeks now, months if she thought back that far, was suddenly strong in her, making her dull and steepy.

"Not to be with your own kind, not to bathe in the air of another, and not to speak the way you all do, such lovely doubling, that is painfully lonely-making, isn't it?"

Her cheeks felt hot. Trinket studied her cheeks. "Your people are so beautiful," he said, his eyes going soft. "I could watch you all day."

"Why?" Stella asked sharply.

"Beg pardon?" Trinket smiled, and this time there was something in the smile that was wrong. Stella did not like being the center of attention. But she wanted to meet the others, more than anything on Earth or in the heavens, as Mitch's father might have said.

Stella's grandfather, Sam, had died five years ago.

"I do not run an accredited school, nor a day care, nor a center of learning," Trinket said. "I try to teach what I can, but mostly I—Mother and I—create a brief refuge, away from the cruel people who hate and fear. We neither hate nor fear. We admire. In my way, I'm an anthropologist."

"Can I meet them now?" Stella asked.

Trinket sat on the couch with a radiant grin. "Tell me more about your mother and father. They're well known in some circles. Your mother discovered the virus, right? And your father found the famous mummies in the Alps. The harbingers of our own fate."

The sweet scents in the room blocked some human odors, but not aggression, not fear. Those she would still be able to smell, like a steel spoon stuck in vanilla ice cream. Trinket did not smell mean or fearful, so she did not feel she was in immediate danger. Still, he wore nose plugs. And how did he know so much about Kaye and Mitch?

Trinket leaned forward on the couch and touched his nostrils. "You're worried about these."

Stella turned away. "Let me see the others," she said.

Trinket snorted a laugh. "I can't be in a crowd of you without these," Trinket said. "I'm sensitive, oh yes. I had a daughter like you. My wife and I acquired the masks and knew the special scents my daughter made. Then, my wife died. She died in pain." He stared at the ceiling, his eyes wet pools of sentiment. "I miss her," Trinket said, and slapped his hand suddenly on the bolster of the couch. "Mother!"

The blank-faced woman returned.

"See if they've finished their lunch," Trinket said. "Then let's introduce Stella."

"Will she eat?" the older woman asked, her eyes unconcerned either way.

"I don't know. That depends," Fred Trinket said. He looked at his watch. "I hope your parents haven't lost their way. Maybe you should call them . . . in a few minutes, just to make sure?"

17

Kaye pulled the Toyota truck to the side of the rutted dirt road and dropped her head onto the wheel. The rain had stopped, but they had nearly gotten their wheels stuck in mud several times. She moaned.

Mitch threw open the door. "This is the road. This is the address. Shit!"

He flung the crumpled piece of paper into a wet ditch. The only house here had been boarded up for a long time, and half of it had slumped into cinders after a fire. Five or six acres of weed-grown farm ground surrounded them, sullen behind a veil of low mist. Streamers of cloud played hide-and-seek with a watery sun. The house was bright, then dark, beneath the coming and going of those wide gray fingers.

"Maybe he doesn't have her." Kaye looked at Mitch through the open door.

"I could have transposed a number," Mitch said, leaning against the cab.

His cell phone rang. They both jerked as if stuck with pins. Mitch pulled the phone out and said, "Yes." The phone recognized his voice and announced that the calling party's number was blocked, then asked if he would take the call anyway.

"Yes," he said, without thinking.

"Daddy?" The voice on the other end was tense, high-pitched, but it sounded like Stella's.

"Where are you?"

"Is that you? Daddy?" The voice went through a digital bird fight and steadied. He had never heard that sort of sound before and it worried him.

"It's me, honey. Where are you?"

"I'm at this house. I saw the house number on the mail box."

Mitch pulled a pen and pad from his inside coat pocket and wrote down the number and road.

"Stay tight, Stella, and don't let anyone touch you," he said, working to steady his voice. "We're on our way." He reluctantly said good-bye and closed the phone. His face was like red sandstone, he was so furious.

"Is she okay?"

Mitch nodded, then opened the phone again and punched in another number.

"Who are you calling?"

"State police," he said.

"We can't!" Kaye cried. "They'll take her!"

"It's too late to worry about that," Mitch said. "This guy's going for bounty, and he wants all of us."

18

So many pictures in the hall leading to the back of the house. Generation after generation of Trinkets, Stella assumed, from faded color snapshots clustered in a single frame to larger, sepia-colored prints showing men and women and children wearing stiff brown clothes and peering with pinched expressions, as if the eyes of the future scared them.

"Our legacy," Fred Trinket told her. "Old genes. All those arrangements, gone!" He grinned and walked ahead, his shoulders rolling with each step. He had a fat back, Stella saw. Fat neck and fat back. His calves were taut, however, as if he did a lot of walking, but pale and hairy. Perhaps he walked at night.

Trinket pushed open a screen door.

"Let me know if she wants lunch," the mother said from the kitchen, halfway up the hall and to the left. As Mrs. Trinket dried a dish, Stella saw a dark, damp towel flick out of the kitchen like a snake's tongue.

"Yes, Mother," Trinket murmured. "This way, Miss Rafelson."

He descended a short flight of wooden steps and walked across the gravel path to a long, dark building about ten paces beyond. Stella saw a doghouse but no dog, and a small orchard of clothes trees spinning slowly in the wind after the storm, their lines empty.

Along would come Mother Trinket, Stella thought, *and pin up the laundry, and it would be clothes tree springtime. When the clothes were dry she would pull them down and stuff them in her basket and it would be winter again.* Expressionless Mother Trinket was the seasonal heart of the old house, mistress of the backyard.

Stella's mouth was dry. Her nose hurt. She touched behind her ears where it itched when she was nervous. Her finger came away waxy. She wanted to take a washcloth and remove all the old scents, clean herself for the people in the long outbuilding. A word came to her: *prensing,* preening and cleansing. It was a lovely word and it made her tremble like a leaf.

Trinket unlocked the door to the rear building. Inside, Stella saw fluorescent lights sputter on, bright and blue, over workbenches, an old refrigerator, stacked cardboard boxes, and, to the right, a strong wire mesh door.

The voices grew louder. Stella thought she heard three or four. They were speaking in a way she could not understand—low, guttural, with piping high exclamations. Someone coughed.

"They're inside," Trinket said. He unlocked the wire door with a brass key tied to a dirty length of twine. "They just finished eating. We'll fetch the trays for Mother." He pulled the mesh door open.

Stella did not move. Not even the promise of the voices, the promise that had brought her this far, could persuade her to take another step.

"There are four inside, just like you. They need your help. I'll go in with you."

"Why the lock?" Stella asked.

"People drive around, sometimes they have guns . . . take potshots. Just not safe," Trinket said. "It's not safe for your kind. Since my wife's death, I've made it one of my jobs, my duty, to protect those I come across on the road. Youngsters like you."

"Where's your daughter?" Stella asked.

"She's in Idaho."

"I don't believe you," Stella said.

"Oh, it's true. They took her away last year. I've never been to visit her."

"They let parents visit sometimes."

"I just can't bear the thought of going." His expression had changed, and his smell, too.

"You're lying," Stella said. She could feel her glands working, itching. Stella could not smell it herself, could not in fact smell anything her nose was so dry, but she knew the room was thick with her persuasion scent.

Trinket seemed to deflate, arms dropping, hands relaxing. He pointed to the wire mesh door. He was thinking, or waiting. Stella moved away. The key dangled from the rope in his hand. "Your people," he said, and scratched his nose.

"Let us go," Stella said. It was more than a suggestion.

Trinket shook his head slowly, then lifted his eyes. She thought she might be having an effect on him, despite his nose plugs and the mints.

"Let us all go," Stella said.

The old woman came in so quietly Stella did not hear her. She was surprisingly strong. She grabbed Stella around the ribs, pinning her arms and making her squeak like a mouse, and shoved her through the door. Her book fell to the floor. Trinket swung up and caught the key on its string, then slammed and locked the gate before Stella could turn around.

"They're lonely in there," Trinket's mother told Stella. She wore a clothespin on her nose and her eyes were watering. "Let my son do his work. Fred, maybe now she'd like some lunch."

Trinket took out a handkerchief and blew his nose, expelling the plugs. He looked at them in disgust, then pushed a button mounted on the wall. A lock clicked and buzzed and another wire door behind her popped open. Stella faced them through the mesh of the first door. She could not make a sound at first, she was so startled and so angry.

Trinket rubbed his eyes and shook his head. He gave a little kick and spun her book into the far corner. "Damn," he said. "She's good. She almost had me. Hellish little skunk."

She stood shivering in the little cubicle. Trinket turned out the fluorescent lights. That left only the reflected glow from the rooms behind her.

A hand touched her elbow.

Stella screamed.

"What?"

She backed up against the mesh and stared at a boy. He was ten or eleven, taller than her by a couple of inches, and, if anything, skinnier. He had scratches on his face and his hair was unkempt and tufty.

"I didn't mean to scare you," the boy said. His cheeks flushed in little spots of pink and brown. His gold-flecked eyes followed her as she sidled to the left, into the corner, and held up her fists.

The boy's nose wrinkled. "Wow," he said. "You're really shook."

"What's your name?" she asked, her voice high.

"What sort of name?" he asked. He leaned over, twisted his head, inhaled the air in front of her, and made a sour face.

"They scared me," she explained, embarrassed.

"Yeah, I can tell."

"Who are you?" she asked.

"Look," he said, leaning forward, and his cheeks freckled again.

"So?"

He looked disappointed. "Some can do it."

"What do your parents call you?"

"I don't know. Kids call me Kevin. We live out in the woods. Mixed group. Not anymore. Trinket got me. I was stupid."

Stella straightened and lowered her fists. "How many are in here?"

"Four, including me. Now, five."

She heard the coughing again. "Somebody sick?"

"Yeah."

"I've never been sick," Stella said.

"Neither have I. Free Shape is sick."

"Who?"

"I call her Free Shape. It's not her name, probably. She's almost as old as me."

"Is Strong Will still here?"

"He doesn't like that name. They call us names like that because they say we stink. Come on back. Nobody's going anywhere soon, right? They sent me out here to see who else old Fred snared."

Stella followed Kevin to the back of the long building. They passed four empty rooms equipped with cots and folding chairs and cheap old dressers.

At the very back, three young people sat around a small portable television. Stella hated television, never watched it. She saw that the television's control panel had been covered with a metal plate. Two—an older boy, Will, Stella guessed, and a younger girl, no more than seven—sat on a battered gray couch. The third, a girl of nine or ten, curled up on a blanket on the floor.

The girl smelled bad. She smelled sick. She coughed into her palm and wiped it on her T-shirt without taking her eyes away from the television.

Will pushed off the couch and stood. He looked Stella over cautiously, then stuck his hands in his pockets. "This is Mabel," he said, introducing the younger girl. "Or Maybelle. She doesn't know. Girl on the floor doesn't say much. I'm Will. I'm the oldest. I'm always the oldest. I may be the oldest alive."

"Hello," Stella said.

"New girl," Kevin explained. "She smells really shook."

"You *do*," Mabel said and lifted her upper lip, then pinched the end of her nose.

Will looked back at Stella. "I can see your freckle name. But what's your other name?"

"I think maybe her name is Rose or Daisy," Kevin said.

"My parents call me Stella," she said, her tone implying she wasn't stuck with it; she could change the name anytime. She knelt beside the sick girl. "What's wrong with her?"

"It isn't a cold and it isn't flu," Will said. "I wouldn't get too close. We don't know where she comes from."

"She needs a doctor," Stella said.

"Tell that to the old mother when she brings your food," Kevin suggested. "Just kidding. She won't do anything. I think they're going to turn us in, all at once, together."

"That's the way Fred makes his moochie," Will said, rubbing his fingers together. "Bounty."

Stella touched the sick girl's shoulder. She looked up at Stella and closed her eyes. "Don't look. Nothing to see," the girl said. Her cheeks formed simple patterns, shapeless. Free Shape. Stella pushed harder on the girl's arm. The arm went limp and she rolled onto her back. Stella shook her again and her eyes opened halfway, unfocused. "Mommy?"

"What's your name?" Stella asked.

"Mommy?"

"What does Mommy call you?"

"Elvira," the girl said, and coughed again.

"Ha ha," Will said without humor. That was a cruel joke name.

"You have parents?" Kevin asked the girl, following Stella's lead and kneeling.

Stella touched Elvira's face. The skin was dry and hot and there was a bloody crust under her nose and also behind her ears. Stella felt beneath her jaw and then lifted her arms and felt there. "She has an infection," Stella said. "Like mumps, maybe."

"How do you know?"

"My mother is a doctor. Sort of."

"Is it Shiver?" Will asked.

"I don't think so. We don't get that." She looked up at Will and felt her cheeks signal a message, she did not know what: embarrassment, maybe.

"Look at me," Will said. Stella got to her feet and faced him.

"You know how to talk this way?" he asked. His cheeks freckled and cleared. The dapple patterns came and went quickly, and synchronized somehow with the irises of his eyes, his facial muscles, and little sounds he made deep in his throat. Stella watched, fascinated, but had no idea what he was doing, what he was trying to convey. "I guess not. What do you smell, little deer?"

Stella felt her nose burn. She drew back.

"Practically illiterate," Will said, but his smile was sympathetic. "It's the Talk. Kids in the woods made it up."

Stella realized Will wanted to be in charge, wanted people to think he was smart and capable. There was a weakness in his scent, however, that made him seem very vulnerable. *He's broken,* she thought.

Elvira moaned and called for her mother. Will knelt and touched the girl's forehead. "Her parents hid her in an attic. That's what the kids in the woods said. Her mom and dad left for California, and she stayed behind with her grandmother. Then the grandmother died. Elvira ran away. She got caught on the street. She was raped, I think, more than once." He cleared his throat and his cheeks were dark with angry blood. "She had the start of this cold or whatever it is, so she couldn't fever-scent and make them stop. Fred found her two days after he found me. He took some pictures. He keeps us here until he has enough to get a good bounty."

"One million dollars a head," Kevin said. "Dead or alive."

"Don't be dramatic," Will said. "I don't know how much he gets, and they don't pay if we're dead. If we're injured, he could even go to jail. That's what I heard in the woods. The bounty is federal not state, so he tries to avoid the troopers."

Stella was impressed by this show of knowledge. "It's awful," she said, her heart thumping. "I want to go home."

"How did Fred catch you?" Will asked.

"I went for a walk," Stella said.

"You ran away from home," Will said. "Do your parents care?"

Stella thought of Kaye waking up to find her gone and wanted to cry. That made her nose hurt more, and her ears started to ache.

The wire mesh door rattled. Will pointed, and Kevin left to see what was going on. Stella glanced at Will and then followed Kevin. Mother Trinket was at the cage door. She had just finished shoving a cafeteria tray under the mesh frame. The tray held a paper plate covered with fried chicken backs and necks, a small scoop of dry potato salad, and several long spears of limp broccoli. The old woman watched them, eyes milky, chin withdrawn, strong mottled arms hanging like two birch logs.

"Yuck," Kevin said, and picked up the tray. He gave it to Stella. "All yours," he said.

"How's the girl?" Mother Trinket asked.

"She's really sick," Kevin said.

"People coming. They'll take care of her," Mother Trinket said.

"What do you care?" Kevin asked.

The old woman blinked. "It's my son," she said, then turned and waddled through the door. She closed and locked it behind her.

The girl, Free Shape, was breathing in short, thick gasps as they carried
Stella's tray into the back room.

"She smells bad," Mabel said. "I'm scared for her."

"So am I," Will said.

"Will is Papa here," Mabel said. "Will should get help."

Will looked miserably at Stella and fell back on the couch. Stella put
the tray on a small folding table. She did not feel like eating. Both she
and Kevin squatted by Elvira. Stella stroked the girl's cheeks, making her
freckles pale. They remained pale. The patches had steadied in the last few
minutes, and were now even more meaningless and vague.

"Can we make her feel better?" Stella asked.

"We're not angels," Will said.

"My mother says we all have minds deep inside of us," Stella said, desperate to find some answer. "Minds that talk to each other through chemicals and—"

"What the hell does she know?" Will asked sharply. "She's human,
right?"

"She's Kaye Lang Rafelson," Stella said, stung and defensive.

"I don't care who she is," Will said. "They hate us because we're new
and better."

"Our parents don't hate us," Stella ventured hopefully, looking at Mabel and Kevin.

"Mine do," Mabel said. "My father hates the government so he hid me,
but he just took off one day. My mother left me in the bus station."

Stella could see that these children had lived lives different from her
own. They all smelled lonely and left out, like puppies pulled from a litter,
whining and searching for something they had lost. Beneath the loneliness
and other emotions of the moment lay their fundamentals: Will smelled rich
and sharp like aged cheddar. Kevin smelled a little sweet. Mabel smelled
like soapy bathwater, steam and flowers and clean, warm skin.

She could not detect Elvira's fundamental. Underneath the illness she
seemed to have no smell at all.

"We thought about escaping," Kevin said. "There's steel wire in all the
walls. Fred told us he made this place strong."

"He hates us," Will said.

"We're worth money," Kevin said.

"He told me his daughter killed his wife," Will said.

That kept them all quiet for a while, all but Free Shape, whose breath rasped.

"Teach me how to talk with my dapples," Stella asked Will. She wanted to take their minds off the things they could not hope to do, like escape.

"What if Elvira dies?" Will asked, his forehead going pale.

"We'll cry for her," Mabel said.

"Right," Kevin said. "We'll make a little cross."

"I'm not a Christian," Will said.

"I am," Mabel said. "Christ was one of us. I heard it in the woods. That's why they killed him."

Will shook his head sadly at this naïveté. Stella felt ashamed at the words she had spoken to the men in the Texaco minimart. She knew she was nothing like Jesus. Deep inside, she did not feel merciful and charitable. She had never admitted that before, but watching Elvira gasping on the floor taught her what her emotions really were.

She hated Fred Trinket and his mother. She hated the federals coming for them.

"We'll have to fight to get out," Will said. "Fred is careful. He doesn't come inside the cage. He won't even call a doctor. He just calls for the vans. The vans come from Maryland and Richmond. Everyone wears suits and carries cattle prods and tranquilizer guns."

Stella shivered. She had called her parents; her parents were coming. They might be captured, too.

"Sometimes when the vans come, the children die, maybe by accident, but they're still dead," Will continued. "They burn the bodies. That's what we heard in the woods." He added, "I don't feel like teaching you how to freckle."

"Then tell me about the woods," Stella said.

"The woods are free," Will said. "I wish the whole world was woods."

19

The rain came back as drizzle. Kaye pulled off and parked just north of the private asphalt road that led to the big, white-pillared brick house and outbuildings. The sky was dark enough that the occupants of the house had turned on the interior lights. The black steel mailbox, mounted on a chest-high brick base, showed five gold reflective numbers.

"This is it," Mitch said. He peered through the wet windshield and rolled down his window. A red pickup and camper had been parked in front. There were no other vehicles.

"Maybe we're too late," Kaye said, fighting back tears.

"It's only been ten or fifteen minutes."

"It took us twenty minutes. The sheriff might have come and gone."

Mitch quietly opened the door. "If I can grab her, I'll come right back."

"No," Kaye said. "I won't be left alone. I don't think I can stand it." Her fingers gripped the steering wheel like cords of rope.

"Stay here, please," Mitch said. "I'll be okay. I can carry her. You can't."

"You'd be surprised," Kaye said. Then, "Why would you have to carry her?"

"For speed," Mitch said. "For speed, that's all."

He opened the glove box and took out a cloth-wrapped bundle, pulled open the cloth, smelling of lubricant, and removed a pistol. He tucked the gun into his suit coat pocket. They had three handguns, all of them unregistered and illegal. Getting charged with gun possession was the last thing Mitch and Kaye lost sleep over. Nevertheless, they both looked on the guns with loathing, knowing that weapons give a false sense of security.

Mitch had cleaned and oiled all three last week.

He took a deep breath and stepped out, walking to the rear of the truck. Kaye released the brake and put the truck into neutral. Mitch pushed, grunting softly in the drizzle. Kaye stepped down and helped, steering with one hand, and together they rolled the truck up the asphalt road, stopping about halfway to the house. Kaye spun the wheel and turned the truck until it blocked the way. Hedges and brick walls lined the drive, and no vehicle would be able to get around the truck going in or out. She sat in the cab. Mitch took her face in his hands and kissed her cheek and she squeezed his arms. Then he walked toward the house, shoving his hands into the pockets of his slacks. He never looked comfortable in a suit. His shoulders and his hands were too big, his neck too long. He did not have the face for a suit.

Kaye watched with heart pounding, her mind a thicket.

The pillars and porch stood dark, the door closed. Mitch walked up the steps as softly as his hard-soled shoes allowed and peered through the tall, narrow window on the right.

Kaye watched him turn without knocking and descend the steps. He walked around the side of the house, out of sight. She started to sob and jammed her knuckles against her teeth and lips. They had been standing on tiptoes for eleven years. It was cruel, and whenever she felt she was used to the extremes of their life together, as she had this morning, almost, so close to feeling normal and productive and contented, working on her scientific paper, napping in front of her computer, she would come up short with some spontaneous vision of how they could lose it all. They had been lucky, she knew.

But rarely did her worst visions meet the level of this nightmare.

Mitch walked along the neatly trimmed grass margin, crouching below the windows along the side of the house. He heard a rasping, flacketing buzz, like a big insect, and glanced up with a scowl into the stormy gloom. Saw nothing.

His heart almost stopped when he realized the cell phone was still on. He reached into his left pocket and switched it off.

A gravel path reached from the back porch out to a long frame outbuilding behind the house. He avoided the path and the scrunching sound his shoes would make there, and walked along the soft margin, stepping from the grass, patchy and dead, onto the outbuilding's concrete stoop. He peered through the small, square window set into the steel door. Why a steel door? And new, at that.

In the room beyond the small window he saw a heavy mesh gate. He quietly tried the doorknob. It was locked, of course. He stepped backward, dropped his heel in a depression in the grass, caught his balance with a hop, then walked around the side, quickening his pace. The sheriff might arrive any second. Mitch preferred recovering Stella without official help. Besides, he knew Kaye could not hold out much longer. He had to finish his reconnaissance in a hurry, locate his daughter, and decide what to do next.

Mitch had never been one to make quick decisions. He had spent too many years patiently scraping and brushing through packed layers of soil, uncovering millennia of silent, unwritten history. The peace that had filled his soul on those digs had turned out not to be a survival trait.

He had thrown that peace away, along with the digging, the history, and almost all of his past life, and replaced it with a desperate and protective fury.

20

Mark Augustine twitched his lips at the arrival of the man and the woman in the old truck. Little Bird gave them a series of clear, frozen pictures, at the ends of blurry swoops, the pictures cameoed on the big screens in blue-wrapped squares.

Two names came up on the last screen. Facial matching had led to an identification that Augustine did not need. The man walking around the house was Mitch Rafelson. The woman in the truck was Kaye Lang Rafelson.

"Good," Browning said. "The gang's all here." She looked up at Augustine.

Augustine pinched his lips. "Enforcement is hardly an exact science," he said. "Where are the vans?"

"About two minutes away," Browning said. Once more, she was completely in control and confident.

21

Kaye heard engines. She looked over the hedge to the road and saw two blue-and-white Virginia State Police patrol cars coming from one direction and from the other, no sirens or flashing lights, a long, blocky white utility van, like a cross between a prison bus and an ambulance. She could not see Emergency Action's red-and-gold shield on the side, but she knew it was there.

She stood quietly as the patrol cars slowed and then nosed off with the van to see who would turn first into the private road.

"No snooping," the old woman said. "You with the gas company?" The woman was forty feet away, nothing more than a frizz-headed silhouette. She had come out of the house very quietly as Mitch had transited the back of the long building. She was carrying a shotgun.

Mitch turned and looked up the right side of the long building, facing the back of the house. He had made his circuit and found no other entrance.

"Don't be silly," he called, trying to sound amiable. "I'm looking for my daughter."

"We don't have parties," the woman said.

"Mother!" A man slammed open the screen door and stood beside her on the back porch. "Put that damned gun away. There are troopers out front."

"Caught him," the woman said. She pointed.

"Come right on up here. Let me see you. You with the troopers?"

"Emergency Action," Mitch said.

"That's not what he said," the woman commented, lowering the shotgun.

The man took the gun away from her with a jerk and stepped back into the house. The woman stood staring at Mitch. "You come to get your daughter," she murmured.

Mitch walked warily around her, then to the left, seeing the headlights of a car and a van at the end of the road behind their old truck.

"Damn it, you've parked all wrong," the man shouted from inside the house. Mitch heard feet stamping on wooden floors, saw lights go on and off through the rooms, heard the door open on the front porch.

As Mitch came around the corner, a plump, active man in shorts stood on the porch between the pillars, hands up as if surrendering. "What are they up to?" the man muttered.

Mitch's hopes were very low. He could not find Stella without making a lot of noise, and there was no way now he could imagine getting her away from the house even if he carried her. The woods behind the house and across a field looked thick. Bugs were humming and chirping all around him now that the rain had let up. The air smelled dusty and sweet with moisture and wet grass and dirt.

Kaye faced the main road and the newly arrived vehicles. Two men in two-tone gray uniforms got out of the patrol cars and walked toward her. The younger man cast a confused backward glance at the van.

"Did you call us, ma'am?" the older trooper asked. He was large, in his late forties, with a deep but crackling bull voice.

"Our daughter's been kidnapped. She's in there," Kaye said.

"In the house?"

"We just got here. She called us and told us where to find her."

The troopers regarded each other briefly, faces professionally blank, then turned toward the two figures emerging from the van: a tall, cadaverous male in a shiny black jumpsuit and a stocky female in plastic isolation whites. They slipped on gloves and face masks and approached the troopers.

"This is our jurisdiction, officers," the thin man said. "We're federal."

"We have a kidnapping complaint," the older trooper said.

"Ma'am, what's your business here?" the woman asked Kaye.

"Show me your ID," Kaye demanded.

"Look at the damned van. They aren't cheap, you know," said the thin man in the black jumpsuit, his voice haughty. "You the mother?"

The troopers stood back. The big one scowled at the thin man.

"You are here to pay bounty," Kaye said, her voice scratchy. "I have no idea how many kids are here, but I know this is not legal. Not in this state."

The big trooper stood his ground with arms folded. "That true?" he asked the woman in the plastic suit.

"We have jurisdiction. This is federal," the tall man repeated. "Sherry," he called out to his partner, "get the office."

"Maryland plates," the younger trooper observed.

Kaye studied the big trooper's face. He was red-cheeked and his nose was a swollen network of broken veins, probably from rosacea, but it could also have been drink.

"Why are you outside of your county?" the big trooper asked the pair from the van.

"It's federal; it's official," the stout little woman said defiantly. "You can't stop us."

"Take off that damned mask. I can't understand you," the big trooper said.

"It's policy to leave the mask on, officer," the woman announced formally. Her outfit rustled and squeaked as she walked. There was an air of disarray about the team that did not inspire confidence. The big trooper's uniform was pressed and fit tightly over a strong frame going to fat. He looked sad and tired, but strong on self-discipline. Kaye thought he looked like an old football player. He was not impressed. He turned his attention back to Kaye. "Who called the state police, ma'am?"

"My husband. Someone snatched our daughter. She's in that house."

"Are we talkin' about virus children?" the trooper asked softly.

Kaye studied his expression, his dark eyes, the lines around his jowls. "Yes," she said.

"How long you been living here?" the big trooper asked.

"In Spotsylvania County, almost four years," Kaye said.

"Hiding out?"

"Living quietly."

"Yeah," the trooper said with somber resignation. "I hear that." He swung around to the Emergency Action team. "You got paperwork?" He waved his hand at his partner. "Check out the house."

"My husband is armed," Kaye said, and pointed toward the house. "They kidnapped our child. Please, he won't shoot at you. Let him surrender his gun."

The big trooper unclipped his pistol with a swift motion of both hands. He squinted at the big pillared house, then saw Mitch and the old woman walking up the side yard.

His partner, younger by at least ten years, stooped and immediately drew his own pistol. "I hate this shit," he said.

"Let us do our work," the stout woman demanded. The mask slipped and she looked even more ridiculous.

"I haven't seen any paperwork, and you are out of your jurisdiction," the big trooper growled, keeping his eyes on the house. "I need to see EMAC documents authorizing this extraction."

Neither responded at once. "We're filling in for the Spotsylvania County team. They're on another assignment," the thin man admitted, some of his bravado gone.

"I know the ones," the big trooper said. He looked sadly at Kaye. "They took my son four years ago. My wife and I haven't seen our boy once, not once, since then. He is in Indiana now, outside Terre Haute."

"You're brave to still be together," Kaye said, as if a spark had passed and they understood each other and their troubles.

The big trooper dropped his chin but still watched everyone with beady, alert eyes. "Don't you know it," he said. He waved his hand at his partner. "William, retrieve the father's little pistol and let's check the house. Let's see what you all have got going here."

Mitch slung his gun by its trigger guard on his pointing finger and held it high up in the air. He regretted carrying it at all now; he felt foolish, like an actor in a cop show. Still, the thought that Stella was inside the house or the long building or somewhere else on the property made him feel volatile and dangerous. Anything might provoke him, and that was frightening. The intensity of his devotion was like a blowtorch in his head, brilliant and blinding.

It had always been that way. There would never be any escape.

The younger trooper slogged across the wet grass in his boots.

The plump man in shorts finally decided to speak. "How can I help, officer?" he asked.

The younger trooper took Mitch's gun and backed away. "Are you holding children on these premises?" he asked the man in shorts.

"We are," the man said. "Strays and runaways. We protect them until the truck comes and takes them to where they can be taken care of. Where they belong."

Mitch looked at the trooper from beneath lowered, bushy brows. He had always possessed what amounted to a single eyebrow over his eyes and with age, the woolly caterpillar of hair had thickened and gone wild. At the best of times, he looked formidable, even a little crazy. "Our daughter is not a runaway," he said. "She was kidnapped."

The big trooper approached with Kaye and the two collectors close behind. "Where are the children?" he asked.

"Round back," said the man in shorts. "Sir, my name is Fred Trinket. I'm a longtime resident, and my mother has lived here all her life."

"To hell with that," the big trooper said. "Show us the kids, now."

Something whickered over their heads like a big insect. They all looked up.

"Damn," the younger trooper said, flinching and dropping his shoulders. "Sounds like federal surveillance."

The big trooper drew himself up and circled his eyes warily around the dark skies. "I do not see a thing," he said. "Let's go."

The arrival of the troopers did not please Rachel Browning.

"I think we should alert the Frederick County office," she said. She blew her nose again. "And let's get the state's attorney general in on this. She'll want to know what her people are up to."

"There won't be time," Augustine said. "It's Virginia, Rachel. They don't like the feds telling them what to do. And the situation is highly irregular, even for an official kidnapping."

Browning tilted her head to one side, jerking her gaze between Augustine and the displays. "I didn't hear what the big guy said." The Little Bird had backed off about fifty feet and was hovering. Its little fuel cell would be depleted soon, and it would have to return or be retrieved by the command vehicle.

"The trooper said his son was taken," Augustine told her. "He is not likely to be sympathetic."

"Shit," Browning said. "You're happy about this, aren't you?"

Augustine did not smile, but his lips twitched.

"I will not take responsibility," Browning insisted.

"Your own machines are recording everything," Augustine said, pointing at the console. "Better whisk Little Bird out of there, and quickly, if you want to escape a district court spanking."

"You're as culpable as I am," Browning said.

"I've never authorized bounty," Augustine reminded her. "That's your division."

The phone on the desk wheedled.

"Whoops," Augustine said. "Someone's been tuning in."

Browning answered. She covered the mouthpiece and looked up desperately at Augustine. "It's the surgeon general," she said, eyes wide.

Augustine expressed his sympathy with a lift of his brows and a sigh. Then he turned and walked toward the door. The rubber tip of his cane made squeaking noises on the hard floor.

Fred Trinket gently pushed his mother aside as he led the group around the right side of the house. Mitch hated this place, the plump man in khaki shorts, the collectors. His head was like a balloon filled with gasoline waiting to be torched off.

Kaye felt his anger like heat from a stove. She gripped his arm. If Stella was harmed, in any way, then . . . If their daughter was harmed, then . . .

She could not finish that sequence of thoughts.

"We've fed the runaways a chicken lunch, very nutritious," Trinket explained. His face was like blotchy marble and he was sweating like a stuck pig. He was beginning to realize the big trooper did not like the way Trinket made money.

Mitch made a jerk in Trinket's direction. Kaye drew him back and squeezed his arm until he winced. He did not object, just looked at the gray, square board face of the long building behind the house, the asphalt shingled roof, the steel door with its tiny window and concrete stoop.

"We keep good, clean facilities," Trinket said. He had moved ahead of Mitch and Kaye and flanked the big trooper. The younger trooper and the collectors took up the rear. "We've had a number of runaways through here," Trinket continued, louder now with the distance to the door decreasing, his secret soon to be revealed. "We're a conscientious clearing house. We take good care of them."

"Shut up," Kaye demanded.

"Keep your temper, ma'am, please," the big trooper requested, but his own voice was shaky.

Stella heard the lock in the big steel door and rushed from Elvira's side down the hall to the inner cage gate. She stood there as the lights came on in the first little room, with the boxes, and saw a big man in a leather jacket and a khaki uniform and behind him, Fred Trinket.

Stella smelled Kaye and Mitch almost immediately.

"Mommy," she said, as if she were three years old again.

"Open that door," the big trooper ordered Trinket. There were tears on the trooper's cheeks. Stella had not seen many police officers in her life, and she had certainly never seen one cry.

Trinket mumbled and drew the brass key on its string.

"Mommy, she's dead!" Stella cried. "She just died, just right now/ We couldn't do anything!" Her voice split and she spoke in two high-pitched, singing, weirdly beautiful streams, as if two young girls stood by the mesh gate, one inside the other. Kaye could not understand, but her heart almost exploded with joy and grief.

"Open it now!" Kaye shouted, pushing through. Her fingernails raked Fred Trinket's cheek. He recoiled, dropped the key and squealed in protest.

Kaye tried to reach Stella through the mesh. The distance between the two doors separated them.

"Lord almighty," the younger trooper said. Mitch scooped up Trinket's key and tossed it to Kaye, then grabbed the man and held him. The big trooper stood back. Kaye opened the mesh gate and then the inner gate and grabbed Stella.

"Get the others," Stella said.

"How many?" the big trooper asked Trinket.

"Five," Trinket said.

"Sir, it's our duty to assemble and transport all virus children," the stocky collector asserted, shouldering into the first room. Her tall, thin colleague remained outside, staring at the ground, the steps, anything but what was happening within the long building.

Kaye, Mitch, and the big trooper walked down the hall. Stella followed her mother closely. Mitch gave his daughter a squeeze around the shoulders and she hugged him close. "I'm sorry," she whispered.

Mabel and Kevin sat on the couch. Will stood by Elvira. The television blared an old episode of *I Love Lucy*. Kaye bent beside the prone girl and examined her, face wrinkling in pity. She saw the bloody crust under the girl's nose, turned her head gently, found more crust behind her ears, felt the lumps under her jaw and in her armpits.

"How long?" Kaye asked Stella.

"Five, six minutes," Stella said. "She just coughed real bad and lay still."

Kaye looked over her shoulder at Mitch and the big trooper. Trinket winced but wisely kept quiet.

"Let me see," the stocky collector said. She knelt briefly beside the girl. Then she pushed to her feet with a whuff of air and a sharp look at the others and stumbled hastily back down the hall.

"Is she sick?" Trinket asked. "Can you help her?"

"What the hell do you care?" the big trooper asked.

Kaye heard the collector calling for the first aid kit. "It's too late," she murmured.

"You a doctor?" the big trooper asked, bending low over Kaye and the girl on the floor.

"Close enough," Kaye said.

"Get your daughter out of here," he said.

"I might help," Kaye suggested, looking up at the big trooper's jowls, his intense blue eyes.

Mitch let go of Trinket and pulled Stella close.

"Just get her out of here," the trooper repeated. "We'll take care of this. Go far away. Stay together."

"Can Will and Kevin and Mabel come?" Stella asked.

Will regarded them all with slit-eyed defiance. Kevin and Mabel focused on the television, their cheeks gold and pink with fear and shame.

"I'm sorry," Kaye said.

"Mother . . ."

"We have to travel light and fast," Kaye said. *And they might all be sick.*

Stella pulled loose from Mitch and ran to Will. She grabbed Will's shoulders and they stared at each other for several seconds.

Kaye and Mitch watched them, Mitch twitching, Kaye oddly calm and fascinated. She hadn't seen her daughter with another *Homo sapiens novus* in two years. She was ashamed it had been so long, but ashamed for whom, she could not say. Maybe for the whole troubled human race.

The two separated. Kaye took Stella by the hand and gave her the secret signal that she had taught her daughter years ago, a scrape of her pointing finger across Stella's palm that meant they had to go now, no questions, no hesitation. Stella jerked but followed.

"Remember the woods," Will sang out. "Woods everywhere. Woods for the whole world."

As they ran down the asphalt road to the truck, they heard the trooper arguing with Trinket and the collectors. "We don't take kindly to child theft, not in this county."

He was buying Stella and her parents time.

So was the dead girl.

•　　•

Mitch drove around the van. The hedge scraped Kaye's door. "We should take them with us, all of them!" she cried, and hugged Stella fiercely. "God, Mitch, we should save them all."

Mitch did not stop.

24

At Dulles, Augustine's limo was flagged through and driven directly to the waiting government jet, its engines idling on the tarmac. As he boarded, an Air Force staff officer handed him a locked attaché case. Augustine asked the attendant for a ginger ale then took his seat midplane, over the wing, and buckled himself in.

He removed an e-sheet from the attaché case and folded the red corner to activate it. A keypad appeared in the lower half. He entered the code of the day and read his briefing from the Emergency Action Special Reconnaissance Office. Interdictions were up 10 percent in the last month, due in large part to Rachel Browning's efforts.

Augustine could no longer bear to watch TV or listen to the radio. So many loud voices shouting lies for their own advantage. America and much of the rest of the world had entered a peculiar state of pathology, outwardly normal, inwardly prone to extraordinary fear and anger: a kind of powder keg madness.

Augustine knew he could take responsibility for a considerable share of that madness. He had once fanned the flames of fear himself, hoping to rise in the ranks to director of the National Institutes of Health and procure more funds from a reluctant Congress.

Instead, the president's select committee on Herod's issues had promoted him laterally to become czar of SHEVA, in charge of more than 120 schools around the country.

Parent opposition groups called him the commandant, or Colonel Klink.

Those were the kind names.

He finished reading, then crimped the corner of the e-paper until it broke, automatically erasing the memory strip. The display side of the paper turned orange. He handed the attendant the scrap and received his ginger ale in exchange.

"Takeoff in six minutes, sir," the attendant said.

"Am I traveling alone?" Augustine asked, looking around the back of his seat.

"Yes, sir," the attendant said.

Augustine smiled, but there was no joy in it. His face was lined and gray. His hair had turned almost white in the past five years. He looked twenty years older than his chronological age of fifty-nine.

He peered through the window at the welcome storm blowing in fits and starts over most of Virginia and Maryland. Tomorrow was going to be dry once again and mercilessly sunny with a high of ninety-three. It would be warm when he gave his little propaganda speech in Lexington.

The South and East were in the fourth year of a dry spell. Kentucky was no longer a state of blue grass. Much of it looked like California at the end of a parched summer. Some called it punishment, though there had been record corn and wheat crops.

Jay Leno had once cracked that SHEVA had pushed global warming onto a back burner.

Augustine fidgeted with the clasp on the attaché case. The plane taxied. With nothing but raindrop-blurred runway visible outside the window, he pulled out the paper edition of the *Washington Post*. That and the Cleveland *Plain Dealer* were the only two true news*papers* he read now. Most of the other dailies around the country had succumbed to the deep recession. Even the *New York Times* was published only in an electronic edition.

Some wags called the online journals "electrons." Whereas paper had two sides, electrons were biased toward the negative. The online journals certainly had nothing good to say about Emergency Action.

"Mea maxima culpa," Augustine whispered, his nervous little prayer of contrition. Infrequently, that mantra of guilt changed places with another voice that insisted it was time to die, to put himself at the mercy of a just God.

But Augustine had practiced medicine, studied disease, and struggled in politics too long to believe in a kind or generous deity. And he did not want to believe in the other.

The one that would be most interested in Mark Augustine's soul.

The plane reached the end of the runway and ascended quickly, efficiently, on the wind from a rich bass roar.

The attendant touched his shoulder and smiled down on him. Augustine had somehow managed a catnap of perhaps ten minutes, a blessing. He felt almost at peace. The plane was at altitude, flying level. "Dr. Augustine, something's come up. We have orders to take you back to Washington. There's a secure satellite channel open for you."

Augustine took the handheld and listened. His face became, if that was possible, even more ashen. A few minutes later, he returned the phone to the attendant and left his seat to walk gingerly down the aisle to the washroom. There, he urinated, bracing the top of his head and one hand against the curved bulkhead. The plane was banking to make a turn.

He was scheduled for an emergency meeting with the secretary of Health and Human Services, his immediate superior, and representatives from the Centers for Disease Control.

He pushed the little flush button, zipped up, washed his hands thoroughly, rinsed his gray, surprisingly corpselike face, and stared at himself in the narrow mirror. A little turbulence made the jet bounce.

The mirror always showed someone other than the man he had wanted to become. The last thing Mark Augustine had ever imagined he would be doing was running a network of concentration camps. Despite the educational amenities and the lack of death houses, that was precisely what the schools were: isolated camps used to park a generation of children at high expense, with no in and out privileges.

No peace. No respite. Only test after test after cruel test for everyone on the planet.

25

Stella watched her parents strip the house. She wept silently.

Kaye dragged a wooden box stacked high with the computer and the most important of their books and papers out to the Dodge. Mitch burned documents in a rusty oil drum in the backyard.

Kaye tersely told Stella to throw the clothes she really wanted into a single small suitcase and anything else into a plastic garbage bag, which they would take if there was room left in the car.

"I didn't mean to do this," Stella said softly. Kaye did not hear or, more likely, did not think it best to listen to her daughter now. Louder, Stella added, "I like this house."

"So do I, honey. So do I," Kaye said, her face stony.

In the kitchen, Mitch smashed the cell phone and pulled out the little plastic circuit boards, then jammed them in his pocket. He would throw them out the window or drop them in a garbage can in another state. He then smashed the answering machine.

"Don't bother," Kaye said as she lugged the plastic bag full of clothes down the hall. "We're probably the most listened-to family in America."

"Old habit," Mitch said. "Leave me to my illusions."

"I've made trouble and I'm putting you in danger," Stella said. "I should just go away. I should just go into a camp."

"Us, in danger?" Kaye stopped and spun around at the end of the hall. "Are you testing me?" she demanded. "We are not worried for *ourselves*, Stella. We have *never been worried about ourselves.*" Her hands moved in small arcs from hips to shoulders, and then she crossed her arms.

"I don't understand why this has to happen," Stella said. "Please, let's stay here and if they come, they come, all right?"

Kaye's face turned white.

Stella could not stop talking. "You say you're afraid for me, but are you really afraid for *yourselves*, for how you'll feel if—"

"Shut up, Stella," Kaye said, shaking, then regretted the sharp words. "Please. We have to get out of here quickly."

"I'd know others like me. I could find out what we really need to do. They have to accept us someday."

"They could just as easily kill you all," Mitch said, standing behind Kaye.

"That's crazy," Stella said. "Their own children?"

Mitch and Kaye faced off against their daughter down the length of the hall. Kaye seemed to recognize this symbolism and turned halfway, not looking directly at Stella, but at the plasterboard, the cornice, the paint, her eyes searching these blank things as if they might be sacred texts.

"I don't think they would," Stella said.

"That is not your concern," Mitch said.

Stella desperately wrinkled her face in what she hoped was a smile. Her tears started to flow. "If it isn't my concern, whose is it?"

"Not yours, alone, not yet," Mitch said, his voice many degrees softer, and so full of painful, angry love that Stella's throat itched. She scratched her neck with her fingers.

Kaye looked up. "Damn," she said, reminded of something. She stared

at her fingers and her nails and rushed into the bathroom. There, she lath-
ered and rinsed her hands for several minutes.

Steam billowed from the sink as Stella stood by the door.

"Fred stuff?" Stella asked.

"Fred," Kaye confirmed grimly.

"You took a good swipe," Stella said.

"Mom cat," Kaye said. She scrubbed back and forth with a stiff little
bristle brush, then looked up at the ceiling through the steam and the laven-
der of the soap. *"I'm going to wash that man right off of my hands,"* she
sang. This was so close to the edge, so fraught, that Stella forgot her guilt
and frustration and reached out for her mother.

Kaye knocked aside her daughter's long arms.

"Mother," Stella said, shocked. "I'm sorry!" She reached out again.
Kaye let out a wail, slapping at Stella's hands until Stella caught her around
her chest. As mother and daughter slumped to the ragged throw rug on the
bathroom floor, too exhausted to do anything but shake and clutch, Mitch
sucked in his breath and finished the work. He loaded a second suitcase
with clothes, zipped it shut, and tossed it into the trunk of the Dodge along
with the garbage bag. He imagined himself a rugged frontier father getting
ready to pull out of the sod house and hightail it into the woods because Indians were coming.

But it wasn't Indians. They had spent time with Indians—Stella had
been born in a reservation hospital in Washington state. Mitch had studied
and admired Indians for decades. He had also dug up ancient North American bones. That had been a long time ago. He didn't think he would do
that now.

Mitch was no longer a white man. He wanted little or nothing to do
with his own race, his own species.

It was the cavalry that he feared.

They took the Dodge and left the old gray Toyota truck in the dirt driveway. Kaye did not look back at the house, but Stella, sitting beside her
mother in the backseat, swung around.

"We buried Shamus there," she said. Shamus had come into their lives
three years ago, an old, battered tomcat with a rope looped around his neck.
Kaye had cut off the rope, sewn up a slashed ear, and put in a shunt to drain
a pus-filled wound behind one eye. To keep the orange tabby from scratch-
ing out the stitches, Mitch had wrapped his head in a ridiculous plastic
shield that had made him look, Stella said, like Frankenpuss.

For a half-wild old tom, he had been a remarkably sweet and affectionate cat.

One evening last winter, Shamus had not shown up for table scraps or his usual siesta on Kaye's lap. The tom had wandered off into the far corner of the backyard, well away from Stella's sense of smell. He had pushed his way under a swelling lobe of kudzu, hidden from crows, and curled up.

Two days later, acting on a hunch, Mitch had found him there, head down, eyes closed, feet tucked under as if asleep. They had buried him a few yards away wrapped in a scrap of knitted afghan he had favored as a bed.

Mitch had said that cats did that, wandered off when they knew the end was near so their bodies would not attract predators or bring disease to the family, the pride.

"Poor Shamus," Stella said, peering out the rear window. "He has no family now."

26

They drove. Stella remembered many such trips. She lay in the backseat, nose burning, arms folded tightly, fingers and toes itching, her head in Kaye's lap and when Kaye drove, in Mitch's.

Mitch stroked her hair and looked down on her. Sometimes she slept. For a time, the clouds and then the sun through the car windows filled her up. Thoughts ran around in her head like mice. Even with her parents, she hated to admit, she was alone. She hated those thoughts. She thought instead of Will and Kevin and Mabel or Maybelle and how they had suffered because their parents were stupid or mean or both.

The car stopped at a service station. Late afternoon sun reflected from a shiny steel sign and hurt Stella's eyes as she pushed through the hollow metal door into the restroom. The restroom was small and empty and forbidding, the walls covered with chipped, dirty tile. She threw up in the toilet and wiped her face and mouth.

Now the backs of her ears stung as if little bees were poking her. In the mirror, she saw that her cheeks would not make colors. They were as pale as Kaye's. Stella wondered if she was changing, becoming more like her mother. Maybe being a virus child was something you got over, like a birthmark that faded away.

•   •

Kaye felt her daughter's forehead as Mitch drove.

The sun had set and the storm had passed.

Stella lay in Kaye's lap, face almost buried. She was breathing heavily. "Roll over, sweetie," Kaye said. Stella rolled over. "Your face is hot."

"I threw up back there," Stella said.

"How far to the next house?" Kaye asked Mitch.

"The map says twenty miles. We'll be in Pittsburgh soon."

"I think she's sick," Kaye said.

"It isn't Shiver, is it, Kaye?" Stella asked.

"You don't get Shiver, honey."

"Everything hurts. Is it mumps?"

"You've had shots for everything." But Kaye knew that couldn't possibly be true. Nobody knew what susceptibilities the new children might have. Stella had never been sick, not with colds or flu; she had never even had a bacterial infection. Kaye had thought the new children might have improved immune systems. Mitch had not supported this theory, however, and they had given Stella all the proper immunizations, one by one, after the FDA and the CDC had grudgingly approved the old vaccines for the new children.

"An aspirin might help," Stella said.

"An aspirin would make you ill," Kaye said. "You know that."

"Tylenol," Stella added, swallowing.

Kaye poured her some water from a bottle and lifted her head for a drink. "That's bad, too," Kaye murmured. "You are very special, honey."

She pulled back Stella's eyelids, one at a time. The irises were bland, the little gold flecks clouded. Stella's pupils were like pinpricks. Her daughter's eyes were as expressionless as her cheeks. "So fast," Kaye said. She set Stella down into a pillow in the corner of the backseat and leaned forward to whisper into Mitch's ear. "It could be what the dead girl had."

"Shit," Mitch said.

"It isn't respiratory, not yet, but she's hot. Maybe a hundred and four, a hundred and five. I can't find the thermometer in the first aid kit."

"I put it there," Mitch said.

"I can't find it. We'll get one in Pittsburgh."

"A doctor," Mitch said.

"At the safe house," Kaye said. "We need a specialist." She was working to stay calm. She had never seen her daughter with a fever, her cheeks and eyes so bland.

The car sped up.

"Keep to the speed limit," Kaye said.

"No guarantees," Mitch said.

27

Christopher Dicken got off the C-141 transport at Wright-Patterson Air Force Base. At Augustine's suggestion, he had hitched a late-afternoon ride from Baltimore with a flight of National Guard troops being moved into Dayton.

He was met on the concrete apron by a neatly dressed middle-aged man in a gray suit, the civilian liaison, who accompanied him through a small, austere passenger terminal to a black Chevrolet staff car.

Dicken looked at two unmarked brown Fords behind the Chevrolet. "Why the escort?" he asked.

"Secret Service," the liaison said.

"Not for me, I hope," Dicken said.

"No, sir."

As they approached the Chevrolet, a much younger driver in a black suit snapped to military attention, introduced himself as Officer Reed of Ohio Special Needs School Security, and opened the car's right rear door.

Mark Augustine sat in the backseat.

"Good afternoon, Christopher," he said. "I hope your flight was pleasant."

"Not very," Dicken said. He hunched awkwardly into the staff car and sat on the black leather. The car drove off the base, trailed by the two Fords. Dicken stared at huge billows of clouds piling up over the green hills and suburbs beside the wide gray turnpike. He was glad to be on the ground again. Changes in air pressure bothered his leg.

"How's the leg?" Augustine asked.

"Okay," Dicken said.

"Mine's giving me hell," Augustine said. "I flew in from Dulles. Flight got bumpy over Pennsylvania."

"You broke your leg?"

"In a bathtub."

Dicken conspicuously rotated his torso to face his former boss and looked him over coldly. "Sorry to hear that."

Augustine met his gaze with tired eyes. "Thank you for coming."

"I didn't come at your request," Dicken said.

"I know. But the person who made the request talked to me."

"It was an order from HHS."

"Exactly," Augustine said, and tapped the armrest on the door. "We're having a problem at some of our schools."

"They are not *my* schools," Dicken said.

"Have we made clear how much of a pariah I am?" Augustine asked.

"Not nearly clear enough," Dicken said.

"I know your sympathies, Christopher."

"I don't think you do."

"How's Mrs. Rhine?"

The goddamned high point of Mark Augustine's career, Dicken thought, his face flushing. "Tell me why I'm here," he said.

"A lot of new children are becoming ill, and some of them are dying," Augustine said. "It appears to be a virus. We're not sure what kind."

Dicken took a slow breath. "The CDC isn't allowed to investigate Emergency Action schools. Turf war, right?"

Augustine tipped his head. "Only in a few states. Ohio reserved control of its schools. Congressional politics," he said. "Not my wish."

"I don't know what I can do. You should be shipping in every doctor and public health worker you can get."

"Ohio school medical staff by half last year, because the new children were healthier than most kids. No joke." Augustine leaned forward in the seat. "We're going to what may be the school most affected."

"Which one?" Dicken asked, massaging his leg.

"Joseph Goldberger."

Dicken smiled ruefully. "You've named them after public health heroes? That's sweet, Mark."

Augustine did not deviate from his course. His eyes looked dead, and not just from being tired. "Last night, all but one of the doctors deserted the school. We don't yet have accurate records on the sick and the dead. Some of the nurses and teachers have walked, too. But most have stayed, and they're trying to take up the slack."

"Warriors," Dicken said.

"Amen. The director, against my express orders but at the behest of the governor, has instituted a lockdown. Nobody leaves the barracks, and no visitors are allowed in. Most of the schools are in a similar situation. That's why I asked you to join me, Christopher."

Dicken watched the highway, the passing cars. It was a lovely afternoon and everything appeared normal. "How are they handling it?"

"Not well."

"Medical supplies?"

"Low. Some interruption in the state supply chain. As I said, this is a state school, with a state-appointed director. I've ordered in federal emergency supplies from EMAC warehouses, but they may not get here until later tomorrow."

"I thought you put together an iron web," Dicken said. "I thought you covered your ass when they handed you all this, your little fiefdom."

Augustine did not react, and that in itself impressed Dicken. "I wasn't clever enough," Augustine said. "Please listen and keep your head clear. Only select observers are being allowed into the schools until the situation is better understood. I'd like you to conduct a thorough investigation and take samples, run tests. You have credibility."

Dicken felt there was little sense in accusing or tormenting Augustine any more. His shoulders drooped as he relaxed his back muscles. "And you don't?" he asked.

Augustine looked down at his hands, inspected his perfectly manicured fingernails. "I am perceived as a disappointed warden who wants out of his job, which I am, and a man who would trump up a health crisis to protect his own hide, which I would not. You, on the other hand, are a celebrity. The press would wash your little pink toes to get your side of this story."

Dicken made a soft nose-blow of dismissal.

Augustine had lost weight since Dicken last saw him. "If I don't get the facts and plug them into some tight little bureaucratic columns in the next few days, we may have something that goes far beyond sick children."

"Goddammit, Mark, we know how Shiver works," Dicken said. "Whatever this is, it is *not* Shiver."

"I'm sure you're right," Augustine said. "But we need more than facts. We need a hero."

28

Grief had been tracking Mitch Rafelson like a hunter. It had him in its eye-beams, painting him like a target, preparing to bring him down and settle in for a long feast.

He felt like stopping the Dodge on the side of the road, getting out, and running. As always, he stuffed these dark thoughts into a little drawer in the basement of his skull. Anything that demonstrated he was other than a loving father, all the emotions that had not been appropriate for eleven years and more, he hid away down there, along with the old dreams about the mummies in the Alps.

All the spooky little guesses about the situation of the long-dead Neandertals, mother and father, and the mummified, modern infant they had made before dying in the cold, in the long deep cave covered with ice.

Mitch no longer had such dreams. He hardly dreamed at all. But then, there wasn't much else left of the old Mitch, either. He had been burned away, leaving a thin skeleton of steel and stone that was Stella's daddy. He did not even know anymore whether his wife loved him. They hadn't made love in months. They didn't have time to think about such things. Neither complained; that was just the way it was, no energy or passion left after dealing with the stress and worry.

Mitch would have killed Fred Trinket if the police and the van hadn't been there. He would have broken the man's neck, then looked into the bastard's startled eyes as he finished the twist. Mitch ran that image through his head until he felt his stomach jump.

He understood more than ever how the Neandertal papa must have felt.

Seven miles. They were on the outskirts of Pittsburgh. The road was surrounded by blaring ads trying to get him to buy cars, buy tract homes, spend money he did not have. The houses beyond the freeway were packed close, crowded and small, and the big brick industrial buildings were dirty and dark. He hardly noticed a tiny park with bright red swings and plastic picnic tables. He was looking for the right turnoff.

"There it is," he told Kaye, and took the exit. He glanced into the backseat. Stella was limp. Kaye held her. Together like that, they reminded him of a statue, a Pietà. He hated that metaphor, common enough on the fringe sites on the Internet: the new children as martyrs, as Christ. Hated it with a passion. Martyrs died. Jesus had died horribly, persecuted by a blind state and an ignorant, bloodthirsty rabble, and that was certainly not going to happen to Stella.

Stella was going to live until long after Mitch Rafelson had rotted down to dry, interesting bones.

The safe house was in the rich suburbs. The tree-filled estates here were nothing like the land around the little frame house in Virginia. Smooth as-phalt and concrete roads served big new houses from the last hot run of the economy. Here the streets were lined on both sides with fresh-cut stone walls set behind mature pines and broken only by black iron gates topped with spikes.

He found the number painted on the curb and pulled the Dodge up to a hooded security keypad. The first time, he fumbled the number and the keypad buzzed. A small red light blinked a warning. The second time, the gate rolled open smoothly. Leaves rustled in the maple trees overarching the driveway.

"Almost there," he said.

"Hurry," Kaye said quietly.

29

Joseph Goldberger School for Children with Special Needs, Emergency Action Ohio, Central District Authority

A small contingent of Ohio National Guard trucks—Dicken counted six, and about a hundred troops—had drawn up at the crossroads. A perennial around the school, blooming every spring and summer, dying back in the winter, protesters stood in clumps away from the troops and the alarm trip wires. Dicken guessed that today they numbered three or four hundred today, more than usual and more energetic as well. Most of the protesters were younger than thirty, many younger than twenty. Some wore brightly tie-dyed T-shirts and baggy slacks and had felted their hair in long bleached dreadlocks. They sang and shouted and waved signs denouncing "Virus Abominations" genetically engineered by corporate mad scientists. Two news trucks poked their white dish antennae at the sky. Reporters were out interviewing the protesters, feeding the hungry broadband predigested opinion and some visuals. Dicken had seen all this many times.

On the news, the protesters' standard line was that the new children were artificial monsters designed to help corporations take over the world. *GM Kids*, they called them, or *Lab Brats*, or *Monsanto's Future Toadies.*

Pushed back almost into the grass and gravel of a makeshift parking lot were a few dozen parents. Dicken could easily tell them apart from the protesters. The parents were older, conservatively dressed, worn down and nervous. For them, this was no game, no bright ritual of youthful passage into a dull and torpid maturity.

The staff car and its two escorts approached the first perimeter gate through a weave of concrete barricades. Protesters swarmed the fence, swinging their signs in the direction of the protected road. The largest sign out front, scrawled in red marker and brandished by a skinny boy with prominent bad teeth, read, HEY HEY USA/ DON'T FUCK WITH NATURE'S DNA!

"Just shoot them," Dicken muttered.

Augustine nodded his tight-lipped concurrence.

Damn, we agree on something, Dicken thought.

In the beginning, the protesters had nearly all been parents, arriving at the schools by the thousands, some hangdog and guilty, some grim and defiant, all pleading that their children be allowed to go home. Back then, the nursery buildings had been filled and the dorms under construction or empty. The parents had mounted their vigils year-round, even in the dead of winter, for more than five years. They had been the best of citizens. They had surrendered their children willingly, trusting government promises that they would eventually be returned.

Mark Augustine had been unable to fulfill that promise, at first because of what he thought he knew, but in later years because of grim political reality.

Americans by and large believed they were safer with the virus children put away. Sealed up, out of sight. Out of range of contagion.

Dicken watched Augustine's expression change from studied indifference to steely impassivity as the staff car climbed the sloping road to the plateau. There the massive complex sat flat and ugly like a spill of children's blocks on the Ohio green.

The car maneuvered around the barricades and pulled up to the dazzling concrete gatehouse, whiter even than the clouds. As the guards checked their schedule of appointments and consulted with the Secret Service agents, Augustine stared east through the car window at a row of four long, ocher-colored dormitories.

It had been a year since Augustine had last inspected Goldberger. Back then, lines of kids had moved between classrooms, dormitories, and cafeteria halls, attended by teachers, interns, security personnel. Now, the dormitories seemed deserted. An ambulance had been parked by the inner gate to the barracks compound. It, too, was unattended.

"Where are the kids?" Dicken asked. "Are they *all* sick?"

30

PENNSYLVANIA

Stella saw and felt everything in ragged jerks. Being moved was an agony and she cried out, but still, the shadows insisted on hurting her. She saw asphalt and stone and gray bricks, then a big upside-down tree, and finally a bed with tight pink sheets. She saw and heard adults talking in the light of an open door. Everything else was dark, so she turned toward the darkness—it hurt less—and listened with huge ears to voices in another room. For a moment, she thought these were the voices of the dead, they were saying such incredible things, harmonizing with a weird joy. They were discussing fire and hell and who was going to be eaten next, and a mad woman laughed in a way that made her flesh crawl.

The flesh did not stop crawling. It just kept on going, and she lay in the bed with no skin, staring up at cobwebs or ghostly arms or just floaters inside her eyeballs, tiny chains of cells magnified to the size of balloons. She knew they were not balloons. It did not matter.

Kaye was beyond exhaustion. Iris Mackenzie sat her down in a chair with a cup of coffee and a cookie. The house was huge and bright inside with the colors and tones rich folks choose: creams and pale grays, Wedgwood blues and deep, earthy greens.

"You have to eat something and rest," Iris told her.

"Mitch . . ." Kaye began.

"He and George are with your girl."

"I should be with her."

"Until the doctor arrives, there's nothing you can do."

"A sponge bath, get that temperature down."

"Yes, in a minute. Now rest, Kaye, please. You nearly fainted on the front porch."

"She should be in a hospital," Kaye said, her eyes going a little wild. She managed to stand, pushing past Iris's gentle hands.

"No hospital will take her," Iris said, turning restraint into a hug and sitting her down again. Iris pressed her cheek against Kaye's and there were tears on it. "We called everyone on the phone tree. Lots of the new children have it. It's on the news already, hospitals are refusing admissions. We're frantic. We don't know about our son. We can't get through to Iowa."

"He's in a camp?" Kaye was confused. "We thought the network was just active parents."

"We are *very* active parents," Iris said with iron in her tone. "It's been two months. We're still listed, and we will stay listed as long as we can help. They can't hurt us any more than they already have, right?"

Iris had the brightest green eyes, set like jewels in a face that was farmer's daughter pretty, with light, florid Irish cheeks and dark brown hair, a slender physique, thin, strong fingers that moved rapidly, touching her hair, her blouse, the tray, and the kettle, pouring hot water into the bone china cups and stirring in instant coffee.

"Does the disease have a name?" Kaye asked.

"No name yet. It's in the schools—the camps, I mean. Nobody knows how serious it is."

Kaye knew. "We saw a girl. She was dead. Stella may have got it from her."

"God *damn* it," Iris said, teeth clenched. It was a real curse, not just an exclamation.

"I'm sorry I'm so scattered," Kaye said. "I need to be with Stella."

"We don't know it isn't catching . . . for us. Do we?"

"Does it matter?" Kaye said.

"No. Of course not," Iris said. She wiped her face. "It absolutely does not matter." The coffee was being ignored. Kaye had not taken a sip. Iris walked off. Turning, she said, "I'll get some alcohol and a bath sponge. Let's get her temperature down."

31

The director greeted the staff car at the tangent where the wide circular drive met the steps to the colonnade of the administration building. He wore a brown suit and stood six feet tall, with wheat-colored hair thinning at the crown, a bulbous nose, and almost no cheek bones. Two women, one large and one short, dressed in green medical scrubs, stood at the top of the steps. Their features were obscured by the shadow of a side wall that blocked the low sun.

Augustine opened the door and got out without waiting for the driver. The director dried his hands on his pants leg, then offered one to shake. "Dr. Augustine, it's an honor."

Augustine gave the man's hand a quick grip. Dicken pushed his leg out, grasped the handle over the door, and climbed from the car. "Christopher Dicken, this is Geoffrey Trask," Augustine introduced him.

Behind them, the two Secret Service cars made a V, blocking the drive. Two men stepped out and stood by the open car doors.

Trask mopped his brow with a handkerchief. "We're certainly glad to have both of you," he said. At six thirty in the evening, the heat was slowly retreating from a high of eighty-five degrees.

Trask flicked his head to one side and the two women descended the steps. "This is Yolanda Middleton, senior nurse and paramedic for the pediatric care center."

Middleton was in her late forties, heavy-set, with classic Congolese features, short-cut wild hair, immense, sad eyes, and a bulldog expression. Her uniform was wrinkled and stained. She nodded at Dicken, then examined Augustine with blunt suspicion.

"And this is Diana DeWitt," Trask continued. DeWitt was small and plump-faced with narrow gray eyes. Her green pants hung around her ankles and she had rolled up her sleeves. "A school counselor."

"Consulting anthropologist, actually," DeWitt said. "I travel and visit the schools. I arrived here three days ago." She smiled sadly but with no hint that she felt put-upon. "Dr. Augustine, we have met once before. This would be a pleasure, Dr. Dicken, under other circumstances."

"We should get back," Middleton said abruptly. "We're very short-staffed."

"These people are essential, Ms. Middleton," Trask admonished.

Middleton flared. "Jesus himself could visit, Mr. Trask, and I'd make him pitch in. You know how bad it is."

Trask put on his most royal frown—a poor performance—and Dicken moved in to defuse the tension. "We don't know," he said. "How bad is it?"

"We shouldn't talk out here," Trask looked nervously at the small crowd of protesters beyond the fence, more than two hundred yards away. "They have those big ears, you know, listening dishes? Yolanda, Diana, could you accompany us? We'll carry on our discussion inside." He walked ahead through the false columns.

One agent joined them, following at a discreet distance.

All of the older buildings were a jarring shade of ocher. The architecture screamed prison, even with the bronze plate on the wall and the sign over the front gate insisting that this was a school.

"On orders from the governor, we have a press blackout," Trask said. "Of course, we don't allow cell phones or broadband in the school, and I've taken the central switchboard offline for now. I believe in a disciplined approach to getting out our message. We don't want to make it seem worse than it is. Right now, my first priority is procuring medical supplies. Dr. Kelson, our lead physician, is working on that now."

Inside the building, the corridors were cooler, though there was no air conditioning. "Our plant has been down, my apologies," Trask said, looking back at Augustine. "We haven't been able to get repair people in. Dr. Dicken, this is an honor. It truly is. If there's anything I can explain—"

"Tell us how bad it is," Augustine said.

"Bad," Trask said. "On the verge of being out of control."

"We're losing our children," Middleton said, her voice breaking. "How many today, Diane?"

"Fifty in the past couple of hours. A hundred and ninety today, total. And sixty last night."

"Sick?" Augustine asked.

"Dead," Middleton said.

"We haven't had time for a formal count," Trask said. "But it is serious."

"I need to visit a sick ward as soon as possible," Dicken said.

"The whole school is a sick ward," Middleton said.

"It's tragic," DeWitt said. "They're losing their social cohesion. They rely on each other so much, and nobody's trained them how to get along when there's a disaster. They've been both sheltered and neglected."

"I think their physical health is our main concern now," Trask said.

"I assume there's some sort of medical center," Dicken said. "I'd like to study samples from the sick children as quickly as possible."

"I've already arranged for that," Trask said. "You'll work with Dr. Kelson."

"Has the staff given specimens?"

"We took samples from the sick children," Trask said, and smiled helpfully.

"But not from the staff?" Dicken blinked impatiently at Trask.

"No." The director's ears pinked. "Nobody saw the need. We've been hearing rumors of a full quarantine, a complete lockdown, everyone, no exceptions. Most of us have families . . ." He let them draw their own conclusions about why he did not want the staff tested. "It's a tough choice."

"You sent samples to the Ohio Department of Health and the CDC?"

"They're waiting to go out now," Trask said.

"You should have sent them as soon as the first child became ill," Dicken said.

"There was complete confusion," Trask explained, and smiled. Dicken could tell Trask was the sort of man who hid doubt and ignorance behind a mask of pleasantry. Nothing wrong here, friends. All is under control. As if expressing a confidence, Trask added, "We are used to them being so healthy."

Dicken glanced at Augustine, hoping for some clue as to what was really going on here, what relationship or control Augustine had over a person like Trask, if any. What he saw frightened him. Augustine's face was as calm as a colorless pool of water on a windless day.

This was not the Mark Augustine of old. And who this new man might become was not something Dicken wanted to worry about, not now.

They passed an elevator and a flight of stairs.

"My office is up there, along with the communications and command center," Trask said. "Dr. Augustine, please feel free to use it. It's on the second floor, with the best view of the school, well, besides the view from the guard towers, which we use mostly for storage now. First, we'll visit the medical center. You can begin work there immediately—away from the confusion."

"I'd like to see the children right away," Dicken insisted.

"By all means," Trask said, eyes shifting. "It will be hard to miss the children." The director walked ahead at a near lope, then looked over his shoulder, saw that Dicken was not nearly as nimble, and doubled back.

DeWitt seemed eager to say something, but not while Trask was in earshot.

"Let me describe our facilities," Trask said. "Joseph Goldberger is the largest school in Ohio, and one of the largest in the country." His hands waved as if outlining a box. "It was built six years ago on the site of the Warren K. Pernicke Corrections Center, a corporate facility administered by Namtex Limited. Pernicke was shut down after the change in drug laws and the subsequent twenty percent drop in the prison population." He was sounding more and more like a tour guide working from a prepared lecture, adding to the surreality. "The contract to convert the complex to hold SHEVA children was let out to CGA and Nortent, and they finished their work in nine months, a record. Four new dorms were erected a hundred yards east of the maximum security building, which was first constructed in 1949. The old hospital and farm buildings were made into research and clinical facilities. The business training building was converted into a nursery, and now it's an education center. The four-hundred-bed special offenders compound now holds our mentally ill and developmentally disabled. We call it our Special Treatment Facility. It's the only one in the state."

"How many children are kept there?" Dicken asked.

"Three hundred and seven," Trask said.

"They were more isolated," Middleton said.

"Dr. Jurie or Dr. Pickman can tell you more about that," Trask said. For the first time, his pleasant demeanor flickered. "Although . . ."

"I haven't seen them," Middleton said.

"Someone told me they left early this morning," DeWitt said. "Perhaps to get supplies," she added hopefully.

"Well." Trask's Adam's apple bobbed like a swallowed walnut and he shook his head with a waxy kind of concern. "As of yesterday, the school housed a total of five thousand four hundred children." He stole a quick look at his watch. "We simply don't have what we need." He escorted them to the west end of the building, and then down a wide connecting corridor lined with old refrigerators. The old white boxes were sealed with black and yellow tape. Empty equipment carts and stacked steel trays littered the passageway. The air was redolent of Pine-Sol.

DeWitt walked beside Dicken like a shipwrecked passenger hoping for a scrap of wood. "They use the Pine-Sol to disrupt scenting and frithing," she said in an undertone. Frithing was a way SHEVA children drew scent into their mouths. They lifted their upper lips and sucked air through their teeth with a faint hiss. The air passed over their vomeronasal organs, glands for detecting pheromones far more sensitive than those found in their parents. "The security and many of the staff wear nose plugs."

"That's pretty standard in the schools," Middleton said to Dicken, with a fleeting look at Augustine. She opened a battered steel storage cabinet and pulled out scrub uniforms and surgical masks. "So far, thank God, none of the staff has gotten sick."

Dicken and Augustine put the uniforms on over their street clothes, strapped on the masks, and slipped their hands into the sterile gloves. They paused as an older man, in his late sixties or early seventies, stooped and eagle-nosed, pushed through the swinging doors at the end of the hall.

"Here's Dr. Kelson now," Trask said, his back stiffening.

Kelson wore a surgical gown and cap, but the gown hung on him, straps loose, and his hands were bare. He approached Augustine, gave him a brusque nod, then turned to Middleton. "Gloves," he demanded. Middleton reached into the locker and handed him a pair of examination gloves. Kelson snapped them on and held them up for inspection. "No go with Department of Health. I asked for a NuTest, antivirals, hydration kits. Not available, they claimed. Hell, I know they have what we need! They're just holding on to them in case this breaks loose."

"It will not break loose," Trask said, his smile faltering.

"Did Trask tell you about our shortage?" Kelson inquired of Augustine.

"We understand it's a crisis," Augustine said.

"It's goddamned *murder*!" Kelson roared. DeWitt jumped. "Three months ago, state Emergency Action officials stripped us of more than half of our medical equipment and drugs. Our entire emergency supply was looted. We have 'healthy children,' they told us. The supplies could be better used elsewhere. Trask did nothing to stop them."

"I would disagree with that characterization," Trask said. "There was nothing I *could* do."

"Last ditch effort, I took a truck into town," Kelson continued. "I smeared mud on the doors and the license plates but they knew. Dayton General told me to stay the hell away. I got nothing. So I came back and slipped in through the Miller's Road entrance. Now even that is blocked." Kelson waved his hand, drunk with exhaustion, and turned his heartsick, skim-milk blue eyes on Dicken. "Who are you?"

Augustine introduced them.

Kelson pointed a knobby gloved finger at Dicken. "You are my witness, Dr. Dicken. The infirmary filled first. It's down this way. We're re-moving bodies by the hundreds. You should see. You should see."

32

Mitch tended to Stella in the bedroom's dim light. She would not hold still. He used all the gentle phrases and tones of voice he could muster; none of them seemed to get through to her.

George Mackenzie watched from the doorway. He was in his early forties and beyond plump. He had a young face with inquiring eyes, his forehead overarched by a styled shock of premature gray hair, and his lip sported a light dust of mustache.

"I need an ear or rectal thermometer," Mitch said. "She might convulse and bite down on an oral one. We'll have to hold her."

"I'll get one," George said, and was gone for a moment, leaving Mitch alone with the tossing child. Her forehead was as dry as a heated brick.

"I'm here," Mitch whispered. He pulled the covers back completely. He had undressed Stella and her bare legs looked skeletal against the pink sheets. She was so sick. He could not believe his daughter was so sick.

George returned holding a blue plastic sheath in one hand and the ther-mometer in the other, followed by the women. Kaye carried a basin of wa-ter filled with ice cubes, and Iris held a washcloth and a bottle of rubbing alcohol. "We never bought an ear thermometer," George said apologeti-cally. "We never felt the need."

"I'm not afraid now," Iris said. "George, I was afraid to touch their lit-tle girl. I am so ashamed."

They held Stella and took her temperature. It was 107. Her normal temperature was 97. They frantically sponged her, working in shifts, and then moved her into the bathroom, where Kaye had filled a tub with water and ice. She was so hot. Mitch saw that she had bleeding sores in her mouth.

Grief looked on, dark and eager.

Kaye helped Mitch take Stella back to the bed. They did not bother to towel her off. Mitch held Kaye lightly and patted her back. George went downstairs to heat soup. "I'll put on some chicken broth for the girl," George said.

"She won't take it," Kaye said.

"Then some soup for us."

Kaye nodded.

Mitch watched his wife. She was almost not there, she was so tired and her face was so drawn. He asked himself when the nightmare would be over. *When your daughter is gone and not before.*

Which of course was no answer at all.

They ate in the darkened room, sipping the hot broth from cups. "Where's the doctor?" Kaye asked.

"He has two others ahead of us," George said. "We were lucky to get him. He's the only one in town who will treat new children."

33

OHIO

The infirmary was on the first floor of the medical center, an open room about forty feet square meant to house at most sixty or seventy patients. The curtained separators had been pushed against the walls and at least two hundred cots, mattresses, and chair pads had been moved in.

"We filled this space in the first six hours," Kelson said.

The smell was overwhelming—urine, vomit, the assaulting miasma of human illness, all familiar to Dicken, but there was more to it—a tang both sharp and foreign, disturbing and pitiful all at once. The children had lost control of their scenting. The room was thick with untranslatable phero-mones, vomeropherins, the arsenal and vocabulary of a kind of human communication that was, if not new, at least more overt.

Even their urine smelled different.

Trask took a handkerchief from his pocket and covered his already masked mouth and nose. Augustine's Secret Service agent took a position in the corner and did the same, visibly shaken.

Dicken approached a corner cot. A boy lay on his side, his chest barely moving. He was seven or eight, from the second and last wave of SHEVA infants. A girl the same age or a little older squatted beside the cot. She held the boy's fingers around a tiny silvery digital music player, to keep him from dropping it. The headphones dangled over the side of the bed. Both were brown-haired, small, with brown skin and thin, flaccid limbs.

The girl looked up at Dicken as he came near. He smiled back at her.

Her eyes rolled up and she tipped her tongue through her lips, then dropped her head on the cot beside the boy's arm.

"Bond friends," DeWitt said. "She has her own cot, but she won't stay there."

"Then move the cots together," Augustine suggested with a brief look of distaste or distress.

"She won't move more than a few inches away from him," DeWitt said. "Their health probably depends on each other."

"Explain," Dicken said softly.

"When they're brought here, the children form frithing teams. Two or three will get together and establish a default scenting range. The teams coalesce into larger groups. Support and protection, perhaps, but mostly I think it's about defining a new language." DeWitt shook her head, wrapped her masked mouth in the palm of one hand, and gripped her elbow. "I was learning so much . . ."

Dicken took the boy's chin and gently turned it: head flopping on a scrawny neck. The boy opened his eyes and Dicken met the blank gaze and stroked his forehead, then ran his rubber-gloved finger over the boy's cheek. The skin stayed pale.

"Capillary damage," he murmured.

"The virus is attacking their endothelial tissues," Kelson said. "They have red lesions between the fingers and toes, some of them vesicular. It's goddamned tropical in its weirdness."

The boy closed his eyes. The girl lifted her head. "I'm not his perf," she said, her voice like a high sough of wind. "He lost his perf last night. I don't think he wants to live."

DeWitt knelt beside the girl. "You should go back to your cot. You're sick, too."

"I can't," the girl said, and again lay down her head.

Dicken stood and tried desperately to clear his mind.

The director tsked in pity. "Absolute confusion," Trask said, voice muffled by the handkerchief. His phone rang in his pocket. He apologized, lowered the cloth, then half turned to answer it. After a few mumbled replies, he closed the phone. "Very good news. I'm expecting a truck filled with supplies from Dayton any minute, and I want to be there. Dr. Kelson, Ms. Middleton—I leave these people with you. Dr. Augustine, do you want to work from my office or would you prefer to stay here? I imagine you have many administrative duties . . ."

"I'll stay here," Augustine said.

"Your privilege," Trask said. With some astonishment, they watched the director toss a nonchalant, almost dismissive wave and make his way around the rows of cots to the door.

Kelson rolled his milky eyes. "Good fucking riddance," he murmured.

"The children are losing all social cohesion," DeWitt said. "I've tried to tell Trask for months that we needed more trained observers, professional anthropologists. Losing bond friends—sometimes they call them perfs—do you realize what that *means* to them?"

"Diana's their angel," Kelson said. "She knows what they're thinking. That may be as important as medicine in the next few hours." He shook his head, jowls jiggling beneath his chin. "They are innocents. They do not deserve this. Nor do *we* deserve Trask. That state-appointed son of a bitch is in on this, I'm sure of it. He's squeezing profits somewhere." Having said his piece, Kelson looked up at the ceiling. "Pardon me. It's the goddamned truth. I have to get back. The medical center is at your disposal, Dr. Dicken, such as it is." He turned and walked down a row of cots, through the door on the opposite side of the infirmary.

"He's a good man," Middleton said. She used a key to open the back door to the main compound, opening on to the infirmary loading dock. She lifted an eyebrow at Dicken. "Used to be pretty cushy around here, room and board, easy work, best school in the world, the kids were so easy, we said. Then *they* up and ran, the bastards."

Middleton led them down the loading ramp to a golf cart parked in the receiving area. DeWitt sat beside her. "Get on, gentlemen."

"Any guesses?" Augustine asked Dicken in an undertone as they climbed onto the middle bench seat. The Secret Service agent, now almost invisible to Dicken, sat on the rear-facing backseat and murmured into a lapel mike.

Dicken shrugged. "Something common—coxsackie or enterovirus, some kind of herpes. They've had trouble with herpes before, prenatal. I need to see more."

"I could have brought a NuTest, if there had been some warning," Augustine said.

"Wouldn't help us much," Dicken said. Something new and unfamiliar had struck the children. If a new virus flooded the first rank of a person's defenses—the innate immune system—and spread to others quickly enough, in close quarters, among confined populations, it could overwhelm any more refined immune response and bring down a huge number of victims in days. He doubted that contact immunity could have had any influence in this outbreak. Another of Mother Nature's little screwups. Or not. He still had a lot to unlearn when it came to viruses and disease, a lot of assumptions to reexamine.

Dicken needed to map the river of this illness before he would venture an answer, chart it back from whatever tributary they were at now to its source. He wanted to know the virus when it was asleep, what he called glacial virus—learn where it hid as frozen snow in the high valleys of the human and animal population, before it melted and became the torrent they were now seeing.

If he found anything closer to that ideal source, that beginning, things might fall into place. He might understand.

Or not.

What they all needed to know as a practical matter was whether this flood would jump its banks and find another run. Taking specimens from the staff would begin to answer that question. But he already had a gut feeling that this disease, attacking a new and juicy population, would not readily cross over to old-style humans.

Proving *that* would, in any sane world, stop the political nightmare building outside.

They passed a crate of body bags the end of the loading dock.

"No trouble getting *those*," Middleton said. "They're going to be filled in a couple of hours."

34

Mitch washed his face for the fourth or fifth time in the bathroom adjacent to the bedroom. He stared at the brass light fixtures, the antique gold faucets, the tile floor. He had never been much for luxuries, but it would have been nice to provide more than just a run-down shack in the Virginia countryside. They had been plagued by ants and by roaches. The big yard had been nice, though. He had liked to sit there with Stella and drag a string for the ever-willing Shamus.

The doctor arrived. He was in his early thirties, hair spiked and frosted. He looked very young. He wore a short-sleeved shirt and carried a black bag and a NuTest diagnostic unit the size of a data phone. He was as worn-out as they were, but he immediately inspected Stella. He took blood and sputum from the girl, who hardly noticed the prick of the little needle. The spit was harder to obtain; Stella's mouth was as dry as a bone. He smeared these fluids on the business end of the NuTest arrays—little sheets of grooved plastic—then inserted them. A few minutes later, he read the results.

"It's a virus," he said. "A picornavirus. No surprise there. Some sort of enterovirus. A variety of Coxsackie, probably. But . . ." He looked at them with a quizzical, worried expression. "There are some polymorphisms that aren't in the NuTest library. I can't make a final determination here."

"Were the baths the right thing to do?" Mitch asked.

"Absolutely," the doctor said. "She's four degrees elevated. Coming down, maybe, but it could spike again. Keep her cool, but don't wear her down. She's skin and bones now."

"She's naturally slender," Kaye said.

"Good. She'll grow up to be a model," the doctor said.

"Not if I can help it," Kaye said.

The doctor stared at Kaye. "Don't I know you?"

"No," she said. "You don't."

"Right," the doctor said, coming to his senses. He gave Stella the first injection, a broad-spectrum antiviral with multiplex immunoglobulin and B vitamins. "Used these when measles hit a bunch of old kids in Lancaster," he said, then grimaced and shook his head. " 'Old kids.' Listen to me. We're talking in tangles. This isn't measles, but the shot can't hurt. It's only good in a series, however. I'll report her arrays anonymously to Atlanta. Part of the field program. Completely anonymous."

Mitch listened without reaction. He was almost beyond caring about anonymity. He looked up as the doctor glanced at the NuTest display and said, "Whoops. Shit." The display was blinking rapidly, reflecting on the doctor's face.

"What?"

"Nothing," the doctor said, but Mitch thought he looked guilty, as if he had screwed up. "Can I have some of that coffee?" the doctor asked. "Cold is fine. I've got two more patients tonight."

He felt Stella under her jaw and behind the ears, then turned her over and inspected her buttocks. A rash was forming on both cheeks. "She's spiking again." He turned her over and helped carry her to the bathtub. George had emptied the kitchen ice machine and driven off to get more from the local grocery. They sponged her down with cold tap water. Stella was convulsing by the time George returned.

Mitch lifted Stella out of the tub by her underarms, soaking his clothes.

George emptied four bags of ice into the water. Then they lowered her in again.

"It's too *cold*," Stella shrieked thinly.

Mitch's daughter seemed to weigh almost nothing. She was ephemeral. The illness was stealing her away so quickly he could not react.

The doctor left to get another injection ready.

Kaye held up her daughter's hand. It was pale and blue. She saw small sores between the girl's fingers. With a gasp, she dropped the hand and leaned to lift Stella's foot. She showed the sole to Mitch. Small lesions spotted the flesh between Stella's toes. "They're on her hands, too," Kaye said.

Mitch shook his head. "I don't know what that is."

George pushed back from the tub and stood, his face showing alarm. The doctor returned with another syringe. As he was injecting Stella he looked at the girl's fingers and nodded. He pulled back Stella's lips and looked into her mouth. Stella moaned.

"Could be herpangina, vesicular stomatitis—" He took a deep breath. "I can't make the call here with just a NuTest. Treatment with a targeted antiviral would work best, and that requires a positive ID. That should be done in a reference lab, and she should be hospitalized. I just don't have that kind of equipment."

"No one will admit her," George said. "Blanket ban."

"Disgraceful," the doctor said, his voice flat from exhaustion. He looked up at George. "It could be communicable. You'll want to sterilize this bathroom and bleach the sheets."

George nodded.

"There's someone who might be able to help," Mitch said to Kaye, taking her aside.

"Christopher?" Kaye asked.

"Call him. Ask him what's happening. You know his phone number."

"His home," Kaye said. "It's an old number. I'm not sure where he works now."

The doctor had dialed up a sentinel CDC report page on his Web phone. "There's no warning posted," he said. "But I've never seen pediatric warnings for virus children."

"New children," George corrected.

"Is it a reportable disease?" Kaye asked.

"It's not even listed," the doctor said, but there was something in his face that disturbed Kaye. *The NuTest. It's got a GPS and a broadband hookup to the Department of Health. And from there, to NIH or the CDC. I'm sure of it.*

But there was nothing they could do. She shrugged it off.

"Call," Mitch told Kaye.

"I don't know who he's working for now," Kaye said.

"We have a secure satellite phone," George said. "No one will back trace. Not that it matters, for us. Our son is already in a camp."

"There is *nothing* secure," Mitch said.

George seemed about to debate this slur on his masculine grasp of crypto-technology.

Kaye held up her hand. "I'll call," she said. It would be the first time she had spoken with Christopher Dicken in over nine years.

But all she got was the answering machine in his apartment. *"This is Christopher. I'm on the road. My house is occupied by cops and wrestlers. Better yet, remember that I collect strange plagues and store them next to my valuables. Please leave your message."*

"Christopher, this is Kaye. Our daughter is sick. Coxsackie something. Call if you have any clues or advice."

And she left the number.

35

OHIO

The infirmary stood adjacent to the southwest corner of the equipment barn: two blocks connected by a short corridor with barred windows. The bright security lights drew angular trapezoids of shadow over the concrete courtyard between the buildings, obscuring a lone boy. Tall and chunky, about ten years old, he leaned or slumped against the door to the research wing, arms folded.

"Who's that?" Middleton called out.

"Toby Smith, ma'am," the boy said, standing straight. He wobbled and stared at them with tired, blank eyes.

"You sick, Toby?"

"I'm fine, ma'am."

"Where's the doctor?" Middleton pulled the cart up ten feet from the boy. Dicken saw the boy's pallid cheeks, almost free of freckles.

The boy turned and pointed into the research wing. "Doctor Kelson is in the gym. My sister's dead," he said.

"I'm sorry to hear that, Toby," Dicken said, swinging out of the seat of the golf cart. "I'm very sorry to hear it. My sister died some time ago."

Dicken approached him. The boy's eyes were rheumy and crusted.

"What did your sister die of?" Toby asked, squinting at Dicken.

"A disease she caught from a mosquito bite. It was called West Nile Virus. May I see your fingers, Toby?"

"No." The boy hid his hands behind his back. "I don't want you to shoot me."

"You ignore that crap, Toby," Middleton said. "I won't let them shoot anybody."

"May I see, Toby?" Dicken persisted. He removed his goggles. Something in his tone, some sympathy, or perhaps the way he smelled—if Toby could still smell him—made the boy look up at Dicken with narrowed eyes and present his hands. Dicken gently reversed the boy's hand and inspected the palm and the skin between the fingers. No lesions. Toby screwed up his face and wriggled his fingers.

"You're a strong young man, Toby," Dicken said.

"I've been in the infirmary, helping, and now I'm on break," Toby said. "I should go back."

"The kids are so gentle," DeWitt said. "They bond so tight, like family, all of them. Tell that to the world out there."

"They don't want to listen," Dicken said under his breath.

"They're scared," Augustine said.

"Of me?" Toby asked.

The cart's small walkie-talkie squawked. Middleton pulled away to answer. Her lips drew together as she listened. Then she turned to Augustine. "Security saw the director's car go out the south entrance ten minutes ago. He was alone. They think he's skipped."

Augustine closed his eyes and shook his head. "Someone alerted him. The governor has probably ordered complete quarantine. We're on our own, for the time being."

"Then we have to move fast," Dicken said. "I need specimens from the remaining staff, and from as many of the children as is practical. I need to learn where this virus came from. Maybe we can get word out and stop this insanity. Have the children in special treatment had contact with the children outside?"

"None that I've heard of," Middleton said. "But I am not responsible for that building. That was Aram Jurie's domain. He and Pickman were part of Trask's inner circle."

"Pickman and Jurie said the specials should be kept separate," DeWitt added. "Something about mental disease being additive in SHEVA children. I think they were interested in the effects of madness and stress."

Viral triggers, Dicken thought. He was torn between disgust and elation. He might find all the clues he needed, after all. "Who's there now?"

"There are six nurses left, I think." Middleton looked away, tears brimming.

"I'll need specimens from those nurses in particular. Nose swabs, fingernail scrapings, sputum, and blood. I think we should do that now."

"Christopher is the point man," Augustine said. "Do whatever he asks."

"I can take you," DeWitt said. She squeezed Middleton's arm supportively. "Yolanda wants to get back to the kids. They need her. I'm baggage for now."

"Let's go," Dicken said. He walked over to Toby. "Thank you, Toby. You've been very helpful."

36

George Mackenzie shook Mitch's shoulder. Mitch lurched up in the bed. The pastel walls of the tidy bedroom swam around him; he did not feel at all rested. He had fallen asleep without pulling back the covers on the bed, still dressed in his rumpled Mr. Smith suit.

"Where's Kaye? How long have I been asleep?"

"She's with your daughter," George said. He looked miserable. "You've been out about an hour. Sorry to wake you. Come take a look at the TV."

Mitch walked into the next room first. Kaye sat on the side of the bed, hands folded between her knees, head bowed. She looked up as Mitch checked Stella, now under the covers. He felt Stella's forehead. "Fever's down."

"Broke about an hour ago. I think. Iris brought some tea and we just sat with her."

Mitch stared at his daughter's sleeping face, so pale on the sky blue pillow, topped by a damp, matted thatch of hair. Her breath came in ragged puffs. "What's with that?"

"She's been breathing that way since the fever broke. She's not badly congested. I don't know what it means. The doctor said he'd be back . . ." She checked the clock on the nightstand. "By now."

"He hasn't come," George said. "I don't think he's going to."

"George wants me to watch the news," Mitch said.

Kaye nodded and waved her hand; she would stay.

George led Mitch down the hall to the den and the flat wall-mounted screen. Huge faces sat behind a fancy rosewood desk, talking . . . Mitch tried to focus.

"I am as liberal as the next fellow, but this scares me," said a middle-aged male sporting a crew cut. Mitch did not watch much television and did not know who this was.

"Brent Tucker, commentator for Fox Broadband," George explained. "He's interviewing a school doctor from Indiana. That's where our son, Kelly, is."

"Haven't we been expecting this?" Tucker was asking. "Isn't this why we've agreed to put the children in these special schools?"

"The footage you've just shown, of parents dropping off their children, finally coming forward and cooperating, is very encouraging—" the doctor said.

Tucker interrupted with a stern expression. "You left your post this morning. Were you afraid?"

"I've been helping explain the situation to the president's staff. I'm going back this afternoon to resume my duties."

"The scientists we've interviewed on this show insist that the children could pose a severe risk to the population at large if allowed to roam free. And there are still tens of thousands of them out there, even now. Isn't it—"

"I cannot agree with that characterization," the doctor said.

"Yes, well, you left your school, and that says it all, don't you think?"

The doctor opened and closed his mouth. Tucker moved in, eyes wide, sensing a kill. "The public can't be fooled. They know what this is about. Let's look at our forum instant messages and what the public is telling us right now."

The figures came up on the screen.

"Ten to one, they want you to arrest parents who don't cooperate, get all the children where we can watch them, and do it now. Ten to one."

"I do not think that is even practicable. We don't have the facilities."

"We built the schools and support your work with taxpayer dollars.

You are a public servant, Dr. Levine. These children are the result of a hideous disease. What if it spreads to all of us, and there are no more normal children born, ever?"

"Do you advocate we should exterminate them, for the public good?" Levine asked.

Mitch watched with grim fascination, jaw clamped, as if witnessing a car crash.

"*Nobody* wants that," Tucker said with an expression of affronted reason. "But there is an imminent health risk. It's a matter of survival."

The doctor put his hands on the rosewood counter. "No illness has spread to staff in any of the schools I'm aware of."

"Then why aren't you in the school now, Dr. Levine?"

"They are *children*, Mr. Tucker. I will be going back to them."

Mitch clenched his fists until his fingernails dug into his palms.

Tucker smiled, showing perfect white teeth, and turned to the camera, which zoomed to a close shot. "I believe in the people and what they have to say. That is the strength of this nation, and it is also the Fox Media philosophy, fair and balanced, and I am not ashamed to agree with it. I believe there is an instinct for preservation at work among the people, and that is *news*. That is *survival*. You'll catch more details here, Fox Multicast, and touch your screen to check our expanded coverage on the Web—"

George turned off the TV. His voice was thin and choked. "Neighbor must have seen you arrive. He told me he's going to turn us in for harboring a virus child. A sick child." He held up and jangled three keys on a ring. "Iris and I have a cabin. It's about two hours from here, up in the mountains. On a small lake. Real nice, away from everybody. There's food for at least a week. You can mail back the keys. Your girl is doing better. I'm sure of it. The crisis is past."

Mitch tried to figure out what their options were—and how adamant Mackenzie was. "She's not breathing right," he said.

"I've been out of work for five months," George said. "We're running out of money. Iris is on the edge of a breakdown. We can't be a safe house anymore. This neighborhood is like Sun City for the wealthy. They're old and scared and mean." George looked up. "If the feds come here and find you, they'll put your daughter someplace where the care is worse than you can imagine. That's where our child is, Mitch."

Kaye stood behind Mitch and touched his elbow, startling him. "Take the keys," she said.

George suddenly fell back into a chair and shook his head. "Stay here until dawn," he said. "The neighbors are asleep. I hope to God everybody is asleep. Get some rest. Then, I'm sorry, you have to leave."

37

OHIO

The Special Treatment center occupied a long, flat, single-story building with reinforced concrete walls. Dicken and DeWitt walked around the empty school trailers and crossed the asphalt square in the brilliant glow of a dozen intense white security lights.

The door to the center hung open. A tangle of sheets and rubber mats had been tossed out like a filthy, lolling tongue. Two iron-barred and wire-reinforced windows gleamed like flat, blank eyes on either side. The building looked dead.

Inside, the air was cooler but not by much, and stank. Beneath the cacophony of stench wavered a weak chord of Pine-Sol. Dicken did not pause, though DeWitt held back and coughed under her mask. He had smelled worse; the professional refrain of a virus hunter.

Beyond the security office and the open double gates of the checkpoint, the doors to all the cells stretched down a long corridor. About half, in no particular order, had been opened. No nurses or guards were in sight.

The body of a boy of eight or nine lay on a mattress in the corridor. Dicken knew the boy was dead from several yards away. He put down his bag of specimen kits, knelt with difficulty beside the soiled mattress, examined the boy with what he hoped was clear-eyed respect, then pushed on the floor and one knee and got up again. He shook his head vigorously at De-Witt's offer of assistance.

"Don't touch anything," he warned. "Yolanda said there were nurses."

"They probably moved the children into the exercise area. The center has its own yard, at the south end."

They checked each room, peering through the observation slit or pushing open the heavy steel doors. Some of the rooms held bodies. Most were empty. A black line drawn on the floor marked the division between rooms equipped for children who need restraints or protection: the padded rooms. All of the doors to these rooms had been opened.

Two rooms contained bodies lying on cots in restraints, one male, one female, both with abnormally large heads and hands.

"It's a condition unique to SHEVA children," DeWitt said. "I've only seen three like this."

"Congenital?"

"Nobody knows."

Dicken counted twenty dead by the time they reached the door at the end. This door was a rolling wall of steel bars covered with thick sheets of acrylic.

"I think this is where Jurie and Pickman ordered the violent children kept," DeWitt said.

Someone had jammed a broken cinder block into the track to prevent the door from automatically closing, and a red light and LED display flashed a security warning. Behind thickly shaded glass, the guard booth was empty, and the alarm had been hammered into silence.

"We don't have to go through here," DeWitt said. "The yard is that way." She pointed down a short hall to the right.

"I need to see more," Dicken said. "Where are the nurses?"

"With the living children, I presume. I hope."

They squeezed through the narrow opening. All the doors beyond were locked by a double bar system, one lateral, one reaching from the ceiling to the floor and slipping into steel-clad holes. Each room held a lone, unmoving child. One stared in frozen surprise at the ceiling. Some appeared to be asleep. It did not look as if they had received any attention. There were at least eight children in these rooms, and no way to confirm they were all dead.

None of them moved.

Dicken stepped back from the last thick view port, shoved his back against the concrete wall, then, with an effort, pushed off and faced DeWitt. "The yard," he said.

About ten paces beyond the door, they met two of the treatment center nurses. They were sharing a cigarette and sprawling on plastic chairs in the shade at the end of a broad corridor lined with padded picnic tables. The two women were in their fifties, very large, with beefy arms and large, fat hands. They wore dark green uniforms, almost black in the overhead glare. They looked up listlessly as Dicken and DeWitt came into view.

"We done everything we could," one of them said, eyes darting.

Dicken nodded, simply acknowledging their presence—and perhaps their courage.

"There are more out there," said the other nurse, louder, as they walked past. "It's damned near midnight. We needed a break!"

"I'm sure you did your best," DeWitt said. Dicken instantly caught the contrast: DeWitt's voice, precise and academic, educated; the nurses', pragmatic and blue collar.

The nurses were townies.

"Fuck you," the first nurse tried to shout, but it came out a wan croak. "Where was everybody? Where're the doctors?"

Brave townies. They cared. They could have bolted, but they had stayed.

Dicken stood in the yard. A canvas tent had been pulled over a concrete quadrangle about fifty feet on a side and surrounded by tan, stucco-covered walls. The lighting was inadequate, just wall-mounted pathway illumination surrounding the open square. The center was a shadowy pit.

Cots and mattresses had been laid out on the concrete in rows that began with some intention of order and ended in scattered puzzles. There were at least a hundred children under the tent, most of them lying down. Four women, two men, and one child walked between the cots, carrying buckets and ladles, giving the children water if they were strong enough to sit up.

Moonlight and starry sky showed through gaps and vent flaps. The quadrangle was still almost unbearably hot. All the water coolers in the building had been carried here, and a few hoses hung out of plastic barrels surrounded by fading gray rings of water slop.

A hardy few of the children, most of them younger than ten, sat under the pathway lights with their backs against the stucco walls, staring at nothing, shoulders slumped.

A woman in a white uniform approached DeWitt. She was smaller than the others, tiny, actually, with walnut-colored skin and black almond eyes and short black hair pushed up under a baseball cap. "You're the counselor, Miss DeWitt?" she asked with an accent. Filipino, Dicken guessed.

"Yes," DeWitt said.

"Are the doctors coming back? Is there more medicine?" she asked.

"We're under complete quarantine," DeWitt said.

The woman looked at Dicken and her face creased with helpless anger. As an outsider, he had failed them all; he had brought nothing useful. "Today and last night was a horror. All my children are gone. I work in special needs. Their only fault was slow wisdom. They were my joy."

"I'm sorry," Dicken said. He held up his bag of specimen kits. "I'm an epidemiologist. I need samples from all of the nurses working here."

"Why? They're afraid it's going to spread outside?" She shook her head defiantly. "None of us is sick. Only the children."

"Knowing what happened here, and how it happened, is important to the children who are still alive."

"Do you justify *this*, Mister . . . whoever the hell you are?" the walnut-colored woman hissed.

"You've done your best," Dicken said. "I know that. We have to keep trying. Keep working." He swallowed. Tonight was already stacking up to be the worst, the most awful he had ever seen. Nightmare bad.

The woman's arms trembled. She turned away, then turned back slowly, and her eyes were as flat and dark as the windows at the entrance. "Food would help" she said as if speaking to one of her less intelligent charges. *Slow wisdom.* "We have to feed those who are still alive."

"I think there's enough food," DeWitt said.

"How many, outside?" the woman asked, hand making a helpless, rotating gesture. "How many have died?"

Dicken had seen such a gesture years ago, at the beginning of all this; he had seen a female chimp reach out for solace and Marian Freedman, who now studied Mrs. Rhine, had grasped the hand and tried to comfort her.

DeWitt held the woman's hand in just that way. "We don't know, honey," she said. "Let's just take of care of our own."

"I'm going to need the doors to the cells opened," Dicken said.

The tiny woman covered her mouth with her hand. "We didn't go in there," she said, staring at him with huge eyes. "We couldn't let them out. Some are violent. Oh, God, I've been afraid to look."

"If they've had no contact with adults, then it's all the more important that I get some specimens," Dicken said.

The woman dropped her hand from her mouth—it shook as if with palsy—and stared at DeWitt.

"Come on," DeWitt said, taking her elbow and guiding her. "I'll help."

"What if some are still alive?" the small woman asked plaintively.

Some were.

38

Mitch glanced down at the digital receiver in the Mackenzies' Jeep. Kaye leaned forward between the seats and touched his arm. "Is that what I think it is?"

"It appears to be," Mitch said. "Webcasts. Catches everything for at least an hour back."

"We've been married too long," Kaye said. "You don't even ask what I'm talking about."

"Do you think?" Mitch said, with precisely Kaye's tone and phrasing.

Stella lay quietly beside Kaye in the backseat. She had gone through one more convulsion, but her fever had not spiked again. She was resting under a thin child's blanket, her head in Kaye's lap.

They had caught less than an hour's nap before leaving the Mackenzie house. Kaye had had a nightmare in which someone very important to her, someone like her father or Mitch, had told her she was a miserable mother, an awful human being, and some shadowy institution was withdrawing all support, which meant life support; she had thought she was running out of oxygen and could not breathe. She had struggled awake and sleep after that was impossible.

The sun was peeking over the highway behind them.

"Turn it on," Kaye said.

Mitch turned on the receiver. The dashboard display showed a map with a red spot, their position, and the radio tuned automatically to a Philadelphia station, giving stock market news for the morning.

"Did he—"

"George turned off the TheftWave years ago," Mitch said. "I checked. It's unplugged. We're just tracking GPS, not sending."

"Good." Kaye reached forward with a grunt, shifting Stella's head, and pulled out a remote folding keypad. "Fancy," she said.

Mitch glanced at her in the rearview mirror. She looked haggard, and her eyes were too bright. He could only see part of the gently breathing, blanketed form beside her.

"Are you all right?" he asked.

"I'm fine." She studied the keypad, then experimented with a few buttons. "Looks like HFMD to me."

"That's not a radio station," Mitch said.

"Hand, foot, and mouth disease. It's usually a minor viral infection in infants and children. I'm sure she's been exposed before. Something's changed. Whatever, we need to stock up on drugs and fluids."

"Drugstore?"

Kaye shook her head. "I'm sure by now they've made this a reportable illness. Every pharmacy in the country will be on the alert, and the hospitals are refusing to take cases . . . Let's hear what the world is saying." The broadband sites were full of digital music, digital advertising, Rush Limbaugh thundering and buzzing away from somewhere in Florida, Dick Richelieu on building that new home, rants by evangelicals, and then BBC World News direct from London. They caught the story in progress. Kaye worked the touch pad and backed up several minutes to the beginning.

"Conditions in Asia and the United States have quickly deteriorated to what can only be described as panic. The prospect of the so-called virus children producing an unknown pathogen capable of causing a pandemic has haunted world governments for a decade, certainly since the strange and disturbing case of Mrs. Rhine seven years ago. And yet the children have remained healthy, in their schools and camps and with their beleaguered families. Now, this new and so-far unexplained illness—given no official diagnosis—is causing widespread disruption in North America, Japan, and Hong Kong. International and even some local airports are blocking flights from affected areas. In the past forty-eight hours, public and private hospitals in the United States have closed their doors to this new illness for fear of becoming part of a proposed general quarantine. Other hospitals in the UK, France, and Italy, announced that should the disease spread to these shores, which some regard as inevitable, they will accept SHEVA children and their relatives only in isolated wards."

"If you see a vet's office, stop," Kaye told him.

"Okay," Mitch said.

"The illness has not yet spread to Africa, which has the smallest population of SHEVA children, some say because of the prevalence of HIV infection. In Washington, Emergency Action denies that it has begun taking measures based on a top-secret presidential decision directive, a confidential order dating from the early years of Herod's plague. On some widely touched Web sites, the specter of bioterrorism is being invoked with alarming frequency."

Kaye turned off the radio and squared her clasped hands in her lap. They were passing through a small town in the middle of fields and grassy plains. "There's a pet hospital," Kaye said, pointing to a strip mall on their right.

Mitch swung off the road into the parking lot and parked opposite a square blue-and-gray stucco building. Kaye drew the sun shades in the Jeep's windows, though the sun was still low in the east and the air was actually cool. "Stay in the back with her," she said as they both got out. Mitch tried to give Kaye a brief, encouraging hug. She squirmed out of his arms like a cat, made a vexed face, and jogged across the asphalt.

Mitch looked over his shoulder to see if they were being watched, then climbed into the backseat, lifted his daughter's head, and placed it on his lap. Stella drew breath in short jerks. Her face was covered with small red spots. She curled her knees up and flexed her fingers. "Mitch, my head hurts," she whispered. "My neck hurts. Tell Kaye."

"Mom will be back in a few minutes," Mitch said, feeling a gnawing helplessness. He might as well have been a ghost watching from the land of the dead.

Kaye peered through the venetian blinds in the glass door and saw lights inside and figures moving in a hallway in the back. She banged on the door until a young woman in a blue medical uniform approached with a puzzled look and opened the door a crack.

"We're just starting the day," the woman said. "Is this an emergency?" She was in her midtwenties, plump but not heavyset, with strong arms, bleached blonde hair, and pleasant brown eyes.

"I'm sorry to bother you, but we have some trouble with our cat," Kaye said, and smiled with her most ingratiating and harried expression. The woman opened the door and Kaye entered the hospital's small lobby. She turned nervously and looked at the admissions counter, the racks of specialized pet food and other products. The woman walked behind the counter, perked up, and smiled. "Well then, welcome. What can we do for you?" Her pocket tag showed a smiling cartoon puppy and the name Betsy.

The good caring women of this Earth, Kaye thought. *They are hardly ever beautiful, they are the most beautiful of all.* She did not know where this came from and shoved it aside, but first used the emotion to put a sympathetic spark into her smile.

"We're traveling," Kaye began. "We're taking Shamus with us, poor thing. He's our cat."

"What's wrong?" Betsy asked with genuine concern.

"He's just old," Kaye said. "Failed kidneys. I thought I brought our supplies with us, but . . . they're back in Brattleboro."

"Do you have a doctor's sheet? A phone number, someone we can talk with?"

"Shamus hasn't seen the doctor in months. We moved recently. We've been taking care of him on our own. We've already been to one pet hospital, up the road a ways . . . They got mad. It's so early, and we've been up all night. They turned me down flat." She wrung her hands. "I was hoping you could help."

Betsy's eyes glinted with the merest shade of suspicion. "We can't supply narcotics or pain killers," she warned.

"Nothing like that," Kaye said, her heart thumping. She smiled and drew a breath. "Oh, forgive me, I'm so worried about the poor thing. We'll need Lactated Ringer's, four or five liters, if you have it, with butterfly clamp, and as many sets of tubes and needles—twenty-five-gauge needles."

"That's a little thin for a cat. Take forever to fill her up."

"It's a he," Kaye said. "It's all he'll put up with."

"All right," Betsy said doubtfully.

"Methyl prednisone," Kaye said. "To calm him while he's traveling."

"We have Depo-Medrol."

"That's fine. Do you have vidarabine?"

"Not for cats," the young woman said, frowning. "I'll have to check all this with the doctor."

"He's at the cabin—our cat. He's doing poorly, and it's all my fault. I should have known better."

"You've handled this before . . . haven't you?"

"I'm an expert," Kaye said, and put on a brave, tearful grin.

The young woman entered the list onto a flat-screen monitor. "I'm not sure I even know what vidarabine is."

Kaye searched her memory, trying to remember the long hours she had spent searching PediaServe, MediSHEVA, and a hundred other sites and databases, years ago, preparing for some unknown disaster. "There's a new one we use sometimes. It's called picornavene, enterovene, something like that?"

"We have equine picornavene. Surely that's not what you're looking for."

"Sounds familiar."

"It comes in quite large doses."

"Fine. Famicyclovir?"

"No," Betsy said, very suspicious now. "Drugstore might have that. What kind of life has your cat lived?"

"He was a wild one," Kaye said.

"If he's that sick . . ."

"He means so much to us."

"You should wait for the vet. He'll be back in an hour."

"I'm not sure we have that long," Kaye said, looking at her watch with a desperate expression she did not have to fake.

"You're positive you've done all this before, you know how it works?"

"We've kept him alive for a year. I've had him for eighteen years. He's a brave old tom. I don't know what I'd do without him."

The assistant shook her head, dubious but sympathetic. "I could get in trouble."

Kaye felt no guilt whatsoever. If she had had a gun, she would have held them up, right now, for everything she needed. "I wouldn't want that," she said, staring right at the woman.

The assistant waggled her head. "What the hell," she said. "Old cats. Pain in the butt, huh?"

"You know it," Kaye said.

"And it's not like we're in the big city. Five liters Ringer's, two hundred mils equine picornavene—that's the smallest we've got—and the Depo-Medrol—" Betsy picked up the printed list. "Credit or debit?"

"Cash," Kaye said.

39

Yolanda Middleton followed Dicken through the school trailers to the old farm buildings. She caught up with him easily and shook out a ring of keys. "We ransacked Trask's office," she said. "Found master keys to all the buildings. There's a tag from when this was a prison. Some of the nurses say there could still be supplies out here, but nobody knows."

"Great. Did Kelson ever come out here?"

"I don't think so. This was Dr. Jurie's lab," Middleton said. "Dr. Pickman was his assistant. Both were authorized to do research. They stayed away from the rest of us."

"What sort of research?" Dicken asked.

Middleton shook her head.

Dicken stood on the asphalt path and tapped his shoe lightly on the curb, thinking. He looked over his shoulder at the converted barn, the old business education building, and the three blank-faced concrete cubes between. Then he set off. Middleton followed.

A double steel door marked one side of the closest cube. This was labeled "NO ADMITTANCE" in white letters on the door's blue enamel.

"What's in here?"

"Well, among other things, a temporary morgue," she said. "That's what they told me. I don't know that it was ever used."

"Why here?"

"Dr. Jurie told us we had to keep the bodies of any children who died. The county coroner wouldn't take them, even though she was supposed to."

"Were the parents notified?"

"We tried," Middleton said. "Sometimes they move without giving any forwarding address. They just leave the children behind."

"Is there a graveyard for the school?"

"Not that I ever heard of. Honestly, Dr. Jurie took care of all that." Middleton looked distinctly uncomfortable. "We assumed they went to a potter's field somewhere outside of town. There weren't that many, really. Two or three, maybe, since the school opened, and only one since I've been here. Trask didn't let word about deaths circulate very far. He called it a private matter."

Dicken rubbed his fingers together. "Key?"

Middleton looked for a newer key on the ring, and held one up for his inspection. It was labeled R1-F, F for Front, presumably—*and R for what, Research?* They agreed with a look that this was the best choice. As she pushed the key into the lock, Dicken turned his gaze up the face of concrete, pale gray in the morning light. He narrowed his eye, as he had learned over the years, to help the fogged lens focus on the vent covers near the top, a few pipes sticking out, a thick power line going to a pole and across to the junction box near the old barn.

Middleton pulled the door open. Inside, it was cool enough to make him shiver.

"The air-conditioner works here, at least," he said.

"It's separate from the main plant," Middleton said. "This building's newer than the rest."

Dicken took a deep breath. He felt as if he were on a wild goose chase.

There might be medicine in these buildings, but he doubted it. More likely they would find laboratory supplies—unless Trask had conspired with the doctors to sell those, too. Still, the lab might be better equipped than the small medical facility adjacent to the infirmary. But these were just excuses.

Something else was bringing him here, an instinctive suspicion that had come to him as he walked among the cots in the special treatment center. *We're curious monkeys,* he thought. *We never miss opportunities.*

He found a light switch on the wall inside the door and pushed it. Fluorescents bathed the interior in a cool, sterile glow. The north wall of the room was covered by stainless steel refrigerators, huge lab units equipped with tiny blue temperature displays. Expensive, and very unlike the small, hump-shouldered units outside the infirmary.

"When did Jurie and Pickman leave?" he asked.

"I'm not sure."

"Did they take anything?"

Middleton shrugged. "I didn't see them go. I can't be everywhere."

"Of course not," Dicken said. The mask itched. He reached up to rub his nose, then thought better of it.

"How long will this take?" Middleton asked.

Dicken ignored her. The refrigerators were locked and equipped with push-button keypads. He ran his fingers across one of the pads and shook his head.

Middleton found a key on the ring that opened the door across the room. This led to a small pathology lab with a single steel autopsy table, shining clean. All the tools lay neatly in their trays or in cabinets along the far wall. Some tools had been left in an autoclave, but otherwise the lab was beautifully organized and maintained.

"When was the last autopsy conducted here?" Dicken asked.

"I don't think there have ever been any," Middleton said. "I haven't heard of any, at least. Wouldn't we have to get permission from the county?"

"Not if they refuse responsibility. Maybe Mark will know." But he was beginning to doubt that Augustine knew anything. It was beginning to look as if his old CDC boss, the putative director of Emergency Action, had finally been hamstrung—perhaps castrated was the better word—by the political wolves in Washington.

Down a short hall and to the right, they came upon the unexpected mother lode: a fully equipped molecular biology and genetics lab, six hundred square feet of space under a high ceiling, crammed with equipment. Tissue centrifuge sorters provided specimen flow to racked analyzers—matrix and variable-probe sequencers specializing in polynucleotides, RNAs and DNAs; proteomizers capable of discerning complete complements of proteins; glycome and lipidome units for isolating and labeling sugars and fats and related compounds. More racks stood at the ends of broad steel lab benches.

The sorter and analyzers were connected by steel and white plastic automated specimen tracks, running like a little railroad through diffraction molecular imagers, inoculator/incubators, and a variety of video microscopes—including two up-to-the-minute carbon force counters. All magnificently automated. A one- or at most two-person lab.

Everything on and around the benches was hooked up to a small, square, bright red Cenomics Ideator, a dedicated computer capable of three-D imaging and real-time gene and protein description and identification.

There was more than a wealth of equipment here: What Dicken saw as he walked around the room amounted to obscene overkill for a typical school medical facility. He had visited labs in rich biotech firms that wouldn't have been able to compete.

"Wow," Dicken said in awe. "This is the whole damned *Delta Queen.*"

Middleton raised an eyebrow. "I beg your pardon?"

"Nothing." He walked between the benches, then paused to reach out with his gloved hand and stroke the Ideator. He had his riverboat. He had everything he needed to track the virus back up the river of disease to the far, frozen north—to its sleeping, glacial form.

If no one else was willing to do it, he was sure he could do it all by himself, right here, and screw the unreasoning outside world. *With the help of a few manuals.* Some of this equipment he had seen only in catalogs.

Dicken leaned over to look at steel tags, identifiers, shipping labels. "Who paid for all this?"

Middleton shook her head. She was as stunned as he, but probably did not fully appreciate the magnitude of their discovery.

He found what he was searching for on the back of one of the carbon force counters. A steel tag read, "PROPERTY OF AMERICOL, INC., U.S.A. FEDERALLY REGISTERED CORPORATE LOAN EQUIPMENT."

"Marge Cross," he said. "Large Marge."

"What?"

Dicken murmured a quick explanation. Marge Cross was the CEO and majority shareholder of both Americol and Eurocol, two of the world's largest pharmaceutical and medical equipment manufacturers. He did not add that for a time Marge Cross had employed Kaye Lang.

Dicken said, "Let's find some way to open those refrigerators. And that." He pointed to the unmarked stainless steel door—more of a hatch, actually—at the back of the lab.

Middleton shuddered. "I'm not sure I want to," she said.

Dicken scowled. "We're tired, aren't we?"

Chastened, she handed him the ring of keys. "I'll look for the codes," she said.

40

Mitch shifted into four-wheel drive, then pushed the Jeep through a previously broken and mangled section of guardrail—just as George had described it. The Jeep rumbled down the embankment.

Kaye cradled Stella once more in the backseat. Stella did not react to the bumps and lurches. Kaye stared straight ahead, through the windshield, seeing nothing, really, and thinking furiously. She could not shut down her mind, filled with scenes and plans that did not connect in any useful way. She was at the end of her rope, about to be jerked up hard; she knew it, and there was nothing she could do about it.

She was more than half convinced they were going to lose Stella. Making plans for a time after Stella certainly seemed appropriate, but she could not bring herself to do so. Her thoughts became jagged and incomplete, painful.

She could feel her throat starting to constrict, as it had in the nightmare.

"There," Mitch said. He pointed.

"What?" Kaye wheezed.

"A road."

As George had told them, they now straddled an almost overgrown path, just barely deserving to be called a road. He swung the Jeep left.

The path wound through scrub forest for a quarter of a mile, then connected to a state highway. This way would avoid quarantine roadblocks on the county line.

Mitch's intuition had been finely honed over the last ten years. He had sharp criminal instincts. He could almost picture Department of Health or FEMA roadblocks, INS agents, or the Philadelphia National Guard checking each vehicle on the main highway, CDC deputy inspectors waiting in the back of an Emergency Action van . . .

He had seen it all before, while traveling, looking for a new home, seven years ago. During the panic after the discovery of Mrs. Rhine.

Kaye crooned to Stella as she had when Stella was a baby. Stella's lips were cracked and her forehead hot. Her head lolled until Kaye cradled it in her elbow. She brushed back the luxurious, short-cut hair with her fingers, watched her daughter's cheeks, alternately flushing and blanching, like a signal light trying to decide whether to stay on. Stella smelled rank in a particularly disturbing way, a *sick offspring* smell that made Kaye deeply uneasy.

Kaye had not entirely lost the enhanced sense of smell she had developed as the mother of a SHEVA infant, even though she could no longer produce her own communicative pheromones. The pores behind her ears had closed up after two years. Mitch's had closed even earlier, and their cheek patches, the variegated melanophores, had faded back to normal as well, though in Kaye's case they had left small, trapped pools of freckles.

Stella's lips moved. She started speaking, babbling really, in two streams at once. Kaye stroked her daughter's chin and lips until they stopped their restless action, and Stella reduced the volume to a whisper:

"I want to see the woods/

"There's so little time/ Leave me in the woods/

"Please./ Please. Please."

"We're in the woods, honey," Kaye told Stella. "We're in the forest."

Stella opened her eyes, then, blinded by the light in her face, swung her arm up, nearly knocking Kaye's nose bloody. Kaye pushed the arm down and covered Stella's eyes with her hand.

"How much longer?" she asked Mitch.

"Not sure. Maybe an hour."

"We might lose her before then."

"She's not going to die," Mitch said. "She's doing better."

"She won't drink."

"You gave her water before we left."

"She peed on the seat. She's hot. She won't drink. How do you know? *I* don't know she won't die."

"I'm the spooky guy," Mitch said. "Remember?"

"This isn't a joke, Mitch," Kaye said, her voice rising.

"Can't you smell her?" Mitch asked.

"I smell her better than you do," Kaye said.

"She isn't dying. I'd know."

"Please stop arguing," Stella murmured, and rolled over, kicking feebly at the door. Her bare feet made the weakest little thumps. "My head hurts. Let me out/ I want to get out."

Kaye held her daughter against her brief struggles. With a discouraged sigh, the girl went limp again. Kaye looked at the back of Mitch's head, the uneven cut of his nape, a bad haircut. You saved money where you could. Mitch had never enjoyed haircuts anyway. For a moment, she hated her husband. She wanted to bite and scratch and hit him.

No one knew more about her daughter than she did. Nobody. If Mitch spoke one more time, Kaye thought she would scream.

41

Trask or someone working for him had shut down the server that handled all the school's internal and external landline and satellite communications, and it would not start up without a password. None of the teachers or nurses or Kelson knew that password, and Trask of course was no longer available.

Augustine could guess on motives, but it did not matter. Nothing mattered but doing whatever he could to shake loose the needed supplies. Dicken did not carry a phone. The only working phone at the moment was Augustine's Web phone.

Personally, and through his secretary in the EMAC office in Indiana, he had sent messages—voice and email—to the heads of all the agencies on his list, confirming his previous calls for supplies. Anything. They had told him they would do their best, but the situation was very tight, and it might take a day or two.

Augustine knew they did not have that long.

One intrepid deputy to an undersecretary at Health and Human Services had suggested he call local media and make his case. "Phones are ringing off the hook over here."

Augustine had declined. He knew how that would go. The beleaguered and unpopular director of Emergency Action would be picked apart by reporters trying to prove him a liar.

He needed facts to avoid panicking the public even further, and Dicken had not yet delivered anything useful.

Now Augustine sat in a worn secretary's chair at a small desk near the corner, and used his Web phone to call up reports on the internal NIH Web site. At least they had not locked out his personal account; he was not completely persona non grata.

He studied the freshly posted morning statistics, the numerical anatomy of the disaster, on the phone's small color screen.

The first case had probably occurred in California, at the Pelican Bay school. Three California penal corporations had won the contracts to house SHEVA children in the Golden State; all had been particularly reluctant to work with any Washington-based authority. Augustine had come to hate those administrators, and those schools; the culture of the California penal system had become inbred, defensive, and arrogant during the last decade of the twentieth century, the Drug War years. He was not surprised that Pelican Bay had not reported the spread of the disease until the day before yesterday. First to notice, next to last to report.

The disease had struck almost simultaneously at fifteen other schools, from Oregon to Mississippi. Dicken would be interested in that fact. Where was the reservoir? Where were the vectors? How had the virus spread before it erupted into pandemic?

How and why had it lain dormant for so long?

Pelican Bay had lost twelve hundred students out of six thousand. One in five. San Luis Obispo and Port Hueneme were reporting smaller percentages, but half the students at Kalispell, almost a thousand, were already gone, and more were expected to die within the next twelve hours. El Cajon, fifty-six out of three hundred.

His eye swept east through the maps and charts. Phoenix, two thousand out of eight thousand. Two thirds had fallen ill in Tucson; half of those were dead. Provo had lost half, but with less than one hundred students. Mormons tended not to hand over their kids without a fight, and there were fewer than a thousand SHEVA children in the three schools in Utah.

Augustine wondered how many of the "home-schooled," as some agencies called them, the underground virus children, had become ill and died. The disease would spread to them soon enough, he guessed.

In Ohio, Iowa, and Indiana, in twelve schools holding sixty-three thousand children gathered from across the Midwest, over thirteen thousand SHEVA children were now dead.

He was looking at the stats for Illinois when the phone beeped. He answered.

It was Rachel Browning from the SRO.

"Hello, Mark. I hear you called. Sad day," Browning said.

"Rachel, how nice to hear from you," Augustine said. "We need supplies here immediately—"

"Hold for a sec. Have to take this one." Light jazz played over the line. That was too much; he almost snapped the phone shut. But he held his palm away from the cover. Patience was the watchword, certainly now, and certainly for a wraith, a wisp whose tenuous authority could simply wink out at any moment.

Browning came back. "One in four, Mark," she began, as if it were a sports score.

"We're counting one in five, averaged across the country, Rachel. We need—"

"You're stuck way out in the middle of it, I hear. Looks like seventy plus percent rate of contagion," Browning interrupted. "Aerosol vital for at least three hours. Horrendous. It's outside of anyone's control."

"It's slowing."

"There aren't many left to infect, not in the schools."

"We could cut the losses to almost nothing with proper medical care," Augustine said. "We need doctors and equipment."

"The Ohio district director is a corrupt son of a bitch," Browning said. "At least we can agree on that. He diverted medical supplies from school warehouses because the kids were so healthy. The rumor is some of his staffers sold the supplies for ten cents on the dollar to Russian bosses in Chicago, and now they're on the black market in Moscow."

"I did not know that," Augustine said, tapping his fingernail on the desktop.

"You should have, Mark. Justice is moving in on little leopard feet," Browning said. "That does not help you or the virus kids. Worse still, there are a lot of brown BVDs in Washington, Mark. They're scared. So am I."

"None of the adults here are ill. It is not a threat to us. We know the etiology and nature of the disease." This was a lie, but he had to show some strength.

"If this illness has anything to do with ancient viruses, and I suspect it does—don't you?—we're going to full-blown biological emergency. PDD 298, Mark."

It had been three years since Augustine had read the details of Presidential Decision Directive 298.

"Hayford has a crisis bill on the House floor now," Browning continued. "No virus child will be tolerated outside a federal school. *None.* Not even on the reservations or in Utah. All schools will come under direct EMAC federal control. You'll like that. The bill increases violation penalties and authorizes *tripling* the staff for interdiction and arrest. We'll be hiring every fat security guard with a bigger gun than a dick, and every yahoo who ever failed cop school. They'll double our budget, Mark."

Augustine looked at his Rolex. "It's eleven in the morning there," he said. "Can anyone in Washington get doctors out here?"

"Not for a day, at least," Browning said. "Everyone's taking care of their own, and the governor of Ohio hasn't asked yet. And, frankly, why should I trust you? You'll help me best where you are—screwing everything up royally. But I don't hold grudges. I'm here to offer some charity. I know where Kaye Lang will be hiding in a couple of hours. Do you?"

"No. I've been busy, Rachel."

"I think you're telling the truth."

Augustine worked quickly through the possible ways Rachel Browning could have discovered such a thing as Kaye's whereabouts. "You squeezed someone?"

"A GPS NuTest report out of Pittsburgh and neighbor complaints led us to a particular house. I got needed medical attention to a particular virus child at a school in Indiana. His parents are very happy. The doctors say he's going to live, Mark." Browning sounded ebullient, relating this tale of detection and shakedown.

"With so much power, I know you could help us here," Augustine said.

"Honestly. I can't. Did you hear that France offered to send in wide-spectrum antivirals, and President Ellington refused?"

"I did not."

"All the precious beltway schools are well-supplied. Nobody raided *their* medical stores. And remember, Ohio did not go for Ellington, last election."

Augustine pinched the bridge of his nose. He had had a headache for the last two hours, and it showed no signs of going away. "I hear no charity, Rachel. Why the call?"

"Because the shit that passes for opinion around here is starting to scare even me. I can't get through to the NRO or NSA bosses. Secretary of Health and Human Services is unavailable. I think they're all in conference in their secure little rabbit holes in Annapolis and Arlington. Mark, you know as well as I do that everyone in the House and Senate had their kids well before SHEVA. Only two senators and four representatives have SHEVA grandkids. Tough luck. Statistically it should be more. Sixty-four percent of our aging electorate favored shoot-on-sight policies against fugitive virus kids in a CNN-Gallup Poll yesterday evening. Two out of three, Mark."

"How secure is this line, Rachel?" Augustine asked.

Browning made a sharp raspberry between her teeth. "Can you guess what's coming down from the beltway?"

The headache pounded. He leaned over the desk. "All too easily."

"Queen's X, Mark?"

"Who's Queen today?"

"That would be me. I'll authorize a special pickup for Kaye Lang and her daughter. People I know and trust."

Augustine thought this over for a few seconds. He had never been angrier in his life, or weaker. "I'm obliged, Rachel."

He could hear the triumph in her voice. "I'm not as stupid as you think I am, Mark. Alive, she's a pain in the ass. Dead, she's a martyr."

"Do what you can, Rachel."

"I always do. No timetables, though. I'll do this on my own schedule and tell you as little as possible."

"All right."

"If this works, you owe me, Mark. Now, here's what—"

Abruptly, the phone died. He shook it and punched the on button several times. The phone flashed to life, but, receiving no signal, turned off again to conserve power.

Very likely, SRO had taken over the wireless networks and shut down cell towers around all the schools. First stage of PDD 298.

Augustine put the phone down just as DeWitt returned to the room.

"Dr. Dicken wants to see you," she said. "They've found something."

"Supplies?" Augustine asked hopefully.

DeWitt shook her head.

42

On the state route, the traffic was light, three or four cars in the last fifteen minutes. Nobody wanted to be caught driving. Simply being out on the road would be suspicious. George had said the turnoff to the cabin was tricky, hard to see. He had nailed a red plastic strip to a large pine tree to mark the spot.

Mitch drove more slowly, looking for the red plastic strip and a wooden plaque that joy-riding vandals tended to splinter with ball bats.

Suddenly, the interior of the Jeep filled with shadow. He felt immersed in inky night. The sensation passed, but it scared him; he could almost smell the darkness, like crankcase oil.

"Too damned tired," he told himself, and wondered whether they had heard him in the backseat. He could feel both of them back there, both alive, both quiet. Stella's breathing had lost some of its harshness, but Mitch knew her fever was high.

Maybe he was coming down with it, too. That would be more than Kaye could stand, he suspected. *So, I will not become sick.*

Whistling in the dark. In the oily dark.

43

"Jurie left the number codes in a desk drawer," Middleton said as Augustine and DeWitt followed her into the concrete cube of the research building. "Dr. Dicken told me to bring you all here."

Dicken came through the opposite door, carrying a thick folder of papers. He glared at Augustine. "You rotten son of a bitch," he said.

Augustine took this without blinking. "You've found something," he said.

"You're goddamned right I've found something. How much did Americol pump into the schools? The *camps*?"

"To my knowledge, nothing."

"You're going to blame it all on Trask, right?"

Augustine shook his head cautiously. He looked around the big room and focused on the wall of steel refrigerators. "I don't even know what *it* is."

"What would Marge Cross want with all these children?" Dicken held out the folder. Augustine reached forward, leaning on his cane, and Dicken pulled it back, then dropped it on a desk next to the stainless steel cold storage units. Photographs spilled out: color photographs of autopsy proceedings. Even from a distance, it was obvious the subjects were children, some of them infants.

Dicken took a step away, as if too disgusted to let Augustine come near him.

Augustine shifted his eyes from face to face, facial lines deepening. He pushed aside the photos, then lifted the cover page on the folder and leafed through it.

"I know you too well," Dicken said. "You wouldn't be stupid enough to just let this happen."

"Show me the rest," Augustine said.

Middleton punched in the code numbers that unlocked the first stainless steel refrigerator door. Fog fell, revealing ranks of jars. Augustine immediately recognized the contents for what they were. The jars on top were small and contained anonymous meaty lumps in colorless fluid.

The jars below, on taller shelves, contained whole internal organs.

Middleton's skin had faded to a sickly shade of olive, and her eyes were almost closed.

"How many?" Augustine asked.

"There're the remains of maybe sixty or seventy children here, and more scattered throughout the building," Dicken said.

"What do you think . . . what purpose?"

"I won't even hazard a guess," Dicken said.

"We never lost this many children," Middleton said, "and Dr. Jurie . . . Dr. Pickman . . . left before . . ." She did not finish. She closed the first door and opened the second. Trays of thousands of frozen tissue samples, mounted on slides or stored in solution in smaller bottles, had been stacked to the top of the compartment.

Augustine surveyed the trays, then stepped forward and motioned for Middleton to open the third door, and the fourth. His cane made rubbery squeaks on the linoleum floor. "You're positive none of these were from the last two days," he said, grasping at some reasonable explanation for all the jars and tubes and dishes sealed, neatly numbered, and marked with yellow-and-red biohazard labels.

"It's a tissue library," Dicken said. "Healthy tissue, pathological specimens, whatever they could get. There's a fully equipped laboratory for analyzing them. Jurie and Pickman autopsied all the children who died at this school, and all the schools in this region. I presume they were bringing the dead here from wherever they could get them," Dicken said. "A central clearing house for cadavers."

"Cross paid for the equipment?" Augustine asked. His demeanor was so quiet, his expression so utterly devastated, that Dicken pushed back his anger.

"Americol," he said.

"Mm hm," Augustine said. He took the list of codes from Middleton and unlocked and examined the next three doors. Two contained the by now familiar stacked trays of specimens. The last contained five cadavers, wrapped in transparent plastic, suspended by hooks and slings from rails at the top of the compartment.

"My God," DeWitt said.

"I should have known," Augustine murmured. "That's certain. I should have known."

Middleton approached the open compartment. "Autopsies would be standard, wouldn't they? Is that what we're looking at, a pathology study being done on behalf of the students, to protect them?"

"No," Augustine said abruptly. "No studies were ever passed up to Washington, and I doubt they were even sent to the Ohio Central authority, or I would have heard of it. Before this week began, a total of three hundred and seventy-nine children in custody of the schools have died. Very low mortality, statistically speaking. Many of them are probably here. They were supposed to be returned to their families or buried if left unclaimed." Augustine closed the door. "I did not authorize this."

Dicken stepped forward. "Was there any value to the children in doing this . . . research?"

"I don't know," Augustine said. "Possibly. Doubtful, however. Anatomically, the children are so much like us that storage of organs or whole cadavers for research never seemed strictly necessary. Biopsies and specific tissue samples from the dead were all I ever authorized. You would have done the same."

Dicken admitted this with a quick nod.

"This implies some sort of large-scale morbidity study. Whole body assessments, thousands of tissue analyses . . . I need to sit down."

DeWitt brought a chair. Augustine slumped into it and leaned forward, shaking his head. "I'm trying to make sense of it," he said.

"Try harder," Dicken urged.

"I know of no reason other than retrovirus expression," Augustine said. "Tracking expression of novel HERV in the new children. A statistical sampling of expression in dozens or hundreds of individuals, correlated with known biographies, stress patterns. That would require an unprecedented effort. Monumental."

"To what end?"

"It could be an attempt to understand the whole process. What the ancient viruses are up to. What dangers they might present."

"To predict incidence of Shiver?" Dicken asked. "That's being done elsewhere. Why do it here, unauthorized?"

"Because nowhere else do they have access to so many new children, dead or alive," Augustine said.

"This is making me sick," DeWitt said, and leaned on the small desk, pushing aside the folder.

Augustine looked up at Dicken. "I'm not the puppet master, Christopher. They broke me in the ranks months ago. I've been trying to keep whatever responsibility was left to me in order to maintain some sense of order." He waved his arm feebly at the stainless steel doors. "People died, Christopher."

"That's what Marian Freedman said, last time I visited Fort Detrick. Some excuse. Anything goes. You're not the bad guy here?" Dicken asked.

"Were they bad guys, really?" Augustine asked. "Do we know that?"

"What about the parents?" DeWitt asked.

"Sentiment must be considered," Augustine said. "Medical ethics should prevail even in an emergency. But we've never faced this kind of problem before."

Dicken took Augustine's arm and lifted him to his feet. "One last bit of evidence," he said.

Augustine walked slowly through the benches in the molecular biology lab, taking in the collection of expensive machinery with impassivity, long past the possibility of surprise. Dicken opened the hatch at the back of the lab and switched on the fluorescent lights, revealing a long, narrow room. All hesitated before entering.

Steel shelves reaching to the ceiling held hundreds of long cardboard boxes. Dicken pulled out one and opened the hinged lid. Within were bones: femurs, tagged and arranged according to size. Another box held phalanges. Bigger boxes on the lower right, none more than four feet in length, held complete skeletons.

Augustine leaned against the edge of the frame. "There's nothing I can do here," he said. "Nothing any of us can do."

"This isn't all," Dicken said. "There's an upper floor. It's still locked."

"What do you think they keep up there?" DeWitt asked, her face ashen.

"No excuses, Christopher," Augustine said. "We should not forget this, but what in hell does anger do for us, now? For the sick children?"

"Not a goddamned thing," Dicken admitted. "Let's go."

44

THE POCONOS, PENNSYLVANIA

Eleven in the morning, the dashboard display said. Mitch looked left on the two-lane asphalt road and saw, about a hundred feet ahead, the red plastic strip hanging on a big old pine. He slowed and rolled down the window.

The signpost was still standing, though it had been knocked askew. The wooden plaque read:

MACKENZIE
George and Iris and Kelly

Mitch got out, unlocked the pipe, and pushed it back through its iron hoop. He took the plaque down from the signpost and stashed it in the back of the Jeep.

The cabin was made of whole stripped logs just beginning to gray with exposure. It sat on the shore of a private half-acre lake, alone in the pines. The air was scented by pine needles and dry dirt. Mitch could smell the moisture from the lake, the greenness of shallows filled with reeds. Sunlight slanted down through the trees onto the Jeep, illuminating Kaye in the backseat.

Mitch walked up onto the porch, his heavy shoes clomping on the wood. He unlocked the door, deactivated the burglar alarm with the six-number code, then returned to the Jeep.

Kaye was already halfway up the walk from the driveway, carrying Stella.

"Get a bag of Ringer's and set up an IV," she said. "A lamp hook, flower-pot hook, anything. I'll spread some blankets." She carried Stella into the cabin. The air inside was cool and sweetly stuffy.

Mitch spread a sleeping bag on the floor behind a big leather couch and took down an empty hanging pot, then slung the bag of Ringer's solution, inserted the long, clear plastic tube into the bag, opened the butterfly clamp, let the clear fluid push through the tube and drip from the needle. Kaye lay Stella on the bag, tapped her arm to bring up a vein, poked in the needle, strapped it to the girl's arm with medical tape.

Stella could barely move.

"She should be in a hospital," Kaye said, kneeling beside her daughter.

Mitch looked down on them both, hands opening and closing help-lessly. "In a better world," he said.

"There is no goddamned better world," Kaye said. "Never has been, never will be. There's just 'suffer the little children.' "

"That's not what that means," Mitch said.

"Screw it, then," Kaye said. "I hope I know what the hell I'm doing."

"Her head hurts," Mitch said.

"She has aseptic meningitis. I'm going to bring the swelling down with prednisone, treat those mouth sores with famicyclovir."

They had found the famicyclovir, medical tape, and other supplies in a small drugstore near the pet hospital. Kaye had also managed to score a box of disposable syringes. Her excuses had worn thin at the last. She had told the pharmacist, perched in his little elevated booth in the back of the store, that she was using the needles for a cloth dyeing project.

That would not have gone over well in the big city.

She prepared to give Stella an injection.

"I'm not even sure about the dose," she murmured.

Mitch was half convinced he could walk out the door, drive off, and Kaye would never notice he was gone. He looked at his hands, smooth from lack of digging. How had this happened? He knew, he remembered, but none of it seemed real. Even the shadow of grief—was that what he had felt in the Jeep?—even that seemed unimportant.

Mitch could feel his soul winking down to nothing.

The drip of lactated Ringer's slid down the long plastic tube.

"I'll watch her," he said.

"Get some sleep," Kaye said. She slipped the used syringe needle into its plastic cap for disposal.

"You first," he said.

"Get some sleep, damn it," Kaye said, and her glance up at him was like the slap of a flat, dull knife.

45

"It begins," Augustine said. "I've dreaded this day for years."

Standing in the number two tower, surrounded by stacked boxes, dusty old desks, and outdated desktop computers, Augustine and Dicken—and Augustine's ever-vigilant agent—watched the Ohio National Guard troops set up their perimeter and cut off the school's entrance. Their view encompassed the main road, the water tower to the west, a barren gravel field broken by lozenges of bare concrete, a line of scrub oaks beyond that, and a state highway slicing through low grassy hills.

DeWitt climbed up the last flight of steps and leaned against the wall, out of breath. DeWitt nodded. "Governor's office called . . . the director's line. The governor is jumping ahead . . . of the feds and declaring," she sucked in her breath with a small whoop, "a stage five public health emergency. We're under complete quarantine. Nobody in or out . . . Not even you, Dr. Augustine." She nailed him with a glare. "Main gate reports twenty more . . . National Guard trucks . . . moving in. They're surrounding the school."

Augustine turned to the Secret Service agent, who tapped his earpiece and made a wry face. "We're in for the duration," the agent affirmed.

"What about the supplies?" DeWitt asked.

"They can drop them off at the entrance and we can send someone to pick them up, no contact," Dicken said. "But they have to get here first."

Augustine seemed less hopeful. "Not difficult to isolate us," he said dryly. "It's a prison to start with. As for supplies—they'll have to go through state lines, state inspection. The state can intercept them and hold them. The governor will try to protect his votes, act ignorant, and shift our supplies to the big cities, the rich neighborhoods, the most visible and well-funded hospitals with the loudest administrators. Stockpile against a potential plague."

"Leave us with nothing? I can't believe they'll be that stupid," DeWitt said. "They'll have a revolt."

"By whom? The parents?" Dicken asked. "They'll hunker down and hope for the best. Dr. Augustine made sure of that years ago."

Augustine looked through the tower window and did not take Dicken's bait. "All it takes to get elected in twenty-first-century America is a mob of frightened sheep and a wolf with a nice smile," he said softly. "We have plenty of sheep. Ms. DeWitt, could I speak with Christopher in private, please? But stay close."

DeWitt looked between them, not knowing what to think, and then left, closing the door behind her.

"It's worse than any of them can imagine," Augustine said, his voice low. "I think the starting pistol has been fired."

"You mentioned that in the car. What in hell does it mean?"

"If we're lucky, the president can put a stop to it . . . But I do not know Ellington. He's kept his distance ever since he was elected. I do not know what he will do."

"Put a stop to what?"

"If the situation gets any worse, I believe the governor will call Washington and ask for permission to clean up the schools. Sterilize the premises. He may ask for sanction to kill the children."

Dicken stood up. "You have got to be shitting me."

Augustine shook his head and looked him steadily in the eye. "State autonomous self-protection, as specified under Presidential Decision Directive 298, Emergency Action Gray Book. It's called the Military and Biological Security Protocol, Part Four. It was enacted seven years ago during a secret session of the Senate oversight committee. It gives discretion to state authorities on the scene to use all necessary force, under well-defined emergency conditions."

"Why was I never told?"

"Because you chose to stay a soldier. The contents of the directive are confidential. At any rate, I opposed the rule as extreme, but there were a lot of scared senators in the room. They were shown pictures of Mrs. Rhine's family, incidents of Shiver in Mexico. They saw pictures of you, Christopher. The statute was signed by the president, and has never been revoked."

"Is there any chance they'll listen to reason?"

"Slim to none. But we have to try. The race is on. You have work to do, and so do I." He raised his voice. "Ms. DeWitt?"

DeWitt opened the door. As requested, she had not gone far; Augustine wondered if she had heard anything.

"I want to talk to Toby Smith."

"Why?" DeWitt asked, as if the thought of Augustine seeing the boy again disgusted her.

"We're going to need their help," he said.

"They're hardly trained for this sort of thing," Dicken said, following Augustine down the concrete stairs. His voice echoed from the hard gray walls.

"You'd be surprised," Augustine said. "We need answers by tomorrow. Is that possible?"

"I don't know." Dicken was amazed at the transformation. This was the old Mark Augustine, jerked back to life like some sort of political zombie. His skin was regaining color, his eyes were hard, and the perpetual grimace of determination had returned.

"If we don't have answers by then, they could move in and kill us all."

Dicken, Augustine, Middleton, DeWitt, Kelson, and Toby Smith gathered in Trask's office.

Toby stood before Augustine with a paper cup of water in one hand. Behind him stood Dr. Kelson and the two remaining school police officers. The officers wore surgical masks. The doctor did not seem to care very much whether he was protected.

"Toby, we're short staffed," Augustine said.

"Yeah," Toby said.

"And we have a lot of sick people to take care of. All of them your friends."

Toby looked around the office. The square, metal-framed windows let in the bright afternoon sun and a whiff of warm air that smelled of the miles of dry grass beyond the compound.

"How many students are healthy enough to help us do some work around here?"

"A few," Toby said. "We're all tired. Pretty koobered."

"Koobered?"

"A word," Toby said, squinting at Dicken, then looking around the room at the others.

"They have a lot of words," DeWitt said. "Most are special to this school."

"We think," Kelson added, and scratched his arm through the sleeve, then looked around to see if anyone had caught him doing this. "I'm fine," he said to Dicken. "Dry skin."

"What does 'koobered' mean?" Augustine asked Toby.

"Not important," Toby said.

"Okay. But we're going to spend a lot of time together, if that's all right with you. I'd like to learn these words, if you're willing to teach me."

Toby shrugged.

"Can you put some teams together and pick up some basic nursing skills from the doctors, from Ms. Middleton and the teachers?"

"I guess," Toby said.

"Some of them are already doing that in the gym and in the infirmary," Middleton said. "Helping keep kids comfortable, deliver water."

Augustine smiled. He had pulled himself together, straightened his rumpled shirt and pants, washed his face in Trask's executive bathroom sink. "Thanks, Yolanda. I'm speaking with Toby now, and I want him to tell me what's what. Toby?"

"I'm not the best at doing that kind of stuff. Not even the best who's still up and standing around."

"Who is?"

"Four or five of us, maybe. Six, if you count Natasha."

"Are you fever-scenting, Toby?" Middleton asked. "Do I have to strap on my sachet again?"

"I'm just seeing if I can, Ms. Middleton," Toby said.

Augustine recognized the chocolate-like scent. Toby was nervous. "I'm glad you're feeling better, Toby, but we all need to think clearly."

"Sorry."

"I'd like for you to represent me and Mr. Dicken and all the school staff, okay? And ask the right kids—the right individuals—to put together teams for more training. Ms. Middleton will help us train, and Dr. Kelson. Toby, can these teams become clouded?"

Toby smiled, one pupil growing larger, the other shrinking. The gold flecks in both irises seemed to move.

"Probably," Toby said. "But I think you mean we should *cloud*. Join up."

"Of course. Sorry. Can you help us learn who's going to get better and who isn't?"

"Yes," Toby said, very serious now, and both irises large.

Augustine turned to Dicken. "I think that's where we should begin. We're not going to get any help from outside, no deliveries, nothing. We're cut off. As far as the children are concerned, we need to focus our efforts and our supplies on those for whom we can do the most good with what we have. The children are better equipped to determine that than we are. Is this clear, Toby?"

Toby nodded slowly.

"I don't like giving children such decisions," Middleton said, eyes thinning. "They are very loyal to each other."

"If we do nothing, more will die. This thing is going through the new children like a crown fire. It's spreading by breath and touch—aerosol."

"What's that mean for us?" Dr. Kelson asked, looking between Dicken and Augustine.

"I don't think we'll catch it from the kids unless we engage in really stupid behavior—pick our noses, that sort of thing," Dicken said, glancing at Augustine. *Damn him, he's pulling us together.* "The aerosol forms of the viruses are probably not infectious for us."

"It has a smell," Toby volunteered. "When it's in the air it smells like soot spread over snow. When someone is going to get sick, and maybe die, they smell like lemons and ham. When they're going to get sick but not die, they smell like mustard and onions. Some of us just smell like water and dust. We won't get sick. That's a good, safe smell."

"What do you smell like, Toby?"

Toby shrugged. "I'm not sick."

Augustine gripped Toby's shoulder. "You're our guy," he said.

Toby returned his stare without expression, but his cheeks flared.

"Let's start," Augustine said.

"It's come to them saving themselves," DeWitt said, finding the logic bitter. "God help us all."

46

The woods became dark and still. The rooms inside the cabin were quiet, stuffy from months of being closed up. Beneath the table lamp in the living room, Stella Nova shuddered at the end of each exhale of breath, but her lungs were not congested, and the air did not go in and out of her with the harsh whicker Kaye had heard earlier.

She changed the bag of Ringer's. Stella still did not awaken. Kaye stooped beside her daughter, listening and watching, then straightened. She looked around the cabin, seeing for the first time the homey and decorative touches, the carefully chosen personal items of the Mackenzie family. On an end table, a silver frame with characters from Winnie-the-Pooh in bas-relief held a picture of George and Iris and their son, Kelly, perhaps three years younger than Stella at the time the picture was taken.

To some, all the new children looked alike. People chose the simplest markers to differentiate between one another. Some people, Kaye had learned, were little more than social drones, going through the motions of being human beings, like little automatons, and teaching these people to see Stella and her kind with any sense of discrimination or understanding was almost impossible.

She hated that amorphous mob, lined up in her imagination like an endless army of unthinking robots, all intent on misunderstanding, hurting, killing.

Kaye checked Stella once again, found her signs steady if not improving, then walked from room to room to find her husband. Mitch sat on the porch in an Adirondack chair, facing the lake, eyes fixed on a point between two big pines. The fading light of dusk made him look sallow and drained.

"How are you?" Kaye asked.

"I'm fine," Mitch said. "How's Stella?"

"Resting. The fever is steady, but not dangerous."

"Good," Mitch said. His hands gripped the ends of the square wooden armrests. Kaye surveyed those hands with a sudden and softening sense of nostalgia. Big, square knuckles, long fingers. Once, simply looking at Mitch's hands would have made her horny.

"I think you're right," Kaye said.

"About what?"

"Stella's going to be okay. Unless there's another crisis."

Mitch nodded. Kaye looked at his face, expecting relief. He just kept nodding.

"We can take turns sleeping," Kaye suggested.

"I won't sleep," Mitch said. "If I sleep, someone will die. I have to stay awake and watch everything. Otherwise, you'll blame me."

This astonished Kaye, to the extent she even had enough energy to feel astonished. "I'm sorry, what?"

"You were angry with me for being in Washington when Stella ran away."

"I was not."

"You were furious."

"I was upset."

"I can't betray you. I can't betray Stella. I'm going to lose both of you."

"Please talk sense. That is *loony,* Mitch."

"Tell me that's not exactly how you felt, because I was away when it began."

Why did the burden rest upon her? How often had Mitch been away, and Stella had decided it was time to pull something, to challenge, stretch, reach out and test? "I was stressed out," Kaye said.

"I've never blamed you. I've tried to do everything you wanted me to do, and be everything I've needed to be."

"I know," Kaye said.

"Then cut me some slack." At another time, those words might have hit Kaye like a slap, but his voice was so drained and desperate, they felt more like the brush of a wind-blown curtain. "Your instincts are no stronger than mine. Just because you are a woman and a mother does not give you the right to . . ." He waved a hand helplessly. "Go off on me."

"I did not 'go off on you,' " Kaye said, but she knew she had, and felt defensively that she did indeed have that right. Yet the way Mitch was behaving, the words he was saying, scared her. He had never been one to complain or to criticize. She could not remember having this sort of conversation in their twelve years of being together.

"I feel things as strongly as you," Mitch said.

Kaye sat on the chair arm, nudging his elbow inward. He folded his arm across his chest. "I know," she said. "I'm sorry."

"I'm sorry, too," Mitch said. "I know it isn't the right time to talk like this." His breath hitched. He was trying to hold back sobs. "But right now I feel like curling up and dying."

Kaye leaned over to kiss the top of his head. His face was cold and hard under her fingers, as if he were already in some other place, dead to her. Her heart started to beat faster.

Mitch cleared his throat. "There's this voice in my head, and it says over and over again, 'You are not fit to be a father.' If that's true, the only option is to die."

"Shush," Kaye said, very cautiously.

"If I go to sleep, I'll let something get in. A little crack. Something will creep in and kill my family."

"The hell with that," she said, again gently, softly, as if her breath might shatter him. "We're tough. We'll make it. Stella's doing better."

"I'm tapped out. Broken."

"Shush, please. You *are* strong, I know you are, and I apologize if I've been acting stupid. It's the situation, Mitch. Don't be hard on either of us."

He shook his head, clearly unconvinced. "I need you to tuck me in," he said, his voice hollow. "Put me in that big bed and pull up the frilly sheets and kiss me on the cheek and say good night. I'll be all right in a little while. Just wake me if Stella has a problem, or if you need me."

"All right," Kaye said. She felt an immense sadness as he looked up and met her eyes.

"I try all the time," he said. "I give you both all I have, all the time."

"I know."

"Without you and Stella, I am a dead man. You know that."

"I know."

"Don't break me, Kaye."

"I won't. I promise."

He stood. Kaye took his hand and led him into the bedroom like a frightened boy or an old, old man. She pulled back the down comforter and the blanket and top sheet. Mitch unbuttoned his shirt and removed his pants and stood by the side of the bed, lost.

"Just lie down and get some rest," she said.

"Wake me if Stella gets any worse," Mitch said. "I want to see her and tell her I love her." He looked at her, eyes unfocused. Kaye tucked the sheets in around him, her heart thumping. She kissed him on the cheek. No tears, his face cold and hard as stone, all Mitch's blood flowing away to somewhere far from her, taking him to where she could not go.

"I love you," Kaye said. "I believe in you. I believe in what we've done."

His eyes focused on hers, then, and she felt embarrassed at the power she had over this large, strong man. The blood returned to his face, and his lips came alive under hers.

Then, like a light going out, he was asleep.

Kaye stood beside the bed and watched Mitch, eyes wide. Her chest felt wrapped in steel bands. She was as frightened as if she had just missed driving them all off a cliff. She stood vigil over him for as long as she could before she had to leave and check on Stella. She hated the conflict, husband or daughter, but went with her judgment and the nature inside her, and crossed the few steps into the living room.

•   •

The cabin was completely dark.

"What?"

Kaye sat up on the floor. She had fallen asleep beside Stella, with only the flap of the sleeping bag between her and the hard wood, and now she had the distinct impression someone other than her daughter was in the room.

It wasn't Mitch. She could see the blanketed hill of his toes through the bedroom door.

"Who's there?" she whispered.

Crickets and frogs outside, a couple of large flies buzzing around the cabin.

She switched on a table lamp, checked her daughter for the hundredth time, found the fever way down, the breathing more regular.

She thought about moving Stella into the second bedroom, but the hook supporting the bag of Ringer's solution would have to be moved as well, and Stella seemed comfortable on the sleeping bag, as comfortable as she would have been in a bed.

Kaye looked in on Mitch. He, too, was sleeping quietly. For a few minutes, Kaye stood in the short, narrow hallway, then leaned against the wall. "It's better," she said to the shadows. "It has got to be better."

She turned suddenly. For a moment, she had thought she might see someone in the hall, someone beloved and familiar. Her father.

Dad is dead. Mom is dead. I'm an orphan. All the family I have is in this house.

She rubbed her forehead and neck. Her muscles were so tense, not least from sleeping beside Stella on the wooden floor. Her sinuses felt congested, as if she had been crying. It was a peculiar, not unpleasant sensation; the byproduct of some deeply buried emotion.

She needed to get some air. She checked Stella again, obsessive; knelt to touch her daughter's forehead and feel her pulse, then walked around the couch, through the porch door, down the steps, and across the path through the grass to the boat dock.

The dock was thirty feet long and ten feet wide, ridiculously large on such a small lake. It supported a single overturned rowboat and a pile of moldy life vests. Grass blades poked out of the vests, shimmering in the moonlight.

Kaye stood at the end of the dock and crossed her arms. Absorbed the night. Crickets stroked out the degrees of heat, frogs thrummed with sexy, alien dignity out there in the shallows, among the reeds. Gnats hummed their desperate little ditties.

"Do any of you know what it is to be sad?" Kaye asked the lake and its inhabitants, then looked back toward the house. "Are *you* sad when your children are ill?" The single lamp in the living room burned golden through the windows of the porch.

She closed her eyes. Something large, completing a connection . . . something *huge* passing over, sweeping the lake, the forest—touching all the living things around her.

The frogs fell silent.

And touching *her.*

Kaye jumped as if someone had cracked through a flimsy wooden wall. Her shoulders rose and her fingers tensed. "Hello?" she whispered.

Any neighbors were at least a mile away, up the road, beyond the thick trees. She saw nothing, heard nothing.

"Wow," she said, and immediately felt stupid. She looked around the lake, toward the reedy shallows, searching for the source of another voice, though no one had spoken. The reeds were empty. The lake fell silent, not even a breath of air. The night was so still Kaye could hear her heart beating in her chest.

Something had *touched* her, not her skin, deeper. At first it was just the awareness that she was not alone. By herself, on the dock, in her bare feet, she now shared her space with someone as real as she—as welcome and strangely familiar as a beloved friend.

She felt years of burden lift. For a moment, she basked in a warm sensation of infinite reprieve.

No judgment. No punishment.

Kaye shivered. Her tongue moved over her lips. A trickle of silvery water seemed to run through her head. The trickle became a rivulet, then an insistent creek flowing down the back of her neck into her chest. It was cool and electric and pure, like stepping out of the sweltering heat of a summer day into an underground spring. But this spring *spoke*, though never with words. It had a particular and distinctive perfume, like astringent flowers.

It was alive, and she could not shake the feeling that she had known about it all along. Like molecules finally fitting, making a whole—yet not. Nothing biological whatsoever. Something *other.*

Kaye touched her forehead. "Am I having a stroke?" she whispered. She fingered her lips. They were trying to form a smile. She bent them straight. "I can't be weak. Not now. Who's there?" she repeated, as if locked into a pointless ritual.

She *knew* the answer.

The visitor, the *caller*, possessed no features, no face or form. Nevertheless, being bathed in this cool, lovely fount was like having all of her great-grandmothers, her great-grandfathers, all the wise and sweet and wonderful and powerful members of her family whom she had never met, all at once and together bestowing the unconditional approval and love they would have bestowed had they cradled her as an infant in their sheltering arms. There was that much in it, and more.

But the caller, at once gentle and unbelievably intense, was nothing like her fleshly kin.

"Please, not now," she begged. With relief came fear that she was losing her tenuous link to reality. The caller was known to her, yet long denied and evaded; but it showed no anger, no resentment. Its only response to her long denial was unconditional sympathy.

Yet was there also trepidation? The caller exposed an extraordinary longing to touch and show itself despite all the rules, the dangers. The caller quite charmingly *yearned*.

Kaye suddenly opened her mouth and let air fill her lungs. Funny, that she had stopped breathing for a moment. Funny, and not scary at all; like a personal joke. "Hello," she said with the exhale, dropping her shoulders and relaxing, pushing aside the doubts and giving up to the sensation. She wanted this to last forever. She knew already it could not. To go back to the way she had felt just a few minutes ago, and all of her life before that, would hurt.

But she knew the pain was necessary. The world was not done with her, and the caller wanted her to be free to make her own choices, without its addictive interference.

Kaye walked back to the cabin to check on the sleeping Stella and to look in on Mitch. Both were quiet. Stella's color seemed to be stronger. Patches of freckles came and went on her cheeks. She was definitely past the crisis.

Kaye returned to the dock and stood staring into the early-morning forest, hoping that the loveliness, the peace, would never leave. She wanted it all, now and forever. There had been so much grief and pain and fear.

But despite her own yearning, Kaye understood.

Can't go on. Not yet. Miles to go before I sleep.

Then, she lost track of time.

Dawn arrived in the east, on the other side of the trees, like gray velvet by candlelight.

She stood beside the overturned rowboat, shivering. How long had it been since she had returned to the dock?

Without words, the fount had spent hours sluicing her soul, (she was not comfortable using that word but there it was), wetting and revealing dusty thoughts and memories, becoming reacquainted in real and human time. Wherever it flowed, she knew its unalloyed delight.

It found her very *good.*

"Is Stella going to be all right?" Kaye asked, her voice soft as a child's in the shaded close of the trees. "Are we all going to be together and well again?"

No response came to these specific questions. The caller did not deal in knowledge, as such, but it did not resent being asked.

She had never imagined such a moment, such a relationship. The few times she had wondered at all what this experience might be like, as a girl, she had conceived of it as guilt and thunder, recrimination, being assigned onerous tasks: a moment of desperate self-deception, justifying years of ignorance and misbegotten faith. She had never imagined anything so simple. Certainly not this intense yet amused upwelling of friendship.

No judgment. No punishment.

And no answers.

I did not call for this. The body has prayed the prayers of desperate flesh, not me.

Her conscious and discerning mind, most concerned with practicalities, the mistress in starched skirts who stared out sternly over Kaye's life, told her, "You're playing Ouija with your brain. It doesn't make sense. This is going to mean nothing but trouble."

And then, as if it were shouting a kind of curse, Kaye's tense and adult voice flew to the trees, "You are having an *epiphany.*"

The crickets and frogs started their racket again, answering.

Finally, the conflict became too much. She dropped slowly to her knees on the dock, feeling that she carried precious cargo, it must not spill. She bent over and laid her hands flat on the rough, weathered wood.

She had to lie down to keep from falling over. With a long, slow release of breath, Kaye stretched out her legs.

Augustine had divided them into two teams, the first with eight students, the second with seven. Toby's team had worked first, from ten in the evening until three in the morning. Teachers and nurses carried those chosen by the team to an exercise field, laying them in rows under the blue glare of tall pole lamps, in the warm early-morning air.

Silently—with little more than a touch of palms and a whiff behind each ear—Toby passed his duties to a girl named Fiona, and the first team fell onto cots laid out in Trask's office.

Fiona and the others on the second team went out with Augustine, back down the steel stairs to the main floor.

Until dawn, Fiona and the six helped Augustine sort through other buildings, walking up to each child on the cots or on bedding spread over concrete or wood floors, on bunks in the former cells and in the dormitories; bending over and smelling above the heads of the sick, showing with one finger, or two, who was strongest, who would probably live another day.

One finger meant the child was likely to die.

After eight hours of work, they had processed about six hundred children, starting with the worst, and consequently, had already visited the most dead and dying, and the children on both teams were quiet and tired.

More children volunteered, forming a third, fourth, and fifth team. Toby did not object, nor did Augustine.

While the first two teams slept, the new teams examined another nine hundred children, separating out four hundred, most of them able to walk with the teachers to the field, where they were assigned to old tents marked "Inmate Overflow."

And round into the dawn and beyond ten o'clock, the kids worked with the remaining teachers, nurses, and security officers—the bravest of the brave—carrying bodies wrapped in sheets or in the last remaining body bags, or even in doubled plastic garbage bags, out to the farthest area within the fence, the employee parking lot, where the dead were laid out between the few and scattered cars.

Middleton worked to rearrange accommodations so that they could set up a morgue in the main gymnasium, adjacent to the infirmary. By eleven, the bodies had been removed from the parking lot and placed out of the sun.

Augustine estimated they had perhaps ten or fifteen hours before the dead would become a horrible nuisance, and twenty before they became a health hazard.

At noon, Augustine fell over after stumbling, half-blind with exhaustion, between a row of inmate tents. The children carried him back to the infirmary, with the help of DeWitt.

There, DeWitt fed Augustine a little canned soup, gave him some water. He said he was feeling better and went back out with the rested first team.

All through the morning and afternoon, their labors were watched by rows of stone-faced National Guard troops patrolling beyond the razor wire perimeter fences.

At two in the afternoon, Augustine was compelled once again to go up to the office and lie down. Dicken emerged from the research lab with another bag full of specimen kits and met him there.

Four children who had worked with the teams slept in the corner, arms around each other, snoring lightly.

Dicken looked down on his former boss. Augustine was trembling, but his face had lost that distant, defeated look.

"You are a surprising fellow, Mark," Dicken admitted.

"Not really," Augustine croaked. He touched his throat. "Sorry. My voice is shot. How's the lab work going?"

"Your turn," Dicken said, and bent down to draw blood. When he was finished, he had Augustine scrape a plastic depressor on his tongue, and sealed that into a little plastic bag.

"Anything conclusive?" Augustine asked.

"Still getting specimens from the staff."

"What next?"

"I'm going out into the field with Toby. Carry on while you rest. Can't let an old bastard like you act the humanitarian all by your lonesome."

Augustine nodded. "Conversion of Saul. Go forth," he advised piously, and crossed the air between them.

Dicken stretched. His whole body felt stiff.

Augustine rolled on his side. "I'm not doing this out of pure charity, I confess," he murmured. Dicken bent over to hear the soft words. "I have done a nasty thing, Christopher. I have played a card I vowed I would never play, to give my enemies—our enemies—the rope I need to hang them all."

"What card?" Dicken said.

"I'm still a bastard. But I do begin to understand them, Christopher."

"The children?"

"All our sweet little albatrosses."

"Good for you," Dicken said, his neck hair prickling, and turned to leave.

48

The sun was high in the sky when Kaye raised her head. She might have slept for another hour or two; she did not remember.

She rolled over on the dock.

It's gone, she said. *It was a dream. Or worse.*

She stood and brushed off her jeans, prepared to feel a resigned sadness. *I should get a checkup. There's been so much stress . . .* Her nose and forehead still felt stuffy. Was that a symptom of embolism or a burst aneurysm? Had wires crossed in her head, pouring signals from one side of the brain to the other? A short circuit?

She turned to look back along the dock at the house, took a step . . .

And let out a squeak like a surprised mouse. She stretched out her arms.

The presence was *still* with her. Quiet, calm, other; patient and real. At the same time Kaye was relieved and terrified.

She ran to the cabin. Mitch knelt on the floor beside Stella. He looked up as she came through the porch door. His hair was tousled and his face looked like a rumpled rag.

"Her fever's gone, I think," Mitch said, searching Kaye's features. His brows twitched. "The spots are smaller. The spots on her butt are gone."

Stella rolled over. Her cheeks had regained more of their color. The sleeping bag was gone, and in its place Mitch had laid out an air mattress covered with a bright yellow sheet and a lime green blanket.

Kaye stared at them both. Her hands hung by her sides, her shoulders slumped.

"Are you all right?" Mitch asked.

Stella rubbed her eyes and reached out to Kaye. Their fingers touched and Kaye moved in and gripped her hand.

"You smell different," Stella said.

Kaye bent down and hugged her daughter as fiercely as she dared.

"She's asleep again." Mitch rejoined Kaye in the cabin's small, neat kitchen. "She looks better, doesn't she?"

"Yes. Much." Kaye bit the inside of her lip and glanced at her husband. "The Mackenzies laid in a wide selection of teas," she said. She opened the box of teabags, confused, desperate.

Mitch returned her look, patient but tired. "Does she need more medicine?"

"Her neck doesn't hurt. Her head doesn't hurt. She's not feverish. I removed the needle because she drank some orange juice. I don't think she'll need any more antiviral."

"She wet the sleeping bag."

"I know. Thank you for changing it."

"You were on the dock. You were asleep."

Kaye looked out the kitchen window at the dock, now bright in the full sun. "You should have awakened me."

"You looked peaceful. I'm sorry if I said anything strange last night."

"You?" She laughed and fumbled the box of tea bags, picked up the spilled ones, then took down two mugs from a rack over the kitchen window. One mug said *Kiss a Clown, You Know You Want to.* The other was from Smith College, gold emblem of a gate on dark blue. "Not at all," Kaye murmured, and filled a kettle with water. Somewhere, a pump started chuckling, and the water jerked from the tap, finally flowing in a steady stream. She swished her hand back and forth, fingers spreading through the coldness.

Not at all the same.

"How are we, Kaye?" Mitch asked, standing beside her at the sink.

"Stella is going to be fine," Kaye said before she could think.

"How are *we,* Kaye?"

Kaye reached out and gripped Mitch's hand on the counter. She had not spent much time lately simply touching her husband. He had been gone so much, and so often, of course.

She must have looked miserable and lost. But what she felt was very, very physical.

Mitch pulled her close. He was always the one to make the first move; except that she had made the move that had produced Stella. Mitch had held back, worried about Kaye, or perhaps just scared at the thought of being a parent to a new kind of human being. They had been so in love, and the problem was, Kaye could not answer Mitch's question now, not truthfully, because she did not know.

There was still love. What kind of love? "We are going to be better," she said into his shoulder. "There is certainly better to be."

"They shouldn't hound us," he said with the boyish sternness of the night before.

"I don't think we have any control over that."

"We won't stay here long," he said, and glared out the window at the woods, the dock, the sunshine. "This place is too nice. I don't trust it."

"It *is* nice. Why not stay a while? The Mackenzies would never tell anyone."

Mitch brushed her cheek with his palm. "Their son is in a camp. The children in the camps are getting sick."

Kaye drew her eyebrows together. She could not follow this line of reasoning.

"Mark Augustine has been looking for you, for us. He's been waiting for the right moment to reel us in. The illness is scaring people badly. This is his moment."

Kaye squeezed his forearm hard, as if to punish him.

"Ow," he said.

She loosened her grip. "We need to keep Stella quiet and calm. She needs to rest for a few days at least. She can't rest in a bouncing Jeep."

"All right," Mitch said.

"We'll stay here," Kaye said. "Will it be okay?"

"It'll have to be," Mitch said.

Kaye leaned her head against Mitch's chest. Her eyes lost focus and then closed. "Is she still asleep?" she asked.

"Let's check," Mitch said, and they walked together into the living room.

She was. Kaye took Mitch's hand and led him into the bedroom. They took off their clothes, and Kaye pulled back the covers on the bed until the bottom sheet was completely revealed.

"I need you," she said.

Her fingers on his lips smelled of tea leaves.

49

Dicken had prepared and racked up his seventy specimen sets. He used a Kim Wipe to take the sting of sweat out of his eyes. His sense of urgency was extreme but counterproductive. He could work no faster than produced good results. Anything less would be worse than not having worked at all.

He had labored nine hours straight, first separating and classifying the specimens based on his labels and field notes, then preparing them for the automated lab equipment. Most of the manual labor involved preparing specimens and racking them up for runs through the instruments.

PCR instruments had been the size of large suitcases when he had been a student. Now he could hold one in the palm of his hand. The racks carried what had been the equivalent of a whole building full of equipment fifteen years ago.

Oligos—small but highly specific segments of DNA mounted in each tiny square cell of the whole-genome array chips—attached themselves to complementary segments of RNA expressed by the cell, including viral genes, if any, and labeled them with fluorescent markers. Scanners would count the markers and approximate their positions in the chromosome sequence.

From a prepared set of serological fractions, the sequencers would amplify and analyze the exact genetic code of any viruses in the samples. The proteomizers would list all proteins found within the targeted cells—both viral and host proteins. Proteins could then be matched by the Ideator to the open reading frames of the sequenced genes.

All this would give him a road map of the disease at the cellular level.

He tapped commands into the server controlling the lab machines. Fortunately, the code gaining entry to this computer had been simple to guess. He had tried combinations of JURIE and ARAM and, finally, ARAM-JURIE#1, and that had worked.

The lab filled with humming and faint clicking, first to his right, then to his left. Dicken stood up and checked the progress of the little plastic tubes marching in their metal tracks one by one into the prissy little mouths of the white-and-silver machines. He had to admire the way the doctors had set up the lab. It was economical, the equipment neatly arranged, with good flow-through from task to task.

Jurie and Pickman had known their business.

Still, virus hunters who fled at the first signs of a disease were not highly regarded by their peers. Very likely, Jurie and Pickman had never chased down viruses in the field. They had behaved more like lab lizards, pale from lack of tropical sun, utter cowards when confronted by their real prey.

For a moment, Dicken felt a chill. How dumb of him not to think of it earlier. Jurie and Pickman had already done the work, discovered the results; that was why they had run away. *The results had been very bad.*

But Dicken had found no sign of specimen kits anywhere in the lab. The equipment had barely been used, it was so new.

The chill passed, but slowly.

An hour later, he tapped the space bar on the keyboard to turn off the screen saver. A flashing green bar with "Eureka!" written across it told him he had results. The results were displayed first as thumbnails on a grid, then, at his command, as a slide show.

With grim satisfaction, Dicken saw that he had isolated a recombined variety of unencapsulated RNA virus from the blood and sputum of all the afflicted children, in titers sufficient to suggest massive infection. No other titers were so prominent.

From the beginning, seeing the buccal lesions and stomatitis, Dicken had suspected coxsackie A, known to cause most of the symptoms in the sick SHEVA children. But this strain was seldom associated with fatal illness. Coxsackie B, however, sometimes produced myocarditis, inflammatory heart disease, in infants and children. According to Dr. Kelson, myocarditis was a possible cause of death in the outbreak. Kelson had said, "There's massive tissue damage. The heart just stops."

Coxsackie A and B typically spread by fecal contact or exchange of saliva. He did not know of any historical instances where it had spread by skin contact or in aerosols—droplets of moisture from breath or sneezing—or through residues left on surfaces, yet those kinds of transmission were necessary to explain the outbreak's rapid and pervasive expansion.

Something had changed. Coxsackie A or B, or both, had suddenly become easier to spread, and targeted to a particular population not heretofore known to be vulnerable to most common childhood viruses.

Now that he knew the type of virus, he could focus on the origin of the disease and its etiology—how it had mutated, how it spread, and where it would be expected to spread next.

Dicken typed in a request for numerical results from each set of specimens, with identification of individuals and their circumstances. The computer prepared a table, but it was complicated and unintuitive.

Dicken took out a piece of paper and began organizing the results in his own favored plot. Using a small marker, he drew three large circles on the paper. Within the first circle he swooped a C, representing the children. Inside he drew a smaller circle, labeled IC for Infected Children. Outside the first, he drew a second large circle and labeled it BT for brave teachers and staff, those who had remained.

The third circle he labeled Tr, for traitors, those who had fled.

He picked up a red felt-tip pen and began categorizing the specimen ID numbers and marking them + or − for their viral status. He then recorded them within the appropriate circles. Two of the circles rapidly filled with numbers and status marks. For now, there were no numbers in the Tr circle—he was leaving that open in case information from outside became available.

He now had points of proximity or actual contact and, presumably, opportunities for viral transmission. The pattern he saw emerging was already clear, but he refused to jump to conclusions. He did not trust either intuition or instinct. He trusted hard facts, indisputable associations, and repeated correlations.

He drew the results a second way, in columns and rows. When he had completed his chart, he drew a new table, reversing the order, and filled the boxes with the categorized numbers.

Dicken cleaned up his work and tapped the plastic end of the pen on the columns, marching down, climbing back up, sweeping the marker to the right across the rows, color-coding the associations.

Any way he drew it out, the pattern was clear.

Within the special treatment center, children who had had no contact with teachers or other students for more than three days had not contracted the virus. Eight children had been in isolation cells and had been abandoned when the staff evacuated. Three had died, but all of their specimens tested negative.

Five hours ago, Middleton had phoned the lab to tell Dicken that one of the rescued children had fallen ill, and Kelson said she was likely to die. That child had almost certainly been exposed after her "rescue."

Dicken had taken specimens from six children who had been locked in a shower room by a fleeing teacher, and not found until late yesterday. One had died from lack of special medication. None had had any contact with teachers or staff for the past forty-eight hours. Their specimens tested negative.

DeWitt and Middleton had identified fifty children whom they knew had had close contact with teachers and staff in the past sixty hours. Of these, forty had fallen ill, and twenty had died. All of their specimens tested positive. Somehow, ten had managed to avoid exposure.

He looked over the results for twenty-two teachers, staff, and security officers. All had had continuous contact with infected children for the past forty-eight hours. They were exhausted, stressed, worn down. Six of these—four nurses from the main pool and one teacher from the special treatment wing, and the counselor, Dewitt—tested positive for the virus, but in low titers compared to infected children. None showed symptoms of infection.

Neither he nor Mark Augustine tested positive.

Dicken held up his chart once more. The conclusions were compelling.

Only infected SHEVA children showed symptoms.

SHEVA children lacking recent adult contact tested negative for the virus and showed no symptoms.

Contagion did not spread from the children to adults with much efficiency, if at all; and if it was passed on, did not cause illness in adults.

Contagion probably *did* spread from child to child, but the chain always began with children who had had recent contact with adults.

He had not gathered specimens from every child, alive or dead, or from all the adults that had been at the school; it was possible that an asymptomatic child was the source; it was also possible that exposed adults would get ill, eventually.

But he doubted it. The children were almost certainly not the source. And adults did not get sick. The river flowed in only one direction, downstream from teachers and staff, adults, to the new children.

The computer chimed again. Dicken looked at the screen. The Ideator had identified a sequence from its standard human genomic library. He touched a box on the screen. It expanded outward, showing a gene map for an obscure and defective HERV. Coxsackie viruses—for that matter, the superfamily of Picornaviridae—had never been known to recombine with legacy retroviral genes. Yet he was looking at a protein traced to a gene from the suspect virus, and it was very similar—90 percent homologous— to a protein once coded for by an ancient human endogenous retrovirus found in two chromosomes.

The presence of the protein converted a relatively benign RNA virus into one that killed, in large numbers.

He typed in another search. The Ideator scanned the Genesys bank for a match within the 52-chromosome genome of the new children. According to the Genesys bank, that particular defective primordial HERV did not exist in any SHEVA child.

Both of its copies had been discarded during the supermitotic splitting and rearrangement of the old chromosomes.

Dicken stared at the screen for several minutes, thinking furiously. His vision blurred. He grabbed the crumpled wipe and dabbed again at his face. His left leg cramped. He pushed away from the bench and walked around the small lab room, bracing on tables, equipment.

What Augustine and the Emergency Action people feared most had happened. Ancient viruses had somehow self-corrected and contributed one or more novel genes to a common virus, producing a deadly disease. But the recombination had not taken place in SHEVA-affected children.

It had begun in adults.

Adults were creating viruses that could infect and kill the SHEVA children. Those same viruses did not harm the adults. Dicken could yet be sure, but he suspected that the viral protein took advantage of yet another protein expressed only in the children—two units not in themselves toxic, but lethal in combination.

A new role for viruses: agents of a species-level immune response. Biological warfare, one generation against another.

An old species trying desperately to kill the new? Or just an awful mistake, a slip-up with deadly consequences?

He secured the samples, backed up the computer files, made a set of printouts, locked up the lab, and brutally shoved the outer door of the research building. It slammed open, and he walked out into the glare of the afternoon sun.

50

PENNSYLVANIA

Mitch had put on one of George Mackenzie's white terry robes to check on Stella. He now lay on the bed beside Kaye, the robe ridiculously short over his long legs. His breathing was even. She could feel his hand, large and wide, with long, thick fingers, resting on her arm.

Kaye rolled over and put her head on his chest, where the robe had pulled open. "Have I been acting a little crazy?" she asked.

Mitch shook his head. "Defensive."

"Do you remember before we were together? You were doing archaeology. I was working away madly, and confused."

"I wasn't doing much archaeology," Mitch said. "I've been out of action for longer than I've known you. My own damned fault."

"I loved your rough hands. All the calluses. What would we be without Stella?"

Mitch's eyes narrowed. Wrong question.

"Right," Kaye said. She lay back on the pillow. "I insisted. We don't have any other life now."

"I helped," Mitch said.

"I've neglected you. In so many ways."

Mitch shrugged.

"What do you want for Stella?" Kaye asked.

"A reasonably normal life."

"What will that be? She isn't like us, not really."

"She's more like us than she's different."

Kaye wiped her eyes with the back of her hands. She could still feel the caller, and when she *touched* it with her thoughts, waves of comfort surged through her and her eyes flowed over. She could not understand this feeling of glorious ease in the midst of their fear.

Mitch touched her cheek. His finger gently dabbed the wet corner of one eye.

"What's it like to have a stroke?" she asked. "Or a seizure?"

"You're the doctor," Mitch said, taken aback.

"Sam had a stroke," Kaye said. Sam was Mitch's father.

"He went down like a tree," Mitch said.

"He was paralyzed and he died in a couple of hours."

"It was fast. What are you getting at?"

"Do people have seizures that make them feel *good*? They wouldn't go to the doctor for that, would they?"

"I've never heard of such a thing," Mitch said.

"But it wouldn't be reported, would it, unless they happened to catch it . . . on an MRI or CAT scan or something. The brain is so mysterious."

"What brings this on?" Mitch asked. "We make love and you talk about having good strokes." He tried to smile. "It's called *having an orgasm*, little lady."

Kaye lifted her head and rolled over to face him, refusing to be amused.

"Have you ever felt something or someone touch your thoughts? Approving of everything about you, filling you with understanding?"

"No-o-oo," Mitch said. He did not like this conversation at all. There was a glow about Kaye's face that reminded him of when she was pregnant, a soft and intimate light in her eyes.

"Is it rare? What do people do, who do they talk to, when it happens that way?"

"What way?"

Kaye sat up and put her hands on his shoulders, staring at him imploringly, helpless. "Is that what makes people religious?"

The look on Mitch's face was so serious, she had to smile. "Maybe I'm becoming a priestess. A shaman."

"Generally," Mitch began, putting on a professorial tone, "shamans are a little crazy. The tribe feeds them and puts them to work. Shamans are more entertaining than reading entrails or tossing knucklebones."

Kaye clenched her jaw. "I'm trying to understand something."

"Out on the dock, did you feel like you were having a stroke?" Mitch asked, unable to keep the concern from his voice.

"I don't know." She smiled as if at a pleasant memory. "It's still with me."

"You're pregnant again, morning sickness?"

"No, damn it," Kaye said, poking his arm. "You're not *listening*."

"I'm not hearing anything I can understand. Tell me, straight . . . did it feel like an episode, a breakdown? We've been under a lot of stress." He stood up by the side of the bed, leaving the short robe behind. Kaye watched him, his forearms and chest and the tops of his shoulders covered with coarse hair, and her gaze dropped to his genitals hanging at postcoital parade rest, waving with the nervous swing of his arms.

She laughed.

This stopped Mitch cold. He stood like a statue, staring down on her. He had not heard Kaye laugh like that, at him, at the ridiculousness of life, in well over a year, maybe two; he couldn't remember the last time.

"You sound happy," he said.

"I'm not *happy*," Kaye insisted indignantly. "Life's a bowl of shit, but our daughter . . ." Her face crumpled. Through her fingers, she sobbed, "She's going to live, Mitch. That's a blessing, isn't it? Is that what I'm feeling—thankfulness, relief?"

"Thankful to what?" Mitch said. "The god who gives little children nasty diseases?"

Kaye spread out her arms, gesturing with her fingers at the bedroom, the lace coverlet, wood-paneled walls, pressed flowers under glass in ornate gold frames, the decorative water pitcher on the little white wicker table by the nightstand. Mitch watched her puffy eyes and red face with real concern. "We *are* luckier than others," she said. "We are so lucky our daughter is alive."

"God didn't do that," Mitch said, his voice turning sour. "We did that. *God* would have killed her. *God* is killing thousands like Stella right now."

"Then what am I feeling?" Kaye asked. She held out her hands and Mitch gripped them. A blackbird sang. Mitch's eyes went to the window.

"You're bouncing back," he said, his anger smoothing. "We can't feel like shit all the time or we'd just give up and die." He pulled her up on her knees on the bed, and expertly hugged her until her back popped.

"Ow," she said.

"That did not hurt," Mitch said. "You feel better now."

"I do," Kaye affirmed, arms around his neck.

Stella pushed through the door. "I've got this thing on my wrist," she said, tugging at the medical tape. "My skin hurts." She stared at them, naked, together. There was no use keeping secrets from her; she could smell everything in the room. Stella had seemed to instinctively understand the whys and wherefores of sex even as a toddler. Nevertheless, Mitch released Kaye, swung his body away, and reached for the robe.

Kaye pulled the coverlet into a wrap and went to her daughter. Stella leaned into her arms and Kaye and Mitch carried her back to her bed.

51

"Our last link to the outside world," Augustine said, holding up a satellite phone. "Secret Service, bless them. But I had to think of it. They're hiding out in their cars, and they did not volunteer." He climbed the flight of steps to Trask's office. Dried vomit—not his own—ran in streaks down his leg.

Dicken sidled up the steps behind Augustine. "The school has a secure server. I have Jurie's password for the lab computers, but not the password to go outside the school."

"I know. What are we looking at, anyway?"

"Coxsackie, a new strain," Dicken said. "The children have hand, foot, and mouth disease."

Augustine pushed the door to the office open. "Like the cattle?"

Dicken shook his head. "You're tired. Listen to me. Not foot and mouth, it's HFMD. Hand, foot, and mouth. Common childhood viral infection."

"Recombined?" Augustine sat behind the desk and propped the phone on the desk. He punched a number, got a rasping and wheedling noise, then swore and punched another.

"Yes," Dicken said.

"With old endogenous viruses?"

"Yes."

"Shit. How is that possible?"

"It's a mechanism I haven't seen before."

"Then why bother to call?" Augustine stopped in mid-dial, disgusted. His fingernails were black with dirt and secretions. "It's all over."

"No, it isn't. The recombined genes can't possibly be from the children," Dicken said. "They don't have them. They were excised and discarded when their chromosomes reformed during supermitosis."

Augustine raised his chin. "*We* helped the virus recombine?"

Dicken nodded. "It may have traveled in us and mutated silently for years. Now it's making its move—against the children."

"Proof?"

"Proof enough," Dicken said. "Most of what we need, anyway. We can send in my results. The CDC just needs to do their own analysis, compare my findings with their own. I'm sure they'll match. Then, we tell Ohio to back off and get Emergency Action to calm down. This is not a killer plague—not for us."

"Will anyone listen?" Augustine asked.

"They have to. It's the truth."

Augustine did not seem convinced that would be enough to turn the tide. "Who's the best contact at CDC?"

Dicken thought quickly. "Jane Salter. She's in charge of statistical analysis at National Center for Infectious Diseases. She never did put in with the Emergency Action people, but they respect her judgment. She's trusted and objective." He took the handset from Augustine and dialed Salter's direct number in Atlanta.

They were in luck, finally. The call went through, and Salter answered in person.

"Jane, it's Christopher."

"The famous Christopher Dicken? Long time, Christopher. Forgive me, I'm a little loopy. I've been up for days, crunching numbers."

"I'm in Ohio, at the Goldberger School. I have something important."

"About a certain recombined Coxsackie virus?"

"That's the one. Population dynamics, virus flow, analysis," Dicken said.

"You don't say."

"You'll want my results."

He heard a click.

"I'm recording, Christopher," Salter said. "Make it quick. There's a key meeting in five minutes. Go or no go, if you know what I mean."

Augustine looked up at a distant roaring noise. He walked to the window and looked across the traffic circle, beyond the main gate. "What the hell is that?" He swung up a pair of binoculars from the windowsill and peered through them. "Helicopters."

DeWitt stamped up the stairs, screaming, "Helicopters are coming!"

"Troops moving in?" Dicken asked.

"They wouldn't dare. We're in quarantine." Augustine tried to hold the image steady. "They're civilian. Who in hell would fly them down here?"

"Someone bringing in supplies," Dicken suggested.

"Is that possible?"

"Someone rich who has a kid here," Dicken said.

"There's two of them," Augustine said. "Not nearly enough." Then, his voice breaking, "Goddamn. I don't believe it. They're shooting. The troops are shooting at them!"

"What's happening?" Salter asked on the phone.

"Just listen to me," Dicken said. He could hear the crackle of assault weapons on the school perimeter. "And for God's sake, work fast."

He began reading her his results.

52

PENNSYLVANIA

The air was cooling and clouds were sliding in above the trees. Mitch sat on the dock. Kaye was in the house, sleeping beside Stella in the big bed, which Stella preferred now that she was feeling a little better.

It could be days before she could travel, but Mitch knew their time would come sooner than that. Somehow, though, he could not bring himself to roust them and pile them in the back of the Jeep.

It wasn't just Stella's health that concerned him.

There was something else, and small as it might seem in retrospect, it disturbed him, the way Kaye had looked, talking about what she had felt on the dock. If after all these years, his partner, his wife, was faltering . . .

Kaye had always been the reservoir of their strength, the rooted tree.

The air was heavy and moist. He watched the overcast move in and felt the first spatters of rain, big drops that changed the air's taste and smell. His nose twitched. He could smell the forest getting ready for the storm. His sense of smell had been sensitive even before they had had Stella. He had once told Kaye "I think with my nose." But that ability had been enhanced by being a SHEVA parent, and for two years after Stella's birth, Mitch had reveled in what it brought into his life. Even now, he smelled things acutely that others could only vaguely detect, if at all.

The lake was not exactly a healthy lake, but sat like a pretty little pocket of green, taking the drainage from the forest during the winter and spring and then drying up and concentrating all the nutrients during the summer, turning ripe with algae. It had no outlet. Still, it was okay; it was pretty. It was probably happy enough, as lakes went, isolated from the big doings of other lakes and rivers, dreaming in its own muted way of the seasons.

Mitch would never have built a cabin on this lake because of the potential for mosquitoes, but was glad the cabin was here, nonetheless. Besides, there were only a few mosquitoes about, he didn't know why.

The last few years, Kaye's scent in his nostrils had been perpetually active, sharp, stressed, and concerned; he had smelled other SHEVA mothers, and mothers in general, and had found a similar watchful odor. In bed a few hours ago, there had been a hint of contentment, of confirmation. Or was he just making that up?

Wishful thinking, that his wife would be happy for a little while?

Stella had noticed it, too.

Perhaps their family had become like the lake, isolated, ingrown, not entirely healthy. And that was why Stella had run away. His thoughts scattered like wavelets under the moving finger of a downdraft.

After a few minutes, Mitch just sat and tried to be empty. Gradually, another concern surfaced, about where they would go when the time came, where they would flee next. He did not know the answer, did not want to believe they were anywhere near the end of their rope, so he put the concern away on a shelf with other impossible worries and looked into the emptiness once more.

The emptiness was comfortable but never lasted long.

He had never asked Kaye how he smelled to her. Kaye did not like to discuss such things. He had fallen in love with a sad and outer-facing Kaye, lived with a woman who had not opened herself to him in months or years, until last night.

Mitch held up his hands and stared at the smooth fingers. He could almost feel himself on a site, with a shovel or trowel or brush or toothbrush in his hand, unearthing some bit of bone or pot. He could almost feel the sweat running down the back of his neck under the hot sun, in the shade of his cap and neck flap.

He wondered what the Neandertal father had thought about, at the last, lying in that Alpine cave, freezing beside his already-dead wife and stillborn child. That was where it had all begun for Mitch, finding the mummies. From that point on, his life had corkscrewed; he had met Kaye, had become part of her world. Mitch's life had acquired tremendous depth but had narrowed in scope and range.

The Neandertal father had never had a chance to feel guilty about the good old lost days of carefree mammoth and bison hunting, cave-bear baiting, swilling fermented berries or bags of honey wine with the boys.

At least once a day, Mitch went through such a sequence of thoughts, interrupting the desired emptiness. Then the thoughts faded and he stared into himself and saw a frightened child hiding among shadows. *You never know what it is like to be a child, even as a child. You have to have one of your own, and then it comes to you.*

You understand for the first time.

The rain pattered on the dock, leaving dark brown splats. Drops beaded in the blades of grass shooting up from the moldering life vests. His hand walked along the wood and found an interesting chunk of bark, about six inches long, weathered and gray. He ran his fingers over the bark, pinched its corky edge.

Kaye stood behind him. He had not heard her until the dock creaked. She moved quietly; she always had. "Did you see a flash out here?" she asked.

"Lightning?"

"No, over there." Kaye pointed into the woods. "Like a glint."

Mitch stared with a frown. "Nothing."

Kaye sighed. "Come inside," she said. "Stella's having some chicken soup. You should eat, too."

Watching his daughter slurp soup would be a treat. Mitch stood and walked with Kaye, arm in arm, back to the house.

A man in a black baseball cap stepped out of the cabin's shadows and met them at the porch door. Kaye gasped. He was young, in his late twenties at most, buff, with tanned arms. He wore a bulletproof vest over a black T-shirt and khaki pants and he carried a small black pistol. Silhouettes moved through the cabin. Mitch instinctively pushed Kaye behind him.

The man in the black cap smelled like burned garlic. He rattled off some words. Mitch's attention was too divided to listen closely.

"Did you hear me? I'm Agent John Allen, Federal Enforcement for Emergency Action. We have an arrest and sequester warrant. Hold out your arms and let me see your hands." The agent looked left, past Mitch. "Are you Kaye Lang?"

Another man, older, walked through the double door. He held out a piece of paper in a blue folder. Mitch glanced at the paper, then focused again on the cabin. Over the young man's shoulder, through the patio doors and past the couch, Mitch saw two men taking Stella out the front door. They had wrapped his daughter in a plastic sheet.

She mewed like a weak kitten.

Mitch raised his hand. Too late, he remembered the piece of bark from the dock, still clenched in his fingers.

The young man jerked up his pistol.

Mitch heard the report and the forest and house spun. The slug felt like a Major League batter connecting with Mitch's arm. The chunk of bark sailed. He landed on his face and chest. A big man sat on him and others planted their running shoes around his head and someone lifted Kaye's feet off the ground. Mitch tried to look up and the big man shoved his face into the pebbled concrete of the walkway. He could not breathe—the whack of the slug and then the fall had pushed out all his air. They twisted his hands behind him. Something parted in his shoulder. That hurt like hell. They were all talking at once, and a couple of people were shouting. He heard Kaye scream. The rain hadn't been so bad. The lake had been fine, and so had the house. He should have known better. Mitch smelled his own blood and started to choke.

53

Stella Nova Rafelson stood on wobbly legs in the long steaming shower stall and watched pink disinfectant swirl down the tile drain. Men and women wearing masks and plastic hoods and rubber gloves walked along the line with clipboards and cameras, recording the children as they stood naked.

"Name," asked a stout young woman with a husky voice.

"Stella," she answered. Her joints ached.

In a clinic somewhere, humans gave her injections and strapped her onto a bed surrounded by curtains. They kept her there for at least a day as she worked through the last obvious signs of her illness. Once, when she was released to use a bedpan, she tried to get up and walk away. A nurse and a police officer stopped her. They did not want to touch her. They used long plastic pipes to prod her back into bed.

The next day, she was tied to a gurney and rolled into the back of a white van. The van took her to a big warehouse. There, she saw hundreds of children lying on rows of camp beds. Crushed and dusty crates had been pushed into a pile at the back of the warehouse. The floor blackened her bare feet. The whole building smelled of old wood and dust and disinfectant.

They gave her soup in a squeeze bottle, cold soup. It tasted awful. All that night she cried out for Kaye and for Mitch in a voice so hoarse and weak she could barely hear it herself.

The next trip—in a bus across the desert and through many towns and cities—took a day and a night. She rode with other boys and girls, sitting upright and even sleeping on a bench seat.

She heard the guard and driver talking about the nearest city, Flagstaff, and understood she was in Arizona. As the bus slowed and jolted off the two-lane highway, Stella saw shiny metallic letters cemented into a brick arch over a heavy steel gate: *Sable Mountain Emergency Action School*.

Time came in confused jerks. Memory and smell mingled and it seemed that her past, her life with Kaye and Mitch, had gone down the drain with the disinfectant.

After they finished taking pictures again and recording their names, the attendants segregated the boys and girls and gave them hospital robes that flapped open at the back and moved the girls in a line across a concrete walkway, under the open evening air, into a mobile trailer unit, twelve new kids in all.

The trailer already held fourteen girls.

One of the girls stood by the bed where Stella lay and said, "Hello/ Sorry."

Stella looked up. The girl was tall and black-haired and had wide, deep brown eyes flecked with green.

"How are you feeling-KUK?" the girl asked her. She seemed to have a speech problem.

"Where am I?"

"It's kind of like-KUK home," the girl said.

"Where are my parents?" Stella asked, before she could stop herself. Her cheeks flushed with embarrassment and fear.

"I don't know," the girl answered.

The fourteen gathered around the new girls and held out their hands. "Touch palms," the black-haired girl told them. "It'll make you feel better."

Stella tucked her hands into her armpits. "I want to know where my parents are," she said. "I heard guns."

The black-haired girl shook her head slowly and touched Stella under the nose with the tip of her finger. Stella jerked her head back.

"You're with us now," she said. "Don't be afraid."

But Stella *was* afraid. The room smelled so strange. There were so many and they were all fever-scenting, trying to persuade the new girls. As she felt the scent doing its job, Stella wanted to get away and run.

This was nothing like she had imagined.

"It's o-KUK-ay," the black-haired girl said. "Really. It's okay here."

Stella cried out for Kaye. She was stubborn. It would be weeks before she stopped crying at night.

She tried to resist joining the other children. They were friendly but she desperately wanted to go back and live in the house in Virginia, the house that she had once tried to run away from; it seemed the best place on Earth.

Finally, as weeks passed into months and no one came for her, she started listening to the girls. She touched their hands and smelled their scenting. She started to belong and did not resist anymore.

The days at the school were long and hot in summer, cold in winter. The sky was huge and impersonal and very different from the tree-framed sky in Virginia. Even the bugs were different.

Stella got used to sitting in classrooms and being visited by doctors.

In a blur of growth and young time, she tried to forget. And even in their sleep, her friends could soothe her.

PART TWO

SHEVA + 15

"Activist SHEVA parents held in federal detention for two years or more without charges, under Emergency Action rules, may finally have their cases reviewed by state circuit courts, in apparent defiance of secret Presidential Decision Directives, says an unnamed source in the office of California's attorney general."

"Visitation rights for SHEVA parents at EMAC schools may be restored on a case-by-case basis, according to Cabinet-level administration officials testifying before Congress. No further details have been made available. Civilian Review of National Health and Safety, a government watchdog group associated with the Green Party, says it will protest this change in policy."

—*New York Times E-line National Crisis Shorts*

" 'They set off bombs. They torch themselves and block traffic. Their children carry diseases we can't begin to imagine. Hell, the parents themselves can make us sick and even kill us. If it's a choice between *their* civil liberties and keeping my own beautiful, normal children disease free, then to hell with liberty. I say screw the ACLU. Always have, always will.' "

—*Representative Harold Barren, R-North Carolina*;
speaking for the House Floor Liberty Minute

"Fifteen years and the strain is killing us. It cannot go on.

"When we suspend habeas corpus and nobody blinks, when our neighbors and relatives and even our children are hauled away in unmarked trucks and we huddle in fearful relief, the end of an entire way of life, of the American philosophy and psychology, is near, too near, perhaps upon us already.

"A government based on fear attracts the worst elements, who corrupt it from within. A shaky edifice, a government against its people, any of its people, must soon collapse."

—Jeremy Willis, *The New Republic*

1

The clouds over the capital were swollen and green with rain. The air felt close and sticky. Kaye took a government car from Dulles. She wore a trim gray suit with a pale yellow blouse, ruffled collar and sleeves, sensible walking shoes, dress pumps in her bag. She had carefully made up her face late in the morning and touched up in a restroom at Dulles. She knew how she looked: pale, thin, face a deeper shade of powdery beige than her wrists. Middle-aged and frail. Too much time spent in laboratories, not enough looking at the sun or seeing the sky.

She could have been any one of ten thousand professional workers leaving the long blocky tan-and-gray buildings around Washington, waiting for traffic to clear, stopping off for a drink or a coffee, meeting coworkers for dinner. She preferred the anonymity.

Last night, Kaye had carefully studied the briefing folio from Senator Gianelli's office. What she had read in that folio she could clearly see on the drive from Dulles. The capital was losing the last of its self-respect. On some streets, garbage pickups had been delayed for weeks without explanation. National guard and regular army troops walked around the streets in trios, firearms slung and clips loaded. Military and security vehicles—Humvees, bomb-squad trucks, armored personnel carriers—sat on key streets, humped up on sidewalks or blocking intersections. Concrete barriers that shifted every day and multiple checkpoints with armored ID kiosks made travel to government buildings tortuous.

The capital even smelled sick. Washington had become a city of long, sad lines, drawn faces, rumpled clothing. Everyone feared people in long coats, delivery trucks, boxes left on streets, and posters taped to walls demanding obscure justice and hiding thin, nasty bombs beneath to blow up those who would try to take them down.

Only the clowns and the monsters looked healthy and happy. Only clowns and monsters found their careers advancing in Washington, D.C., in the fifteenth year of SHEVA.

The driver told her the hearing had been delayed and they had some time to kill. Kaye asked him to stop in front of a Stefano's bookstore on K Street. She thought about eating but she could not rouse an appetite. She just wanted to be alone for a few minutes to think.

Kaye pulled up the strap on her shoulder bag and entered the retail-grade checkpoint outside the bookstore. A large, heavy guard in an ill-fitting uniform with all the buttons straining looked her over with a blank expression and motioned for her to apply thumb to scanner, then waved her through the metal detector. Sniffers whuffed, checking for traces of explosives or suspicious volatiles.

Perfume had become a no-no in the city.

"Clear," the guard said, his voice like soft thunder. "Y'all have a good evening."

Outside, the rain began to fall. Kaye looked back through a display window and saw trash floating down the gutters, paper bags and cups bobbing along. The gutters were clogging and water would soon back up.

She knew she needed some food. She should not attend the hearing on an empty stomach, and she had not eaten since ten that morning. It was five now. Soup and sandwiches were available at a small café inside the store. But Kaye walked past the menu board without stopping, on some sort of autopilot. Her walking shoes made damp sucking sounds on the linoleum as she passed several deep aisles of bookshelves. Fluorescent lights flickered and buzzed overhead. A young man with long felted hair sat on a patched chair, half-empty knapsack crumpled in his lap, asleep. A paperback Bible lay open facedown on the arm of the chair.

God sleeping.

Without thinking, Kaye turned right and found herself in the religion section. Most of the shelves were filled with brightly colored apocalypse novels. E-paper holograms leaped from lurid covers as she passed: end time, rapture, revelation, demons and dark angels. Most of the books had speaker chips that could read out the entire story. The same chips replaced jacket copy with vocal come-ons. The shelves murmured softly in a wave, like ghosts triggered by Kaye's brief passage.

Serious theology texts had been crowded out. She found a single shelf concealed high in the back, near the brick wall. It was cold in that corner and the books were worn and dusty.

Eyes wide, ill at ease, Kaye touched the spines and read one title, then another. None seemed right. Most were contemporary Christian commentaries, not what she was looking for. Some lashed out angrily at Darwinism and modern science.

She turned slowly and looked down the aisle, listening to the books, their competing voices sibilant like falling leaves. Then she frowned and returned to the lone shelf. She was determined to find something useful. She tugged out a book called *Talking With the Only God.* Skimming through five pages, she found big print, wide margins, self-righteous but simple instructions on how to live a Christian life in troubled times. *Not good. Not what I need.*

She replaced the book with a grimace and turned to leave. An older man and woman blocked the aisle, smiling at her. Kaye held her breath, eyes shifting. She was sure her driver had come into the store but could not remember seeing him.

"Are you seeking?" the man asked. He was tall and skeletally thin with a short cap of braided white hair. He wore a black suit. The way his coat sleeves rode up his wrists reminded Kaye of Mitch, but the man himself did not. He looked determined and a little fake, like a mannequin or a bad actor. The woman was equally tall, thin through the waist but with fleshy arms. She wore a long dress that clung to her thighs.

"I beg your pardon?" Kaye asked.

"There are better places to seek, and better texts to find," the man said.

"Thanks, I'm fine," Kaye said. She looked away and reached for another book, hoping they would leave her alone.

"What *are* you seeking?" the woman asked.

"I was just browsing. Nothing specific," Kaye said, avoiding their eyes.

"You won't find answers here," the man said.

The driver was not in sight. Kaye was on her own, and this probably wasn't serious anyway. She tried to appear friendly and unconcerned.

"There's only one valid translation of the Lord's words," the man said. "We find them in the King James Bible. God watched over King James like a holy flame."

"I've heard that," Kaye said.

"Which church do you attend?"

"No church," she said. She had come to the end of the aisle and the pair had not moved. "Excuse me. I have an appointment." Kaye clutched her purse to her side.

"Have you made peace with God?" the woman asked.

The man lifted his hand as if in benediction. "We lose our families, the families of God. In our sin, in homosexuality and promiscuity and following the ways of the Arab and the Jew, the pagan gods of the Web and TV, we stray from the path of God and God's punishment is swift." He swept his hand with a scowl at the whispering books on the shelves. "It is useless to seek His truth in the voices of the devil's machines."

Kaye's eyes crinkled. She suddenly felt angry and perversely in control, even predatory, as if she were the hawk and *they* were the pigeons. The woman noticed the change. The man did not. "Terence," the woman said and touched the man's elbow. He looked down from the ceiling, meeting Kaye's steady glare and reeling in his spiel with a surprised galumph and a bobble of his Adam's apple.

"I'm alone," Kaye said. She offered this like bait, hoping they would bite and she would have them. "My husband just got out of prison. My daughter is in a school."

"I'm so sorry. Are you all right?" the woman asked Kaye with an equal mix of suspicion and solicitude.

"What *kind* of daughter?" the man asked. "A daughter of sin and disease?" The woman tugged hard on his sleeve. His Adam's apple bobbled again, and their eyes darted over her clothes as if looking for suspicious bulges.

Kaye squared her shoulders and shoved out her hand to get through.

"I know you," the man continued, despite his wife's tugging. "I recognize you now. You're the scientist. You discovered the sick children."

Confined by the aisle, Kaye's throat closed in. She coughed. "I have to go."

The man made one last attempt, brave enough, to get through to her. "Even a scientist in self-centered love with her own mind, suffocating in the fame of television exposure, can learn to know God."

"You've spoken to Him?" Kaye demanded. "You've talked to God?" She grabbed his arm and dug into the fabric and the flesh beneath with her fingernails.

"I pray all the time," the man said, drawing back. "God is my Father in Heaven. He is always listening."

Kaye tightened her grip. "Has God ever answered you?" she asked.

"His answers are many."

"Do you ever feel God in your head?"

"Please," the man said, wincing.

"Let him *go*," the woman insisted, trying to push her arm between them.

"God doesn't talk to you? How *weird*." Kaye advanced, pushing both back. "Why wouldn't God talk to *you*?"

"We fear God, we pray, and He answers in many ways."

"God doesn't stick around when things get ugly. What kind of God is that? He's like a recorded message, some sort of God service that puts you on hold when you're screaming. Explain it to me. God says he loves me but dumps me into a world of pain. You, so full of hate, so ignorant, he leaves alone. Self-righteous bigots he doesn't even touch. *Explain that to me!*"

She let go of the man's arm.

The couple turned with stricken looks and fled.

Kaye stood with the murmuring books lapsing into silence behind her. Her chest heaved and her cheeks were flushed and moist.

"All right," she said to the empty aisle.

After a decent interval, to avoid meeting the couple outside, she left the store. She ignored the guard's irritated glower.

She stood under the eaves breathing in the heat and the humidity and listening to real thunder, far off over Virginia. The government car came around the corner and stopped at the black-striped yellow curb in front of the store. "Sorry," the driver said. Kaye looked through the limo's window and saw for the first time how young the driver was, and how worried. "Store security ignored my license. No place to park. Goddamned guard fingered his holster at me. Jesus Christ, Mrs. Rafelson, I'm sorry. Is everything okay?"

2

Hart Senate Office Building
Plenary session of the Senate Emergency Action Oversight Committee,
closed hearing
WASHINGTON, D.C.

Mark Augustine waited patiently in the antechambers until called to take his seat. It was duly noted that he was the former director of Emergency

Action. The nine senators assembled for this unusual evening session—five Republicans and four Democrats—exchanged edgy pleasantries for a few minutes. Two of the Democrats observed, for the record, that the current director was late. As well, Senator Gianelli was not present.

The chair, Senator Julia Thomasen of Maryland, expressed her aggravation and wondered who had called the meeting. No one was clear on that.

The meeting began without the director and Gianelli, and lacking any obvious point or focus, soon devolved into a testy debate about the events that had led to Mark Augustine's dismissal three years earlier.

Augustine sat back in his chair, folded his hands in his lap, and let the senators argue. He had come to the Hill to testify fifty-three times in his career. Power did not impress him. Lack of power impressed him. Everyone in this room, as far as he was concerned, was almost completely powerless.

And—if the rumors were true—what they did not know was about to bite them right on the ass.

The minority Democrats held sway for a few minutes, deftly entering their comments into the record. Senator Charles Chase of Arizona began the questioning of Augustine as a matter of senatorial courtesy. His questions soon led to the role of the state of Ohio in the death of SHEVA children.

"Madam Chair," bellowed Senator Percy from Ohio, "I resent the implication that the state of Ohio was in any way responsible for this debacle."

"Senator Percy, Senator Chase has the floor," Senator Thomasen reminded him.

"I resent the entire subject area," Percy bellowed.

"Noted. Please continue, Senator Chase."

"Madam Chair, I am only following the line of questioning begun last week by Senator Gianelli, who is not, I hope, indisposed today, not with a virus, at least."

No laughter in the Senate chamber. Chase continued without missing a beat. "I mean no disrespect to the honorable senator from Ohio."

Senator Percy flipped his hand out over the chamber as if he would have gladly tossed them all through a window. "Personal corruption should not reflect ill on such a fine state."

"Nor am I impugning the reputation of Ohio, which is where I was born, Madam Chair. May I continue my questions?"

"What in hell made you move, Charlie?" Percy asked. "We could use your eagle eye." He grinned to the nearly empty room. Only a grandstanding senator—or an aging vaudevillian—could imagine an audience where there was none, Augustine mused. He unfolded his hands to tap his finger lightly on the table.

"Chair asks for a minimum of unchecked camaraderie."

"I'm done, Madam Chair," Percy announced, sitting back and wrapping his hands behind his neck.

Augustine sipped slowly from a glass of water.

"Perhaps our questions should be more pointed, dealing more with responsibility and less with geography," Thomasen suggested.

"Hear, hear," Percy said.

"When you were in charge of the school system for Emergency Action, did you supply all schools—even state-controlled schools—with the federally mandated allotments for medical supplies?" Chase continued.

"We did, Senator," Augustine said.

"These supplies included the very antivirals that might have saved these unfortunate children?"

"They did."

"In how many states was there sufficient supply of these antivirals to treat sick children?"

"Five; six, if we include the territory of Puerto Rico."

"My state, doctor, was one of those five?"

"It was, Senator," Augustine said.

The senator paused to let that sink in. "The supply of antivirals was sufficient to take care of the children in our custody—our care. Arizona did not lose nearly as many children as most. And that supply was insured because Arizona did not seek to control and divert the federal allotments and allocations for Emergency Action schools, a hijacking sponsored by the Republican majority, if I remember correctly?"

"Yes, Senator." Augustine tapped his finger again on the table. Now was not the time to bring up Arizona's current record. There were rumors that the children of dissidents were being warehoused in schools there. He no longer had access to the lists, of course.

"Is it fair to say that you lost your job because of this fiasco?" Chase asked.

"It was part of the larger picture," Augustine said.

"A large part, I presume."

Augustine gave the merest nod.

"Do you continue to consult for the Emergency Action Authority?"

"I serve as adviser on viral affairs to the director of the National Institutes of Health. I still have an office in Bethesda."

Chase searched his papers for more material, then added, "Your star is not completely out of the firmament in this matter?"

"I suppose not, Senator."

"And what is the authority's budget this year?" Chase looked up innocently.

"You of all people should know that, Charlie," Senator Percy grumbled.

"Emergency Action's budget is not subject to yearly congressional review, nor is it available for direct public scrutiny," Augustine said. "I don't have exact figures myself, but I would estimate the present budget at over eighty billion dollars—double what it was when I served as director. That includes research and development in the private and public sector."

Thomasen looked around the room with a frown. "The director is tardy."

"She is not here to defend herself," Percy observed with amusement. Thomasen nodded for Chase to continue, and then conferred with an intern.

Chase closed in on his favorite topic. "Emergency Action has become one of the biggest government programs in this nation, successfully fighting off all attempts to limit its scope and investigate its constitutionality in a time of drastic fiscal cutbacks, has it not?"

"All true," Augustine said.

"And with this budget, approved by both Republican and Democratic administrations year after year, EMAC has spent tens of millions of dollars on lawyers to defend its questionable legality, has it not?"

"The very best, Senator."

"And does it pay any attention to the wishes of Congress, or of this oversight committee? Even to the extent that the director arrives on time when summoned?"

Senator Percy from Ohio exhaled over his microphone, creating the sensation of a great wind in the chamber. "Where are we going, Madam Chair? Haven't we enough black eyes to go around?"

"We lost seventy-five thousand children, Senator Percy!" Chase roared.

Percy riposted immediately. "They were killed by a *disease*, Senator Chase, not by my constituents, nor indeed by any of the normal citizens—the true citizens—of my great state, or this fine country." Percy avoided the hawklike gaze of the senator from Arizona.

"Dr. Augustine, is it not the scientific conclusion that this new variety of virus—hand, foot, and mouth disease—arose within the so-called normal adult population, in part through recombination of ancient viral genes not found within SHEVA children?" Chase asked.

"It is," Augustine said.

"Many prominent scientists disagree," Percy said, and lifted his hand as if to fend off the sudden rap of the gavel.

"And did you predict that just the reverse would happen, fourteen years ago, a statement that practically led to the creation of Emergency Action?"

"The reverse being . . ." Augustine said, lifting his brows.

"That the children would create new viruses that would kill *us,* Doctor."

Augustine nodded. "I did."

"And is that not still a scientific possibility, Dr. Augustine?" Percy demanded.

"It hasn't happened, Senator," Augustine said mildly.

Percy moved in. "Come on, Dr. Augustine. It's your theory. Is it not likely that this deadly viral outbreak will happen soon, given the possibility that these children might perceive that they are under *threat,* and that many of these old viruses respond to the chemicals, steroids, or whatever, that we make when we are unhappy or stressed?"

Augustine subdued a twitch of his lips. The senator was showing some education. "I suggest that perhaps the children have already turned the other cheek, and it is time now for us to show some charity. We could relieve some of their stress. And we *should* recognize them for what they are, not what we fear they might become."

"They are the mutated products of a deadly viral disease," Percy said, straightening his microphone with a scraping noise.

"They are our children," Augustine said.

"Never!" Percy shouted.

3

Sable Mountain Emergency Action School

ARIZONA

Without explanation, Stella's evening study hour had been canceled and she had been told to go to the gym. The building was empty and the basketball made a clapping echo with each resonant bounce.

Stella ran toward the end of the court, worn sneakers squeaking on the rubbery paint that covered the hard concrete. She spun around for a layup and watched the ball circle the hoop, hiccup, then drop through. There was no net to slow its fall. She deftly grabbed the ball as it fell and ran around the court to do it again. Mitch had taught her how to shoot hoops when she was eight. She remembered a little about the rules, though not much.

Stella's bunkmate, black-haired Celia Northcott, wandered into the gym fifteen minutes later. Celia was a year younger but seemed more mature. She had been born as a twin but her sister had died while only a few months old. This was common among SHEVA twins; usually, only one survived. Celia made up for a tendency toward sadness with a brittle cheer that sometimes irritated Stella. Celia was full of schemes, and was probably the most avid constructor of demes—social groupings of SHEVA children—and plans about how to live when they grew up.

She was nursing her arm—a bandage covered her wrist—and grimaced as Stella held the ball and queried her with a freckle flash and stare.

"Blood," Celia said, and sat cross-legged on the side of the court. "About a gallon."

"Why?" Stella asked.

"How should I know? KUK/ I had a nightmare last night." Celia's tongue caught and she made her signature glottal click, which almost obscured her underspeech. Celia was not very good at double speaking. Someone, she never said who, had tried to mutilate her tongue when she was eight years old. This she had revealed to Stella late at night, when Stella had found her huddled in a corner of the barracks, crying and smelling of electric onions. The facile ridge found in most of the children was a white scar on Celia's tongue, and she sometimes slurred her words, or inserted a hard clucking sound.

Stella squatted beside Celia and lightly bounced her palm off the ball, held in the nest of her legs. Nobody knew why the counselors took so much blood, but visits to the hospital usually followed upsets or unusual behavior; that much Stella had deduced. "How long did they keep you?"

"Until morning."

"Anything new in the hospital?" That was what they called the administration building, adjacent to the counselor and teacher dormitories, all beyond a razor-wire topped fence that surrounded the boys' and girls' compounds.

Celia shook her head. "They gave me oatmeal and eggs for breakfast," she said. "And a big glass of orange juice."

"Did they do a biopsy?"

Celia bit her lip and let her eyes grow large. "No. Who's had-KUK a biopsy?"

"Beth Fremont says one of the boys told her. Right out of his . . . you know." She pointed down and tapped the basketball.

"*Kweeee,*" Celia whistle-tongued.

"What did you dream?" Stella asked.

"I don't remember. I just woke up with a screech."

Stella licked her palms, tasting the paint on the court and the old rubber of the ball and a little of the dust and dirt of other shoes, other players. Then she held out her palms for Celia to clasp. Celia's palms were damp. Celia squeezed and rubbed their hands together, sighed, and let go after a moment. "Thanks," she said, eyes downcast. Her cheeks turned a steady mottled copper and stayed that way for a while.

Stella had learned the spit trick from another girl a few weeks after her arrival.

The door to the gym opened and Miss Kinney came in with ten other girls. Stella knew LaShawna Hamilton and Torry Butler from her dorm; she knew most of the others by name, but had never shared a deme with any of them. And she knew Miss Kinney, the girl's school coach. Miss Kinney led the other girls onto the court. Slung over her shoulder was a duffel bag filled with more balls.

"How about a little practice?" she asked Celia and Stella.

"Her arm hurts," Stella said.

"Can you bounce and throw?" Miss Kinney asked Celia. Miss Kinney stood about five feet nine inches tall, a little shorter than Stella. The gym teacher was thin and strong, with a long, well-shaped nose and large green eyes, like a cat's.

Celia got to her feet. She never turned down a challenge from a counselor or a teacher. She thought she was tough.

"Good," Miss Kinney said. "I brought some jerseys and shorts. They're ragged, but they'll pass. Let's go put them on. Time to see what you can do."

Stella adjusted the baggy shorts with a grimace and tried to focus on the ball. Miss Kinney shouted encouragement from the sidelines to Celia. "Don't just sniff the breeze. Take a shot!"

All the girls on the court had come to a halt in the middle of hoop practice. Stella looked to Celia, the best at sinking baskets in her group of five.

Miss Kinney strode forward, exasperated, and put on her best *I'm being patient* face. Stella would not meet her steady gaze.

"What is so hard about this?" Miss Kinney asked. "Tell me. I want to know."

Stella lowered her eyes farther. "We don't understand the point."

"We're going to try something different. You'll *compete*," Miss Kinney said. "You'll play against each other and get exercise and learn physical coordination. It's fun."

"We could all make more baskets if we formed our own teams," Stella said. "One team could have three slowing others down, if they were coming in too fast. Seven could play opposite and make baskets." Stella wondered if she sounded obtuse, but she truly wasn't understanding what Miss Kinney expected of them.

"That isn't the way it's done," Miss Kinney said, growing dangerously patient. Miss Kinney never got really angry, but it bothered Stella that she could hold in so much irritation and not express it. It made the teacher smell unpleasant.

"So, tell us how it's-KUK done," Celia said. She and LaShawna approached. Celia stood an inch taller than Stella, almost five eleven, and LaShawna was shorter than Miss Kinney, about five seven. Celia had the usual olive-to-brown skin and flyaway reddish hair that never seemed to know what to do or how to hold together on her head. LaShawna was darker, but not much, with finely kinked black hair that formed a slumped nimbus around her ears and down to her shoulders.

"It's called a game. Come on, girls, you know what a game is."

"We play," Stella said defensively.

"Of course you play. All of us monkeys *play*," the teacher said.

Stella and LaShawna smiled. Sometimes Miss Kinney was more open and direct than the other teachers. They liked her, which made frustrating her even more distressing.

"This is *organized* play. You guys are good at organizing, aren't you? What's not to understand?"

"Teams," LaShawna said. "Teams are like demes. But demes choose themselves." She lifted her hands and spread them beside her temples, making little elephant ears. It was a sign; many of the new children did such things without really understanding why. Sometimes the teachers thought they were acting smart; but not Miss Kinney.

She glanced at LaShawna's "ears," blinked, and said for the tenth time, "Teams are not demes. Work with me here. A team is temporary and fun. *I* choose sides for you."

Stella wrinkled her nose.

"I pick players with complementary abilities. I can help sculpt a team. You understand how that works, I'm sure."

"Sure," Stella said.

"Then you play against another team, and that makes all of you better players. Plus, you get exercise."

"Right," Stella said. So far, so good. She bounced the ball experimentally.

"Let's try it again. Just the practice part. Celia, cover Stella. Stella, go for the basket."

Celia stood back and dropped into a crouch and spread her arms, as Miss Kinney had told her to do. Stella bounced the ball, made a step forward, remembered the rules, then dribbled toward the basket. The floor of the court was marked with lines and half circles. Stella could smell Celia and knew what she was going to do. Stella moved toward her, and Celia stepped aside with a graceful sweep of her arms, but without any signs or suggestions for adjustment, and Stella, in some confusion, threw the ball. It bounced off the backboard without touching the basket.

Stella made a face at Celia.

"You are supposed to try to *stop* her," Miss Kinney told Celia.

"I didn't *help* her." Celia glanced apologetically at Stella.

"No, I mean, actively *try to stop her.*"

"But that would be a foul," Celia said.

"Only if you chop her arms or push her or run into her."

Celia said, "We all want to make baskets and be happy, right? If I stop her from getting a basket, won't that reduce the number of baskets?"

Miss Kinney raised her eyes to the roof. Her face pinked. "You want to get the most baskets for your team, and keep the other team from getting *any* baskets."

Celia was getting tired of thinking this through. Tears started in her eyes. "I thought we were trying to get the most baskets."

"For your *team*," Miss Kinney said. "Why isn't that clear?"

"It hurts to make others fail," Stella said, looking around the court as if to find a door and escape.

"Oh, puh-*leeze*, Stella, it's *only* a game! You play against one another. It's called *sport*. Everyone can be friendly afterward. There's no harm."

"I saw soccer riots on TV once," LaShawna said. Miss Kinney lifted her eyes to the ceiling. "People got hurt," LaShawna added doubtfully.

"There's a lot of passion in sport," Miss Kinney admitted. "People care, but usually the players don't hurt each other."

"They run into each other and lay down for a long time. Someone should have warned them they were about to collide," said Crystal Newman, who had silver-white hair and smelled like some new kind of citrus tree.

Miss Kinney motioned the twelve girls to go over to the metal chairs lined up outside the lines. They pulled the chairs into a circle and sat.

Miss Kinney took a deep breath. "I think maybe I'm missing something," she said. "Stella, how would you *like* to play?"

Stella thought about this. "For exercise, we could push-pull and swing, mosey, you know, like a dance. If we wanted to learn how to run better, or make baskets better, we could set up running academies. Girls could form wavy channels and ovals and others could run the channels. The girls in the wavy channels could tell them how they aren't doing it right." She pointedly did not tell Miss Kinney about spit-calming, all the players slapping palms, which she had seen athletes do in human games. "Then the runners could shoot baskets from inside the channels and at different distances, until they could sink them from all the way across the court. That's more points, right?"

Miss Kinney nodded, going along for the moment.

"We'd switch out a runner and a channel each time. In a couple of hours, I bet most of us could sink baskets really well, and if we added up the points, the teams would have more points than if they, you know, fought with each other." Stella thought this over very earnestly for an instant and her face lit up. "Maybe a thousand points in a game."

"Nobody would want to watch," Miss Kinney said. She was showing her exhaustion now, but also making a funny little grin that Stella could not interpret. Stella looked at the blinking red light on the nosey on Miss Kinney's belt. Miss Kinney had turned off the nosey before practice, perhaps because the girls often triggered its tiny little wheeping alarm when they exercised, no matter how much self-control they displayed.

"I would watch!" Celia said, leaning into the words. "I could learn how to train people in motion with, you know, signs." Celia glanced at Stella conspiratorially, and undered, /*Signs and smells and spit, eyes that twirl and brows that knit*. It was a little song they sometimes sang in the dorm before sleep; softly. "That would really be fun."

The other girls agreed that they understood that sort of game.

Miss Kinney lifted her hand and twisted it back and forth like a little flag. "What is it? You don't like competition?"

"We like push-pull," Stella said. "We do it all the time. On the playground, in the walking square."

"Is that when you do those little dances?" Miss Kinney asked.

"That's mosey or maybe push-pull," said Harriet Pincher, the stockiest girl in the group. "Palms get sweaty with mosey. They stay dry with push-pull."

Stella did not know how to begin to explain the difference. Sweaty palms in a group touch could make all sorts of changes. Individuals could become stronger, more willing to lead, or less aggressive in their push to lead, or simply sit out a deme debate, if one happened. Dry palms indicated a push-pull, and that was less serious, more like play. A deme needed to adjust all the time, and there were many ways to do that, some fun, some more like hard work.

Rarely, a deme adjustment involved stronger measures. The few attempts she had seen had resulted in some pretty nasty reactions. She didn't want to bring that up now, though Miss Kinney seemed genuinely interested.

Adjusting to humans was a puzzle. The new children were supposed to do all the adjusting, and that made it hard.

"Come on," said Miss Kinney, getting up. "Try again. Humor me."

4

Pathogenics Center
Viral Threat Assessment Division
Sandia Labs
NEW MEXICO

"**W**e trade a lot of aptronyms to let off steam," Jonathan Turner said as he spun the golf cart up to the concrete guard box.

"Aptronyms?" Christopher Dicken asked.

The sun had set in typical New Mexico fashion—suddenly and with some drama. Halogen lamps were switching on all over the facility, casting the plain and often downright ugly architecture into stark artificial day.

"Names that suit the job. I'll give you an example," Turner said. "We have a doctor here at Sandia named Polk. Asa Polk."

"Ah," Dicken said. The guard box stood empty. Something small and white moved back and forth behind smoked glass windows. A long steel tube jutted from the side. He used a handkerchief to wipe sweat from his cheeks and forehead. The sweat was not just from the heat. He did not like this new role. He did not like secrets.

In particular, he did not like stepping into the belly of the beast.

Turner followed his gaze. "Nobody home," he said. "We still use people at the main gates, but here it's an automated sentry." Dicken caught a glimpse of a grid of purple beams scooting over Turner's face, then his own.

A green light glowed beside the gate.

"You are who we say you are, Dr. Dicken," Turner said. He reached into a small box under the dash and took out a plastic bag marked BIO-HAZARD. "The rag, please, Kleenex in your pockets, anything used to sop. Nothing like that is allowed in or out. Clothing is bad enough."

Dicken dropped the handkerchief into the bag, and Turner sealed it and slipped it into a small metal drop box. The concrete and iron barriers sank and drew back.

"In accounting, we have Mr. Ledger," Turner said as he drove through. "And in statistics, Dr. Damlye."

"I once worked with a pathologist named Boddy," Dicken said.

Turner nodded provisional approval. "One of our arbovirus geniuses is named Bugg."

The cart hummed past a dark gray water tower and five pressurized gas cylinders painted lime green, then crossed a median to a fenced enclosure containing a large white satellite dish. With a flourish, Turner did a 360 around the dish, then drove up to a row of squat bungalows. Behind the bungalows, and beyond several electrified fences topped with razor wire, lay five concrete warehouses, all of them together code-named Madhouse. The fences were patrolled by squat gray robots and soldiers toting automatic weapons.

"I once knew a plastic surgeon named Scarry," Dicken said.

Turner smiled approval. "An auto mechanic named Torker."

"A nuclear chemist named Mason."

Turner grimaced. "You can do better. It may be essential to your sanity, working here."

"I'm fresh out," Dicken admitted.

"I could go on for days. Hundreds and hundreds, all on file and verified. None of this urban legend crap."

"I thought you said just personal acquaintances."

"I may have been handicapping you," Turner admitted, and pulled the cart into a parking space marked in cargo letters on a white placard: #3 MADHOUSE HONCHO. "A gynecologist named Box."

"An anthropologist named Mann," Dicken said, peering right at the sunning cages for the more hirsute residents of the Madhouse, now empty. "Mustn't let down the team."

"A dog trainer named Doggett."

"A traffic cop named Rush." Dicken felt himself warming to the game.

"A cabby named Parker," Turner countered.

"A compulsive gambler named Chip."

"A proctologist named Poker," Turner said.

"You used that one."

"Scout's honor, it's another," Turner said. "And I *was* a scout, believe it or not."

"Merit badge in hemorrhagic fevers?"

"Lucky guess."

They walked toward the plain double doors and the white-lit corridor beyond. Dicken's brow furrowed. "A pathologist named Thomas Shew," he said, and smiled sheepishly.

"So?"

"T. Shew."

Turner groaned and opened the door for Dicken. "Welcome to the Madhouse, Dr. Dicken. Initiation begins in half an hour. Need to make a pit stop first? Restrooms to your right. The cleanest loos in Christendom."

"Not necessary," Dicken said.

"You should, really. Initiation begins with drinking three bottles of Bud Light, and ends with drinking three bottles of Becks or Heinekens. This symbolizes the transition from the halls of typical piss-poor science to the exalted ranks of Sandia Pathogenics."

"I'm fine." Dicken tapped his forehead. "A libertarian named State," he offered.

"Ah, that's a different game entirely," Turner said.

He rapped on the closed door to an office and stood back, folding his hands. Dicken looked along the cinder block hallway, then down to the concrete gutters on each side, then up at sprinkler heads mounted every six feet. Long red or green tags hung from the sprinkler heads, twisting in a slow current of air flowing north to south. The red tags read: CAUTION: ACID SOLUTION AND DETERGENT. A second pipe and sprinkler system on the left side of the corridor carried green tags that read: EXTREME CAUTION: CHLO-RINE DIOXIDE.

At the southern end of the corridor, a large fan mounted in the wall slowly turned. During an emergency, the fan would switch off to allow the corridor to fill with sterilizing gas. Once the area had been decontaminated, the fan would evacuate the toxic atmosphere into big scrubbing chambers.

The office door opened a crack. A plump man with thick black hair and beard and critical dark green eyes watched them suspiciously through the crack, then smiled and stepped into the hall. He quietly closed the door behind him.

"Christopher Dicken, this is Madhouse Honcho number five, or maybe number four, Vassili Presky," Turner said.

"Proud to meet you," Presky said, but did not offer his hand.

"Likewise," Dicken said.

"He happens *not* to be a computer geek," Turner added.

Dicken and Presky stared at him with quizzical half-smiles. "Pardon?" Presky said.

"Press-key," Turner explained, astounded by their density.

"We will pardon Dr. Turner," Presky said with a pained expression.

"We're at step two of the initiation," Turner said. "On our way to the party. Vassili is Speaker to Animals. He runs the zoo and does research, as well."

Presky smiled. "You want it, we have it. Mammals, marsupials, mono-tremes, birds, reptiles, worms, insects, arachnids, crustaceans, planaria, nematodes, protists, fungi, even a horticultural center." He snapped his fingers and opened his door again. "I forgot, this is formal. Let me get my coat."

He emerged wearing a gray tweed jacket with worn cuffs.

The labs spun out like spokes from a hub. Turner and Presky led Dicken through broad double glass doors, then navigated in quicktime a maze of corridors, guiding him toward the center of Sandia Pathogenics. Dicken's ears throbbed with the surge in air pressure as the doors hissed shut behind them.

All the buildings and connecting corridors were equipped with sprin-klers and evacuation fans, emergency personnel showers—stainless steel–lined alcoves with multiple showerheads, decontamination rooms with re-mote manipulators, color-coded red-and-blue containment and isolation suits hanging behind plastic doors, and extensive collections of emergency medical supplies.

"Pathogenics is bug motel," Presky said. Dicken was trying to place his accent: Russian, he thought, but modified by many years in the U.S. "Bugs come in, they do not go out."

"Dr. Presky never gets our jingles right," Turner said.

"I have no mind for trivia," Presky agreed. Then, proudly, "Also, not watching TV all my life."

A group of five men and three women awaited them in the lounge. As Dicken and his two escorts entered, the group lifted bottles of Bud Light in salute and gave him a rousing, "Hip, hip, hurrah!"

Dicken stopped in the doorway and rewarded them with a slow, awkward grin. "Don't scare me," he admonished. "I'm a shy guy."

"Wouldn't dream of it," said a very young man with long blond hair and thick, almost white eyebrows. He wore a well-tailored gray suit that took a stylish drape on his substantial frame, and Dicken pegged him as the dandy. The others dressed as if they wanted covering and nothing more.

The dandy whistled a short tune, held out a strong, square-fingered hand, crossed two fingers, shook the hand in the air before Dicken could grip it, then backed away, bowing obsequiously.

"The secret handshake, unfortunately," Turner said, lips pressed together in disapproval.

"It symbolizes lies and deceit and no contact with the outside world," the dandy explained.

"That's not funny," said a tall, black-haired woman with a distinct stoop and a pleasant, homely face with beautiful blue eyes. "He's Tommy Powers, and I'm Maggie Flynn. We're Irish, and that's the extent of what we share. Let me introduce you to the rest."

They passed him a bottle of beer. Dicken made his greetings all around. Nobody shook hands. This close to the center, it was apparent people avoided direct contact as much as possible. Dicken wondered how much their love lives had suffered.

Thirty minutes into the party, Turner took Dicken aside, using the pretext of swapping the half-consumed Bud for a bottle of Heineken. "Now, Dr. Dicken," he said. "It's official. How do you like our players?"

"They know their stuff," Dicken said.

Presky approached, bottle of Becks lifted in salute. "Time to meet the master, gentlemen?"

Dicken felt his back stiffen. "All right," he said.

The group fell silent as Turner opened a side door leading off the lounge and marked by a large red square at eye level. Dicken and Presky followed him down another corridor of offices, innocuous in itself but apparently rich in symbolism.

"The rest back there don't usually get this far," Turner said. He walked slowly beside Dicken, allowing for his pace. "It's tough recruiting for the inner circle," he admitted. "Takes a certain mindset. Curiosity and brilliance, mixed with an absolute lack of scruples."

"I still have scruples," Dicken said.

"I had heard as much," Turner said, dead serious and a little critical. "Frankly, I don't know why in hell you're here." He grinned wolfishly. "But then, you have connections and a certain reputation. Maybe they balance out."

Presky tried for an ironic smile. They came to a broad steel door. Turner ceremoniously removed a plastic tag from his pocket and let it dangle from the end of a red lanyard imprinted with *Sandia* in white letters. "Never tell the townies you work here," he advised.

He lifted his arms. Dicken lowered his head, and Turner slung the lanyard around his neck, then backed off. "Looks good on you."

"Thanks," Dicken said.

"Let's make sure you're in the system before we enter."

"And if I'm not?"

"If lucky," Presky said, "you are hit by Tazer before they use bullets."

Turner showed him how to press his palm against a glass pad and stare into a retinal scanner. "It knows you," Turner said. "Better still, it likes you."

"Thank god," Dicken said.

"Security *is* god here," Turner said. "The atomic age was a firecracker compared with what's on the other side of that door." The door opened. "Welcome to ground zero. Dr. Jurie is looking forward to meeting you."

5

WASHINGTON, D.C.

Gianelli swept through the waiting room of his office, accompanied by Laura Bloch, his chief of staff. His face was red and he looked just as Mitch had once described him: on the edge of a heart attack, with a big, friendly expression topped by shrewd eyes.

Kaye stood up beside the long wrought iron-and-marble coffee table that held center position in the lobby. Even though she was alone, she felt like a card being forced from a deck.

"They're wrangling," Laura Bloch told Gianelli in an undertone. "The director is late."

"Perfect," Gianelli said. He looked at a clock on the wall. It was eleven. "Where's my star witness?" He gave Kaye a lopsided smile, his expression combining both sympathy and doubt. She knew she did not look prepared. She did not feel prepared. Gianelli sneezed and walked into his office. A young male Secret Service agent closed the door and stood guard beside it, hands folded in front of him, eyes unreadable behind smoked glasses.

Kaye let out her breath.

The maple-and-glass door opened almost immediately and the senator poked his head out.

"Dr. Rafelson," he called, and crooked his finger.

The office beyond was stacked with newspapers, magazines, and two antiquated desktop computers perched on three desks. The huge desk nearest the window was covered with law books and leftover boxes of Chinese food.

The agent closed the door behind Kaye. The air was close and mustily cool. Laura Bloch, in her forties, small and plump, with intense, bulging black eyes and a halo of frizzy black hair, stood and handed papers from a briefcase to Gianelli.

"Pardon our mess," he said.

"He says that to everyone," Bloch said. Her smile was at once friendly and alarming; her expression reminded Kaye of a pug or a Boston terrier, and she could not seem to look directly at anyone.

"This has been my home away from home the last few days. I eat, drink, and sleep here." Gianelli offered his hand. "Thank you for coming."

Kaye shook the hand lightly. He let her determine the strength and duration of the grip.

"This is Laura Bloch. She's my right hand . . . *and* my left hand."

"We've met," Bloch said, and smiled. Kaye shook Laura's hand; it was soft and dry. Laura seemed to stare at Kaye's forehead and her nose. Suddenly, irrationally, Kaye liked and trusted her.

Gianelli she was not so sure about. He had moved up awfully fast in the last few years. Kaye had become suspicious of politicians who prospered in bad times.

"How's Mitch?" he asked.

"We haven't spoken for a few weeks," Kaye said.

"I like Mitch," Gianelli said with an undulating shrug of his shoulders, apropos of nothing. He sat behind his desk, stared over the crusted boxes, and frowned. "I hated to hear about what happened. Awful times. How's Marge?"

Kaye could tell he did not really give a damn about Marge Cross, not at the moment. He was mentally preparing for the committee meeting.

"She sends her regards," Kaye said.

"Good of her," Gianelli said.

Kaye looked up at a framed portrait to the right of the big desk. "We were sorry to hear of Representative Wickham's death," she said.

"Shook up everything," Gianelli murmured, appraising her. "Gave me the boost I needed, however, and here I am. I am a whelp, and many kind folks in this building are bound and determined to teach me humility."

He leaned forward, earnest now and fully focused. "Is it true?"

Kaye knew what he meant. She nodded.

"Based on what data sets?"

"Americol pharmacy tracking reports. Drop-in data collection systems in two thousand area hospitals servicing epidemiology contracts with Americol." Kaye swallowed nervously.

Gianelli nodded, his eyes shifting somewhat spookily over her shoulder as he thought this through. "Any government sources?" he asked.

"RSVP Plus, Air Force LEADER 21, CDC Virocol, NIH Population Health Monitor."

"But no sources exclusive to Emergency Action."

"No, though we suspect they listen in on some of our proprietary tracking systems."

"How many will there be?" Gianelli asked.

"Tens of thousands," Kaye said. "Maybe more."

"Jesus, Homer, and Jethro Christ," Gianelli said, and leaned back, his tall chair creaking on old steel springs. As if to calm himself, he raised his arms and folded his hands behind his head. "How's your daughter?"

"She's in a camp in Arizona," Kaye said.

"Good old Charlie Chase and his wonderful state of Arizona. But how *is* she, Dr. Rafelson?"

"Healthy. She's found friends."

Gianelli shook his head. Kaye could not tell what he was thinking or feeling. "It could be a rough meeting," he said. "Laura, let's give Dr. Rafelson a quick tour of the subcommittee's players."

"I was briefed in Baltimore," Kaye said.

"Nobody knows 'em better than we do, right, Laura?"

"Nobody," Laura Bloch said.

"Laura's daughter, Annie, died at Joseph Goldberger," the senator said.

"I'm sorry," Kaye said, and suddenly her eyes filled with tears.

Bloch patted Kaye's arm and set her face in grim reserve. "She was a sweet kid," she said. "A little dreamy." She drew herself up. "You are about to testify before a baboon, two cobras, a goose, a certified bull ape, and a spotted leopard."

"Senator Percy is the baboon," Gianelli said. "Jakes and Corcoran are the cobras, lying low in the grass. They hate being on this committee, however, and I doubt they'll ask you anything."

"Senator Thomasen is chairperson. She's the goose," Bloch said. "She likes to think she's keeping the other animals in order, but she has no fixed opinions herself. Senator Chase claims to be on our side—"

"He's the bull ape," Gianelli said.

"But we don't know how he'll vote, push comes to shove," Bloch finished.

Gianelli glanced at his watch. "I'm going to bring you in first. Laura tells me the director is still stuck in traffic."

"Twenty minutes away," Bloch said.

"She's working hard to get the directorship of EMAC legislated into a Cabinet-level position, giving her sole budgetary control. The director is our leopard." Gianelli scratched his upper lip with a forefinger. "We expect you to help us counter her suggestions, which are bound to be nasty beyond belief."

"All right," Kaye said.

"Mark Augustine will be there," Bloch said. "Any problem with that?" she asked Kaye.

"No," Kaye said.

"You two get along?"

"We disagreed," said Kaye, "but we worked together."

Bloch made a fleeting face of dubiety.

"We'll take our chances," Gianelli said with a snuffle.

"You should never take chances," Bloch advised, producing another handkerchief from her purse.

"I *always* take chances," Gianelli said. "That's why I'm here." He blew his nose. "Goddamned allergies," he added, and watched Kaye's reaction. "Washington is full of snotty noses."

"No problem," Kaye said. "I'm a mommy."

"Good," Bloch said. "We need a pro."

6

Dr. Jurie's office was small and crammed with boxes, as if he had arrived only a few days before. Jurie pushed back his old Aeron chair as Dicken and Turner entered.

The shelves around the office were lightly populated with a few battered college texts, favorites for quick reference, and binders filled with what Dicken assumed were scientific papers. He counted seven metal lab stools in the small room, arranged in a cramped half-circle around the desk. The desk supported a flat top computer with two panels popped up, displaying results from two experiments.

"Acclimatizing, Dr. Dicken?" Jurie asked. "Altitude treating you well?"

"Doing fine, thank you," Dicken said. Turner and Presky assumed relaxed hunched positions on their stools.

Jurie motioned for Dicken to sit in a second old Aeron, on the other side of the desk. He had to push past a stack of boxes to fit into the chair, which bent his leg painfully. Once he sat, he wondered if he would be able to get up again.

Jurie wore brown oxfords, wool slacks, a dark blue shirt with a broad collar, and a sleeveless, cream-colored knit sweater, all clean but rumpled. At fifty-five, his features were still youthfully handsome, his body lean. He had the kind of face that would have fit well right above the collar of an Arrow shirt in a magazine ad. Had he smoked a pipe, Dicken would have thought him a cliché scientist. His body was too small, however, to complete the Oppenheimer effect. Dicken guessed his height at barely five feet three inches.

"I've invited more of our research group heads to join us. I apologize for showing you off, Dr. Dicken." Jurie reached over to send the flat top into sleep mode, then rotated in his chair, back and forth.

A woman's head poked through the door and pushed a fist in to rap on the inside wall.

"Ah," Jurie said. "Dee Dee. Dr. Blakemore. Always prompt."

"To a fault," the woman said. In her late thirties, comfortably rotund, with long mousy hair and a self-assured expression, she pushed through the door and sat with some difficulty on a stool. In the next few minutes, four others joined them in the room, but remained standing.

"Thank you all for coming," Jurie started the meeting. "We are all here to greet Dr. Dicken."

Two of the men had entered holding cans of beer, apparently cadged from the party. Dicken noted that one—Dr. Orlin Miller, formerly of Western Washington University—still favored Bud Light over Heineken.

"We're a relaxed group," Jurie said. "Somewhat informal." He never smiled, and as he spoke, he made small, unexpected hesitations between words. "What we're essentially interested in, here at Pathogenics, is how diseases use us as genetic libraries and reservoirs. Also, how we've adapted to these inroads and learned to use the diseases. It doesn't really matter whether viruses are rogue genes from inside us, or outside invaders—the result is the same, a constant battle for advantage and control. Sometimes we win, sometimes we lose, right?"

Dicken could not disagree.

"I've listened to all the media babble about virus children, and frankly I don't give a damn whether they're the products of disease or evolution. Evolution *is* a disease, for all I know. What I want to learn is how viruses can recombine and kill us.

"Not coincidentally, if we learn how that works, we have a pretty important weapon for both national defense and offense. This is the age of gene and germ, and whatever subtle little perversions we can think of, our enemies can also think of. Which is a pretty good reason to keep Sandia Pathogenics funded and running at fool steam, which we all will benefit from."

"Amen," said Turner.

I heard "fool steam," Dicken thought, and looked around the room. *Did anybody else? Fool steam ahead.*

"Dr. Presky, shall we show Dr. Dicken our zoo?" Jurie asked.

7

Mitch had lost everything important, but once again he had dirt and bone chips and pottery. He was back in the field, carrying a small spade and a kit full of brushes. Starting from scratch was an archaeologist's definition of workaday life, and he was definitely starting from scratch, all over again.

Around him, a neat square hole in the earth had been sculpted into many terraces on which sat fragments of flint, the crushed remains of what might have once been a wicker basket, a rough oval of shards from a small pot, and the thing that had absorbed his attention all day: an engraved shell.

The sun had set several hours ago and he was working by the light of a Coleman lantern. Down in the hole, all colors had long since turned to gray and brown. Brown was the color he knew best. Beige, gray, black, brown. The brown dust in his nose made everything smell like dry earth. A brown, neutral smell.

The shell lay in three pieces and was crudely engraved with what looked like a crosshatched bird's wing. Mitch had a hunch it might be similar to the shells found at the Craig mound in Spiro, Oklahoma. If it was, that might generate enough publicity that they could persuade the contractors to pause for a few weeks.

The generator in the back of the truck had broken down the night before. Now, the lantern's gas was running out.

With a sigh, he turned the lantern off, laid his spade and kit on the side of the hole and climbed out carefully, feeling his way in the dark, putting a strain on his good arm.

As with most university-sponsored digs, the budget was minimal and equipment was precious, usually secondhand, and seldom reliable. Time was important, of course. In two more weeks bulldozers would move in and cover hundreds of acres with fill and concrete slabs for a housing tract.

The twelve students working the site had gathered under a tent and were sipping beer in the cooling twilight. Some things never changed. He accepted a freshly popped can from a twenty-year-old brunette named Kylan, then sat with a groan in a camp chair reserved for him in part because he was the most experienced and in part because he was the oldest and the kids thought he might require the bare minimum of comfort to keep functioning.

The gimpy arm drew sympathy, too. Mitch could only dig effectively with one hand, propping the handle of the shovel under his armpit.

The others squatted on the dirt or on the two rugged wooden benches pulled from the back of the single battered pickup, the same one that held the useless generator.

"Any luck?" Kylan asked. They were not very talkative this evening, perhaps because they saw the imminent dashing of their hopes and dreams. This dig had become their lives in the past few weeks. Two couples were already lovers.

Mitch held up his hand, made a grasping motion. "Flashlight," he said.

Tom Pritchard, twenty-four, skinny, with a head of dusty and tousled blond hair, tossed him a black aluminum flashlight.

The students looked at each other, blank-faced in the way kids have of hiding what might be an inappropriate emotion: hope.

"What is it?" asked tall, stout Caitlin Bishop, far from her native New York.

Mitch lifted his head and sighed. "Probably nothing," he said.

They crowded around, all pretense and weariness gone. They needed hope as much as they needed rehydrating fluids. "What?" "What is it?" "What did you find?"

Mitch said it was probably nothing; probably not what he thought it was. And even if it was, how did that figure into his plans? There were hundreds of shells from Spiro scattered in private and university collections. So what if he had just found one more?

What sort of prize was that to replace his family?

He waved them off with the flashlight, then aimed the beam up at the first star to appear in the sky. The air was dry and the beam was only visible because the dust they had been raising all day lingered in the still air.

"Anyone know about Spiro, Oklahoma? The Craig mound?" he asked.

"Mississippian civilization," said Kylan, the best student in the group but hardly the best digger. "Opened during the nineteen thirties by the Pocola Mining Company. A disaster. Burials, pottery, artifacts, all gone, all sold to tourists."

"A famous source for engraved conch shells," Mitch added. "Decorated with birds and snakes and such, vaguely Mesoamerican designs. Probably part of an extensive bartering community spread through a number of cultures in the East and South and Midwest. Anybody know about these shells?"

They all shook their heads.

"Show us," said Bernard Rowland and stepped forward, as tall as Mitch and broader across the shoulders. He was a Mormon and did not drink beer; Iced Sweat, a wickedly green drink in a large plastic bottle, was his liquid of choice.

Mitch led them back through the ranks of holes in the ground. Flies were starting to zizz and hum after hiding out during the heat of the day. The cattle feed lots near Lubbock were less than ten miles away. When the wind was right, the smell was impressive. Mitch wondered why anyone would want to build homes here, so close to that smell and the flies.

They came to his hole and the students stood a foot back from the dry edges. He climbed into the hole and pointed the flashlight at the terrace that held the shell, painstakingly revealed by his brush and dental pick work of the last six hours.

"Wow," Bernard said. "How did it get out here?"

"Good question," Mitch said. "Anybody have a camera?"

Kylan handed him her digital, Dyno-labeled "Potshooter." Mitch drew out the marker strings with length measurements in small squares of tape, handed them to the students, who set them at right angles and weighted them with rocks, and then snapped a series of flash pictures.

Bernard helped Mitch out of the hole. They stood solemnly for a moment.

"Our treasure," Mitch said. Even to himself, he sounded cynical. "Our only hope."

Fallon Dupres, a twenty-three-year-old from Canada, who looked like a fashion model and kept severely aloof from most of the men, handed him another can of Coors. "Actually, the Craig mound shells weren't conchs," she told Mitch in an undertone. "They were whelks."

"Thanks," Mitch said. Fallon tilted her head, blasé. She had made a pass at Mitch three days before. Mitch had suspected her of being the type of attractive woman that instantly gravitated to age and authority, however weak that authority might be. In the near vacuum of the little dig, he was the most authoritative male, and he was certainly the oldest. He had politely declined and told her she was very pretty, and under other circumstances he might oblige. He had hinted, in as roundabout a way as possible, that that part of his life was over. She had ignored the evasions and told him bluntly that his attitude was not natural.

In fact, Mitch had not had a woman since he and Kaye had parted last year in Phoenix, shortly after his release from prison. They had agreed to go their strategic ways. Kaye had gone to work for Americol in Maryland, and Mitch had gone on the road, looking for holes in the Earth to hide in.

"I thought Spiro was, like, a corrupt vice president," said Larry Kelly, the dimmest and funniest of the crew. "How's a shell going to save our dig?"

Fallon, surprisingly, set herself to gently explain.

Mitch wandered off to check his cell phone. He had turned it off for the morning work hours, and forgotten to switch it on during the nap he had taken at the burning center of the day. There was one message. He vaguely recognized the number. With an awkward pass, he punched in the retrieval code.

The voice was instantly recognizable. It was Eileen Ripper, a fellow archaeologist and friend. Eileen specialized in Northwestern digs. They had not spoken in more than ten years. "Mitch, something dishy. Are you busy? Better not be. This is, as I said, *dishy*. I am stuck here with a bunch of women, can you believe it? Want to upset some more apple carts? Call me."

Mitch looked across the darkening plateau and the black ditches to where Fallon was explaining the Spiro shells to a group of bone-weary students, about to have their dig closed and covered over by lawns and concrete slabs. He stood with the phone in his weak hand, clenching his strong hand. He could not stand the thought of having this dig closed, however trivial it was, of having another part of his life be judged useless.

He had been put away for two years for assault with a deadly weapon—a large wood chip. He had not seen Kaye for more than a year. She was working on viruses for Marge Cross, and in Mitch's judgment, that was a kind of defeat as well.

And there was Stella, stashed away by the government in a school in Arizona.

Fallon Dupres walked up behind him. He turned just as she folded her arms, watching him carefully. "It isn't a whelk, Mitch," she said. "It's a broken clamshell."

"I could have sworn," he said. He had seen the Mesoamerican design so plainly.

"It's scratched up like a doodle pad," the young woman said. "But it's not a whelk. Sorry." She turned away, glanced at him one more time, smiled perhaps more in regret than pity, and walked off.

Mitch stood under the blue-black sky for a few minutes, wondering how many wish-thinks he had left in him before he lost it completely. Another door closing.

He could head north. Drop off and visit Stella along the way—if they let him. You could never find out in advance.

He called Eileen's number.

8

Gianelli entered at the back of the chamber, carrying a stack of papers. Thomasen looked up. Augustine glanced over his shoulder. The last senator on the committee was followed by a Secret Service agent, who took a position with another agent by the door, and then by a small, intense-looking woman. Augustine recognized Laura Bloch. She was the main reason Gianelli was a senator, and she was a formidable political mind.

Augustine had also heard that Bloch was a bit of a spymaster.

"Glad you could make it, Dick," Chase called out across the chamber. "We were worried."

Gianelli smiled foxily. "Allergies," he said.

Kaye Lang Rafelson entered after Bloch. Her presence surprised Augustine. He recognized a setup and suspected that the current director of EMAC would regret not arriving on time.

Kaye moved up to the witness table. A chair and microphone awaited her. She was introduced to the committee, all of whom knew her by name and reputation.

Senator Percy looked disconcerted. He, too, could smell a setup. "Dr. Rafelson is not on our list, Dick," he said as Bloch helped Gianelli settle himself at the dais.

"She brings important news," Gianelli said brusquely.

Kaye was sworn in. Not once did she look at Augustine, though he sat fewer than five feet away.

Senator Thomasen stifled a yawn. She seemed perfectly happy to take her cues from Gianelli. There was some procedural wrangling, more interruptions by Percy and counterarguments by Chase, and finally Percy held up his hands and let her testimony proceed. He was clearly unhappy that the director was still not present.

"You work at Americol, correct, Dr. Rafelson?" Thomasen said, reading from the witness sheet handed to her by Gianelli.

"Yes, Senator."

"And what is your group doing?"

"We're studying ERV knockout techniques in mice and chimpanzees, Senator," Kaye said.

"Bravo," Senator Percy said. "A worthy effort, to rid the world of viruses."

"We're working to understand the roles viruses play in our genome and in our everyday lives," Kaye corrected. The distinction seemed lost on Percy.

"You also work with the Centers for Disease Control," Thomasen continued. "Serving as a go-between for Marge Cross and Fern Ridpath, the director of SHEVA affairs at the CDC?"

"Occasionally, but Dr. Ridpath spends more time with our PI."

"PI?"

"Principal Investigator."

"And that is?"

"Dr. Robert Jackson," Kaye said.

Thomasen looked up, as did the others, at the sound of the door at the back of the chamber opening once more. Rachel Browning marched down the aisle, wearing a black dress with a wide red belt. She glanced at Augustine, then looked over the senators on the dais with what she meant to be a puzzled smile. To Kaye, the smile appeared predatory. Two steps behind walked her counsel, a small, gray-haired woman in a beige cotton summer suit.

"You're late, Ms. Browning," Senator Thomasen said.

"It was my understanding Dr. Browning was to be testifying alone to the committee, in closed session," the counsel said, her voice commanding.

"The hearing *is* closed," Gianelli said with another sniff. "Senator Percy invited Dr. Augustine, and I invited Dr. Rafelson."

Browning sat at the end of the table and smiled calmly as her counsel leaned over to set up a small laptop on the desk. The counsel then unfolded blinders, to prevent the computer display from being visible to either side, and took her seat on Browning's left.

"Dr. Rafelson was interrupted," Senator Gianelli reminded the chair.

Thomasen smirked. "I'm not sure which tune we're supposed to be dancing to. Who's the fiddler?"

"You are, as always, Madam Chair," Gianelli said.

"I sincerely doubt that," Thomasen said. "All right, go ahead, Dr. Rafelson."

Kaye did not like going up against the director of Emergency Action in this way, but she clearly had no choice. She was being squeezed between lines of scrimmage in a game far rougher than football.

"Yesterday evening, a meeting was held in Baltimore to discuss the results of a proprietary Americol health survey. You were present," Gianelli said. "Tell us what's happening, Kaye."

Browning's look was a warning.

Kaye ignored her. "We have conclusive evidence there have been new first-stage SHEVA deliveries, Senator," she said. "Expulsion or abortion of interim daughters."

A hush fell over the chamber. All the senators looked up and around, as if a strange bird had flown into the room.

"I beg your pardon?" Chase said.

"There will be new SHEVA births. We are now in our third wave."

"Is there not a security protocol?" Percy asked, regarding his fellow senators on the committee with a look of astonishment. "This committee is not known for its discretion. I ask you to consider the political and social fallout—"

"Madam Chair," the senator from Arizona demanded, exasperated.

"Dr. Rafelson, please explain," Gianelli said, ignoring the ruckus.

"Blood samples from more than fifty thousand males in committed relationships are again producing SHEVA retroviruses. Current CDC estimates are that more than twenty thousand women will give birth to second-stage SHEVA infants over the next eight to twelve months in the United States. In the next three years, we may have as many as a hundred thousand SHEVA births."

"My God," Percy called out, "Will it never end?" His voice made the sound system ring.

"The big ball rolls again," Gianelli said.

"Is this true, Ms. Browning?" Senator Percy demanded.

Browning drew herself up. "Thank you, Senator. Emergency Action is well aware of these cases, and we have prepared a special plan to counteract their effect. True, there have been miscarriages. Subsequent pregnancies have been reported. There is no proof that these children will have the same kind of virally induced mutations. In fact, the retrovirus being shed by males is not homologous to the SHEVA viruses we are familiar with. We may be witnessing a novel resurgence of the disease, with new complications."

Senator Percy moved in. "This is awesome and awful news. Ms. Browning, don't you think it is high time that we free ourselves of these invaders?"

Browning arranged her papers. "I do, Senator Percy. A vaccine has been developed that confers substantial resistance to transmission of SHEVA and many other retroviruses."

Kaye held onto the edge of the table to keep her hands from shaking. There was no new vaccine; she knew that for a fact. This was the purest scientific bullshit. But now was certainly not the time to call Browning to account. Let her spin her web.

"We expect to be able to stop this new viral phase in its tracks," Browning continued. She slipped on granny reading glasses and read from notes on her data phone. "We are also recommending quarantine and GPS-chipping and tracking of all infected mothers, to prevent further outbreaks of Shiver. We hope to eventually get court permission to chip all SHEVA children."

Kaye looked along the row of faces behind the dais, seeing only fear, and then turned to Browning again.

Browning held Kaye's gaze for a long moment, eyes square and forthright over the granny glasses. "Emergency Action has the authority, under Presidential Decision Directives 298 and 341, and the authority conferred by Congress in our original charter, to announce a full quarantine of all affected mothers. We are ordering separate house arrest for males shedding the new retrovirus, removing them from households where they may infect their partners. The bottom line is we do not want any more SHEVA-affected children to be born."

Chase had gone pale. "How do we prevent that, Ms. Browning?" he asked.

"If chipping cannot be implemented immediately, we'll resort to older methods. Ankle bracelets will be attached to monitor the activities of affected males. Other plans are being drawn up even now. We *will* prevent this new surge of disease, Senator."

"How long until we can cleanse our bodies of these viruses completely?" Senator Percy asked.

"That's Ms. Lang's area of expertise," Browning said, and turned to her with an ingenuous expression, one professional to another. "Kaye? Any progress?"

"Our division is trying new procedures," Kaye said. "So far, we have been unable to remove legacy retroviruses—ERVs—from mouse or chimpanzee embryos and proceed to live birth. Removing most or all of the ancient viral genes, including SHEVA genes, produces gross chromosomal abnormalities following mitosis, failure of fertilized eggs to implant, early absorptions, and miscarriages. As well, we have not made progress at Americol with any effective vaccine. There's a lot to be learned. Viruses—"

"There it is," Browning interrupted, turning back to the senators. "Utter failure. We have to move now with practical remedies."

"One wonders, Dr. Rafelson, whether or not you are to be trusted with this work, given your sympathies?" Senator Percy said, and mopped his forehead.

"That's uncalled for, Senator Percy," Gianelli said sharply.

Browning swept on. "We hope to share all scientific data with Americol and with this committee," she said. "We sincerely believe that Ms. Lang and her fellow scientists should be as forthcoming with us, and perhaps a tad more diligent."

Kaye folded her hands on top of the table.

After the session was gaveled to a close, Augustine sipped a glass of water in the waiting room. Browning walked briskly by.

"Did you have anything to do with this, Mark?" she asked in an undertone, pouring herself a glass from the frosted pitcher. Three years ago, he had underestimated the fear and hatred of which Americans were capable. Rachel Browning had not. If the new director of Emergency Action trailed any rope, Augustine could not see it.

Many more years might pass before she hanged herself.

"No," Augustine said. "Why would I?"

"Well, the news will get out soon enough."

Browning turned away from the door to the waiting room as Kaye was ushered in by Laura Bloch, and slipped away with her counsel. Bloch quickly secured Kaye a cup of coffee. Augustine and Kaye stood less than a pace apart. Kaye lifted her cup. "Hello, Mark."

"Good evening, Kaye. You did well."

"I doubt that, but thank you," Kaye said.

"I wanted to tell you I'm sorry," Augustine said.

"For what?" Kaye asked. She did not know, of course, all that had happened on that day when Browning had called and told him about the possible acquisition of her family.

"Sorry you had to be their decoy," he said.

"I'm used to it," Kaye said. "It's the price I'm paying for being out of the loop for so long."

Augustine tried for a sympathetic grin, but his stiff face produced only a mild grimace. "I hear you," he said.

"Finally," Kaye said primly, and turned to join Laura Bloch.

Augustine felt the rebuff, but he knew how to be patient. He knew how to work in the background, silently and with little credit.

He had long since learned how to emulate the lowly viruses.

9

To enter the Pathogenics zoo, they had to pass through a room with bare concrete walls painted black and dip their shoes in shallow trays of sweet, cloying yellow fluid—a variation on Lysol, Turner explained.

Dicken awkwardly swirled his shoes in the fluid.

"We do it on the way out, too," Presky said. "Rubber soles last longer."

They scraped and dried their shoes on black nylon mats and slipped on combination cotton booties and leggings, cinched around the calf. Presky gave each a snood and fine mesh filter masks to cover their mouths, and instructed them to touch as little as possible.

The zoo would have made a small town proud. It filled four warehouses covering several acres, steel and concrete walls lined with enclosures containing loose facsimiles of natural environments. "Comfortable, low stress," Turner pointed out. "We want all our ancient viruses calm and collected."

"Dr. Blakemore is working with vervets and howler monkeys," Jurie said. "Old World and New World. Their ERV profiles are vastly different, as I'm sure you know. We hope soon to have chimps, but perhaps we can just piggyback on Americol's chimp project." He glanced at Dicken with speculative brown eyes. "Kaye Lang's work, no?"

Dicken nodded absently.

The five large primate cages had most of the amenities: tree limbs, swings and rings, floors covered with rubber matting, multiple levels for pacing and climbing, a wide selection of plastic toys. Dicken counted six howler monkeys segregated male and female in two cages, with perforated plastic sheeting between: They could see and smell each other, but not touch.

They walked on and paused before a long, narrow aquarium containing a happily swimming platypus and several small fish. Dicken loved platypuses. He smiled like a little boy at the foot-long juvenile as it breached and dove several times through the clear green water, silvery lines of bubbles streaming from its slick fur.

"Her name is Torrie," Presky said. "She's pretty, no?"

"She's wonderful," Dicken said.

"Anything with fur, scales, or feathers, has viral genes of interest," Jurie said. "Torrie's rather a dud, at the moment, but we like her anyway. We've just finished sequencing and comparing the allogenomes of echidnas and, of course, platypuses."

"We're taking a census of monotreme ERVs," Turner explained. "ERVs are useful during viviparous development. They help us subdue our mothers' immune systems. Otherwise, her lymphocytes would kill the embryos, because in part they type for the father's tissue. However, like birds, monotremes lay eggs. They should not use ERVs so extensively during early development."

"The Temin-Larsson-Villarreal hypothesis," Dicken said.

"You're familiar with TLV?" Turner asked, pleased. TLV stood for a theory of virus-host interactions concocted from work done over decades, at different institutions, by Howard R. Temin, Eric Larsson, and Luis P. Villarreal. TLV had gained a lot of favor since SHEVA.

Dicken nodded. "So, do they?"

"Do who, what?" Presky asked.

"Do echidnas and birds express ERV particles to protect their embryos?"

"Ah," Presky said, and smiled mysteriously, then wagged his finger. "Job security." He faced Turner. Wherever his head moved, his body moved as well, like a clocktower figure. "Torrie will have a mate soon. That effects many changes intriguing to us."

"Intriguing to Torrie, as well, presumably," Jurie added, deadpan.

They moved on to a concrete enclosure with a convincing, though small grove of conifers. "No lions or tigers, but we have bears," Presky said. "Two young males. Sometimes they're out sparring with each other. They are brothers, they like to play fight."

"Bears, raccoons, badgers," Turner added. "Peaceful enough critters, virally, at least. Apes, including us, seem to have the most active and numerous ERV."

"Most plants and animals have their own capabilities in biological propaganda and warfare. War happens only if the populations are pressed hard," Jurie said. "Shall we hear Dr. Turner's favorite example?"

Turner took them across to a large enclosure containing three rather mangy-looking European bison. Four large, shaggy animals, fur hanging in patches, regarded the human onlookers with ageless placidity. One shook its head, sending dust and straw flying. "Fresh in modern memory, for hamburger eaters anyway: Toxin gene transfer to *E. coli* bacteria in cattle," Turner began. "Modern factory farming and slaughterhouse technique puts severe stress on the cattle, who send hormonal signals to their multiple tummies, their rumen. *E. coli* react to these signals by taking up phages—viruses for bacteria—that carry genes from another common gut bacteria, *Shigella*. Those genes just happen to code for Shiga toxin. The exchange does not hurt the cow, fascinating, no? But when a predator kills a cow-like critter in nature, and bites into the gut—which most do, eating half-digested grass and such, wild salad it's called—it swallows a load of *E. coli* packed with Shiga toxin. That can make the predators—and us—very sick. Sick or dead predators reduce the stress on cows. It's a clever relief valve. Now we sterilize our beef with radiation. *All* the beef."

"Personally, I never eat rare meat," Jurie said with a contemplative arch of his brows. "Too many loose genes floating around. Dr. Miller, our chief botanist, tells me I should be concerned about my greens, as well."

Orlin Miller raised his hands in collegial defense. "Equal time for veggies."

They entered Building Two, the combination aviary and herpetarium. Mounted on benches beside the large sliding warehouse door, glass boxes housed king snakes coiled beneath red heat lamps.

"We have evidence of a slow but constant lateral flow of genes between species," Jurie said. "Dr. Foresmith is studying transfer of genes between exogenous and endogenous viruses in chickens and ducks, as well as in the Psittaciformes, parrots."

Foresmith, an imposing, gray-haired fellow in his early fifties, formerly of the Massachusetts Institute of Technology—Dicken knew him for his work on minimum genome bacteria—took up the topic. "Flu and other exogenous viruses can exchange genes and recombine within host or reservoir populations," he said, his voice a bass rumble. "New strains of flu used to come rumbling out of Asia every year. Now, we know that exogenous and endogenous viruses—herpes, poxviruses, HIV, SHEVA—can recombine in us. What if these viruses make a mistake? Slip a gene into the wrong location in a cell's DNA . . . A cell starts to ignore its duties and grows out of control. Voilà, a malignant tumor. Or, a relatively mild virus acquires one crucial gene and flips from a persistent to an acute infection. One really *big* mistake, and *pow*," he slapped his fist into his palm, "we suffer one hundred percent mortality." His smile was at once admiring and nervous. "One of our paleo guys figures we can explain a lot of mass extinctions that way, in theory. If we could resurrect and reassemble the older, extremely degraded ERVs, maybe we would learn what actually happened to the dinosaurs."

"Not so fast," Dicken said, raising his hands in surrender. "I don't know anything about dinosaurs or stressed cows."

"Let's hold off on the wilder theories for now," Jurie admonished Foresmith, but his eyes gleamed. "Tom, you're next."

Tom Wrigley was the youngest in the group, in his mid-twenties, tall, dark-haired, and homely, with a red nose and a perpetually pleasant expression. He smiled shyly and handed Dicken a coin, a quarter. "That's roughly what a birth control pill costs. My group is studying the effect of birth control on endogenous retrovirus expression in women between the ages of twenty and fifty."

Dicken rolled the quarter in his hand. Tom held out his palm, lifting his eyebrows, and Dicken returned the coin.

"Tell them why, Tom," Jurie prodded.

"Twenty years ago, some researchers found that HIV infected pregnant women at a higher rate. Some human endogenous retroviruses are closely related to HIV, which goes after our immune systems with a vengeance. The fetus within the mother expresses lots of HERV from its placenta, which some think helps subdue the mom's immune system in a beneficial way—just enough so that it won't attack the developing fetus. TLV, as you know, Dr. Dicken."

"Howard Temin is a god in this place," Dee Dee Blakemore said. "We've set up a little shrine in C wing. Prayers every Wednesday."

"Birth control pills produce conditions in women similar to pregnancy," Wrigley said. "We decided that women on birth control would make an excellent study group. We have twenty volunteers, five of them our own researchers."

Blakemore raised her hand. "I'm one," she said. "I'm feeling testy already." She growled at Wrigley and bared her canines. Wrigley held up his hands in mock fright.

"Eventually, SHEVA females will be getting pregnant," Wrigley said, "and some may even use birth control pills. We want to know how that will effect production of potential pathogens."

"Sexual maturity and pregnancy in the new children is likely to be a time of great danger," Jurie said. "Retroviruses released in the natural course of a second generation SHEVA pregnancy could transfer to humans. The result could be another HIV-like disease. In fact, Dr. Presky here, among others, believes something similar explains how HIV got into the human population."

Presky weighed in. "A hunter in search of bush meat could have slaughtered a pregnant chimp." He shrugged; the hypothesis was still speculation, as Dicken knew well. As a postdoc in the late 1980s, Dicken had spent two years in the Congo and Zaire tracking possible sources for HIV.

"And last but not least, our gardens. Dr. Miller?"

Orlin Miller pointed to flats of greenery and flower gardens spread out under skylights and artificial sun bulbs hanging in imposing phalanxes, like great glassy fruit, on the north side of the warehouse. "My group studies transfer of viral genes between plants and insects, funguses and bacteria. As Dr. Jurie hinted earlier, we're also studying human genes that may have originated in plants," Miller added. "I can just see the Nobel hanging from that one."

"Not that you'll ever go up on stage to collect," Jurie warned.

"No, of course not," Miller said, somewhat deflated.

"Enough. Just a taste," Jurie said, stopping in front of a basin containing a thick growth of young corn. "Seven other division heads who could not be here tonight extend their congratulations—to me, for landing Dr. Dicken. Not necessarily do they congratulate Dr. Dicken."

The others smiled.

"Thanks, gentlemen," Jurie said, and waved bye-bye, as if to a group of school children. The directors said their farewells and filed out of the warehouse. Only Turner remained.

Jurie fixed Dicken with a gaze. "NIH tells me I can find a use for you at Pathogenics," Jurie said. "NIH funds a substantial portion of my work here, through Emergency Action. Still, I'm curious. Why did you accept this appointment? Not because you love and respect me, Dr. Dicken." Jurie loosely crossed his arms and his bony fingers engaged in a fit of searching, marching along toward the elbows, drawing the arms into a tighter hug.

"I go where the science is," Dicken said. "I think you're primed to discover some interesting things. And I think I can help. Besides . . ." He paused. "They gave you a list. You picked me."

Jurie lifted one hand dismissively. "Everything we do here is political. I'd be a fool not to recognize it," he said. "But, frankly, I think we're winning. Our work is too important to stop, for whatever reason. And we might as well have the best people working with us, whatever their connections. You're a fine scientist, and that's the bottom line." Jurie strolled before a plastic-wrapped greenhouse filled with banana trees, obscured by the translucent plastic. "If you think you're ready, I have a theoretical problem for you."

"Ready as I'll ever be," Dicken said.

"I'd like for you to start with something a little off the beaten path. Up for it?"

"I'm listening," Dicken said.

"You can work with Dr. Wrigley's volunteers. Assemble a staff from our resident postdocs under Dee Dee's supervision, no more than two to begin with. They're analyzing ancient promoter regions associated with sexual characteristics, physiological changes in humans possibly induced by retroviral genes." Jurie swallowed conspicuously. "Viruses have induced changes quite evident in our SHEVA children. Now, I'd like to study more mundane instances in humans. Can you think of the fold of tissue of which I'm suspicious?" Jurie asked.

"Not really," Dicken said.

"It's like an alarm mounted on a gate kept closed until maturity. When the gate is breached, that announces a major accomplishment, a crucial change; announces it with a burst of pain and a whole cascade of hormonal events. The hormones generated by this experience appear to activate HERV and other mobile elements, preparing our bodies for a new phase of life. Reproduction is imminent, this breach tells the body. Time to prepare."

"The female hymen," Dicken guessed.

"The female hymen," Jurie said. "Is there any other kind?" He was not being sarcastic. It was a straight question. "Are there other gates to be opened, other signals? . . . I don't know. I'd like to know." Jurie studied Dicken, eyes glittering with enthusiasm once again. "I'm supposing that viruses have altered our phenotype to produce the hymen. Rupturing the hymen gives them warning that sex is taking place, so they can prepare to do all that they do. By altering expression of key genes, promoting or blocking them, the viruses may change our behavior as well. Let's find out how." He reached into his jacket pocket, removed a small plastic case, and handed the case to Dicken. "My notes. If you find them useful, I'll be content."

"Good," Dicken said. He knew very little about hymens; he wondered what his other resources would be.

"SHEVA females don't have hymens, you know," Jurie said. "No such membranes. Comparison should bring up fascinating divergences in hormonal pathways and viral activations. And viral activations are what concern me."

Dicken found himself nodding. He was almost hypnotized by the audacity of the hypothesis. It was perverse; it was perversely brilliant. "You think menarche in SHEVA females will switch on viral mutations?" he asked.

"Possibly," Jurie said evenly, as if discussing the weather. "Interested?"

"I am," Dicken said after a thoughtful pause.

"Good." Jurie reached up and pulled his head to one side, making the bones in his neck pop. His eyes turned elsewhere, and he nodded once and walked away, leaving Turner and Dicken alone in the warehouse between the trailers and the gardens.

The interview was over.

Turner escorted Dicken back through the zoo, the foot baths, and the corridors to the steel door. They stopped off at the maintenance office to get the key to Dicken's dorm room.

"You've survived meeting the Old Man," Turner said, then showed Dicken the way to the dorm wing for new residents. He held up a key, pinched the key's tag, turning it from blue to red, and dropped it into Dicken's palm. He stared at Dicken for a long, uncomfortable moment, then said, "Good luck."

Turner walked back down the hall, shaking his head. Over his shoulder, he called out, "Jesus! Hymens. What next?"

Dicken closed the door to the room and switched on the overhead light. He sat on the narrow, tightly made-up bed, and rubbed his temples and jaw muscles with trembling fingers, dizzy from repressed emotion.

For the first time in his life, the prey Dicken was after was not microbial.

It was a disease, but it was entirely human.

10

Stella awoke to the sound of an over-under songfest between barracks. The wake-up bell had not yet rung. She rolled between the crisp white sheets of the top bunk and stared up at the ceiling tiles. She was familiar with the routine: A few dozen boys and girls were hanging out of the windows of their barracks, singing to each other across the razor-wire fence. The *over* was loud and almost tuneless; the under was *subtle* and not very clear from where she lay. She had no doubt it carried a lot of early-morning gossip, however.

She closed her eyes for a moment and listened. The singers in the barracks tended to slip into harshly sweet and sky-shaking laments, pushing sounds around both sides of their ridged tongues, circulating breath through nose and throat simultaneously. The two streams of song began to play counterpoint, weaving in and out in a way designed to prevent any eavesdropping by the counselors.

Not that the counselors had yet figured out how to interpret underspeech.

Stella heard loud clanging. She closed her eyes and grinned. She could see it all so clearly: Counselors were going through the barracks, banging metal trash-can lids and shouting for the children to shut up. Slowly, the songs scattered like gusts of scented air. Stella imagined the heads withdrawing from the windows, children rushing to their bunks, climbing under their covers.

Tomorrow, other barracks would take their turns. There was a kind of lottery; they tried to predict how long it would take the counselors to get from their compound to the guilty barracks, and how long they could be fooled as to which were the offending barracks. Her barracks might join in and undergo the same trash-can-lid response. Stella would be part of the songfest. She did not look forward to the challenge. She had a high, clear overvoice, but needed work on her underspeech. She was not quite as facile as the others.

Silence returned to the morning. She sank under the covers, waiting for the alarm bell. New uniforms had been deposited at the end of each bunk. The bunks were stacked three high, and the kids began each morning with a shower and a change of clothes, to keep the scent from building on their bodies or what they wore.

Stella knew that her natural smell was not offensive to humans. What concerned the camp counselors and captains was persuasion.

The girls below her, Celia and Mandy, were stirring. Stella preferred to be among the first in the showers. The wake-up bell at the south end of the hall went off as she ran toward the gate to the showers. Her thin white robe flapped at mid-thigh level.

Fresh towels and brushes were provided every day. She took a towel and a toothbrush but avoided using toothpaste. It had a lingering smell that she suspected was meant to confuse. Stella stood at the long basin with the polished steel mirror and ran the moist brush over her teeth, then massaged her gums with one finger, as Mitch had showed her how to do almost ten years ago.

Twenty other girls were already in the shower room, most from other barracks. Stella's building—barracks number three—tended to be slow. It contained the older girls. They were not as chipper or enthusiastic as the younger girls. They knew all too well what the day had in store—boredom, ritual, frustration. Stagnation.

The youngest girl in the camp was ten. The oldest was fifteen.

Stella Nova was fourteen.

After she finished, Stella returned to her bunk to dress. She looked down the lines of bunks. Most of the girls were still in the showers. It was her day to act as monitor for the barracks. She had to be inconspicuous—simply walking from bunk to bunk, bending over, and taking a big whiff would probably land her in detention, with Miss Kantor asking pointed questions. But it had to be done.

Stella carried a stack of school newspapers printed the day before. She walked from bunk to bunk, placing a paper on each bunk and gently sniffing the unmade sheets without bending over.

Within ten minutes, as the girls returned from the showers and began to dress, Stella had a good picture of the health and well-being of the barracks. Later, she would report to her deme mentor. The mentors changed from day to day or week to week. Underspeech or cheek-flashes would tell her who was responsible today. She would make a quick report with underspeech and scenting, before the heavily supervised, once-a-week, coed outdoor activity began.

The girls had thought this procedure up all by themselves. It seemed to work. The bed check was not just useful in knowing how each member was faring, it was also an act of defiance.

Defiance was essential to keeping their sanity.

Perhaps they would have early warning if the humans passed along any more diseases. Perhaps it was just a way of feeling they had some control over their lives. Stella didn't care.

Catching the scent of her barracks mates was reward enough. It made her feel as if she were a part of something worthwhile, something not human.

11

"Elcob hobe!"

Liz Cantrera rushed past Kaye, a rack of clear plastic trays clattering in her arms beneath the flopping edge of a folder clamped between her teeth. She deposited the rack near the safety sink and pulled the black-bound folder from her mouth. "This just in from La Robert."

Kaye hung her coat on the knobs behind the lab door. "Another salvo?"

"Mm hmm. I think Jackson is jealous you were asked to testify and not he."

"Nobody should envy me that." Kaye waggled her fingers. "Give it to me."

Cantrera smirked and handed her the folder. "He'll be pushing a disease model long after the Karolinska hangs gold on you."

Kaye leafed through the fifty-page brief and response to their work of the last two years. This was the big one. Robert Jackson, PI for the larger group and in some respects her boss, was working very hard to get Kaye out of his labs, out of the building, out of the way.

The expected publication date for Jackson's paper in the *Journal of Biologics and Epigenetics* was sticky-tabbed to the last page: December. "How nice he's passed peer review," Kaye said.

Liz put her hands on her hips and stood in an attitude of defiant expectation. She pushed back a strand of curly strawberry blonde hair and loudly chewed a wad of gum. Her eyes were bright as drops of fresh blue ink. "He says we're removing necessary transcription factors surrounding our ERV targets, throwing out the baby with the contaminated bathwater."

"A lot of those factors are transactivated by ERV. You can't have it both ways, Dr. Jackson. Well, at least we can shoot that one down." Kaye slumped on a stool. "We're not getting anywhere," she muttered. "We're taking out the viruses and not getting any baby chimps. What does it take for him to come around?" She glanced up at Liz, who was still waggling her hips and snapping her chewing gum in mock defiance of La Robert.

Liz cracked a big sappy smile. "Feel better?"

Kay shook her head and laughed despite herself. "You look like a Broadway gamine. Who are you supposed to be, Bernadette Peters?"

Liz cocked her hips and fluffed her hair with one hand. "She's a corker. Which play?" she demanded. "Revival of *Mame?*"

"Sweeney Todd," Kaye said.

"That would be Winona Ryder," Liz countered.

Kaye groaned. "Where do you get so much energy?"

"Bitterness. Seriously, how did it go?"

"I'm being used as a prop by one side and a patsy by the other. I feel like Dorothy in the tornado."

"Sorry," Liz said.

Kaye stretched and felt her back pop. Mitch used to do that for her. She riffled through Jackson's folder again and found the page that through instinct, and a touch of luck, had caught her eye a moment before: suspect lab protocols.

As ever, Jackson was trapped in a maze of in vitro studies—test-tube and petri dish blind alleys using Tera2 tumor cell lines—proven traps for making mistakes with ERV. *Hell, he's even using chicken embryos,* she thought. *Egglayers don't use ERVs the same way we do.*

"Jackson's vaccines kill monkeys," Kaye said softly, tapping the page. "Marge doesn't like projects that never get past animal studies."

"Shall we play another game of Gotcha with Dr. Jackson?" Liz asked innocently.

"Sure," Kaye said. "I am almost cheered by this." She dropped the folder on her small, crowded desk.

"I'm off to check our arrays, and then I'm going home," Liz called out as she pushed through the door with the tray. "I've been working all night. You in for the week?"

"Until they fire me," Kaye said. She rubbed her nose reflexively. "I need to look over the fragile site studies from last week."

"Prepped and digitized. They're on the photobase," Liz said. "There's some leftover spaghetti in the fridge."

"Heavenly," Kaye said.

"Bye," Liz called as the door swung closed behind her.

Kaye got up and rubbed her nose again. It felt slightly stuffy, not unpleasantly so. The lab smelled unusually sweet and fresh, not that it ever smelled dirty. Liz was a stickler for cleanliness.

The scent was hard to place, not at all like perfume or flowers.

There was a long day's work ahead, preparing for tomorrow's morning meeting. Kaye closed her eyes, hoping to find her calm spot; she needed to focus on the chromosome results from last week. Get the sour clamp of Washington off her gut.

She pulled the stool over to the workstation and entered her password, then called up the tables and photos of chimpanzee chromosome mutations.

Early-stage embryos modified for lab work had had all of their single-copy ERVs deleted, but all multicopy ERVs, LINEs, and "defective" ERVs left intact. They had then been allowed to develop for forty-eight hours. The chromosomes, bunched up by mitosis, were removed, photographed, and crudely sequenced. What Kaye was looking for were anomalies around fragile sites and hot spots in the chromosomes—regions of genes that responded quickly to environmental change, suggesting rapid adaptive response.

The modified chimp chromosomes were severely distorted—she could tell that just by looking at the photos. The fragile sites were all screwed up, broken and rearranged incorrectly. The embryos would never have implanted in the womb, much less gone to term. Even single-copy ERVs were important to fetal development and chromosome adaptation in mammals, perhaps especially so in primates.

She looked over the analysis and saw random and destructive methylation of genes that should be actively transcribing, necessary lengths of DNA mothballed like a fleet of old ships, curling the chromatin into an agony of alternating misplaced activity and dark, inactive lassitude.

They looked *ugly*, those chromosomes, ugly and unnatural. The early-stage embryos, growing under the tutelage of such chromosomes, would die. That was the story of everything they had done in the lab. If, by rare chance, the ERV-knockout embryos managed to implant and begin development, they were invariably resorbed within the first few weeks. And getting that far had required giving the chimp mothers massive drug regimens developed for human mothers at fertilization clinics to prevent miscarriages.

The ERVs served so many functions in the developing embryos, including mediating tissue differentiation. And it was already obvious that TLV—the Temin-Larsson-Villarreal conjecture—was correct. Highly conserved endogenous retroviruses expressed by the trophectoderm of the developing embryo—the portion that would develop into the surrounding amnion and placenta—protected against attacks by the mother's immune system. The viral envelope proteins selectively subdued the mother's immune response to her fetus without weakening the mother's defenses against external pathogens, an exquisite dance of selectivity.

Because of the protective function of legacy retroviruses, ERV knockout—the removal or stifling of most or all of the genome's "original sins"—was invariably fatal.

Kaye vividly remembered the chill she had felt when Mitch's mother had described SHEVA as "original sin." How long ago had that been— fifteen years? Just after they had conceived Stella.

If SHEVA and other ERV constituted original sin, then it was starting to look as if all placental mammals, perhaps all multicelled life forms, were filled with original sin, required it, died without it.

And wasn't that what the Garden of Eden was all about? The beginning of sex and self-knowledge and life as we know it.

All because of viruses.

"The hell with that," Kaye muttered. "We need a new name for these things."

12

Roll call was Stella's least favorite time of day, when the girls were all gathered together and Miss Kantor walked between the rows under the big tent.

Stella sat cross-legged and drew little figures of flowers and birds in the dust with her finger. The canvas flapped with the soft morning breeze. Miss Kantor walked between the lines of seated, cross-legged adolescents and leafed through her daybook. She relied entirely on paper, simply because losing an e-pad or laptop in the reserve was a severe offense, punishable by dismissal.

The dormitories held no phones, no satellite feeds, no radios. Television was limited to educational videos. Stella and most of the other children here had come to abhor television.

"Ellie Ann Garcia."

"Here."

"Stella Nova Rafelson."

"Here," Stella called out, her voice silvery in the cool desert air.

"How's your cold, Stella?" Miss Kantor asked as she walked down the row.

"Done," Stella answered.

"Eight days, wasn't it?" Miss Kantor tapped her pen on the daybook page.

"Yes, ma'am."

"That's the fifth wave of colds we've had this year."

Stella nodded. The counselors kept careful and tedious track of all infections. Stella had spent several hours being examined, five days ago; so had two dozen other children with similar colds.

"Kathy Chu."

"Here!"

Miss Kantor walked by Stella again after she had finished. "Stella, are you scenting?"

Stella looked up. "No, Miss Kantor."

"My little sensor tells me you are." She tapped the nosey on her belt. Stella was not scenting, and neither was anybody around her. Miss Kantor's electronic snitch was wrong, and Stella knew why; Miss Kantor was having her period and that could confuse the nosey. But Stella would never tell her that.

Humans hated to be clued when they produced revealing odors.

"You'll never learn to live in the outside world if you can't control yourself," Miss Kantor said to Stella, and knelt in front of her. "You know the rules."

Stella got to her feet without being prompted. She did not know why she was being singled out. She had done nothing unusual.

"Wait over by the truck," Miss Kantor said.

Stella walked to the truck, brilliant white under the morning sun. The air over the mountains was intense and blue. It was going to be hot in a few hours, but it might rain heavily later; that would make the late-afternoon air perfect for catching up. She did not want to miss that.

Miss Kantor finished her count and the kids filed off to the morning classes in the trailers and bungalows scattered over the dusty grounds. The counselor and her assistant, a quiet, plump young woman named Joanie, walked across the gravel to the truck. Miss Kantor would not look straight at Stella.

"I know it wasn't just you," Miss Kantor said. "But you're the only one I could catch. It has to stop, Stella. But I'm not going to punish you this time."

"Yes, ma'am." Stella knew better than to argue. When things went her way, Miss Kantor was reasonable and fairly easygoing, but any show of defiance or contradiction and she could get harsh. "Can I go to classes now?"

"Not yet," Miss Kantor said, placing her notepad in the truck. She opened the rear door of the truck. "Your father is visiting," she said. "We're going back to the infirmary."

Stella sat in the back of the truck, behind the plastic barrier, feeling confused. Miss Kantor climbed into the front seat. Joanie closed the door for her and went back to the tent. "Is he there, now?" Stella asked.

"He'll arrive in an hour or so," Miss Kantor said. "You two just got approval. That's pretty good, isn't it?"

"What do they want?" Stella asked suddenly, before she could control her tongue.

"Nothing. It's a family visit."

Miss Kantor switched on the truck motor. Stella could feel her disapproval. Parental visits were futile at the best of times, Miss Kantor believed. The children would never be fully integrated into human society, no matter what the school policy said. She knew the children too well. They just could not behave appropriately.

Worse still, Miss Kantor knew that Stella's father had served time in prison for assaulting Emergency Action enforcement officers. Having him as a visitor would be something of an affront to her. She was a holdover from the times when Sable Mountain School had been a prison.

Stella had not seen Mitch in three years. She hardly remembered what he smelled like, much less what he looked like.

Miss Kantor drove over the gravel to the paved road, and then between the brush half a mile to the brick building they called the hospital. It wasn't really a hospital. As far as Stella knew, for sure, the hospital was just the administration and detention center for the school. It had been a hospital once, for the prison. Some kids claimed the hospital was where they injected salt into your cheeks, or resected your tongue, or Botoxed the new facial muscles that made your expressions so compelling.

It was the place they tried to turn SHEVA kids into humans. Stella had never met a kid who had undergone such torments, but that was explained, some said, by the fact that they sent those kids away to Suburbia, a town made up of nothing but SHEVA kids trying to act just like humans.

That was not true, as far as Stella knew, but the hospital was where they sent you when they wanted to draw blood. She had been there many times for that purpose.

There were lots of stories in the camps. Few of them were true, but most were scary, and the kids could get ominously bored.

As they drove through a razor-wire fence and over a moat, Stella felt something sad and cold grow in her.

Memory.

She did not want to lose her focus. She stared through the window, resenting Mitch for coming. Why now? Why not when she had her act together and could tell him she had accomplished something worthwhile? Life was still too confused. The last visit with her mother had been painful. Stella had not known what to say. Her mother had been so sad and full of needs neither could satisfy.

She hoped Mitch would not just sit and stare at her over the table in the family conference room. Or ask pointed questions. Or try to tell Stella there was hope they would get together again. Stella did not think she could stand that.

Stella dipped her head and rubbed her nose. She touched the tip of her finger to the corner of her eye and then to her tongue, out of sight of the rearview mirror. Her eyes were moist and the tears tasted of bitter salt. She would not cry openly, however. Not in front of a human.

Miss Kantor stopped the truck in the parking lot of the flat brick building, got out, and opened Stella's door. Stella followed her into the hospital. As they turned a corner, through a gap in the brick breezeway she saw a long yellow bus drawn up beside the processing office. A load of new kids had arrived. Stella hung back a few steps from Miss Kantor as they passed through the glass doors and walked to the detention center.

The door to the secretary's office was always open, and through the wide window beyond, Stella thought she would catch a glimpse of the new kids from the shipment center. That would be something to take back to the deme; possible recruits or news from outside.

Suddenly, irrationally, she hated Mitch. She did not want him to visit. She did not want any distractions. She wanted to focus and never have to worry about humans again. She wanted to lash out at Miss Kantor, strike her down to the linoleum floor, and run away to anywhere but here.

Through Stella's brief, fierce scowl—a more intense scowl than most humans could manage—she caught a glimpse of the lineup of children beyond the secretary's window. Her scowl vanished.

She thought she recognized a face.

Stella dropped to remove her shoe and turned it upside down, shaking it. Miss Kantor looked back and stopped with hands on hips.

The nosey on her belt wheeped.

"Are you scenting again?" she asked.

"No, ma'am," Stella said. "Rock in my shoe." This pause gave her time enough to chase down the memory of the face in the lineup. She stood, shuffled awkwardly for a moment until Miss Kantor glanced away, then shot a second look through the window.

She *did* know the face. He was taller now and skinnier, almost a walking skeleton, his hair unruly and his eyes flat and lifeless in the bright sun. The line began to move and Stella flicked her gaze back to the corridor and Miss Kantor.

She no longer worried about Mitch.

The skinny kid outside was the boy she had met in Fred Trinket's shed in Virginia, when she had run away from Kaye's and Mitch's house.

It was Will. Strong Will.

13

BALTIMORE

Kaye shut down the displays and removed the specimens, then carefully returned them to a preservation drawer in the freezer. She knew for the first time that she was close to the end of her work at Americol. Three or four more experiments, six months at most of lab work, and she could go back to Congress and face down Rachel Browning and tell the oversight subcommittee that all apes, all monkeys, all mammals, probably all vertebrates, even all animals—and possibly all forms of life above the bacteria—were genetic chimeras. In a real sense, we were all virus children.

Not just Stella. Not just my daughter and her kind.

All babies use viruses to get born. All senators and all representatives and the president and all of their wives and children and grandchildren, all the citizens of the United States, and all the people of the world, are all guilty of original sin.

Kaye looked up as if at a sound. She touched the bridge of her nose and peered around the lab, the ranks of white and beige and gray equipment, black-topped tables, lamp fixtures hanging from the ceiling like upside-down egg cartons. She felt a gentle pressure behind her eyes, the cool, liquid silver trickle down the back of her head, a growing awareness that she was not alone in the room, in her body.

The caller was back. Twice in the past three years, she had spent as much as three days in its presence. Always before, she had been traveling or working on deadline and had tried to ignore what she had come to regard as a pointless distraction.

"This isn't a good time," she said out loud and shook her head. She stood up and stretched her arms and bent to touch her toes, hoping exercise might push the caller into the background. "Go away." It did not go away. Its signal came in with even greater conviction. Kaye started to laugh helplessly and wiped away the tears. "Please," she whispered, leaning against a lab bench. She tipped a stack of petri dishes with her elbow. As she was re-arranging them, the caller struck full force, flooding her with delicious approval. Kaye shut her eyes and leaned forward, her entire body filled with that extraordinary sensation of oneness with something very close and intimate, yet infinitely creative and powerful.

"It feels like you love me," she said, shaking with frustration. "So why do you torment me? Why don't you just tell me what you want me to do?" Kaye slid down the bench to a chair near a desk in the corner of the lab. She put her head between her knees. She did not feel weak or even woozy; she could have walked around and even gone about her daily work. She had before. But this time it was just too much.

Her anger swelled even over the insistent waves of validation and approval. The first time the caller had touched her, Mitch and Stella had been taken away. That had been so bad, so unfair; she did not want to remember that time now. And yet this affirmation forced her to remember.

"Go away. Please. I don't know why you're here. This world is cruel, even if you aren't, and I have to keep working."

She looked around, biting her lip, seeing the lab, the equipment, so neatly arranged, the dark beyond the window. The wall of night outside, the bright rationality within.

"Please."

She felt the voice become smaller, but no less intense. *How polite,* she thought. Abruptly, panicked at this new loss, this possible withdrawal, she jumped to her feet.

"Are you trying to clue me in to something?" she asked, desperate. "Reward me for my work, my discoveries?"

Kaye received the distinct impression that this was not the case. She got up and made sure the door was locked. No sense having people wander in and find her talking to herself. She paced up and down the aisles. "So you're willing to communicate, just not with words," she said, eyes half-closed. "All right. I'll talk. You let me know whether I'm right or wrong, okay? This could take a while."

She had long since learned that an irreverent attitude had no effect on the caller. Even when Kaye had loathed herself for what she had done by abandoning Mitch in prison and her daughter in the schools, ruining all their lives in a desperate gamble to use all the tools of science and rationality, the caller had still radiated love and approval.

She could punish herself, but the caller would not.

Even more embarrassing, Kaye had come to think of the caller as definitely not female, and probably not neuter—but *male.* The caller was nothing like her father or Mitch or any other man she had ever met or known, but it seemed strangely masculine nonetheless. What that meant psychologically, she was most unwilling to discover. It was a little too *de rigueur*, a little too churchy, for comfort.

But the caller cared little about her qualms. He was the most consistent thing in her life—outside of her need to help Stella.

"Am I doing the right thing?" she asked, looking around the lab. Her tremors stopped. She let the extraordinary calm wash over her. "That means yes, I suppose," she said tentatively. "Are you the Big Guy? Are you Jesus? Or just Gabriel?"

She had asked these questions before, and received no response. This time, however, she felt an almost insignificant alteration in the sensations flooding through her. She closed her eyes and whispered, "No. None of the above. Are you my guardian angel?"

Again, a few seconds later, she closed her eyes and whispered, "No.

"Then what are you?"

No response at all, no change, no clues.

"God?"

Nothing.

"You're inside me or up there or someplace where you can just pump out love and approval all day long, and then you go away and leave me in misery. I don't understand that. I need to know whether you're just something in my head. A crossed nerve. A burst blood vessel. I need solid reassurance. I hope you don't mind."

The caller expressed no objection, not even to the extent of withdrawing under the assault of such questioning, such blasphemies.

"You're really something else, you know that?" Kaye sat before the workstation and logged on to the Americol intranet. "There's nothing Sunday school about you."

She glanced at her watch—6 P.M.—and looked up the roster that recorded who was in the building at this hour.

On the first floor, chief radiologist Herbert Roth was still at his post, working late. Just the man she needed. Roth was in charge of the Noninvasive Imaging Lab. She had worked with him two weeks ago taking scans of Wishtoes, their oldest female chimp.

Roth was young, quiet, dedicated to his craft.

Kaye opened the lab door and stepped out into the hall. "Do you think Mr. Roth will want to scan *me*?" she asked no one in particular.

14

They did not let Stella see Mitch for hours. First Stella was visited by a nurse who examined her, took a cheek swab, and drew a few cc's of blood.

Stella looked away as the nurse lightly jabbed her with the needle. She could smell the nurse's anxiety; she was only a few years older than Stella and did not like this.

Afterward, Miss Kantor took Stella to the visitor's area. The first thing Stella noticed was that they had removed the plastic barrier. Tables and chairs, nothing more. Something had changed, and that concerned her for a moment. She patted the cotton patch taped to the inside of her elbow. After an hour, Miss Kantor returned with a pile of comic books.

"*X-Men*," she said. "You'll like these. Your father's still being examined. Give me the cotton."

Stella pulled off the tape and handed it to Miss Kantor, who opened a plastic bag to store it.

"He'll be done soon," Miss Kantor said with a practiced smile.

Stella ignored the comics and stood in the bare room with its flowered wallpaper and the single table and two plastic chairs. There was a water cooler in the corner and a couple of lounge chairs, patched and dirty. She filled a paper cup with water. A window opened from the main office, and another window looked out over the parking lot. No hot coffee or tea, no hot plate for warming food—no utensils. Family visits were not meant to last long or to be particularly comfortable.

She curled the paper cup in her hand and thought alternately about her father and about Will. Thinking about Will pushed her father into the background, if only for a moment, and Stella did not like that. She did not want to be chaotic. She did not want to be unpredictable; she wanted to be faithful to the goal of putting together a stable deme, away from the school, away from human interference, and that would require focus and an emotional constancy.

She knew nothing about Will. She did not even know his last name. He might not remember her. Perhaps he was passing through, getting a checkup or going through some sort of quarantine on his way to another school.

But if he was staying . . .

Joanie opened the door. "Your father's here," she said. Joanie always tried to hide her smell behind baby powder. Her expression was friendly but empty. She did what Miss Kantor wanted and seldom expressed her own opinions.

"Okay," Stella said, and took a seat in one plastic chair. The table would be between them, she hoped. She squirmed nervously. She had to get used to the thought of seeing Mitch again.

Joanie pointed the way through the door and Mitch came in. His left arm hung by his side. Stella looked at the arm, eyes wide, and then at Mitch's denim jacket and jeans, worn and a little dusty. And then she looked at his face.

Mitch was forcing a nervous smile. He did not know what to do, either.

"Hello, sweetie," he said.

"You can sit in the chair," Joanie said. "Take your time."

"How long do we have?" Mitch asked Joanie. Stella hated that. She remembered him as being strong and in charge, and his having to ask about such a thing was wrong.

"We don't have many visits scheduled today. There are four rooms. So . . . take your time. A couple of hours. Let me know if you need anything. I'll be in the office right outside."

Joanie shut the door and Mitch looked at the chair, the table. Then, at his daughter.

"Don't you want a hug?" he asked Stella.

Stella stood, her cheeks tawny with emotion. She kept her hands by her sides. Mitch walked across the room slowly, and she tracked him like a wild animal. Then the currents of air in the room brought his scent, and the cry came up out of her before she could stop it. Mitch took the last step and grabbed her and squeezed and Stella shook in his arms. Her eyes filled with tears that dripped on Mitch's jacket.

"You're so tall," Mitch murmured, swinging her gently back and forth, brushing the tips of her shoes against the linoleum.

She planted her feet and pushed him back and tried to pack in her emotions, but they did not fit. They had exploded like popcorn.

"I've never given up," Mitch said.

Stella's long fingers clutched at his jacket. The smell of him was overwhelming, comfortable and familiar; it made her feel like a little girl again. He was basic and simple, no elaborations, predictable and memorable; he was the smell of their home in Virginia, of everything she had tried to forget, everything she had thought was lost.

"I couldn't come to see you," he said. "They wouldn't let me. Part of probation."

She nodded, bumping her chin gently against his shoulder.

"I sent your mother messages."

"She gave them to me."

"There was no gun, Stella. They lied," Mitch said, and for a moment he looked no older than her, just another disappointed child.

"I know. Kaye told me."

Mitch held his daughter at arm's length. "You're gorgeous," he said, his thick brows drawing together. His face was sunburned. Stella could smell the damage to his skin, the toughening. He smelled like leather and dust above the fundamental of just being Mitch. In his smell—and in Kaye's—she could detect a little of her own fundamental, like a shared license number in the genes, a common passkey to the emotions.

"They want us to sit . . . here?" Mitch asked, swinging one arm at the table.

Stella wrapped her arms around herself, still jammed up inside. She did not know what to do.

Mitch smiled. "Let's just stand for a while," he said.

"All right," Stella said.

"Try to get used to each other again."

"All right."

"Are they treating you well?" Mitch asked.

"They probably think so."

"What do you think?"

Shrug, long fingers wrapping around her wrists, making a little cage of her hands and arms. "They're afraid of us."

Mitch clenched his jaw and nodded. "Nothing new."

Stella's eyes were hypnotic as she tried to express herself. Her pupils shifted size and gold flecks passed like fizz in champagne. "They don't want us to be who we are."

"How do you mean?"

"They move us from one dorm to another. They use sniffers. If we scent, we're punished. If we cloud-scent or fever scent, they break us up and keep us in detention."

"I've read about that," Mitch said.

"They think we'll try to persuade them. Maybe they're afraid we'll try to escape. They wear nose plugs, and sometimes they fill the dorms with fake strawberry or peach smell when they do a health inspection. I used to like strawberry, but now it's awful. Worst of all is the Pine-Sol." She shoved her palm against her nose and made a gagging sound.

"I hear the classes are boring, too."

"They're afraid we'll learn something," Stella said, and giggled. Mitch felt a tingle. That sound had changed, and the change was not subtle. She sounded wary, more mature . . . but something else was at work.

Laughter was a key gauge of psychology and culture. His daughter was very different from the little girl he had known.

"I've learned a lot from the others," Stella said, straightening her face. Mitch traced the faint marks of lines under and beside her eyes, at the corners of her lips, fascinated by the dance of clues to her emotions. Finer muscle control than she had had as a youngster . . . capable of expressions he could not begin to interpret.

"Are you doing okay?" Mitch asked, very seriously.

"I'm doing better than they want," she said. "It isn't so bad, because we manage." She glanced up at the ceiling, touched her earlobe, winked. Of course, they were being monitored; she did not want to give away any secrets.

"Glad to hear it," Mitch said.

"But of course there's stuff they already know," she added in a low voice. "I'll tell you about that if you want."

"Of course, sweetie," Mitch said. "Anything."

Stella kept her eyes on the top of the table as she told Mitch about the groups of twenty to thirty that called themselves demes. "It means 'the people,' " she said. "We're like sisters in the demes. But they don't let the boys sleep in the same dorms, the same barracks. So we have to sing across the wire at night and try to recruit boys into our demes that way."

"That's probably for the best," Mitch said. He lifted one eyebrow and pinched his lips together.

Stella shook her head. "But they don't *understand*. The deme is like a big family. We help each other. We talk and solve problems and stop arguments. We're so smart when we're in a deme. We feel so right together. Maybe that's why . . ."

Mitch leaned back as his daughter suddenly spoke in two bursts at once:

"We need to be together/We're healthier together

"Everyone cares for the others/Everyone is happy with the others

"The sadness comes from not knowing/The sadness comes from being apart."

The absolute clarity of the two streams astonished him. If he caught them immediately and analyzed, he could string them together into a serial statement, but over more than a few seconds of conversation, it was obvious he would get confused. And he had no doubt that Stella could now go on that way indefinitely.

She looked at him directly, the skin over the outside of her eye orbits drawing in with a pucker he could neither duplicate nor interpret. Freckles formed around the outside and lower orbits like little tan-and-gold stars; she was sparking in ways he had never seen before.

He shivered in both admiration and concern. "I don't know what that means, when . . . you do that," he said. "I mean, it's beautiful, but . . ."

"Do what?" Stella asked, and her eyes were normal again.

Mitch swallowed. "When you're in a deme, how many of you talk that way . . . at once?"

"We make circles," Stella said. "We talk to each other in the circle and across the circle."

"How many in the circle?"

"Five or ten," Stella said. "Separately, of course. Boys have rules. Girls have rules. We can make new rules, but some rules already seem to be there. We follow the rules most of the time, unless we feel there's an emergency—someone is feeling steepy."

"Steepy."

"Not part of cloud. When we cloud, we're even more like brothers and sisters. Some of us become mama and papa, too, and we can lead cloud, but mama and papa never make us do what we don't want to do. We decide together."

She looked up at the ceiling, her chin dimpling. "You know about this. Kaye told you."

"Some, and I've read about some of it. I remember when you were trying out some of these . . . techniques on us. I remember trying to keep up with you. I wasn't very good. Your mother was better."

"Her face . . ." Stella began. "I see her face when I become mama in cloud. Her face becomes my face." Her brows formed elegant and compelling double arches, grotesque and beautiful at once. "It's tough to explain."

"I think I understand," Mitch said. His skin was warming. Being around his own daughter made him feel left out, even inferior; how did it make the counselors feel, their keepers?

In this zoo, who were the animals, really?

"What happens when someone disagrees? Do you compel her? Him?"

Stella thought about this for a few seconds. "Everyone is free in cloud, but they cooperate. If they don't agree, they hold that thought until the time is right, and then cloud listens. Sometimes, if it's an emergency, the thought is brought up immediately, but that slows us down. It has to be good."

"And you enjoy being in the cloud?"

"Being *in* cloud," Stella corrected. "All clouds are part of each other, just smeared out. We sort the differences and stuff later, when the demes catch up. But we don't get to do that often, so most of us don't know what it's really like. We just imagine. Sometimes they let it happen, though."

She did not tell Mitch that those were the times when nearly everybody got taken to the hospital to be sampled, after.

"Sounds very friendly," Mitch said.

"Sometimes there's hate," Stella said soberly. "We have to deal with it. A cloud feels pain just like an individual."

"Do you know what I'm feeling, right now?"

"No," Stella said. "Your face is kind of a blank." She smiled. "The counselors smell like cabbages when we do something unexpected./ They smelled like broccoli when we caught colds a few days ago./

"I'm over my cold now and it wasn't serious but we acted sicker to worry them."

Mitch laughed. The crossed intonations of resentment and wry superiority tickled him. "That's pretty good," he said. "But don't push it."

"We know," Stella said primly, and suddenly Mitch saw Kaye in her expression, and felt a rush of real pride, that this young woman still came of them, from them. *I hope that doesn't limit her.*

He also felt a sudden burst of longing for Kaye.

"Is prison like this?" Stella asked.

"Well, prison is a bit harder than here, even."

"Why aren't you with Kaye, now?"

Mitch wondered how he could possibly explain. "When I was in prison—she was going through rough times, making hard decisions. I couldn't be a part of those decisions. We decided we'd be more effective if we worked separately. We . . . couldn't cloud, I guess you'd say."

Stella shook her head. "That's *fit*, like drops of rain hitting each other. *Slipskin* is when the drops fall apart. Cloud is a bigger thing."

"Oh," Mitch said. "How many words for snow?"

Stella's expression became one of a simple lack of comprehension, and for a moment Mitch saw his daughter as she had been even ten years ago, and loved her fiercely. "Your mother and I talk every few weeks. She's busy now, working in Baltimore. Doing science."

"Trying to turn us back into humans?"

"You *are* human," Mitch said, his face going red.

"No," Stella said. "We aren't."

Mitch decided this wasn't the time or the place. "She's trying to learn how we make new children," he said. "It's not as simple as we thought."

"Virus children," Stella said.

"Yes, well, if I understand it correctly, viruses play all sorts of roles. We just discovered that fact when we looked at SHEVA. Now . . . it's pretty confused."

Stella seemed, if anything, offended by this. "We're not new?"

"Of course you're new," Mitch said. "I really don't understand it very well. When we all get together again, your mother will know enough to explain it to us. She's learning as fast as she can."

"We're not taught biology here," Stella said.

Mitch clamped his teeth together. *Keep them down. Keep them under lock and key. Otherwise, you might prime their fuse.*

"That makes you angry?" Stella asked.

He could not answer for a moment. His fists knotted on the top of the table. "Of course," he said.

"Make them let us go. Get us all out of here," Stella said. "Not just me."

"We're trying," Mitch said, but knew he wasn't being entirely truthful. As a convicted felon, he had a limited range of options. And his own sense of resentment and damage reduced his effectiveness in groups. In his darkest moods, he thought that was why he and Kaye were no longer living together.

He had become a political liability. A lone wolf.

"I have lots of families here, and they're growing," Stella said.

"*We're* your family," Mitch said.

Stella watched him for a moment, puzzled.

Joanie opened the door. "Time's up," she said.

Mitch spun around in his chair and tapped his watch. "It's been less than an hour," he said.

"There'll be more time tomorrow if you can come back," Joanie said.

Mitch turned to Stella, crestfallen. "I can't stay until tomorrow. There's something . . ."

"Go," Stella said, and stood. She came around the table as Mitch got to his feet and hugged her father again, brisk and strong. "There's lots of work for all of us."

"You are so adult now," Mitch said.

"Not yet," Stella said. "None of us knows what that will be like. They probably won't let us find out."

Joanie tsked, then escorted Mitch and Stella from the room. They parted in the brick corridor. Mitch gave her a small wave with his good arm.

•   •

Mitch sat in the hot interior of his truck, under the low Arizona sun, sweating and near despair, lonelier than he had ever been in his life.

Through the fence and across the brush and sand, he saw more children—hundreds of them—walking between the bungalows. His hand drummed on the steering wheel.

Stella was still his daughter. He could still see Kaye in her. But the differences were startling. Mitch did not know what he had expected; he had expected differences. But she was not just growing up. The way Stella behaved was sleek and shiny, like a new penny. She was unfamiliar, not distant in the least, not unfriendly, just focused elsewhere.

The only conclusion he could come to, as he turned over the big engine in the old Ford truck, was a self-observation.

His own daughter scared him.

After the nurse filled another tube with her blood, Stella walked back to the bungalow where they would watch videos after dinner of human children playing, talking, sitting in class. It was called civics. It was intended to change the way the new children behaved when they were together. Stella hated civics. Watching people without knowing how they smelled, and watching the young human faces with their limited range of emotions, disturbed her. If they did not face the televisions, however, Miss Kantor could get really ugly.

Stella deliberately kept her mind clear, but a tear came out of her left eye and traveled down her cheek. Not her right eye. Just her left eye.

She wondered what that meant.

Mitch had changed so much. And he smelled like he had just been kicked.

15

The imaging lab office was separated from the Magnetic Resonance Imager—the Machine—by two empty rooms. The forces induced by the toroidal magnets of the Machine were awesome. Visitors were warned not to go down the hall without first emptying their pockets of mechanical and electronic devices, pocket PCs, wallets, cell phones, security name tags, eyeglasses, watches. Getting closer to the Machine required exchanging day clothes for metal-free robes—no zippers, metal buttons, or belt buckles; no rings, pins, tie clasps, or cuff links.

Everything loose within a few meters of the Machine was made of wood or plastic. Workers here wore elastic belts and specially selected slippers or athletic shoes.

Five years ago, right in this facility, a scientist had forgotten the warnings and had her nipple and clitoris rings ripped out. Or so the story went. People with pacemakers, optic nerve rewiring, or any sort of neural implants could not go anywhere near the Machine.

Kaye was free of such appliances, and that was the first thing she told Herbert Roth as she stood in the door to the office.

Slight, balding, in his early forties, Roth gave her a puzzled smile as he put down his pencil and pushed a batch of papers aside. "Glad to hear it, Ms. Rafelson," he said. "But the Machine is turned off. Besides, we spent several days imaging Wishtoes and I already know that about you."

Roth pulled up a plastic chair for Kaye and she sat on the other side of the wooden desk. Kaye touched the smooth surface. Roth had told her that his father had crafted it from solid maple, without nails, using only glue. It was beautiful.

He still has a father.

She felt the cool river in her spine, the sense of utter delight and approval, and closed her eyes for a moment. Roth watched her with some concern.

"Long day?"

She shook her head, wondering how to begin.

"Is Wishtoes pregnant?"

"No," Kaye said. She took the plunge. "Are you feeling very scientific?"

Roth looked around nervously, as if the room was not completely familiar. "Depends." His eyes squinched down and he could not avoid giving Kaye the once-over.

"Scientific and discreet?"

Roth's eyes widened with something like panic.

"Pardon me, Ms. Rafelson—"

"Kaye, please."

"Kaye. I think you're very attractive, but . . . If it's about the Machine, I've already got a list of Web sites that show . . . I mean, it's already been done." He laughed what he hoped was a gallant laugh. "Hell, I've done it. Not alone, I mean."

"Done what?" Kaye asked.

Roth flushed crimson and pushed his chair back with a hollow scrape of the plastic legs. "I have no idea what in hell you're talking about."

Kaye smiled. She meant nothing specific by the smile, but she saw Roth relax. His expression changed to puzzled concern and the excess color faded from his face. *There is something about me, about this,* she thought. *It's a charmed moment.*

"Why are you down here?" Roth asked.

"I'm offering you a unique opportunity." Kaye felt impossibly nervous, but she was not going to let that stop her. As far as she knew, there had never been an opportunity like this in the history of science—nothing confirmed, at least, or even rumored. "I'm having an epiphany."

Roth raised one eyebrow, bewildered.

"You don't know what an epiphany is?" Kaye asked.

"I'm Catholic. It's a feast celebrating Jesus' divinity. Or something like that."

"It's a manifestation," Kaye said. "God is inside me."

"Whoa," Roth said. The word hung between them for several seconds, during which time Kaye did not look away from Roth's eyes. He blinked first. "I suppose that's great," he said. "What does it have to do with me?"

"God comes to most of us. I've read William James and other books about this kind of experience. At least half of the human race goes through it at one time or another. It's like nothing else I've ever felt. It's life changing, even if it is very . . . very inconvenient. And inexplicable. I didn't ask for it, but I can't, I *won't* deny that it is real."

Roth listened to Kaye with a fixed expression, brow wrinkled, eyes wide, mouth open. He sat up in the chair and folded his arms on the desk. "No joke?"

"No joke."

He considered further. "Everyone is under pressure here."

"I don't think that has anything to do with it," Kaye said. Then, slowly, she added, "I've considered that possibility, I really have. I just don't think that's what it is."

Roth licked his lips and avoided her stare. "So what does it have to do with me?"

She reached out to touch his arm, and he quickly withdrew it. "Herbert, has anyone ever imaged a person who's being touched by God? Who's having an epiphany?"

"Lots of times," Roth said defensively. "Persinger's research. Meditation states, that sort of thing. It's in the literature."

"I've read them all. Persinger, Damasio, Posner, and Ramachandran." She ticked the list off on her fingers. "You think I haven't researched this?"

Roth smiled in embarrassment.

"Meditation states, oneness, bliss, all that can be induced with training. They are under some personal control . . . But not *this*. I've looked it up. It can't be induced, no matter how hard you pray. It comes and it goes as if it has a will of its own."

"God doesn't just *talk* to us," Roth said. "I mean, even if I believed in God, such a thing would be incredibly rare, and maybe it hasn't happened for a couple of thousand years. The prophets. Jesus. That sort of thing."

"It isn't rare. It's called many things, and people react differently. It does something to you. It turns your life around, gives it direction and meaning. Sometimes it breaks people." She shook her head. "Mother Teresa wept because she didn't have God making regular visits. She wanted continuing confirmation of the value of her work, her pain, her sacrifices. Yet no one actually knows if Mother Teresa experienced what I'm experiencing . . ." She took a deep breath. "I want to learn what is happening to me. To us. We need a baseline to understand."

Roth tried to fit this into some catalog of social quid pro quos, and could not. "Kaye, is this really the place? Aren't you supposed to be doing research on viruses? Or do you think God is a virus?"

Kaye stared at Roth in disbelief. "No," she said. "This is not a virus. This is not something genetic and it's probably not even biological. Except to the extent that it touches me."

"How can you be so sure?"

Kaye closed her eyes again. She did not need to search. The sensation rolled on, coming in waves of amazement, of childlike glee and adult consternation, all of her emotions and reactions met not with tolerance, nor even with amusement, but with an equally childlike yet infinitely mature and wise *acceptance.*

Something was sipping from Kaye Lang's soul, and found her delicious.

"Because it's bigger than anything I know," she said finally. "I have no idea how long it's going to last, but whatever it is, it's happened before to people, many times, and it's shaped human history. Don't you want to see what it looks like?"

Roth sighed as he examined the images on the large monitor.

Two and a half hours had passed; it was almost ten o'clock. Kaye had been through seven varieties of NMR, PET, and computerized tomography scans. She had been injected, shielded, injected again, rotated like a chicken on a spit, turned upside down. For a while, she wondered if Roth was bent on taking revenge for her imposition.

Finally, Roth had wrapped her head in a white plastic helmet and put her through a final and, he claimed, rather expensive CT-motion scan, capable, he muttered vaguely, of extraordinary detail, focusing on the hippocampus, and then, in another sweep, the brain stem.

Now she sat upright, her wrist wrapped in a bandage, her head and neck bruised from clamps, feeling a vague urge to throw up. Somewhere near the end of the procedures, the caller had simply faded, like a shortwave radio signal from across the seas. Kaye felt calm and relaxed, despite her soreness.

She also felt sad, as if a good friend had just departed, and she was not sure they would ever meet again.

"Well, whatever he is," Roth said, "he isn't talking. None of the scans show extensive speech processing, above the level of normal internal dialog and my own datum of questions. You seem, no surprise, a little nervous—but less so than other patients. Stoic might be the word. You show a fair amount of deep brain activity, signifying a pretty strong emotional response. Do you embarrass easily?"

Kaye shook her head.

"There's a little indication of something like arousal, but I wouldn't call it sexual arousal, not precisely. Nothing like orgasm or garden-variety ecstasy such as, for example, you might find in someone using consciousness-altering drugs. We have recordings—movies—of people meditating, engaging in sex, on drugs, including LSD and cocaine. Your scans don't match any of those."

"I can't imagine having sex in that tube."

Roth smiled. "Mostly enthusiastic young people," he explained. "Here we go—CT motion scans coming up." He became deeply absorbed in the false-color images of her brain on the display: dark fields of gray overlaid with symmetric, blossoming Rorschach birds, touched here and there with little coals of metabolic activity, maps of thought and personality and deep subconscious processes. "All right," he said to himself, pausing the scroll. "What's this?" He touched three pulsing yellow splotches, a little bigger than a thumbnail, points on a scan taken midway through their session. He made small humming sounds, then flipped through an on-line library of images from other explorations, some of them years and even decades old, until he seemed satisfied he had what he wanted.

Roth pushed his chair back with an echoing scrape and pointed to a blue-and-green sagittal section of a head, small and oddly shaped. He filled in and rotated the image in 3-D, and Kaye made out the outlines of an infant's skull and the fog of the brain within. Radiating fields of mental activity spun within ghostly curves of bone and tissue.

An indefinite grayish mass seemed to issue from the infant's mouth.

"Not so much detail, but it's a pretty close match," Roth said. "Famous experiment in Japan, about eight years ago. They scanned a normal birthing session. Woman had had four kids previously. She was an old pro. The machines didn't bother her."

Roth studied the image. He hummed for a moment, then clicked his fingernails like castanets. "This is a scan of the infant's brain while he or she was getting acquainted with mom. Taking the teat, I'd say." He used his finger to point out the gray mass, magnified the activity centers in the infant's brain, rotated them to the proper azimuth, then superimposed the baby's scan on Kaye's.

The activity centers lined up neatly.

Roth smiled. "What do you think? A match?"

Kaye was lost for a moment, remembering the first time Stella had suckled, the wonderful sensation of the baby at her nipple, of her milk letting down.

"They look the same," she said. "Is that a mistake?"

"Don't think so," Roth said. "I could make some animal brain comparisons. There's been some work in the last few years on bonding in kittens and puppies, even some in baboons, but not very good. They don't hold still."

"What does it mean?" Kaye asked. She shook her head, still lost. "Whatever He is, He's not using speech—that much has been clear from the start. Irritating, actually."

"Mumbles from the burning bush?" Roth said. "And no stone tablets."

"No speeches, no proclamations, nothing," Kaye confirmed.

"Look, this is the closest I can come to a match," Roth said.

With her finger, Kaye traced the Rorschach birds inside the infant's brain. "I still don't understand."

Roth tilted his head. "Looks to me like you've made a big connection. You're imprinting on someone or something big-time. You've become a baby again, Ms. Rafelson."

16

Kaye unlocked her apartment, entered, and used her briefcase to block the front door from closing. She punched in her six-number code to deactivate the alarm, then took off her sweater, hung it in the closet, and stood in the hallway, breathing deeply to keep from sobbing. She wasn't sure how much longer she could endure this. The voids in her life were like deserts she could not cross.

"What about *you?*" she asked the empty air. She walked into the darkened living room. "The way I see it, if you're some kind of big daddy, you *protect* those you love, you keep them from harm. What's the God ... what's the *damned*," she finally shouted it, "the *God damned* excuse?"

The phone beeped. Kaye jumped, pulled her eyes away from the corner of the ceiling she had been addressing, stepped to the kitchen counter, and reached across to pick up the handset.

"Kaye? It's Mitch."

Kaye drew in another breath, almost of dread, certainly of guilt, before speaking. "I'm here." She sat stiffly upright in the easy chair and covered the mouthpiece as she told the lights to switch on. The living room was small and neat, except for stacks of journals and offprints arrayed at angles to each other on the coffee table. Other piles spilled across the floor beside the couch.

"Are you all right?"

"No-o-o," she said slowly. "I'm not. Are you?"

Mitch did not answer this. *Good for him,* Kaye thought.

"I'm on the road again," he said.

A pause.

"Where are you?" she asked.

"Oregon. My horse broke down and I thought I'd give you a call, ask if you had some extra . . . I don't know. Horseshoes." He sounded even more exhausted than she was. Kaye intercepted something else in his tone and zeroed in with sudden hope.

"You saw Stella?"

"They let me see Stella. Lucky guy, right?"

"Is she well?"

"She gave me a big hug. She's looking pretty good. She cried, Kaye."

Kaye felt her throat catch. She held the phone aside and coughed into her fist. "She misses you. Sorry. Dry throat. I need some water." She walked into the kitchen to take a bottle from the refrigerator.

"She misses both of us," Mitch said.

"I can't be there. I can't protect her. What's to miss?"

"I just wanted to call and tell you about her. She's growing up. It makes me feel lost, thinking that she's almost grown and I wasn't around."

"Not your fault," she said.

"How's the work?"

"Finished soon," Kaye said. "I don't know if they'll believe it. So many are still stuck in old ruts."

"Robert Jackson?"

"Yeah, him, too."

"You're lucky to be working at what you do best," Mitch said. "Listen, I'm—"

"You don't deserve what happened, Mitch."

Another pause. *You didn't deserve being dumped,* she added to herself. Kaye looked back to that empty corner of wall and ceiling and continued, "I miss you." She tightened her lips to keep them from trembling. "What's in Oregon?"

"Eileen's got something going, very mysterious, so I left the dig in Texas. I mistook a clamshell for a whelk. I'm getting old, Kaye."

"Bullshit," Kaye said.

"You give me the word, I'll drive straight to Maryland." Mitch's voice steeled. "I swear. Let's go get Stella."

"Stop it," Kaye said, though with sudden gentleness. "I want to, you know that. We have to keep to our plan."

"Right," Mitch said, and Kaye was acutely aware he had had no part in making the plan. Perhaps until now Mitch had not really been informed there *was* a plan. And that was Kaye's fault. She had not been able to protect her husband or her daughter, the most important people on Earth. *So who am I to accuse?*

"What are the kids up to? How has she changed?" Kaye asked.

"They're forming groups. Demes, they call them. The schools are trying to keep them broken up and disorganized. I'd guess they're finding ways around that. There's a lot of scenting involved, of course, and Stella talks about new kinds of language, but we didn't have time for details. She looks healthy, she's bright, and she doesn't seem too stressed out."

Kaye fixed on this so intensely her eyes crossed. "I tried to call her last week. They wouldn't put me through."

"The bastards," Mitch said, his voice grating.

"Go help Eileen. But keep in touch. I really need to hear from you."

"That's good news."

Kaye let her chin drop to her chest, and stretched out her legs. "I'm relaxing," she said. "Listening to you relaxes me. Tell me what she looks like."

"Sometimes she moves or acts or talks like you. Sometimes she reminds me of my father."

"I noticed that years ago," Kaye said.

"But she's very much her own person, her own type," Mitch said. "I wish we could run our own school, bring lots of kids together. I think that's the only way Stella would be happy."

"We were wrong to isolate her."

"We didn't have any choice."

"Anyway, that's not an issue now. Is she happy?"

"Maybe happier, but not exactly *happy*," Mitch said. "I'm calling on a landline now, but let me give you a new phone code."

Kaye took up a pad and wrote down a string of numbers keyed to a book she still kept in her suitcase. "You think they're still listening?"

"Of course. Hello, Ms. Browning, you there?"

"Not funny," Kaye said. "I ran into Mark Augustine on Capitol Hill. That was . . ." It took her a few seconds to remember. "Yesterday. Sorry, I'm just tired."

"What about him?"

"He seemed apologetic. Does that make sense?"

"He was busted to the ranks," Mitch said. "He deserves to be apologetic."

"Yeah. But something else . . ."

"You think the atmosphere is changing?"

"Browning was there, and she treated me like a Roman general standing over a dying Gaul."

Mitch laughed.

"God, that is *so* good to hear," Kaye said, tapping her pen on the message pad and drawing loops around the numbers, across the pad.

"Give me the word, Kaye. Just one word."

"Oh, Jesus," Kaye said, and sucked in a breath against the lump in her throat. "I hate it so much, being alone."

"I know you're on the right course," Mitch said, and Kaye heard the reserve in his voice, filling in, *even if it means leaving me outside.*

"Maybe," Kaye said. "But it is so hard." She wanted to tell him about the other things, the imaging lab, chasing down her visitor, the caller, and finding nothing conclusive. But she remembered that Mitch had not reacted well to her attempts to talk about it on their last night together in the cabin.

She remembered as well the love-making, familiar and sweet and more than a little desperate. Her body warmed. "You know I want to be with you," Kaye said.

"That's my line." Mitch's voice was hopeful, fragile.

"You'll be at Eileen's site. It is a site, I assume?"

"I don't know yet."

"What do you think she's found?"

"She's not telling," Mitch said.

"Where is it?"

"Can't say. I get my final directions tomorrow."

"She's being more cagey than usual, isn't she?"

"Yeah." She heard Mitch moving, breathing into the handset. She could hear as well the wind blowing behind and around him, almost picture her man, rugged, tall, his head lit up by the dome light in the booth. If it was a booth. The phone might be next to a gas station or a restaurant.

"I can't tell you how good this is," Kaye said.

"Sure you can."

"It is *so* good."

"I should have called earlier. I just felt out of place or something."

"I know."

"Something's changed, hasn't it?"

"There's not much more I can do at Americol. Showdown is tomorrow. Jackson actually dropped off his game plan today, he's that cocky. They either listen to the truth or they ignore it. I want to . . . I'll just fly out to see you. Save me a shovel."

"You'll get rough hands."

"I love rough hands."

"I believe in you, Kaye," Mitch said. "You'll do it. You'll win."

She did not know how to answer but her body quivered. Mitch murmured his love and Kaye returned his words, and then they cut off the connection.

Kaye sat for a moment in the warm yellow glow of the small living room, surveying the empty walls, the plain rented furniture, the stacks of white paper. "I'm imprinting," she whispered. "Something says it loves me and believes in me but how can anything fill an empty shell?" She rephrased the question. "How can anyone or anything believe in an empty shell?"

Leaning her head back, she felt a tingling warmth. With some awe she realized she had not asked for help, yet help had arrived. Her needs—some of them, at least—had been answered.

At that, Kaye finally let down her emotions and began to weep. Still crying, she made up her bed, fixed herself a cup of hot chocolate, fluffed a pillow and set it against the headboard, disrobed and put on satin pajamas, then fetched a stack of reprints from the living room to read. The words blurred through her tears, and she could hardly keep her eyes open, but she needed to prepare for the next day. She needed to have all her armor on, all her facts straight.

For Stella. For Mitch.

When she could stand it no more and sleep was stealing the last of her thoughts, she ordered the light to turn off, rolled over in bed, and moved her lips, *Thank you. I hope.*

You are hope.

But she could not help asking one more question. *Why are you doing this? Why talk to us at all?*

She stared at the wall opposite the bed, then dropped her focus to the cover rising with her knees above the bed. Her eyes widened and her breath slowed. Through the shadowy grayness of the cover, Kaye seemed to look into an infinite and invisible fount. The fount poured forth something she could only describe as *love*, no other word was right, however inadequate it was; love never-ending and unconditional. Her heart thudded in her chest. For a moment, she was frightened—she could never deserve that love, never find its like again on this Earth.

Love without condition—without desire, direction, or any quality other than its purity.

"I don't know what that means," she said. "I'm sorry."

Kaye felt the vision, if that was what it was, withdraw and fade—not out of resentment or anger or disappointment, but just because it was time to end. It left a mellow, peaceful glow behind, like candles thick as stars behind her eyes.

The wonder of that, the awesome wonder, was too much for her.

She laid her head back and stared into the darkness until she drifted off to sleep.

Almost immediately, it seemed, she dreamed of walking over a field of snow high in the mountains. It did not matter that she was lost and alone. She was going to meet someone wonderful.

17

The high desert morning was warm and it was barely seven o'clock. Mitch walked across the motel parking lot, swung his bag into the battered old truck's side seat and shielded his eyes against the sun over the low, gray eastern hills. An hour to the Spent River. Half an hour to the outlying camp. He had his instructions from Eileen, and one more warning: *Don't breathe a word to anyone. No students, no wives, no girlfriends, no dogs, no cats, no guinea pigs: Got it?*

He got it.

He pulled out of the Motel 50 parking lot, scraping his bumper on the way. The old truck was on its last few thousand miles; it smelled of singed oil and was starting to cough blue smoke on the grades. Mitch loved big old trucks and cars. He would be sad to see the truck die.

The motel's red sign grew tiny in his mirror. The road was straight and on either side lay rolling brown terrain daubed with greasewood and sage and low, stubby pines and an occasional sketchy line of fence posts, leaning and forlorn, the wire broken and coiled like old hair.

The air got cooler as the truck climbed the gentle grade into the high country. The Spent River was not on the itinerary of most tourists. Surrounded by forest, in the long shadow of Mount Hood, it consisted of a winding, flat sandy bed cutting through black lava cliffs, leaving tufty islands and curving oxbows. The river itself hadn't flowed for many thousands of years. It was not well known to archaeologists, and with good reason; the geological history of alternating floods—gravel beds filled with pebbly lava and rounded bits of granite and basalt—and periodic eruptions of lava made it hellacious to dig and disappointing to those who did. Indians had not built or stayed much in these areas over the last few thousand years.

Out of time, out of human interest, but now Eileen Ripper had found something.

Or she had looked into the sun too long.

The road mesmerized him after a while, but he was jounced to full alertness when it started to get rough from washouts. The land had taken on a five o'clock stubble of trees and grass. The asphalt switched to gravel.

A small state sign came and went: SPENT RIVER RECREATION AREA: THREE MILES. The sign looked as if it had been out in the sun for at least fifty years.

The road curved west abruptly, and as he turned, Mitch caught a gleam about a mile ahead. It looked like a car windshield.

The old truck barked out blue smoke as he took a short grade, then he spotted a white Tahoe and saw a stocky figure standing up and waving from the open driver's door. He pulled over to the side of the road and draped his arm out the window. Enough grip remained in his hand to clutch the door frame and make the gesture look casual.

Eileen had gone completely gray. Her clothes and skin and hair had weathered to the color of the land out here.

"I recognized your taste in trucks," Eileen said as she walked across the gravel shoulder. "God, Mitch, you're as obvious as a sailor with a stack of two-dollar bills."

Mitch smiled. "You're a regular Earth mother," he said. "You should at least wear a red scarf."

Eileen pulled a rag from her pocket and draped it from her belt. "Better?"

"Just fine."

"How's your arm?" she asked, patting it.

"Limp," Mitch said.

"We'll put you on toothbrush detail," she said.

"Sounds good. What have you got?"

"It's *dishy*," Eileen said. "It's grand." She did a little jig on the gravel. "It's deadly dangerous. Want to come see?"

Mitch squint-eyed her for a moment. "Why not?" he said.

"It's just over there," she said and pointed north, "about ten more miles."

Mitch scowled. "I'm not sure my truck will make it."

"I'll follow and scoop up parts."

"How can you tell me when to turn?" Mitch asked.

"It's a game, old friend," Eileen said. "You'll have to sniff it out, same as I did." She smiled wickedly.

Mitch squinted harder and shook his head. "For Christ's sake, Eileen."

"Older than Christ by at least eighteen thousand years," she said.

"You should wear thicker hats," he said.

Eileen looked tired beneath the bravado. "This is the big one, Mitch. In a couple of hours, I swear to God you won't even know who you are."

18

ARIZONA

At eleven in the morning, Stella walked with all the girls from their barracks through a gate in the razor wire fence to the open field, attended by Miss Kantor and Joanie and five other adults.

Once a week, the counselors and teachers let the SHEVA children mingle coed on the playground and under the lunch table awnings.

The girls were uncharacteristically quiet. Stella felt the tension. A year ago, going through the fence to socialize with the boys had been no big deal. Now, every girl who imagined herself a deme maker was plotting with her partners as to which boys would be best in their group. Stella did not know what to think about this. She watched the demes form and disintegrate and reform in the girl's dorms, and her own plans changed in her head from day to day; it was all so confusing.

The sky was sprinkled with broken clouds. She shaded her eyes and looked up and saw the moon hanging in the pure summer blueness, a wan face blankly amused by their silliness. Stella wondered what the moon smelled like. It looked kindly enough. It looked a little simple, actually.

"Single file. We're going to South Section Five," Miss Kantor told them all, and waved her hand to give them direction. The girls shuffled where she pointed, cheeks blank.

Stella saw the boys come through their own fence line from the opposite rows of barracks. They were more touching heads and weaving and pointing out the girls they noticed. They smiled like goofs, cheeks brown at this distance with indistinguishable color.

"Oh, joy," Celia said listlessly. "Same old."

The sexes would be allowed to mingle with heavy supervision for an hour.

"Is he here?" Celia asked. Stella had told her last night about Will.

Stella did not know. She hadn't seen him yet. She didn't think it likely.

She indicated all this with a low whistle, a few desultory freckles, and a twitch of her shoulders. "My, you're-KUK touchy," Celia said. She bumped shoulders with Stella as they walked. Stella did not mind.

"I don't know what they expect us to do in an hour," Stella said.

Celia giggled. "We could try to-KUK kiss one of them."

Stella's brows formed an uneven pair of curves and her neck darkened. Celia ignored this. "I could kiss James Callahan. I almost let him hold my hand last year."

"We were kids last year," Stella said.

"What-KUK are we now?" Celia asked.

Stella was looking down a line of boys drawn up in the sun beside the lunch table awnings. The tallest she recognized immediately.

"There he is," she said, and pointed him out to Celia. Three other girls moved in and followed her point, all smelling of aroused curiosity—smoke and earth.

Will stood, looking at the ground with shoulders slumped and hands stuck firmly in his pockets. The other boys seemed to be ignoring him, which was to be expected; boys didn't cloud as quickly with newcomers as girls did. It would take Will a few days to form tight bonds with his barracks partners.

Or maybe not, Stella thought, watching him. Maybe he never would.

"He's not very pretty," said Felice Miller, a small, brown-haired girl with thin, strong arms and thicker legs.

"How do you know?" asked Ellie Gow. "You can't smell him from here."

"He wouldn't smell pretty, either," Felice said disdainfully. "He's too tall."

Ellie winced. She was known for her sensitivity to sounds and a preference for talking while lying under a blanket. "What's that got to do with a cat's fart?"

Felice smiled tolerantly. "Whiskers," she said.

Stella paid no attention to them.

"Someone you met when you were young can exert a profound influence," Felice continued.

"I didn't see him for very long," Stella admitted.

Celia quickly told them the story of Stella and Will, speaking in her halting double, while the counselors and teachers huddled and arranged the rules of the confab. The rules changed week to week. Today, on the outskirts of the field, three men stood watching them with binoculars.

Nine months ago, Stella had been taken aside and driven to the hospital with five other girls after such a meeting. They had all given blood and one, Nor Upjohn, had suffered other indignities she would not describe, and afterward she had smelled like a mildewed orange, a warning scent.

The girls made their formation, four long columns of fifty each. The counselors did not try to stop them from talking, and Stella saw that some of them—possibly all—had turned off their nosies.

Will looked across the brown grass and gravel at the lines of girls. His brows drew into a narrow straight line and he seemed to be sucking on something sour. His matted hair was cut jagged and his cheeks were hollow pits, as if he had lost some teeth. He looked older than the others, and tired. He looked defeated.

"He's not pretty, he's *ugly*," Felice said, and with a shrug turned her attention to the other boys they had not seen before. Stella had counted the new arrivals on the bus: fifty-three. She had to agree with Felice. Whatever her memory of Strong Will, this fellow was no one's idea of a good deme partner.

"You want to cloud with *him*?" Celia asked in disbelief.

"No," Stella said, and looked away with a sharp pang of disappointment.

The woods were far away now for both of them.

"What's anything got to do with toad skin?" Ellie asked nervously as the teachers started to shoo the rows and columns toward each other.

"Crow on the road," Felice replied.

"What's that have to do with apple feathers?" Ellie riposted by reflex.

"Oh, just-KUK *grow*," Celia said. Her face wrinkled like a dried peach in a sudden despair of shyness. "Grow big and *hide me*."

The lines drew up before the concrete lunch tables and the boys were pushed to go and sit, three to one side, leaving the opposite side of each table empty.

"What'll we say?" Ellie asked, hiding her eyes as their turn approached.

"Same thing we always say," Stella said. "Hello and how are you. And ask how their demes are growing and what they're doing on the other side of the wire."

"Harry, Harry, quite contrary," Felice sang in an undertone, "how does your garden grow? Pubic hairs and wanton stares, making the hormones flow."

Ellie told her to shush. Miss Kantor walked in front of the rows from their barracks. "All right, girls," she said. "You may talk, you may look. You may not touch."

But the nosies are turned off, Stella thought. The girls fanned out from the lines. Stella looked up at the cameras mounted on the long steel poles, swinging slowly right and left.

Ellie's turn came and she ran off to join a table of boys whom, as far as Stella knew, she had never visited before. So much for shyness. Stella's turn came, and of course whatever she had thought earlier, she moved toward the table where Will sat with two smaller boys.

Will hunched over the table, looking at the old food stains. The two smaller and younger males watched her approach with some interest and freckled each other. She thought she heard some under, difficult to be sure at this distance, and Will looked up. He did not seem to recognize her.

Stella was the only girl to sit at their table. She said hello to the two boys, and then focused on Will. Will rested his cheeks in the palms of his hands. She could not see his patterns, though she saw his neck darken.

"He's in our barracks," said the boy on the right, strong but short, Jason or James; the boy to the left of Will was named Philip. Stella had sat with Philip three weeks ago. He was pleasant enough, though she had learned quickly she did not want to cloud with him. Neither Jason/James nor Philip smelled right. She freckled Philip a butterfly greeting, friendly but not open, meaning no offense, etc.

"Why did you sit here?" Philip asked with a frown. "Doesn't somebody *else* want to sit here?"

"I want to talk to him," Stella said. She was not very good at dealing with the boys, but then few of the girls were. There were unspoken, unwritten rules, rules yet to be discovered, but this way of doing things was never going to make the rules any plainer.

"He doesn't talk much," Jason/James said.

"Girls play games," Philip said resentfully.

"Nothing like *human* girls," Will murmured, and looked up at her. The glance was brief, but Stella knew he remembered their last meeting. "They cut you like knives and you never know why."

"Right," Philip said. "Will lived among the savages." Jason/James giggled at this, and made a gesture of tangled fingers Stella could not interpret.

"I passed," Will said.

"Was it the woods?" Stella asked, hope flickering like a small ember.

"What?" he asked.

"They scrubbed him before he came to our barracks," Philip said, just being informative. "His skin was red from soap."

"Did you stay with your parents?" Will asked. He looked up and let her see his cheeks. They were blank, dark and raw. Most of Will's neck and face were red and rough. Stella inhaled, only what was polite under the circumstances, and could still smell the Lysol and soap on his skin and clothes.

"Only for a few days," Stella said. "I got sick."

"I missed out on getting scabs," Will said, touching between his fingers. The SHEVA kids referred to the disease that had killed so many of them as "scabs" or "the ache."

"We're going to another table," Jason/James and Philip said, almost in unison.

"You two should be alone," Philip added brusquely. "We can tell."

Stella wanted to ask them to stay, but Will shrugged, so she shrugged as well. "They're breaking the rules," she said after they were gone.

"They can find a table with not enough boys," Will suggested. "They're making up rules in the barracks. Something about demes. What are demes?"

"Demes are families," Stella said. "New families. We're trying to figure out what they'll look like when we're grown up."

Will looked directly at her once more, and Stella looked away, then covered her own cheeks. "It doesn't matter," Will said. "I don't care."

"I came over to say hello," Stella said. He could not know what his words had meant to her. "You must have got away." She watched him eagerly, hoping for his story.

"We're talking human talk. Do you know the under and the over?"

"Yes," Stella said. "Do you speak it the same way?"

"Not the way they do in the barracks," Will admitted with a twitch of one arm. "Out on the road . . . It's different. Stronger, faster."

"And in the woods?" Stella asked.

"There are no woods," Will said, face crinkling as if she had spoken some obscenity.

"When you got away, where did you go?"

Will looked up at the sky. "I can eat lots here," he said. "I'll get better, stronger, learn the smell, talk the two tongues." He balled up his hands and bounced them lightly on the table, then against each other, thumb to thumb, as if playing a game. "Why are they letting us get together, boy-girl?"

"I don't know. Sometimes they draw blood and ask questions."

Will nodded.

"Do you know what they're doing?" Stella asked.

"Not a clue," Will said. "They teach nothing, like all the schools. Right?"

"We read some books and learn some skills. We can't cloud or scent or we're punished."

Will smiled. "Stupid blanks," he said.

Stella winced. "We try not to call them names."

Will looked away.

"How long were you free?" Stella asked.

"They caught me a week ago," Will said. "I've lived on my own and with runaways and street kids. Covered my cheeks with henna tattoos. Neck, too. Some human kids mark their faces to look like us, but everyone knows. They also claim to read thoughts and have better brains. Like they think we do. They say it's cool, but their freckles don't move."

Stella could see some brown still staining the raw patches on Will's face. "How many of us are outside?"

"Not many," Will said. "I got turned in by a human for a pack of cigarettes, even after I saved him from getting beat up." He shook his head slowly. "It's awful out there."

Stella smelled Joanie nearby, under her signature mask of baby powder. Will straightened as the stout young counselor approached.

"No one-on-one," Stella heard Joanie say. "You know the rules."

"The others left," Stella said, turning to explain, stopping only when Joanie gripped Stella's shoulder. Touched and held, she refused to meet the counselor's eyes.

Will stood. "I'll go," he said.

Then, speaking two streams at once, the over a flow of young gibberish, he said, "See you, say hi to Cory in Six" (there was no Cory and no Six) and "keep it low, keep it topped, shop with pop, nay?"

The under:

"What do you know about a place called Sandia?"

He mixed the streams so expertly that it took Stella a moment to know he had delivered the question. To Joanie, it probably sounded like a slur in the gibberish.

Then, with a toss of his hand, as Joanie led Stella away, Will said, in one stream, "Find out, hey?"

Stella watched Ellie be led away to give blood. Ellie pretended it was no big deal, but it was. Stella wondered if it was because Ellie had attracted a lot of boys today, five at the table where she and Felice had sat. The rest of the girls went to their late morning classrooms, where they were shown films about the history of the United States, guys in wigs and women in big dresses, wagon trains, maps, a little bit about Indians.

Mitch had taught Stella about Indians. The film told them nothing important.

Felice was sitting in the aisle next to her. "What's a green bug got to do with anything?" she whispered, making up for Ellie's absence.

Nobody answered. The game had gone sour. This time, being with the boys had hurt, and somehow Stella and the others knew it would only get worse. The time was coming when they would all need to be left alone, boys and girls together, to work things out for themselves.

Stella did not think the humans would ever let that happen. They would be kept apart like animals in a zoo, forever.

"You're scenting," Celia warned in a whisper behind her. "Miss Kantor turned her nosey on."

Stella did not know how to stop. She could feel the changes coming.

"You're doing it, too," Felice whispered to Celia.

"Damn," Celia said, and rubbed behind her ears, eyes wide.

"Girls," Miss Kantor called from the front of the classroom. "Be quiet and watch the film."

19

Promptly at eleven, Kaye entered the Americol twentieth-floor conference room, Liz close behind. Robert Jackson was already in the room. His hair had turned salt and pepper over the years but otherwise he had not matured much either in behavior or appearance. He was still handsome, skin pale to the point of blueness, with a sharply defined nose and chin and a glossy five o'clock shadow. His quartzlike eyes, dark gray, bored into Kaye whenever they met, occasions she tried to keep to a minimum.

Angled on either side of Jackson at the corner position he favored were two of his postdocs—research interns from Cornell and Harvard, in their late twenties, compact fellows with dark brown hair and the nervous aloofness of youth.

"Marge will be here in a few minutes," Jackson told Kaye, briefly half-standing.

He had never forgiven her an awkward moment in the early days of SHEVA, sixteen years ago, when it seemed that Marge and Kaye had ganged up on him. Jackson had won that round in the long run, but grudges came naturally to him. He was as passionate about office politics and the social side of research as he was about science as an ideal and an abstraction.

With so keen a sense of the social, Kaye wondered why Jackson had been other than brilliant in genetics. To Kaye, the processes behind both were much the same; to Jackson, that idea was heresy of a disgusting magnitude.

The representatives from three other research divisions had also arrived before Kaye and Liz. Two men and one woman, all in their late forties, bowed their heads as they pored over touch tablets, getting through the perpetual network-enabled tasks of their day. They did not look up as Kaye entered, though most of them had met her and conversed with her at Americol mixers and Christmas parties.

Kaye and Liz sat with their backs to a long window that looked out over downtown Baltimore. Kaye felt a breeze go up her back from a floor vent. Jackson had taken pole position, leaving Liz and Kaye with the air conditioning.

Marge Cross entered, alone for once. She seemed subdued. Cross was in her middle sixties, portly, her short-cut, scraggly hair brilliantly hennaed, her face jowly, her neck a landscape of hanging wrinkles. She possessed a voice that could carry across a crowded conference hall, yet carried herself with the poise of a ballet dancer, dressed in carefully tailored pant suits, and somehow could charm the butterflies out of the skies. It was difficult to know when she did not like what she was hearing. Like a rhino, Cross was said to be at her most dangerous when she was still and quiet.

The CEO of Americol and Eurocol had grown stouter and more beefy-faced over the years, but still walked with graceful confidence. "Let the games begin," she said, her voice mellow as she made her way to the window. Liz moved her chair as Cross passed.

"You didn't bring your lance, Kaye," Jackson said.

"Behave, Robert," Cross warned. She sat beside Liz and folded her hands on the table. Jackson managed to look both properly chastened and amused by the jabbing familiarity.

"We're here to judge the success so far of our attempts to restrict legacy viruses," Cross began. "We refer to them generically as ERV— endogenous retroviruses. We've also been concerned with their close relations, transgenes, transposons, retrotransposons, LINE elements, and what have you—all mobile elements, all jumping genes. Let's not confuse our ERV with someone else's ERV—*equine rhinovirus,* for example, or *ecotropic recombinant retrovirus,* or, something we've all experienced in these sessions, a sudden loss of *expiratory reserve volume.*"

Polite smiles around the room. A little shuffling of feet.

Cross cleared her throat. "We certainly wouldn't want to confuse anybody," she said, her voice dropping an octave. Most of the time, it hovered between a quavering soprano and a mellow alto. Many had compared her to Julia Child, but the comparison was surface only, and with age and hennaed hair, Cross had gone well beyond Julia and into her own stratospheric realm of uniqueness. "I've looked over the team reports from our vaccine project, and of course the chimpanzee and mouse ERV knockout projects. Dr. Jackson's report was very long. Also, I've looked over the research reviews and audits from the fertility and general immunology groups." Cross's arthritis was bothering her; Kaye could tell from the way she massaged the swollen knuckles on her hands. "The consensus is, we seem to have failed at everything we set out to do. But we're not here for a postmortem. We need to decide how to proceed from where we are at this moment. So. Where are we?"

Glum silence. Kaye stared straight ahead, trying to keep from biting her lip.

"Usually, we toss a coin and let the winner start. But we're all familiar with this debate, up to a point, and I think it's time we begin with some probing questions. I'll choose who goes first. All right?"

"Fine," Jackson said nonchalantly, lifting his hands from the tabletop.

"Fine," Kaye echoed.

"Good. We all agree it sucks," Cross said. "Dr. Nilson, please begin."

Lars Nilson, a middle-aged man with round glasses, had won a Nobel twenty years ago for his research in cytokines. He had once been heavily involved in Americol's attempts to resolve retroviral issues in xenotransplants—

the transplanting of animal tissues into human recipients—a prospect that had come to a drastic halt with the appearance of SHEVA and the case of Mrs. Rhine. He had since been reassigned to general immunology.

Nilson peered around the room with a wry expression, looking to Kaye like a gray and disconsolate pixie. "I presume I'm expected to speak first out of some notion of Nobel *oblige* or something more awful still, like seniority."

A small, very slim elderly man in a gray suit and yarmulke entered the room and looked around through friendly, crinkled brown eyes, his face wreathed in a perpetual smile. "Don't mind me," he said, and took a chair in the far corner, crossing his legs. "Lars is no longer senior," he added quietly.

"Thank you, Maurie," Nilson said. "Glad you could make it." Maurie Herskovitz was another of Cross's Nobel laureates, and perhaps the most honored biologist working at Americol. His specialty was loosely labeled "genomic complexity"; he now functioned as a roving researcher. Kaye was startled and a little unnerved by his presence. Despite his smile—built-in, she suspected, like a dolphin's—Herskovitz was known to be a demanding tyrant in the lab. She had never seen him in person.

Cross folded her arms and breathed loudly through her nose. "Let's move on," she suggested.

Nilson looked to his right. "Dr. Jackson, your SHEVA vaccines have unexpected side effects. When you work to block transmission of ERV particles between cells in tissue, you kill the experimental animals— apparently in part because of a massive overreaction of their innate immune system—whether they be mice, pigs, or monkeys. That seems counterintuitive. Can you explain?"

"We believe our efforts interfere with or mimic some essential processes involving the breakdown of pathogenic messenger RNA in somatic cells. The cells seem to interpret our vaccines as a byproduct of the appearance of viral RNA, and stop all transcription and translation. They die, apparently to protect other cells from infection."

"I understand there may also be a problem with shutting down function of transposases in T cells," Nilson continued. "RAG1 and RAG2 are apparently affected by nearly all the candidate vaccines."

"As I said, we're still tracking that connection," Jackson said smoothly.

"Most expression of ERVs doesn't trigger cell suicide," Nilson said.

Jackson nodded. "It's a complicated process," he said. "Like many pathogens, some retroviruses have developed a cloaking ability and can avoid cell defenses."

"So the model that all viruses are interlopers or invaders may not apply in these cases?"

Jackson vehemently disagreed. His argument was rigidly traditional: DNA in the genome was a tightly constrained and efficient blueprint. Viruses were simply parasites and hangers-on, causing disorder and disease but, in rare instances, also creating useful novelty. He explained that putting viral promoters in front of a necessary cellular gene could cause more of that gene's products to be manufactured at a key moment in the cell's history. More rarely, within germ cells—egg or sperm progenitors— they might land, randomly, in such a way as to cause phenotypic or devel- opmental variation in the offspring. "But to call any such activity orderly, part of some cellular reaction to the environment, is ridiculous. Viruses have no awareness of their actions, nor are the cells specifically activating viruses for some wonderful purpose. That has been obvious for more than a century."

"Kaye? Do viruses know what they're doing?" Cross asked, turning in her chair.

"No," Kaye said. "They're nodes in a distributed network. Greater pur- pose as such lies with the network, not the node; and not even the network can be described as self-aware or deliberately purposeful, in the sense that Dr. Jackson has purpose."

Jackson smiled.

Kaye went on. "All viruses appear to be descendants, directly or indi- rectly, of mobile elements. They did not pop up from outside; they broke free from inside, or evolved to carry genes and other information between cells and between organisms. Retroviruses like HIV in particular seem closely related to retrotransposons and ERV in the cells of many organisms. They all use similar genetic tools."

"So a flu virus, with eight genes, is derived from a retrotransposon or retrovirus with two or three genes?" Nilson asked with some disdain. His brows dropped into a puzzled and stormy expression at this patent absurdity.

"Ultimately, yes," Kaye said. "Gaining or mutating genes, or losing them, is mediated by necessity. A virus entering a new and unfamiliar host might take up and incorporate useful genes found within the host cell, but it's not easy. Most of the viruses simply fail to replicate."

"They go in, hoping for a handout at the gene table?" Jackson asked. "That's what Dr. Howard Urnovitz believed, isn't it? Vaccinations led to HIV, Gulf War Syndrome, and every other illness known to modern man?"

"Dr. Urnovitz's views seem closer to yours than to mine," Kaye replied evenly.

"That was more than twenty years ago," Cross said, yawning. "Ancient history. Move on."

"We know many viruses can incorporate genes from ERVs," Kaye said. "Herpes, for example."

"The implications of that process are not at all clear," Jackson said, a rather weak-kneed response, Kaye thought.

"I'm sorry, but it simply is not controversial," she persisted. "We know that is how Shiver arose in all its variety, and that is how the virus mutated that gave our children lethal HFMD. It picked up endogenous viral genes found only in non-SHEVA individuals."

Jackson conceded these points. "Some of our children," he amended quietly. "But I'm willing to concede that viruses may be enemies from within. All the more reason to eradicate them."

"Just *enemies*?" Cross asked. She propped her chin in one palm, and looked up at Jackson from beneath her bushy eyebrows.

"I did say 'enemies,' not handmaids or subcontractors," Jackson said. "Jumping genes cause problems. They are rogues, not handmaids. We know that. When they're active, they produce genetic defects. They activate oncogenes. They're implicated in multiple sclerosis and in schizophrenia, in leukemia and all manner of cancers. They cause or exacerbate autoimmune diseases. However long they can lie dormant in our genes, they're part of a panoply of ancient plagues. Viruses are a curse. That some are now tame enough to get by without causing their hosts major damage is just the way disease evolution works. We know that HIV retroviruses mutated and jumped from one primate species to another, to us. In chimps, the HIV precursor evolved to be neutral, a genetic burden and little more. In us, the mutation proved to be highly immunosuppressive and lethal. SHEVA is little different. The ERV we are fighting are simply not useful to the organism in any fundamental way."

Kaye felt as if she had traveled back in time, as if thirty years of research had never happened. Jackson had refused to change despite massive strides; he simply ignored what he could not believe in. And he was not alone. The number of papers produced each year in virology alone could fill the entire meeting room. To this day, most such papers stuck to a disease model for both viruses and mobile elements.

Jackson felt safely enclosed by thick walls of tradition, away from Kaye's mad, howling winds.

Cross turned to the sole woman on the review committee, Sharon Morgenstern. Morgenstern specialized in fertility research and developmental biology. A nervous-looking, thin woman, reputedly a spinster, with a withdrawn chin, prominent teeth, wispy blonde hair, and a soft North Carolina accent, she also chaired the Americol jury that approved papers before they were submitted to the journals—in-house peer review set up in part to quash publications that might reveal corporate secrets. "Sharon? Any questions while we're jumping up and down on Robert?"

"Your test animals, when given candidate vaccines, have also been known to suffer the loss or reduction of key sexual characteristics," Morgenstern began. "That seems exceptionally odd. How do you plan to get around those problems?"

"We have noticed reduction of certain minor sexual characters in baboons," Jackson said. "That may have no relevance to human subjects."

Nilson moved in once more, ignoring Morgenstern's irritated expression. *Let the woman finish,* Kaye thought, but said nothing.

"Dr. Jackson's vaccine could be of immense importance in our attempts to neutralize viruses in xenotransplant tissues," Nilson said. "Dr. Rafelson's endeavors also hold tremendous promise—to knock out all ERV genes in these tissues has been one of our holy grails for at least fifteen years. To say we're disappointed by these failures is an understatement." Nilson shifted in his seat and referred to his notes by leaning over sideways and looking through the edge of his glasses, like a bird examining a seed. "I'd like to ask some questions about why Dr. Jackson's vaccines fail."

"The vaccines do not fail. The organisms fail," Jackson said. "The vaccines succeed. They block intercellular transmission of all ERV particles."

Nilson smiled broadly. "All right. Why do the *organisms* fail, time after time? And, in particular, why do they become sterile if you're blocking or otherwise frustrating a viral load—all the disease-causing elements within their genomes? Shouldn't they experience a burst of energy and productivity?"

Jackson asked that the overhead projector be lowered. Liz sighed. Kaye kicked her gently under the table.

Jackson's presentation was classic. Within three minutes, he had used nine acronyms and six made-up scientific terms with which Kaye was un-familiar, without defining any of them; he had entangled them all in an ingenious map of pathways and byproducts and some deep evolutionary suppositions that had never been demonstrated outside a test tube. When he was on the defensive, Jackson invariably reverted to tightly controlled *in vitro* demonstrations using the tumor cell cultures favored for lab research. All the experiments he cited had been tightly designed and controlled and had, all too often, led to predicted results.

Marge Cross gave him five minutes. Jackson noticed her impatience and drew his sidebar to a close. "It's obvious that ERVs have devised ways to worm themselves into the machinery of their host's genome. We know of many instances in nature where trying to remove a parasite can kill a host. It's even likely they've created safeguards against removal—pseudogenes, multiple copies, disguised or compressed copies that can be reassembled later, methylation to prevent restriction enzyme activity, all sorts of clever tricks. But the prime proof of the malevolent nature of all retroviruses, even the so-called benevolent or benign, is what HIV and SHEVA have done to our society."

Kaye looked up from her notes.

"We have a generation of children who can't fit in," Jackson con-tinued, "who arouse hatred and suspicion, and whose so-called adaptive characteristics—randomly invoked from a panoply of possible distortions—only cause them distress. Viruses cause us grievous harm. Given time, our group will overcome these unfortunate delays and eliminate all viruses from our lives. Genomic viruses will be nightmares from a rough and nasty past."

"Is that a conclusion?" Cross asked without letting Jackson's dramatic effect sink in.

"No," Jackson said, leaning back in his chair. "Something of an out-burst. I apologize."

Cross looked at the questioners. "Satisfied?" she asked.

"No," Nilson said, once again with that special Olympian frown Kaye had only seen in older male scientists, winners of Nobel prizes. "But I have a question for Dr. Rafelson."

"Lars can always be relied upon to keep these sessions lively," Cross said.

"I'm hoping Dr. Nilson will ask equally probing questions of Kaye," Jackson said.

"Count on it," Nilson said dryly. "We realize how difficult it is to work with early-stage embryos in mammals, mice for example, and how much more difficult it is to work with primates and simians. As far as I have been able to review, your lab techniques have been creative and skilled."

"Thank you," Kaye said.

Nilson waved this off with another frown. "We also know that there are many ways in which embryos and their hosts, their mothers, work together to prevent rejection of the paternal components of embryonic tissues. Isn't it possible that by removing known ERVs in chimpanzee embryos, you have also shut down genes crucial to these other protective functions? I am thinking in particular of FasL, triggered by CRH, corticotropin releasing hormone, in the pregnant female. FasL causes cell death in maternal lymphocytes as they move in to attack the embryo. It is essential to getting born."

"FasL is unaffected by our work," Kaye said. "Dr. Elizabeth Cantrera, my colleague, spent a year proving that FasL and all other known protective genes remain intact and active after we knock out ERVs. In fact, we're tracking the possibility now that a LINE element transactivated by the pregnancy hormone in fact regulates FasL."

"I do not see that in your references," Nilson said.

"We published three papers in *PNAS*." Kaye gave him the citations, and Nilson patiently wrote them down. "The immunosuppressive function of particles derived from endogenous retroviruses is indisputably part of an embryo's protective armament. We've proven that over and over."

"I'm concerned in particular about evidence that a drop in corticotropin releasing hormone after pregnancy induces rapid expression of ERV responsible for triggering arthritis and multiple sclerosis," Nilson said. "The ERV in this case are reacting to a sharp *drop* in hormones, not a rise, and they appear to cause disease."

"Interesting," Cross said. "Dr. Rafelson?"

"It's a reasonable hypothesis. The triggering of autoimmune disorders by ERV is a rich area for research. Such expression could be regulated by stress-related hormones, and that would explain the role such hormones—and stress in general—play in such disorders."

"Then which is it, Dr. Rafelson?" Nilson asked, his eyes sharp upon her. "Good virus, or bad virus?"

"Like everything else in nature, one or the other or even both, depending on the circumstances," Kaye said. "Pregnancy is a tough time for both the infant and the mother."

Cross turned to Sharon Morgenstern. "Dr. Morgenstern showed me some of her questions earlier," she said. "They are cogent. They are in fact excellent."

Morgenstern leaned forward and looked at Kaye and Liz. "I will state up front that although I often agree with Dr. Nilson, I do not find Dr. Rafelson's laboratory procedures free from bias or error. I suspect that Dr. Rafelson came here to prove that something could *not* be done, not that it *could* be done. And now we are supposed to believe that she has proven that embryos cannot proceed to live birth, or even grow to pubescence, without a full complement of old viruses in their genes. In short, working backwards, she is trying to prove a controversial theory of virus-based evolution that could conceivably elevate the social status of her own daughter. I am suspicious when such strong emotional motivations are involved in a scientist's work."

"Do you have a specific criticism?" Cross asked mildly.

"A number of them, actually," Morgenstern said. Liz handed Kaye a note. Kaye looked over the quickly scrawled message. *Morgenstern published twenty papers with Jackson over the last five years. She's his contact on the Americol jury.*

Kaye looked up and stuffed the note in her coat's side pocket.

"My first doubt—," Morgenstern continued.

This was the true beginning of the frontal assault. All that had come before was just the softening up. Kaye swallowed and tried to relax her neck muscles. She thought of Stella, far across the continent, wasting her time in a school run by bigots. And Mitch, driving to rejoin an old lover and colleague on a dig in the middle of nowhere.

For one very bad moment, Kaye felt she was about to lose everything, all at once. But she drew herself up, caught Cross's gaze, and focused on Morgenstern's stream of precisely phrased, mind-numbing technicalities.

20

They had left the dirt road twenty minutes ago and Mitch still had not seen anything compelling. The game was beginning to wear. He slammed on the brakes and the old truck creaked on its shocks, swayed for a moment, then stalled out. He opened the door and mopped his forehead with a paper towel from the roll he kept under his front seat, along with a squeegee to remove mud.

Dust billowed around them until a stray draft between narrow rills spirited it away.

"I give up," Mitch said, walking back to stare into Eileen's window. "What am I supposed to be looking for?"

"Let's say there's a river here."

"Hasn't been one for a few centuries, by the looks of things."

"Three thousand years, actually. Let's go back even further—say, more than ten thousand years."

"How much more?"

Eileen shrugged and made an "I'm not telling" face.

Mitch groaned, remembering all the troubles that came with ancient graves.

Eileen watched his reaction with a weary sadness that he could not riddle. "Where would you set up some sort of long-term fishing camp, say, during the fall salmon run? A camp you could come back to, year after year?"

"On hard ground above the river, not too far."

"And what do you see around here?" Eileen asked.

Mitch scanned the territory again. "Mostly mudstone and weak terraces. Some lava."

"Ash fall?"

"Yeah. Looks solid. I wouldn't want to dig it out."

"Exactly," Eileen said. "Imagine an ash fall big enough to cover everything for hundreds of miles."

"Broken flats of ash. That would have to be above this bed, of course. The river would have worn through."

"Now, how would an archaeologist find something interesting in all that confusion?"

He frowned at her. "Something trapped by ash?"

Eileen nodded encouragement.

"Animals? People?"

"What do you think?" Eileen peered through the dusty windshield of the Tahoe. She looked sadder and sadder, as if reliving an ancient tragedy.

"People, of course," Mitch said. "A camp. A fishing camp. Covered by ash." He shook his head, then mockingly smacked his forehead, *Such a dummy.*

"I'm practically giving it away," Eileen said.

Mitch turned east. He could see the dark gray-and-white layers of the old ash fall, buried under ten feet of sediments and now topped by a broken wall of pines. The ash layer looked at least four feet thick, mottled and striated. He imagined walking over to the cut and fingering the ash. Compacted by many seasons of rain, held in place by a cap of dirt and silt, it would be rock hard at first, but ultimately frangible, turning to powder if he hit it vigorously with a pick.

Big fall, a long time ago. Ten thousand and more years.

He looked north again, up a wash and away from the broad mud and gravel bed of the long-dead river, spotted with hardy brush and trees, a course now cut off even from snow melt and flash floods. Undisturbed by heavy erosion for a couple of thousand years.

"This used to be a pretty good oxbow, I'd say. Even in the Spent River heyday, there'd have been shallows where you could walk across and spear fish. You could have set up a weir in that hollow, under that boulder." He pointed to a big boulder mostly buried in old silt and ash.

Eileen smiled and nodded. "Keep going."

Mitch tapped his lips with his finger. He circled the Tahoe, waving his arms, making swooshing sounds, kicking the dirt, sniffing the air.

Eileen laughed and slapped her knees. "I needed that," she said.

"Well, shucks," Mitch said humbly. "If I'm tapping into mystic spirits, I got to act the part." He fixed his gaze on a gap that led to higher ground, above the ash. His head leaned to one side and he shook out his bad arm, which was starting to ache. He got the look of a hound on the scent. Eyes sweeping the rough ground, he walked up the wash and climbed around the boulder.

Eileen yelled, "Wait up!"

"No way," Mitch called back. "I'm on it."

And he was.

He spotted the camp ten minutes later. Eileen came up beside him, breathless. On a level plateau only thinly forested, marked by patches of gray where the deep ash layer had been exposed by erosion, he saw twelve low-slung, light-weather tents covered with netting, dead branches, and bushes uprooted from around the site. A pair of old Land Rovers had been parked together and disguised as a large boulder.

Mitch had taken a seat on a rock, staring glumly at the tents and vehicles. "Why the camouflage?" he asked.

"Satellites or remoters doing searches for the BLM and Army Corps, protecting Indian rights under NAGPRA," Eileen said. Federal interpretation of the complaints of certain Indian groups, citing NAGPRA—the Native American Graves Protection Act—had been the nemesis of American archaeologists for almost twenty years.

"Oh," Mitch said. "Why take the chance? Do we need that now? Having the feds cover your dig with concrete?" That was how the Army Corps of Engineers had protected Mitch's dig against further intrusion, more than a lifetime ago, it seemed now. He waved his hand at the site and made a face. "Not very smart, staying hidden like this, hoping to avoid the Big Boys."

"Isn't that what you did?" Eileen asked.

Mitch snorted with little humor. "It's a fair cop," he admitted.

"These are not rational times," Eileen said. "You'll understand soon enough. Don't we all need to know what it means to be human? Now more than ever? How we got to where we are, and what's going to come later?"

"What are a few old Indian bones going to tell us that we don't already know?" Mitch asked, feeling his sense of discovery start to sputter and stall.

"Would I have called you out here if that was all we had at stake?" Eileen said. "You know me better than that, Mitch Rafelson. I hope you do."

Mitch wiped his hand on his pants leg and looked over his shoulder at the long fan of the wash. They had climbed about twenty feet, but he could still see evidence of ancient bank erosion. "Big river, way back when," he said.

"It was smaller at the time of our site," Eileen said. "Just a broad, shallow stream filled with salmon. Bears used to come down and fish. One of my students found an old male on the other side. Killed by an early phase of the ash fall, stage one of the eruption."

"How long ago?" Mitch asked.

"Twenty thousand years, we're estimating. Ash gives a good potassium-argon result. We're still refining with carbon dating."

"Something more than just a dead grizzly?"

Eileen nodded like a little girl confirming that there were, indeed, more dolls in her room. "The bear was female. She was missing her skull. It had been cut off, the bones hacked through with stone axes."

"Twenty thousand years ago?"

"Yeah. So my student crossed the Spent River and started looking at other reveals. Just killing time until the Land Rover came to pick her up. She found an eroded layer of high-silica ash, right down there, about fifty meters from where the camp is now." Eileen pointed. "She almost stepped on a human toe bone mixed with some gravel. Nothing spectacular, really. But she tracked down where it had weathered out, and she found more."

"Twenty thousand years," Mitch said, still incredulous.

"That isn't the half of it," Eileen said.

Mitch took a huge leap of supposition and bent backwards, then did a little dip of disbelief. "You are not suggesting . . ."

Eileen stared at him keenly.

"You found *Neandertals*?"

Eileen shook her head, a strong *no*, then rewarded him with a teary-eyed smile that gave some hint of the distress she had gone through, at night, lying awake and thinking things over.

Mitch let out his breath. "What, then?"

"I don't want to be coy," she said primly, and took his hand. "But you're not nearly crazy enough. Come on, Mitch. Let's go meet the girls."

21

Morgenstern's questions were spot on and difficult to answer. Kaye had done her best, but she felt she had goofed a few of her responses rather badly. She felt like a mouse in a room full of cats. Jackson appeared more and more confident.

"The fertility group concludes that Kaye Rafelson is not the proper individual to continue research in ERV knock outs," Morgenstern concluded. "She has obvious bias. Her work is suspect."

A moment of silence. The accusation was not rebutted; everyone was considering their options and the map of the political minefield around them.

"All right," Cross said, her face as serene as a baby's. "I still don't know where we stand. Should we continue to fund vaccines? Should we continue to look for ways to create organisms without any viral load?" Nobody answered. "Lars?" Cross inquired.

Nilson shook his head. "I am perplexed by Dr. Morgenstern's statements. Dr. Rafelson's work looks impressive to me." He shrugged. "I know for a fact that human embryos implant in their mothers' wombs with the aid of old viral genes. Dr. Morgenstern is undoubtedly familiar with this, probably more than I."

"Very familiar," Morgenstern said confidently. "Utilization of endogenous viral syncytin genes in simian development is interesting, but I can quote dozens of papers proving there is no rhyme or reason to this random occurrence. There are even more remarkable coincidences in the long history of evolution."

"And the Temin model of viral contributions to the genome?"

"Brilliant, old, long since disproved."

Nilson pushed his scattered notes and papers into a stack, squared them, and thumped them lightly on the table top. "All my life," he said, "I have come to regard the basic principles of biology as tantamount to an act of faith. *Credo,* this I believe: that the chain of instruction arising from DNA to RNA to proteins never reverses. The Central Dogma. McClintock and Temin and Baltimore, among many others, proved the Central Dogma to be wrong, demonstrating that genes can produce products that insert copies of themselves, that retroviruses can write themselves to DNA as proviruses and stay there for many millions of years."

Kaye saw Jackson regarding her with his sharp gray eyes. He tapped his pencil silently. They both knew Nilson was grandstanding and that this would not impress Cross.

"Forty years ago, we missed the boat," Nilson continued. "I was one of those who opposed Temin's ideas. It took us years to recognize the potential of retroviruses to wreak havoc, and when HIV arrived, we were unprepared. We did not have a crazy, creative bouquet of theories to choose from; we had killed them all, or ignored them, much the same. Tens of millions of our patients suffered for our own stubborn pride. Howard Temin was right; *I* was wrong."

"I would not call it faith, I'd call it process and reason," Jackson interrupted, tapping his pencil harder. "It's kept us from making even more horrible blunders, like Lysenko."

Nilson was having none of this. "Ah, get thee behind me, Lysenko! Faith, reason, dogma, all add up to stubborn ignorance. Thirty years before that, we had missed the boat with Barbara McClintock and her jumping genes. And how many others? How many discouraged postdocs and interns and researchers? It was prideful, I see now, to hide our weaknesses and spite our fundamentalist enemies. We asserted our infallibility before school boards, politicians, corporations, investors, patients, whomever we thought might challenge us. We were arrogant. We were *men*, Ms. Cross. Biology was an incredible and archaic patriarchy with many of the aspects of an old boy network: secret signs, passwords, rituals of indoctrination. We held down, for a time at least, some of our best and brightest. No excuses. And once again we failed to see the coming juggernaut. HIV rolled over us, and then SHEVA rolled over us. It turned out we knew nothing whatsoever about sex and evolutionary variation, *nothing*. Yet some of us still act as if we know it all. We attempt to assess blame and escape our failures. Well, we *have* failed. We have failed to see the truth. These reports sum up our failure."

Cross seemed bemused. "Thank you, Lars. Heartfelt, I'm sure. But I still want to know, *where do we go from here?*" She hammered her fist on the table with each emphatic word.

Still stuck in his chair in the far corner, pushed back from the table, wearing his trademark gray jacket and yarmulke, Maurie Herskovitz raised his hand. "I think we have a clear-cut problem in epistemology," he said.

Cross squeezed her eyes shut and pressed the bridge of her nose. "Oh, please, Maurie, anything but *that*."

"Hear me out, Marge. Dr. Jackson tried to create a positive, a vaccine against SHEVA and other ERV. He failed. If, as Dr. Morgenstern accuses, Dr. Rafelson came to Americol to demonstrate that no babies would be born if we suppressed their genomic viruses, she has made her point. None have been born. Regardless of her motivations, her work is thorough. It is scientific. Dr. Jackson continues to put forth an hypothesis that the results of his labors seem to have disproved."

"Maurie, *where do we go from here?*" Cross repeated, her cheeks pinking.

Herskovitz lifted his hands. "If I could, I would put Dr. Rafelson in charge of viral research at Americol. But that would only be to curse her with more managerial duties and less time in the laboratory. So, I would give her what she needs to conduct her research on her own terms, and let Dr. Jackson focus on what he is best suited for." He peered happily at Jackson. "Administration. Marge, you and I can make sure he does it right." Herskovitz then looked at everyone around the room, trying hard to appear serious.

The faces at the table were stony.

Jackson's skin had turned a bluish shade of ivory. Kaye worried for a second that he might be on the verge of a heart attack. He ticked his pen in a brisk shave-and-a-haircut-two-bits. "I welcome, as always, Dr. Nilson's and Dr. Herskovitz's opinions. But I don't think Americol wants a woman who may be losing her mind in charge of this particular area of research."

Cross leaned back as if caught in a cold wind. Morgenstern's watery gaze finally settled on Jackson with an attitude of dread expectancy.

"Dr. Rafelson, last night you spent some hours with our chief radiologist in the imaging lab. I noticed the billing request when I was picking up results from radiology this morning. I asked what the billing was for, and I was told that you were looking for God."

Kaye managed to hold on to her pencil and not let it drop to the floor. Slowly, she brought her hands up to the tabletop. "I was having an unusual experience," she said. "I wanted to find out what the cause might be."

"You told the radiologist you felt God was inside your head. You had been having these experiences for some time, ever since the removal of your daughter by Emergency Action."

"Yes," Kaye said.

"Seeing God?"

"I've been experiencing certain psychological states," Kaye said.

"Oh, come on, we've just been lectured by Dr. Nilson about truth and honesty. Will you deny your God three times, Dr. Rafelson?"

"What happened was private and has no influence on my work. I am appalled that it should be brought up at this meeting."

"None of this is relevant? Other than the expense, some seven thousand dollars of unauthorized tests?"

Liz seemed thunderstruck.

"I'm willing to pay for that," Kaye said.

Jackson lifted a paper-clipped set of invoices and rippled it in the air. "I see no evidence of your picking up the bill."

Cross's calm look was replaced by indignant irritation—but at whom, Kaye could not tell. "Is this true?"

Kaye stammered, "It is a personal state of mind, of scientific interest. Almost half—"

"Where will you find God next, Kaye?" Jackson asked. "In your cunning viruses, shuffling around like holy ratchets, obeying rules only you can understand, explaining everything you can't? If God was my mentor, I'd be thrilled, it would all be so easy, but I am less fortunate. I have to rely on *reason*. Still, it is an honor to work with someone who can simply ask a higher authority where truth waits to be discovered."

"Astonishing," Nilson said. In the corner, Herskovitz sat up. His smile appeared cut in plaster.

"It is not like that," Kaye said.

"That's enough, Robert," Cross said.

Jackson had not moved since beginning his accusation. He sat half-slumped in his chair. "None of us can afford to give up our scientific principles," he said. "Especially not now."

Cross stood abruptly. Nilson and Morgenstern looked at Jackson, then at Cross, and got to their feet, pushing back their chairs.

"I have what I need," Cross said.

"Dr. Rafelson, is God behind evolution?" Jackson called out. "Does he hold all the answers, does he jerk us around like puppets on a string?"

"No," Kaye said, eyes unfocused.

"Are you really sure, now, in a way none of the rest of us can be, with your *special knowledge*?"

"Robert, that is enough!" Cross roared. Seldom had any of them heard Cross when she was angry, and her voice was painful in its crackling intensity. She let the stack of papers in her hands slip back to the table and spill onto the floor. She glared at Jackson, then shook her fists at the ceiling. "Absolutely unbelievable!"

"Astonishing," Nilson repeated, much quieter.

"I apologize," Jackson said, not at all chastened. His color had returned. He looked vigorous and healthy.

"This is over," Cross declared. "Everyone go home. Now."

Liz helped Kaye from the room. Jackson did not deign to look at them as they left.

"What in hell is going on?" Liz asked Kaye in an undertone as they walked toward the elevator.

"I'm fine," Kaye said.

"What in hell was La Robert on about?"

Kaye did not know where to begin.

22

Eileen escorted Mitch down the slope on a crude stairway made of boards hammered into the dirt. As they walked through a copse of pines and up a short embankment, gaining a closer view of the camp, Mitch saw that a large excavation of about ten thousand square feet, L-shaped and covered by two joined Quonset huts, had been hidden by brush arranged over netting. From the air, the entire site would be little more than a smudge in the landscape.

"This looks like a terrorist base, Eileen. How do you conceal the heat signature?" he asked half-seriously.

"It's going to terrorize North American anthropology," Eileen said. "That's for sure."

"Now you're scaring me," Mitch said. "Do I have to sign an NDA or something?"

"I trust you," Eileen said. She rested a hand on his shoulder.

"Show me now, Eileen, or just let me go home."

"Where *is* home?" she asked.

"My truck," Mitch said.

"That heap?"

Mitch mockingly implored forgiveness with his broad-fingered hands.

Eileen asked, "Do you believe in providence?"

"No," Mitch said. "I believe in what I see with my eyes."

"That may take a while. We're into high-tech survey for now. We haven't actually pulled up the specimens. We have a benefactor. He's spending lots of money to help us. I think you've heard of him. Here's his point man now."

Mitch saw a tent flap open about fifty feet away. A lean, red-headed figure poked out, stood, and brushed dust from his hands. He shaded his eyes and looked around, then spotted the pair on the bluff and lifted his chin in greeting. Eileen waved.

Oliver Merton jogged toward them across the pale, rugged ground.

Merton was the science journalist who had dogged Kaye's career and footsteps during the SHEVA discoveries. Mitch had never been sure whether to look on Merton as a friend or an opportunist or just a damned fine journalist. He was probably all three.

"Mitch!" Merton called. "How grand to see you again!"

Merton stuck out his hand. Mitch shook it firmly. The writer's hand was warm and dry and confident. "My god, all Eileen told me was she was going to fetch someone with experience. How absolutely, bloody appropriate. Mr. Daney will be delighted."

"You always seem to get there ahead of me," Mitch said.

Merton shaded his eyes against the sun. "They're having a kind of midafternoon powwow, if that's the right word, back in the tents. Bit of a knockdown, really. Eileen, I think they're going to decide to uncover one of the girls and take a direct look. You have perfect timing, Mitch. I've had to wait days to see anything but videos."

"It's a committee decision?" Mitch asked, turning to Eileen.

"I couldn't stand having all of this on my shoulders," Eileen confessed. "We have a fine team. Very argumentative. And Daney's money works wonders. Good beer at night."

"Is Daney here?" Mitch asked Merton.

"Not yet," Merton said. "He's shy and he hates discomfort." They hunkered their shoulders against a gritty swirl blowing up the gully. Merton wiped his eyes with a handkerchief. "Not his kind of place at all."

The wide, bush-studded net flapped in the afternoon breeze, dropping bits of dry branch and leaf on them as they stooped to enter the pit. The excavation stretched about forty feet north, then branched east to form an L. Mottled sunlight filtered through the net. They descended four meters on a metal ladder to the floor of the pit.

Aluminum beams crossed the pit at two-meter intervals. Rises in the pit, like little mesas, were topped with wire grids. Over the mesas, some of the beams supported white boxes with lenses and other apparatus jutting from the bottoms. As Mitch watched, the closest box slowly railed right a few centimeters and resumed humming.

"Side scanner?" he asked.

Eileen nodded. "We've scraped off most of the mud and we're peeking through the final layer of tephra. We can see about sixty centimeters into the hard pack." She walked ahead.

The Quonset structure—arched wooden beams covered by sheets of stamped, ribbed steel and a few milky sheets of fiberglass—sheltered the long stroke of the L. Sunlight poured through the fiberglass sheeting. They walked over flat, hard dirt and haphazard cobbles of river rock between the high, irregular walls. Eileen let Mitch go first, ascending a dirt staircase to the left of a flat-topped rise being surveyed by two more white boxes.

"I don't dare walk under these damned things," Eileen said. "I have enough skin blotches as is."

Mitch knelt beside the mesa to look at alternating layers of mud and tephra, capped by sand and silt. He saw an ash fall—tephra—followed by a lahar, a fast-moving slurry of hot mud made of ash, dirt, and glacier melt. The sand and silt had arrived over time. At the bottom of the mesa, he saw more alternating layers of ash, mud, and river deposits: A deep book going back far longer than recorded history.

"Computers do some really big math and show us a picture of what's down there," Eileen said. "We actually debated whether to dig any deeper or just cover it over again and submit the videos and sensor readings. But I guess the committee is going for a traditional invasion."

Mitch moved his hand in a sweeping motion. "Ash came down for several days," he said. "Then a lahar swept down the river basin. Up here, it slopped over but didn't carry off the bodies."

"Very *good*," Merton said, genuinely impressed.

"Want to see our etchings?" Eileen asked.

Eileen unrolled a display sheet in the conference tent and tuned it to her wrist computer. "Still getting used to all this tech," she murmured. "It's wonderful, when it works."

Merton watched over Mitch's shoulder. Two women in their thirties, dressed in jeans and short-sleeved khaki shirts, stood at the rear of the long, narrow tent, debating in soft but angry voices. Eileen did not see fit to introduce them, which clued Mitch that she was not the only high-powered anthropologist working the dig.

The screen glowed faintly in the tent's half-light. Eileen told the computer to run a slide show.

"These are from yesterday," she said. "We've done around twenty-seven complete scans. Redundancy upon redundancy, just to be sure we're not making it up. Oliver says he's never seen a more frightened bunch of scientists."

"I haven't," Merton affirmed.

The first image showed the pale ghost of a skeleton curled in fetal position, surrounded by what looked like sheets of grass matting, a few stones, and a cloud of pebbles. "Our first. We're calling her Charlene. As you can see, she's fairly modern *Homo sap*. Prominent chin, relatively high forehead. But here's the tomographic reconstruction from our multiple sweeps." A second image came up and showed a dolichocephalic, or long-headed, skull. Eileen told the computer to rotate this image.

Mitch scowled. "Looks Australian," he said.

"She probably is," Eileen said. "About twenty years of age. Trapped and asphyxiated by hot mud. There are five other skeletons, one close to Charlene, the others clustered about four meters away. All are female. No infants. And no sign of males. The grass matting has decayed, of course. Just molds remain. We have a shadow mold around Charlene, a cast of fine silt from seepage through the mud and ash showing the outlines of her body. Here's a tomographic image of what that cast would look like, if we could manage to pry it loose from the tephra and the rest of the overburden."

A distorted ghost of a head, neck, and shoulders appeared and rotated smoothly on the display sheet. Mitch felt odd, standing in a tent that would have been familiar to Roy Chapman Andrews or even to Darwin himself, while staring down at the rolled-out sheet of the computer display.

He asked Eileen to rotate the image of Charlene again.

As the image swung around and around, he began to discern facial features, a closed eye, a blob of ear, hair matted and curled, a hint of cooked and distorted flesh slumped from the back of the skull.

"Pretty awful," Merton said.

"They suffocated before the heat got to them," Eileen said. "I hope they did, anyway."

"Early-stage Tierra del Fuegan?" Mitch asked.

"That's what most of us think. From the Australian migration out of South and Central America."

Such migrations had been charted more and more often in the last fifteen years; Australian skeletons and associated artifacts found near the tip of South America had been dated to older than thirty thousand years BP, before the present.

The two other women walked around them to reach the exit, as serious and unsocial as porcupines. A plump, red-faced woman a few years younger than Eileen held the flap open for them then stepped in and stood before Mitch. "Is this the famous Mitch Rafelson?" she asked Eileen.

"Mitch, meet Connie Fitz. I told her I'd bring you here."

"Delighted to meet you, after all these years." Fitz wiped her hands on a dusty towel hanging from her belt before shaking hands. "Have you showed him the good stuff?"

"We're getting there."

"Best picture of Gertie is on sweep 21," Fitz advised.

"I know," Eileen said testily. "It's my show."

"Sorry. I'm the mother hen," Fitz said. "The others are still arguing."

"Spare me," Eileen said. Another image cast their faces in a pale greenish light.

"Say hello to Gertie," Merton said. He glanced up at Mitch, waiting to see his reaction.

Mitch poked the surface of the screen, making the light pool under his finger. He looked up, on the edge of anger. "You're kidding me. This is a joke."

"No joke," Merton said.

Eileen magnified the image. Then, clearing his throat, Mitch asked, "Fraud?"

"What do you think?" Eileen asked.

"They're in close association? Not in different layers?"

Eileen nodded. "They were buddies, probably traveling together. No infants, but as you can see, Gertie was maybe fifteen or sixteen, and she was probably gravid when the ash covered her."

"Either that or she ate babies," Merton said. Another twitch of the lip from Eileen.

"Oliver's on borrowed time," Fitz said.

"Matriarchy," Merton accused, deadpan.

The tent suddenly seemed very stuffy. Mitch would have sat down had there been a convenient chair. "She looks early. Different from Charlene. Is she a hybrid?" he asked.

"No one's willing to say," Eileen replied. "You'll like our late-night debates. A few weeks back, when I wanted you to join us, everyone shouted me down. Now, we're all at each other's throats, and Oliver, I'm told, convinced Daney it was time."

"I did," Merton said.

"Personally, I'm glad you're here," Eileen added.

"I'm not," Fitz said. "If the feds find out about you, if there's any publicity at all, we're NAGPRA toast."

"Tell me more, Mitch," Eileen suggested.

Mitch massaged the back of his neck and for the ninth time watched the image of the skull grow and rotate. "Skull seems compressed. She's long-headed, more even than the Australian. There's a flint implement near her hand, and she's carrying some sort of grass bag over her shoulder, if I'm not mistaken."

"You're not."

"Filled with what looks like bush or small tree roots."

"Desperation diet," Fitz said.

"Maybe that was just her assignment, gathering roots for the stone soup."

Merton looked puzzled. Eileen explained stone soup.

"How colonial," Merton said.

"Ever the B-movie Brit, aren't you?" Fitz said.

"Please, children," Eileen warned.

"Relatively tall, taller than Charlene, maybe, and pretty robust, heavy boned," Mitch continued, trying to talk himself out of what he was see-ing. "Sloping forehead, mid-sized to small brain case, but the face is fairly flat. Impressive supraorbital torus. A bit of a sagittal keel, even an occipital torus. I'd love to get a better look at the incisors."

"Shovel-shaped," Eileen said.

Mitch rubbed his limp hand to still the tingling and looked at the others as if all of them might be crazy. "Gertie is much too early. She looks like Broken Hill 1. She's *Homo erectus*."

"Obviously," Fitz said with a sniff.

"They've been extinct for more than three hundred thousand years," Mitch said.

"Apparently not," Eileen said.

Mitch laughed and stood back with a snap as if he had been leaning over a wasp that had suddenly taken flight. "Jesus."

"Is that it?" Eileen asked. "Is that the most you can say?" She was kid-ding, but her tone had an edge.

"You've had longer to get used to it," Mitch said.

"Who says we're used to it?" Eileen asked.

"What about the fetus?"

"Too early and too little detail," Fitz said. "It's probably a lost cause."

"I'm thinking we should drive a tube, take a thin core sample, and PCR mitochondrial DNA from the remaining integuments," Merton said.

"Dreamer," Fitz said. "They're twenty thousand years old. Besides, the lahar cooked them."

"Not to mush," Merton countered.

"Think like a scientist, not a journalist."

"Shh," Eileen said in deference to Mitch, who was still staring at the rolled-out screen, mesmerized. "Here's what we have on the central group," she said, and paged through another set of ghostly images. "Gertie and Charlene are outliers. These four are Hildegard, Natasha, Sonya, and Penelope. Hildegard was probably the oldest, in her late thirties and already racked with arthritis."

Hildegard, Natasha, and Sonya were clearly *Homo sapiens*. Penelope was another *Homo erectus*. They lay entwined as if they had died hugging each other, a mandala of bones, elegant in their sad way.

"Some of the hardliners are calling this a flood deposition of unassociated remains," Fitz said.

"How would *you* answer them?" Eileen challenged Mitch, reverting to his teacher of old.

Mitch was still trying to remember to breathe. "They're fully articulated," he said. "They have their arms around each other. They don't lie at odd angles, tossed together. This is in no way a flood deposit."

Mitch was startled to watch Fitz and Eileen hug each other. "These women *knew* each other," Eileen agreed, tears of relief dripping down her cheeks. "They worked together, traveled together. A nomadic band, caught in camp by a burp from Mount Hood. I can feel it."

"Are you with us?" Fitz asked, her eyes bright and suspicious.

"*Homo erectus*. North America. Twenty thousand years ago," Mitch said. Then, frowning, he asked, "Where are the males?"

"To hell with that," Fitz fumed. "Are you with us?"

"Yeah," Mitch said, sensing the tension and Eileen's discomfort at his hesitation. "I'm with you." Mitch put his good arm around Eileen's shoulders, sharing the emotion.

Oliver Merton clasped his hands like a boy anticipating Christmas. "You realize that this could be a political bombshell," he said.

"For the Indians?" Fitz asked.

"For us all."

"How so?"

Merton grinned like a fiend. "Two different species, living together. It's as if someone's teaching us a lesson."

23

Dicken showed his pass at the Pathogenics main gate. The three young, burly guards there—machine pistols slung over their shoulders—waved him through. He drove the cart to the valet area and presented the pass for his car.

"Going for a drink," he told the serious-faced middle-aged woman as she inspected his release.

"Did I ask?" She gave him a seasoned, challenging smile.

"No," he admitted.

"Don't tell us anything," she advised. "We have to report every little thing. Vodka, white wine, or local beer?"

Dicken must have looked flustered.

"I'm joking," she said. "I'll be back in a few minutes."

She returned driving his leased Malibu, adapted for handicapped drivers.

"Nice setup, all the stuff on the wheel," she said. "Took me a bit to figure it out."

He accepted the inspection pass, made sure it was completely filled out—there had been some trouble with such things yesterday—and slipped it into a special holder in the visor. The sun was lingering over the rocky gray-and-brown hills beyond the main Pathogenics complex. "Thanks," he said.

"Enjoy," the valet said.

He took the main road out of the complex and drove through rush hour traffic, following the familiar track into Albuquerque, then pulled into the parking lot of the Marriott. Crickets were starting up and the air was tolerable. The hotel rose over the parking lot in one graceless pillar, tan and white against the dark blue night sky, proudly illuminated by big floodlights set around stretches of deep green lawn. Dicken walked into a low-slung restaurant wing, visited the men's room, then came out and turned left to enter the bar.

The bar was just starting to crowd. Two regulars sat at the bar—a woman in her late thirties, looking as if life and her partners had ridden her hard, and a sympathetic elderly man with a long nose and close-set eyes.

The worn-down woman was laughing at something the long-nosed man had just said.

Dicken sat on a tall stool by a high, tiny table beside a fake plant in an adobe pot. He ordered a Michelob when the waitress got around to him, then sat watching the people come and go, nursing his beer and feeling miserably out of place. Nobody was smoking, but the air smelled cold and stale, with a tang of beer and liquor.

Dicken reached into his pocket and withdrew his hand, then, under the table, unfolded a red serviette. He palmed the serviette over the damp napkin on the table, also red, and left it there.

At eight, after an hour and a half, his beer almost gone and the waitress starting to look predatory, he pushed off the stool, disgusted.

Someone touched his shoulder and Dicken jumped.

"How does James Bond do it?" asked a jovial fellow in a green sport jacket and beige slacks. With his balding pate, round, red Santa nose, lime green golf shirt bulging at the belly, and belt tightened severely to reclaim some girth, the middle-aged man looked like a tourist with a snootful. He smelled like one, too.

"Do what?" Dicken asked.

"Get the babes when they all know they're just going to die." The balding man surveyed Dicken with a jaundiced, watery eye. "I can't figure it."

"Do I know you?" Dicken asked gravely.

"I've got friends watching every porthole. We know the local spooks, and this place is not as haunted as some."

Dicken put down his beer. "I don't know what you're talking about," he said.

"Is Dr. Jurie your peer?" the man asked softly, pulling up another stool.

Dicken knocked his stool over in his haste to get up. He left the bar quickly, on the lookout for anyone too clean-cut, too vigilant.

The balding man shrugged, reached across the table to grab a handful of peanuts, then crumpled Dicken's red serviette and slipped it into his pocket.

Dicken drove away from the hotel and parked briefly on a side street beside a used car lot. He was breathing heavily. "Christ, Christ, Cheee-rist," he said softly, waiting for his heart to slow.

His cell phone rang and he jumped, then flipped it open.

"Dr. Dicken?"

"Yes." He tried to sound coldly professional.

"This is Laura Bloch. I believe we have an appointment."

Dicken drove up behind the blue Chevrolet and switched off his engine and lights. The desert surrounding Tramway Road was quiet and the air was warm and still; city lights illuminated low, spotty cumulus clouds to the south. A door swung open on the Chevrolet and a man in a dark suit got out and walked back to peer into his open window.

"Dr. Dicken?"

Dicken nodded.

"I'm Special Agent Bracken, Secret Service. ID, please?"

Dicken produced his Georgia driver's license.

"Federal ID?"

Dicken held out his hand and the agent whisked a scanner over the back. He had been chipped six years ago. The agent glanced at the scanner display and nodded. "We're good," he said. "Laura Bloch is in the car. Please proceed forward and take a seat in the rear."

"Who was the guy in the bar?" Dicken asked.

Special Agent Bracken shook his head. "I'm sure I haven't the faintest idea, sir."

"Joke?" Dicken asked.

Bracken smiled. "He was the best we could do on short notice. Good people with experience are kind of in short supply now, if you get my meaning. Slim pickings for honest folks."

"Yeah," Dicken said. Special Agent Bracken opened the door and Dicken walked to the Chevrolet.

Bloch's appearance was a surprise to him. He had never seen pictures and at first he was not impressed. With her prominent eyes and fixed expression, she resembled a keen little pug. She held out her hand and they shook before Dicken slid in beside her on the rear seat, lifting his leg to clear the door frame.

"Thank you for meeting with me," she said.

"Part of the assignment, I guess."

"I'm curious why Jurie asked for you," Bloch said. "Any theories?"

"Because I'm the best there is," Dicken said.

"Of course."

"And he wants to keep me where he can see me."

"Does he know?"

"That NIH is keeping an eye on him? No doubt. That I'm speaking with you, now, I certainly hope not."

Bloch shrugged. "Matters little in the long run."

"I should get back soon. I've been gone a little too long for comfort, probably."

"This will just take a few minutes. I've been told to brief you."

"Who told you?"

"Mark Augustine said you should be prepped before things start happening."

"Say hello to Mark," Dicken said.

"Our man in Damascus," Bloch said.

"Beg your pardon? I don't get the reference."

"Saw the light on the road to Damascus." She regarded Dicken with one eye half closed. "He's being very helpful. He tells us Emergency Action is soon going to be forced to do some questionable things. Their scientific underpinnings are coming under severe scrutiny. They have to hit pay dirt within a certain window of public fear, and that window may be closing. The public is getting tired of standing on tiptoes for the likes of Rachel Browning. Browning has put all her hopes on Sandia Pathogenics. So far, she's keeping the Hill off her back by appealing to fear, national security, and national defense, all wrapped in tight secrecy. But it's Mark's belief that Pathogenics will have to violate some pretty major laws to get what they want, even should it exist."

"What laws?"

"Let's leave that open for now. What I'm here to tell you is that the political winds are about to shift. The White House is sending out feelers to Congress on rescinding Emergency Action's blanket mandate. Cases are coming up in the Supreme Court."

"They'll support EMAC. Six to three."

"Right," Bloch said. "But based on our polling, we're pretty sure that's going to backfire. What's the science look like so far, from the Sandia perspective?"

"Interesting. Nothing very useful to Browning. But I'm not privy to what's going on with all the samples brought in from Arizona—"

"The Sable Mountain School," Bloch said.

"That's the main source."

"Goddamned bastard is consistent."

Dicken sat back and waited for Bloch's face to clear an expression of angry disgust, then concluded, "There's no evidence that social interaction or stress is causing viral recombination. Not in SHEVA kids."

"So why is Jurie persisting?"

"Momentum, mostly. And fear. Real fear. Jurie is convinced that puberty is going to do the trick. That, and pregnancy."

"Jesus," Bloch said. "What do you think?"

"I doubt it. But it's still a possibility."

"Do they suspect you're working with outside interests? Beyond NIH, I mean?"

"Of course," Dicken said. "They'd be fools not to."

"So, what is it with Jurie—a death wish?"

Dicken shook his head. "Calculated risk. He thinks I could be useful, but he'll bring me into the loop only when it's necessary and not a second before. Meanwhile, he keeps me busy doing far-out stuff."

"How do the others feel about what Pathogenics is doing?"

"Nervous."

Bloch clenched her teeth.

Dicken watched her jaw muscles work. "Sorry not to be more helpful," he said.

"I will never understand scientists," she murmured.

"I don't understand people," Dicken said. "Anybody."

"Fair enough. All right," Bloch said. "We have about a week and a half. Supreme Court is scheduled to release their decision on *Remick v. the state of Ohio*. Senator Gianelli wants to be ready when the White House is forced to cut a deal."

Dicken fixed her gaze and raised his hand. "May I have my say?"

"Of course," Bloch said.

"No half measures. Bring them down all at once. Tell the big boys Department of Health and Human Services needs to revoke EMAC's blanket national security exception to 45 CFR 46, protection of human subjects, and exceptions to 21 CFR parts 50 and . . . amended, what is it, 312? 321? Informed consent waiver for viral national emergency," Dicken said. "Are they going to do that?"

Bloch smiled, impressed. "21 CFR 50.24 actually applies. I don't know. We've got some institutional review boards coming over to our side, but it's a slow process. EMAC still funds a boatload of research. Get us whatever you can for ammunition. I don't want to sound crass, but we need outrage, Dr. Dicken. We need more than just pitiful bones in a drawer."

Dicken tugged nervously on the door handle.

"We're on the knife edge of public opinion here. It could go either way. Understand?" Bloch added.

"I know what you need," Dicken said. "I'm just disgusted that it's gone this far, and we've become so difficult to shock."

"We don't claim any moral high ground, but neither the senator nor I are in this for political advancement," Bloch said. "The senator's approval rating is at an all-time low, thirty-five percent, twenty percent undecided, and it's because he's outspoken on this issue. I'm beginning to take a dislike to our constituents, Dr. Dicken. I really am."

Bloch offered him her small, pale hand. He paused, looking into her steady black eyes, then shook it and returned to his car.

Special Agent Bracken closed his door for him and leaned down to window level. "Some friends in the New Mexico State Police tell me that citizens around here aren't happy about what's going on at Sandia," he said. "They—the police, and maybe the citizens—plan to engage in some civil disobedience, if you know what I mean. Not much we can do about it, and damned few details. Just a heads up."

"Thanks," Dicken said.

Bracken tapped the roof of the car. "Free to go, Dr. Dicken."

24

ARIZONA

Stella awoke before dawn and stared at the acoustic tile ceiling over her bunk. She was instantly vigilant, aware of her surroundings. The dormitory was quiet but she smelled something funny in the air: an absence. Then she realized she couldn't smell anything at all. A peculiar sensation of claustrophobia came over her. For a moment, she thought she saw a pattern of dark colors form a circle over her bunk. Little flashes of red and green, like distant glowing insects, illuminated the circle, became tiny faces. She blinked, and the circle, the lights, the faces faded into the shadowy void of the ceiling tiles.

Stella felt a chill, as if she had seen a ghost.

Her thighs were damp. She reached under the covers with her hand and brought up her finger, curling it to keep the sheet clean. The finger was tipped with a smudge of black in the moonlight shining through the windows. Stella made a little sound, not of fear—she knew what it probably was, Kaye had explained it years ago to her—but of deeper recognition.

Just that afternoon, she had seen spots of blood on a toilet lid in the bathroom. Not her own; some other girl's. She had wondered if somebody had cut herself.

Now she knew.

With a sigh, she wiped the blood on her nightgown, beneath the fabric of her short sleeve, then thought for a moment, and touched the finger to the tip of her tongue. The sensation—taste was not really the right word—was not entirely pleasant. She had done something that seemed to violate her body's rules. But slowly her sense of smell returned. The sensation on her tongue lingered, sharp with an undertone of mystery.

I'm not ready, she thought. And then remembered what Kaye had told her: *You won't believe you're ready. The body propels us.*

She lifted the sheets with her knees and then let them drop, wafting her own scent through the small gaps around her midriff. She smelled different, not unpleasant, a little sour, like yogurt. She liked her earlier smell better. She recognized it. This new smell was not welcome. She did not need any more difficulties.

I don't care. I'm just not ready.

She shivered suddenly, as if a ropey loop of emotion had been pulled, rasping, through her body, then felt a sudden contraction of muscles around her abdomen, a cascade of unexpected pleasure. The tip of her tongue seemed to expand. Her entire body flushed. She did not know whether she was dreaming or what was happening.

Stella kicked back the covers, then rolled on her side, wincing at the stickiness, wanting to get up and get clean, wash away the new smell. Slowly, as the minutes passed, she relaxed, closed her eyes. *Natural stuff. Not so bad. Mother told me.*

Her nostrils flared. Currents of slow air moved around the dormitory, propelled by drafts through the doorways, cracks in the ceiling; at night, it was possible sometimes for girls to scent and communicate, reassure each other, without getting out of bed. Stella was reasonably familiar with the circulation patterns of the building at different hours and with the wind outside coming from different directions.

Around the room, she smelled the other girls on their bunks and heard them moving quietly in the bars and shadows of moonlight. Some of them moaned. One and then another coughed and softly called out her friends' names.

Celia rolled out of the bottom bunk and stood up beside Stella. Her eyes were large in the dim light, her face a moving blob of paleness framed by wild black hair. "Did you feel that?" she whispered.

"Shh," Stella said.

Felice's face joined Celia's beside Stella's bed.

"I think it's okay," Stella said, almost too softly for them to hear.

"We're getting-KUK our first periods," Celia said.

"All *together*?" Felice asked, squeaking.

Someone in another bunk heard and giggled.

"Shh," Stella insisted, wrinkling her face in warning. She sat up and looked along the rows of bunks. Some of the younger girls—a year or more younger—were still asleep. Then, her back tingling, Stella looked up at the video cameras mounted in the rafters. Moonlight reflected from the linoleum floor glinted in their tiny plastic eyes.

Four girls left their bunks and padded into the bathroom, walking bowlegged.

Useless to hide it, Stella thought. *They're going to know.*

And they would be even more frightened. She could predict that easily and with assurance. Everything different frightened the humans, and this was going to be very different.

25

OREGON

Eileen set the Coleman lantern on a metal table and laid out the cold dinner: a nearly frozen loaf of white bread, Oscar Meyer bologna in a squat, rubbery cylinder, American cheese, and a chilled, half-eaten tin of Spam. A Tupperware box, yellow with age, contained cut celery stalks. She positioned two apples, three tangerines, and two cans of Coors beside this assortment. "Want to see the wine list?" she asked.

"Beer will do. Breakfast of diggers," Mitch said. The plastic roof of the hut over the long reach of the L-shaped excavation rattled in the wind rolling down the old riverbed.

Eileen sat in the canvas seat of her camp chair and let out her breath in a sigh that was halfway to a shriek. But for them and the still-hidden bones, the excavation was empty. It was almost midnight. "I am *dead*," she proclaimed. "I can't take this anymore. Dig 'em out, don't dig 'em out, keep your cool when the academics start to scrap about emergence violations. The whole goddamned human race is so *primitive*."

Mitch cracked his can and tossed back a long gulp. The beer, almost tasteless but for a prolonged fizz, satisfied him intensely. He put down the can and picked up a slice of cheese, then prepared to peel back the wrapping. He turned it into a grand gesture. Eileen watched as he lifted the slice, rotated it on tripod fingers, and then, using his teeth, delicately lifted and pulled off the intercalary paper. He glanced at her with narrowed eyes and raised one thick eyebrow. "Expose 'em," he said.

"Think so?" Eileen asked.

"Give me that old-time revelation. I'd rather see them personally than trust future generations to do it better. But that's just me." The beer and exhaustion both relaxed Mitch and made him philosophical. "Bring them into the light. Rebirth," he said. "The Indians are right. This is a sacred moment. There should be ceremonies. We should be appeasing their troubled spirits, and our own. Oliver is right. They're here to teach us."

Eileen sniffed. "Some Indians don't want their theories contradicted," she said. "They'd rather live with fairy tales."

"The Indians in Kumash gave us shelter when Kaye was pregnant. They still refuse to hand their SHEVA kids over to Emergency Action. I've become more understanding of anybody the U.S. government has repeatedly lied to." Mitch raised his beer in toast. "Here's to the Indians."

Eileen shook her head. "Ignorance is ignorance. We can't afford to hang on to our childhood blankies. We're big boys and girls."

Mostly girls, Mitch thought. "Are anthropologists any more likely to see what's under their noses?"

Eileen pursed her lips. "Well, no," she said. "We've already got two in camp who insist these can't possibly be *Homo erectus*. They're creating a tall, stocky, thick-browed variety of homo sap on their laptops even as we speak. We're having a hell of a time convincing them to keep their mouths shut. Ignorant bitches, both of them. But don't tell anybody I said so."

"Absolutely," Mitch said.

Eileen had finished assembling a Spam and American cheese sandwich, with two stalks of celery sticking out like lunate Gumby feet from the pressed layers of perfect crust. She bit into a corner and chewed thoughtfully.

Mitch wasn't particularly hungry, not that he minded the food. He had eaten much worse on previous sites—including a meal of roasted grubs on toast.

"Was it another SHEVA episode?" Eileen mused. "A massive leap between *Homo erectus* and *Homo sapiens*?"

"I wouldn't think so," Mitch said. "A little too radical even for SHEVA."

Eileen's speculative gaze rose beyond the rattling plastic roof. "Men," she said. "Men behaving badly."

"Uh-oh," Mitch said. "Here it comes."

"Men raiding other groups, taking prisoners. Not very choosy. Gathering up all the females with the appropriately satisfying orifices. Females only, whomever and whatever they might be."

"You think our absent males were raiders and rapists?" Mitch asked.

"Would *you* date a *Homo erectus*? I mean, if you weren't at the absolute bottom of any social hierarchy?"

Mitch thought of the mother in the cave in the Alps, more than a lifetime ago, and her loyal husband. "Maybe they were more gentle."

"Psychic flower children, Mitch?" Eileen asked. "I say these gals were all captives and they were abandoned when the volcano blew. Anything else is pure William Golding bullshit." Eileen was pushing the matter deliberately, playing both proponent and devil's advocate, trying to clear her head, or possibly his.

"I suppose the *Homo erectus* members of the group might have been slaves or servants—captives," Mitch said. "But I'm not so sure social life was that sophisticated back then, or that there were such fine gradations of status. My guess is they were traveling together. For protection, maybe, like different species of herd animals on the veldt. As equals. Obviously, they liked each other enough to die in each other's arms."

"Mixed species band? Does that fit anything in your experience with the higher apes?"

Mitch had to admit it did not. Baboons and chimps played together when they were young, but adult chimps ate baby baboons and monkeys when they could catch them. "Culture matters more than skin color," he said.

"But *this* gap . . . I just don't see it being bridgeable. It's too huge."

"Maybe we're tainted by recent history. Where were you born, Eileen?"

"Savannah, Georgia. You know that."

"Kaye and I lived in Virginia." Mitch let the thought hang there for a moment, trying to find a delicate way to phrase it.

"Plantation propaganda from my slave-owner ancestors, my thrice-great grandpappy, has tainted the entire last three hundred years. Is that what you're suggesting?" Eileen asked, lips curling in a duelist's smile, savoring a swift and jabbing return. "What a goddamned Yankee thing to say."

"We know so little about what we're capable of," Mitch continued. "We are creatures of culture. There are other ways to think of this ensemble. If they weren't equals, at least they worked together, respected each other. Maybe they smelled right to each other."

"It's becoming personal, isn't it, Mitch? Looking for a way to turn this into a *real* example. Merton's political bombshell."

Mitch agreed to that possibility with a sly wink and a nod.

Eileen shook her head. "Women have always hung together," she said. "Men have always been a sometime thing."

"Wait till we find the men," Mitch said, starting to feel defensive.

"What makes you think they stuck around?"

Mitch stared grimly at the plastic roof.

"Even if there *were* men nearby," she said, "what makes you think we'll be lucky enough to find them?"

"Nothing," he said, and felt hazily that this was a lie.

Eileen finished her sandwich and drank half her can of Coors to chase it down. She had never liked eating very much and did it only to keep body and soul together. She was hungry and deliberate in bed, however. Orgasms allowed her to think more clearly, she had once confessed. Mitch remembered those times well enough, though they had not slept together since he had been twenty-three years old.

Eileen had called her seduction of the young anthropology grad student her biggest mistake. But they had stayed friends and colleagues all these years, capable of a loose and honest interaction that had no pretense of sexual expectation or disappointment. A remarkable friendship.

The wind rattled the roof again. Mitch listened to the hiss of the Coleman lantern.

"What happened between you and Kaye, after you got out of prison?" Eileen asked.

"I don't know," Mitch said, his jaw tightening. Her asking was a weird kind of betrayal, and she could sense his sudden burn.

"Sorry," she said.

"I'm prickly about it," he acknowledged. He felt a waft of air behind him before he saw the woman's shadow. Connie Fitz stepped lightly over the hard-packed dirt and stood beside Eileen, resting a hand on her shoulder.

"Our little stew pot is about to boil over," Fitz said. "I think we can hold the lid down for another two or three days, max. The zealots want to issue a press release. The hardliners want to keep it covered up."

Eileen looked at Mitch with a crinkled lower lip. All that was outside her control, her expression said. "Enslaved women abandoned in camp by cowardly males," she resumed, getting back to the main topic, her eyes bright in the Coleman's pearly light.

"Do you really believe that?" Mitch asked.

"Oh, come on, Mitch. I don't know what to believe."

Mitch's stomach worked over the meal with no conviction. "You should at least tell the students that they need to expand the perimeter," he said. "There could very well be other bodies around, maybe within a few hundred yards."

Fitz made a provisional moue of interest. "We've talked about it. But everybody wants a piece of the main dig, so nobody was enthusiastic about fanning out," she said.

"You feel something?" Eileen asked Mitch. She leaned forward, her voice going mock-sepulchral. "Can you read these bones?"

Fitz laughed.

"Just a hunch," Mitch said, wincing. Then, more quietly, "Probably not a very good one."

"Will Daney continue to pay if we dawdle and poke around a couple of more days?" Fitz asked.

"Merton thinks he's patient and he'll pay plenty," Eileen said. "He knows Daney better than any of us."

"This could become every bit as bad as archaeology in Israel," said Fitz, a natural pessimist. "Every site loaded with political implications. Do you think Emergency Action will come in and shut us down, using NAGPRA as an excuse?"

Mitch pondered, slow deliberation being about all he was capable of this late, this worn down by the day. "I don't think they're that crazy," he said. "But the whole world's a tinderbox."

"Maybe we should toss in a match," Eileen said.

26

Kaye woke to the sound of the bedside phone dweedling, sat straight up in bed, pulled her hair away from her face, and peered through sleep-fogged eyes at the edge of daylight slicing between the shutters. The clock said 5:07 A.M. She could not think who could be calling her at this hour.

Today was not going to be a good day, she knew that already, but she picked up the phone and plumped the pillow behind her into a cushion. "Hello."

"I need to speak with Kaye Lang."

"That's me," she said sleepily.

"Kaye, this is Luella Hamilton. You got in touch with us a little while ago."

Kaye felt her adrenaline surge. Kaye had met Luella Hamilton fifteen years ago, when she had been a volunteer subject in a SHEVA study at the National Institutes of Health in Bethesda. Kaye had taken a liking to the woman, but had not heard from her since driving west with Mitch to Washington state. "Luella? I don't remember . . ."

"Well, you did."

Suddenly Kaye held the phone close. She had heard something about the Hamiltons being connected to Up River. It was reputed to be a very choosy organization. Some claimed it was subversive. She had forgotten all about her letter; that had been the worst time for her, and she had reached out to anyone, even the extremists who claimed they could track and rescue children.

"Luella? I didn't—"

"Well, since I knew you, they told me to make the return call. Is that okay?"

She tried to clear her head. "It's good to hear your voice. How are you?"

"I'm expecting, Kaye. You?"

"No," Kaye said. Luella had to be in her middle fifties. Talk about rolling the dice.

"It's SHEVA again, Kaye," Luella said. "But no time to chat. So listen close. You there, Kaye?"

"I hear you."

"I want you to get to a scrambled line and call us again. A *good* scrambled line. You still have the number?"

"Yes," Kaye said, wondering if it was in her wallet.

"You'll get a cute mechanical voice. Our little robot. Leave your number and we might call you back. Then, we'll go from there. All right, honey?"

Kaye smiled despite the tension. "Yes, Luella. Thank you."

"Sorry to ring so early. Good-bye, dear."

The phone went dead. Kaye immediately swung her legs out of bed and walked into the kitchen to fix coffee. Thought about trying to reach Mitch and tell him.

But it was too early, and probably not a good idea to spread such news around when any phone call was risky.

She stood by the window looking out over Baltimore and thought about Stella in Arizona, wondering how she was doing, and how long it would be until she saw her again.

Something snapped and she heard herself making little growls, like a fox. For a moment, clutching the coffee cup in her trembling hand, Kaye felt a blind, helpless rage. "*Give me back my daughter,* you FUCKHEADS," she rasped. Then she dropped back into the nearest chair, shaking so hard the coffee spilled. She set the cup on a side table and wrapped herself in her arms. With the thick terry sleeve of her robe, she wiped tears of helplessness from her eyes. "Calm down, *dear,*" she said, trying to copy Mrs. Hamilton's strong contralto.

It was not going to be an easy day. Kaye strongly suspected she was going to be put at liberty. Fired. Ending her life as a scientist forever, but opening up her options so she could go get her daughter and reunite her family.

"Dreamer," she said, with none of the conviction of Luella Hamilton.

27

They pumped a thick strawberry smell into the dorm at eight in the morning. Stella opened her eyes and pinched her nose, moaning.

"What now?" Celia asked in the bunk below.

The humans did that whenever they wanted to do something the children might object to. Shots, mass blood samples, medical exams, dorm checks for contraband.

Next came a wave of Pine-Sol, blowing in through the vent pipes slung under the frame roof. The smell came in through Stella's mouth when she breathed, making her gag.

She sat on the edge of the bed in her nightgown, her stomach twisting and her chest heaving. Three men in isolation suits walked down the center aisle of the dormitory. One of the men, she saw, was not a man; it was Joanie, shorter and stockier than the others, her blank face peering through the plastic faceplate of the floppy helmet.

Joanie reminded Stella of Fred Trinket's mother; she had that same calm, fated expectancy of everything and anything, with no emotional freight attached.

The suited trio stopped by a bed four down from Stella's. The girl in the top bunk, Julianne Nicorelli, not a member of Stella's deme, climbed down at a few soft words from Joanie. She looked apprehensive but not scared, not yet. Sometimes the counselors and teachers ran drills in the camp, odd drills, and the kids were never told what they were up to.

Joanie turned and walked deliberately toward Stella's bunk. Stella slid down quickly, not using the ladder, and flattened her nightgown where it had ridden up above her knees. She hid her chest with her hands; the fabric was a little sheer, and she didn't like the way the men were looking at her.

"You, too, Stella," Joanie said, her voice hollow and hissy behind the helmet. "We're going on a trip."

"How many?" Celia asked.

Joanie smiled humorlessly. "Special trip. Reward for good grades and good behavior. The rest get to eat breakfast early."

This was a lie. Julianne Nicorelli got terrible grades, not that anyone cared.

28

"**H**eads up. Marge will be here in twenty minutes." Liz Cantrera said. "Ready?"

"Ready as I'll ever be," Kaye said, and took a deep breath. She looked around the lab to see if there was anything that could be put away or cleaned up. Not that it mattered. It was her last day.

"You look fine," Liz said sadly, straightening Kaye's lapels.

Marge Cross understood the messy bedrooms of science. And Kaye doubted that she wanted to check up on their housekeeping.

Around Kaye, Cross was almost always cheerful. She seemed to like Kaye and to trust her as much as she trusted anybody. Today, however, Cross was saying little, tapping her lip with her finger and nodding. She lifted her head to peer at the pipes hanging from the ceiling. She seemed to study a series of red tags hanging from various pressurized lines.

Only three people accompanied Cross. Two handsome young men in charcoal gray suits made notes on e-tabs. A slender young woman with long, thin blonde hair and a short, upturned nose took photos with a pen-sized camera.

Liz kept to the background, conspicuously allowing Kaye the point position. She gave them all a brief tour, well aware they were taking inventory in preparation for a transfer or a shutdown.

"We've lost," Cross said. "Everything this company has been charged to do by the government and by the people has turned into a can of worms," she added quietly, and chewed her lower lip. "I hear you did a good job on the Hill this week." Cross regarded Kaye with a faint smile.

"It went okay." Kaye shifted her eyes to one side and shrugged. "Rachel Browning tried to pull down my shorts."

"Did she succeed?" Cross asked.

"Got them down to my curlies," Kaye said.

The young men looked ready to appear shocked, should Cross be. Cross laughed. "Jesus, Kaye. I never know what I'm going to hear from you. You drive my PR folks nuts."

"That's why I try to keep my head down and stay quiet."

"We're not learning how to stop SHEVA," Cross said reflectively, still examining the ceiling pipes.

"That's true," Kaye said.

"You're glad."

Once again, Kaye felt it was not her place to answer, that she had responsibilities to others besides herself.

"La Robert is failing, too, but he won't admit it," Cross said. She waved her hands at the others in the lab. "Time to go, kiddies. Leave us sacred monsters alone for a while."

The young men filed through the door. The slender blond tried to remind Cross of appointments later in the morning.

"Cancel them," Cross instructed her.

Liz had stayed behind, solicitous of Kaye. The way she twitched, Kaye thought her assistant might try to physically intervene to protect her.

Cross smiled warmly at Liz. "Honey, can you add anything to our duet?"

"Not a thing," Liz admitted. "Should I go?" she asked Kaye.

Kaye nodded.

Liz picked up her coat and purse and followed the blond through the door.

"Let's take the express to the top floor," Cross suggested pleasantly, and put her arm around Kaye's shoulder. "It's been far too long since we put our heads together. I want you to explain what happened. What you thought you'd find in radiology."

The Americol boardroom on the twentieth floor was huge and extravagant, with a long table cut lengthwise from an oak trunk, handmade William Morris–style chairs that seemed to float on their slender legs, and walls covered with early twentieth-century illustrative art.

Cross told the room what to do and two of the walls folded up, revealing electronic whiteboards. Sections of the table rose up like toy soldiers, thin personal monitors.

"If I were starting over again," Cross said, "I'd turn this into a kindergarten classroom. Little chairs and wagons with little cartons of milk. That's how ignorant we are. But . . . We do cling to our beauty and wealth. We like to feel we are in control and always will be."

Kaye listened attentively, but did not respond.

Cross pushed another button and the whiteboards replayed long strings of scrawled notes. Kaye guessed these were a frozen record of several late-night and early-morning pacing sessions, Cross alone up here in the heights, wielding her little pen wand, moving along the boards like a sorcerous queen scattering spells on the walls of her castle.

Kaye could decipher very few of the scrawls. Cross's handwriting was notorious.

"Nobody's seen this," Cross murmured. "It's hard to read, isn't it?" she asked Kaye. "I used to have perfect penmanship." She held up her swollen knuckles.

Kaye wondered where Cross intended to go with this. Was it all some devious way of letting her go gracefully, with a hearty handshake?

"The secret of life," Cross said, "lies in understanding how little things talk to each other. Correct?"

"Yes," Kaye said.

"And you've maintained, from before the beginnings of SHEVA, that viruses are part of the arsenal of communications our cells and bodies use to talk."

"That's why you brought me to Americol."

Cross dismissed that with a slight frown and a lift of one shoulder. "So you turned yourself into a laboratory to prove a point, and gave birth to a SHEVA child. Gutsy, and more than a little stupid."

Kaye clenched her jaw.

Cross knew she had touched an exposed nerve. "I think the Jackson clique is right on the money. Experience biases you in favor of believing SHEVA is benign, a natural phenomenon that we'll just have to knuckle under and accept. Don't fight it. It's bigger than all of us."

"I'm fond of my daughter," Kaye said stiffly.

"I don't doubt it. Hear me out. I'm going somewhere with this, but I don't know where just yet." Cross paced along the whiteboards, arms folded, tapping one elbow with the remote. "My companies are my children. That's a cliché, but it's true, Kaye. I am as stupid and gutsy as you were. I have turned my companies into an experiment in politics and human history. We're very much alike, except I had neither the opportunity—nor, frankly, the inclination—to put my body on the line. Now, we both stand to lose what we love most."

Cross turned and flicked the whiteboards clean with the press of a button. Her face curled in disgust. "It's all shit. This room is a waste of money. You can't help but think that whoever built all this knew what they were

doing, had all the answers. It's an architectural lie. I *hate* this room. Everything I just erased was drivel. Let's go somewhere else." Cross was visibly
angry.

Kaye folded her hands cautiously. She had no idea what was going to
happen, not now. "All right," she said. "Where?"

"No limos. Let's lose the luxuries for a few hours. Let's get back to
little chairs and cookies and cartons of milk." Cross smiled wickedly,
revealing strong, even, but speckled teeth. "Let's get the hell out of this
building."

A gray, drizzly light greeted them as they pushed through the glass doors to
the street. Cross hailed a cab.

"Your cheeks are pinking," she told Kaye as they climbed into the
backseat. "Like they want to say something."

"That still happens," Kaye admitted with some embarrassment.

Cross gave the driver an address Kaye did not recognize. The gray-
haired man, a Sikh wearing a white turban, looked over his shoulder.

"I will need card in advance," he said.

Cross reached for her belt pouch.

"My treat," Kaye said, and handed the driver her credit card. The cab
pushed off through traffic.

"What was it like, having those cheeks—like signboards?" Cross
asked.

"It was a revelation," Kaye said. "When my daughter was young, we
practiced cheek-flashing. It was like teaching her how to speak. I missed
them when they faded."

Cross watched her absorbedly, then gave a little start and said, "I
learned I couldn't have children when I was twenty-five. Pelvic inflammatory disease. I was a big, ungainly girl and had a hard time getting dates. I
had to take my men where I found them, and one of them . . . Well. No children, and I decided not to reverse the scarring, because there was never
a man I trusted enough to be a father. I got rich pretty early and the men
I was attracted to were like pleasant toys, needy, eager to please, not very
reliable."

"I'm sorry," Kaye said.

"Sublimation is the soul of accomplishment," Cross said. "I can't say I
understand what it means to be a parent. I can only make comparisons with
how I feel about my companies, and that probably isn't the same."

"Probably not," Kaye said.

Cross clucked her tongue. "This isn't about funding or firing you or anything so simple. We're both explorers, Kaye. For that reason alone, we need to be open and frank."

Kaye peered out the taxi window and shook her head, amused. "It isn't working, Marge. You're still rich and powerful. You're still my boss."

"Well, hell," Cross said with mock disappointment, and snapped her fingers.

"But it may not matter," Kaye said. "I've never been very good at concealing my true feelings. Maybe you've noticed."

Cross made a sound too high-pitched to be a laugh, but it had a certain eccentric dignity, and probably wasn't a giggle, either. "You've been playing me all along."

"You knew I would," Kaye said.

Cross patted her cheek. "Cheek-flashing."

Kaye looked puzzled.

"How can something so wonderful be an aberration, a disease? If I could fever scent, I would be running every corporation in the country by now."

"You wouldn't want to," Kaye said. "If you were one of the children."

"Now who's being naïve?" Cross asked. "Do you think they've left our monkey selves behind?"

"No. Do you know what a *deme* is?" Kaye asked.

"Social units for some of the SHEVA kids."

"What I'm saying is a deme might be the greedy one, not an individual. And when a deme fever scents, we lesser apes don't stand a chance."

Cross leaned her head back and absorbed this. "I've heard that," she said.

"Do you know a SHEVA child?" the driver asked, looking at them in the rearview mirror. He did not wait for an answer. "My granddaughter, a SHEVA girl, is in Peshawar, she is charmer. Real charmer. It is scary," he added happily, proudly, with a broad grin. "Really scary."

29

Stella sat with Julianne Nicorelli in a small beige room in the hospital. Joanie had separated them from the other girls. They had been waiting for two hours. The air was still and they sat stiff as cold butter on their chairs, watching a fly crawl along the window.

The room was still thick with strawberry scent, which Stella had once loved.

"I feel awful," Julianne said.

"So do I."

"What are they waiting for?"

"Something's screwy/ Made a mistake," Stella said.

Julianne scraped her shoes on the floor. "I'm sorry you aren't one of my deme," she said.

"That's okay."

"Let's make our own, right here. We'll/ Like us/ join up with anyone else/ locked away/ who comes in."

"All right," Stella said.

Julianne wrinkled her nose. "It stinks so bad/ Can't smell myself think."

Their chairs were several feet apart, a polite distance considering the nervous fear coming from the two girls, even over the miasma of strawberry. Julianne stood and held out one hand. Stella leaned her head to one side and pulled back her hair, exposing the skin behind her ear. "Go ahead."

Julianne touched the skin there, the waxy discharge, and rubbed it under her nose. She made a face, then lowered her finger and frithed—pulling back her upper lip and sucking air over the finger and into her mouth.

"Ewww," she said, not at all disapprovingly, and closed her eyes. "I feel better. Do you?"

Stella nodded and said, "Do you want to be deme mother?"

"Doesn't matter," Julianne said. "We're not a quorum anyway." Then she looked alarmed. "They're probably recording us."

"Probably."

"I don't care. Go ahead."

Stella touched Julianne behind her ear. The skin was quite warm there, hot almost. Julianne was fever scenting, desperately trying to reach out and both politely persuade and establish a bond with Stella. That was touching. It meant Julianne was more frightened and insecure than Stella, more in need.

"I'll be deme mother," Stella said. "Until someone better comes in."

"All right," Julianne said. It was just for show, anyway. No quorum, just whistling down the wind. Julianne rocked back and forth. Her scent was changing to coffee and tuna—a little disturbing. It made Stella want to hug somebody.

"I smell bad, don't I?" Julianne said.

"No," Stella said. "But we both smell different now."

"What's happening to us?"

"I'm sure they want to find out," Stella said, and faced the strong steel door.

"My hips hurt," Julianne said. "I am so miserable."

Stella pulled their chairs closer. She touched Julianne's fingers where they rested on her knee. Julianne was tall and skinny. Stella had more flesh on her frame though as yet no breasts, and her hips were narrow.

"They don't want us to have children," Julianne said, as if reading her mind, and her misery crossed over into sobs.

Stella just kept stroking her hand. Then she turned the girl's hand over, spit into her palm, and rubbed their palms together. Even over the strawberry smell, she got through to Julianne, and Julianne began to settle down, focus, smooth out the useless wrinkles of her fear.

"They shouldn't make us mad," Julianne said. "If they want to kill us, they better do it soon."

"Shhh," Stella warned. "Let's just get comfortable. We can't stop them from doing what they're going to do."

"What are they going to do?" Julianne asked.

"Shh."

The electronic lock on the door clicked. Stella saw Joanie in her hooded suit through the small window. The door opened.

"Let's go, girls," Joanie said. "This is going to be fun." Her voice sounded like a recording coming out of an old doll.

A yellow bus, like a small school bus, waited for them on the drive in front of the hospital. The bus that had brought Strong Will had been a different bus, secure and shiny, new; she wondered why they were not using that bus.

Four counselors in suits moved five girls and four boys forward, toward the door of the bus. Celia and LaShawna and Felice were in the group once again. Julianne walked ahead of Stella, her loose clogs slapping the ground.

Strong Will was among the boys, Stella saw with both apprehension and an odd excitement. She was pretty sure it wasn't a sexual thing—based on what Kaye had told her—but it was something *like* that. She had never felt such a thing before. It was new.

Not just to her.

She thought maybe it was new to the human race, or whatever the children were. A virus kind of thing, maybe.

The boys walked ten feet apart from the girls. None of them were shackled, but where would they run? Into the desert? The closest town was twenty miles away, and already it was a hundred degrees.

The counselors held little gas guns that filled the air with a citrus smell, oranges and limes, and a perennial favorite, Pine-Sol.

Will looked dragged down, frazzled. He carried a paperback book without a cover, its pages yellow and tattered. He did not look at the girls; none of the boys did. They appeared to be okay physically, but shuffled as they walked. She could not catch their scent.

The door to the bus opened and the boys were led in first, taking seats on the left-hand side. Through the windows, Stella saw plastic curtains being drawn and fastened. They looked flimsy, like shower curtains. Joanie moved the girls up to the door. They walked to the right of the curtain and sat in the five middle rows of slick blue plastic bench seats, one girl to each seat.

Stella squirmed and her pants stuck to the plastic. The seat felt funny, tacky and oily. It exuded a peculiar smell, like turpentine. They had sprayed the interior of the bus with something.

Celia sat directly in front of her and leaned forward to talk to LaShawna.

"Stay where you are," Joanie instructed them in a monotone. "No talking." She surveyed the children on both sides of the curtain, then walked forward and took Julianne by the arm. She removed Julianne, backing out of the bus. Julianne shot a frightened but relieved look at Stella, then stood outside, arms straight by her sides, shivering.

A security guard came aboard. He was in his middle forties, stocky and bare-armed, wearing a pair of khaki pants and a short-sleeved white shirt that clung to his shoulders. He carried a small machine pistol in a holster on his belt. He glanced back at the boys, then leaned to one side, and peered along the right side of the bus at the girls.

Everyone on the bus was silent.

Stella's stomach seemed to shrink inside her.

The door closed. Will swung his hand against the plastic curtain and made the hooks rattle on the rail bolted to the roof. The guard leaned forward and frowned.

Stella couldn't smell a thing now. Her nose was completely clogged.

"Am I allowed to read on the bus?" Will yelled.

The guard shrugged.

"Thank you," Will shouted, and the girls giggled. "Thank you very much."

The man obviously did not like this duty. He faced forward, waiting for the driver.

"What about lunch?" Will shouted. "Are we going to eat?"

The boys laughed. The girls sank back into their seats. Stella thought maybe they were being taken away to be killed and dissected. Felice was clearly thinking the same thing. Celia was shivering.

Finally, Will stopped yelling. He pulled a page from the paperback, crumpled it into a ball, and tossed it over three seats into the well next to the driver's window. Tongue between his lips and making a clownish grin, he pulled out another page, crumpled it, and lobbed it into the empty driver's seat. Then another, which fell to the floor in front of the driver's seat. Stella watched through the transparent sheeting between the rows, embarrassed and exhilarated by this show of defiance.

The driver climbed up the steps. He picked up the crumpled paper with his gloved hand, made a face, then tossed it out the door. It bounced from the chest of the second security guard as she came aboard. She was also large and in her forties. The female guard muttered something Stella could not hear. Both guards were equipped with noseys pinned to their breast pockets. The noseys were switched off, Stella noticed.

The driver took his seat.

"Let's go!" Will shouted. Behind him, one of the boys began to hoot. The female guard swiveled and glared at them, just in time to be hit by another crumpled ball of paper.

The male guard walked to the back along the boys' side of the plastic barrier.

"Go! Go!" Will shouted, and bounced in his seat.

"Sit down, damn it," the first guard said.

"Why not tie us down?" Will asked. "Why not strap us in?"

"Shut up," the guard said.

Stella felt a chill. They were being taken somewhere by a team that had had little experience with SHEVA children. She had an instinct for such things. These two, and the driver, looked even dumber than Miss Kantor. None of the humans inside or outside of the bus looked happy; they looked as if something had gone wrong.

Stella wondered what had happened to that other bus, the one they usually used.

Will was watching the guards and the driver like a hawk, eyes steady. Stella tried to keep his face in focus through the plastic, but he leaned back and got fuzzy.

The wire-reinforced plastic windows were locked shut from the outside; this was the kind of bus she had seen as a child carrying prisoners to pick up trash or cut down brush along the highways. She stared out through the window and shivered.

Her body ached. In front of her, Celia hunched forward, whispering to herself, her hands clasping the padded rail. LaShawna was yawning, pretending not to care. Felice had wrapped herself in her arms and was trying to go to sleep.

"Go, go, go!" the boys hooted, bouncing in their seats. Felice laid her head against the window. Stella wanted the boys to be quiet. She wanted everything to be quiet so she could close her eyes and pretend she was somewhere else. She felt betrayed by the school, by Miss Kantor, by Miss Kinney.

That was stupid, of course. Being at the school was a betrayal in the first place. Why would leaving be any worse? She leaned her head back to keep from feeling nauseated.

The female guard told the driver to close and lock the door. The driver started the bus and put it in gear. It lurched forward.

Celia began to throw up. The driver jerked the bus to a halt at the end of the concrete apron before the main road.

"Never mind!" the female guard shouted, her face a mask of disgust. "We'll clean it up when we get there. Just go!"

"Go, go, go!" the boys chanted. Will glanced at Stella, straightened his lips, and began to peel another page from the paperback.

Once the bus was under way, air began to move through small vents above the windows and Stella felt better. Celia stayed quiet, and the two other girls sat stiffly in their seats. Stella was thinking over their situation and decided it was all very clumsy and badly planned, probably last-minute. They were being transported like lobsters in a tank. Time was of the essence. Someone was eager to get to them while they were still fresh.

Stella tried to make some spit to moisten her mouth. The taste on her tongue was terrible.

"This will take about an hour and ten minutes," the driver said as they pulled out of the school parking lot. "There's water in bottles below each seat. We'll make one bathroom stop."

Stella reached below the blue seat and picked up a plastic bag with a bottle of water inside. She looked down at it, wondering what it held besides water; what was going to happen at the end of the ride, their treat for being such good little boys and girls? To stay calm, she thought of Kaye, and then she thought about Mitch. Last, but not least, she remembered holding their old orange cat, Shamus, and stroking him while he purred.

If she was going to die, she could at least be as dignified as old Shamus.

30

OREGON

Mitch got up before sunrise, dressed without waking Merton, and left the tent they shared to stand at the rim of the Spent River gulley. He watched the early-morning sun try to spread light over the shaded landscape. He could clearly see Mount Hood, twenty miles away, its snows purple in the dawn.

He found a twig and stuck it between his lips, then bit it with his teeth.

Mitch had never thought he was prescient, sensitive, psychic, whatever name one gave to having second sight. Kaye had told him, years ago, that scientists and artists shared similar origins for creative thinking—but that scientists had to prove their fancies.

Mitch had never told Kaye what he had gotten out of that conversation, but in a way it had helped him put things in perspective—to see the artistic side of how he came to his own, often logically unsupportable conclusions. It wasn't ESP.

He was just thinking like an artist.

Or a cop. Nature was the world's most efficient serial killer. An anthropologist was a kind of detective, not so much interested in justice—that was entirely too abstract in the face of time's immensity and so many deaths—but in figuring out how the victims had died and, more important, how they had lived.

He wiped his eyes with one finger and looked north along the gulley, to the deeper gorge that had long ago been cut through alternating layers of mud and lava and ash. Then he turned and peered at the L-shaped site with its array of canvas and plastic covers, concealed by camouflage netting.

"Shit," he said, almost in wonder at the way his feet began to walk him along the rim of the gulley, away from the main dig.

That bear. That damned, enigmatic bear that had started it all.

The bear had come down to the river to do some fishing and had been suffocated by a fall of ash—but several days before the humans had arrived. The humans typically tracked bears, he was almost sure of it, relying on them to find good fishing. Someone had claimed the skull, but had not butchered the carcass—there were no cut marks on the bones—which meant it was probably in an unappetizing condition by the time they found it.

Salmon came back in the spring, summer, and fall to spawn and die, different groups and different species at different seasons. Nomadic bands had timed their journeys and arranged their settlements to take advantage of one or more of these returns, when the rivers ran thick with rich, red-fleshed fish.

Leaves changing color. Water running crisp and cold. Salmon wriggling over the rocky streambeds like big red pull toys. Bears waiting to march across the stream and grab them.

But most of the bears had probably left with the first ash fall, leaving behind one old male too sick to travel far, maybe chewed up in a fight, waiting to die.

Guessing. Just guessing, goddamnit.

Why would people walk up the river and ignore the ash fall? Not even hunger could have driven them into that landscape, or made them stay once there. Unless it had been raining, every step would have brought up a cloud of choking ash. Setting up a fishing camp would have been stupid in the extreme.

Like the bear, they were being followed.

He had dreamed about the bones in the night. He did not know whether artists dreamed their work—or whether detectives dreamed solutions to their cases. But the way he worked was, he often dreamed of the people he found, in their graves or where they had fallen and died.

And sometimes he was right.

Often he was right.

Hell, nine times out of ten, Mitch's dreams turned out to be right—so long as he waited for them to evolve, to ripple through their necessary variations and reach their inevitable conclusion. That was how it had been with the Alpine mummies. He had dreamed about them for months.

But now there was not enough time. He had to rely on what amounted to a hunch.

The Australians had clued him, even more than the *Homo erectus* skeletons. They were very far north. Only now was anthropology accepting the many tides and clashes of peoples in the Americas—the early arrival by storm-driven boats of a few Australians in the south, the later and frequent arrivals of the Asians moving along and over the land and ice bridges in the north.

The Australoids had been in South America—and now it was apparent North America—for tens of thousands of years before they met the Asians. The Asians conquered and killed, subdued, pushed them back south from whatever northern territories they might have explored. It must have been a monumental war, spread out over millions of square miles and many thousands of years, race-based and violent.

In the end, the Australians had all but vanished—leaving only a few mixed-race descendants on the eastern coast of South America: the Tierra del Fuegans familiar to Darwin and other explorers.

They were being chased. They partnered with the Homo erectus *individuals because they faced a common enemy.*

Mitch stepped out like an automaton, eyes sweeping the ground ahead, ignoring everything but the pound of his boots on the old rounded river rocks. It was no place to take a tumble, especially with one bum arm.

Too far north. In dangerous territory, surrounded by Asians. They had come up here for the rich runs of fish, following the bears; men and women, an extended family group. Perhaps united under one powerful male—and maybe he did like dabbling with the Homo erectus *females. No sense being naïve.*

But his women did not care. No babies ever resulted. Mitch could almost see the Homo erectus *males and females tagging along, behind the Australians, begging at first, then being set up to do work for the women, then offering themselves to the men, their own males indifferent to the exchange. Attitudes of a hungry, dying people.*

In the end, there had been some measure of affection, perhaps more than masters for their pets. Equals? Probably not. But the Homo erectus *members of the group were not stupid. They had survived for more than a million years.* Homo sap *was just a newcomer in the equation.*

Mitch snuffed air and blew his nose into his handkerchief; the warming air was thick with grass pollen. He was not normally susceptible, but his years in prison, with musty air and lots of mold, had exaggerated his reactions.

If the men are out here—and no guarantee of that—they couldn't save the women. They failed, and they probably died, too. Or they hightailed it out of this miserable place ahead of the wave of hot mud—leaving the women behind.

How am I any better?

I left my women behind, and they took Stella.

What if I do find the males, what of it? What in hell am I looking for? Salvation? An excuse?

He glanced up at the sun, then shaded and dropped his eyes. The thickest deposit of mudstone had set in a dark brown layer all around the banks of the old river, weathered in spots to soil rich enough to support shrubs and trees, hard and stripped and barren elsewhere. Boulders the size and shape of soccer balls pocked the ground, and nowhere any clue as to where an elusive collection of fossils might just poke up underfoot.

He sat on a weather-split boulder and lifted his left elbow onto his knee to get the tingle out of his slack arm. Sometimes the blood just cut off in that arm, and then the nerves, and after a while the arm jerked awake and hurt like hell.

It wasn't easy staying attentive and on point. Something insisted on getting in the way, perhaps an all-too-real sense of the complete futility of what he was trying to do. "Where would you go?" he whispered. He hunched his knees slowly around the rock, turning his eyes to sweep the rugged land, up the high ground and down into the swales filled with brush. "Where would you weather out twenty thousand years after you died? Come on, guys. Help me out."

A light breeze whistled through the brush and touched his hair like phantom fingers. He blew a fly away from his lips and brushed the hair out of his eyes. Kaye had always chided him about getting haircuts. After a while she had just let it drop, giving up, and Mitch wondered what he resented more—being treated like a little boy or being given up on by his own wife.

His teeth ground lightly, like a beast scaring away enemies. His chest ached from loneliness and guilt.

Wandering.

His eyes could tell a chip of bone from a pebble at a dozen paces, even now. He could set mental filters to ignore squirrel and rabbit bones, any recent subset of bleached, chewed, or sinew-darkened remnant.

His eyes narrowed to slits.

An experienced band of males might have seen or heard the lahar and become frightened, tried to make it to high ground. That's where he was now, where his feet had taken him, to the highest ground in the area, a ridge of hard rock and cupped pockets of soil and brush. He could see the camp, or at least where he knew it was, about half a mile away, obscured by tall brush and trees.

And north, the ever-present sentinel of Mount Hood, a quiet, squat dunce cap of repressed Earth energy, hissing faint plumes of steam but confessing nothing about past tantrums, past crimes.

Mitch closed his eyes completely and visualized the head male of the band. The picture cleared. Mitch went away, and in his place stood the band's lead hunter, the chief.

The chief's face was dark and intent, hair flecked with ash, skin streaky gray with ash, like a ghost. In Mitch's imagination, the chief started out purple-brown and quite naked, but pieced skins suddenly appeared on his lanky, stooped frame, not crude rags even twenty thousand years ago, because people were savvy about fashion and utility even then; leggings and tunic tied at the waist, pouch for flints and obsidian tips or whatever they might have with them.

Their hearts beat fast seeing the pallor on their skins, they already look dead. They're afraid of each other. But the chief holds them together. He jumps and makes faces until they crow at their ashen complexions. The chief is more than smart; he cares about the anomalous little group of males, partners in this harsh land; and he is solicitous of the females, the chewers of skins and makers of the clothing he wears.

Never underestimate your ancestors, your cousins. They lasted a long, long time. And even then they loved, they cared, they protected.

31

The bus cut through a Flagstaff suburb, low, flat, brown brick, and, stucco houses surrounded by dusty gravel yards. Stella had lived in such a suburb as a girl. She laid her head back on the plastic seat and stared at the passing homes. Even with air-conditioning, the bus was hot inside and her water was running out fast.

The boys had stopped talking and Will seemed to be asleep next to a small pile of crumpled yellow pages from his old paperback book.

Someone tapped her shoulder. It was the male guard. He had a larger plastic bag from which he pulled another bottle of water.

"Not long now," he said, and stuck the bottle into her hand. "Give me the empties." The girls handed him their empties and he passed them to the female guard, who stuck them into another bag and sealed it. Then he stepped around the curtain at the front of the bus and gave the boys fresh bottles, again collecting the empties.

The male guard shook his head and glared down disapprovingly at Will's mess before giving the boy a bottle.

"Having fun?" he asked Will.

Will stared up at him and shook his head slowly.

The bus driver was making lots of turns, taking them up and down many streets as if he were lost. Stella did not think the driver was lost. They were trying to avoid someone or something.

That made her sit up. She looked behind. The bus was being followed by a small brown car. Up front, as they turned a corner she saw another car, this one green, with two people in the front seat. The bus was following the lead car. They had escorts.

Nothing too unexpected about that. Why, then, did Stella feel that none of this had been planned out well, that something had gone awry?

Will was watching her. He pushed close to the plastic curtain and moved his lips but she could not hear what he was saying over the road noise; they were on gravel now, rumbling across a farm track through a fallow dirt field to a state road. The bus bounced up onto the asphalt and swung left. The lead car slowed for the bus to catch up.

She tracked Will's lips more carefully now that the bouncing had stopped: *Sandia,* he was mouthing silently. She remembered him asking earlier if she had heard of it, but she still did not know what Sandia was.

Will drew his finger across his throat. Stella closed her eyes and turned away. She could not watch him now. She did not need to be any more scared than she already was.

Another hour, and they rode on a straight stretch of highway between rocky desert with low red mountains on the horizon. The sun was almost directly overhead. The trip was taking a lot longer than Joanie had said it would.

The highway was almost empty, only a few cars going either way. A small red BMW with New Mexico plates swung around to the left of the short caravan and zoomed by. The boys tracked its speedy passage listlessly, then held up their hands with crooked finger signs and laughed.

Stella did not know what they meant. The laughter sounded harsh. The boys worried her. They seemed wild.

The long, sandy, rocky stretches beside the highway hypnotized her. The mountains were always far away. She wondered what *Sandia* meant once more, then stuffed the word away, hating the sound of it, more so because it was actually a pretty word.

Screech of tires.

She was jerked up out of a doze by a sudden swerve. Stella clung to the seat back in front of her as the bus veered left, then right, then tilted. Tires kept on screaming over the asphalt. Celia's head and shoulders bounced one way then another, and as Stella looked right, the outside world flew up and dropped down, mountains and desert and all. Then everything shoved sideways, and she slipped along the plastic seat and crashed down on the window, jamming her head, neck, and shoulder against the plastic. Plastic crazed and peeled away in wire-clasped ripples and her shoulder pressed into dirt and gravel.

For a moment, the bus was very quiet. It seemed to be lying on one side, the right side, her side. The light was not very good and the air was thick and still and full of the smell of burned rubber.

She tried to move and found that she still could, which caused a surge of excitement. Her body was still working, she was still alive. She pushed up slowly and heard jingling and ripping sounds. Then, a boy fell onto the curtain and jammed his knee into her side. Through the taut veil of plastic above her, she saw another boy's denim-clad butt and a vague, contorted face. *Will,* she thought, and with a grunt, pushed up against the body, but could not move it.

"Please, get off," she demanded, her voice muffled.

Stella was in pain. She thought for a minute she was going to panic, but she closed her eyes and made that go away. She could not bring her hand around to feel her shoulder, but she thought it might be bleeding, and her blouse seemed to be ripped. She could feel gravel or something sharp against her bare skin.

Outside, she heard some voices, men talking, one man yelling. They seemed far away. Then a door squealed open. The knee on her chest drew up and a foot came down hard on her ankle, pressing it into the frame of the seat in front. She screamed; that really hurt.

"Sorry," a boy said, and the foot was lifted. She saw shadows moving over her, clumsy, dazed, pressing against the plastic curtain. Will's face seemed to blur and fade, and he was gone. The curtain lay lightly around her. Something sighed, a brake cylinder maybe, or a boy. She rolled enough to finally touch her shoulder and lifted her hand against the curtain to see a bit of blood there, not a lot. Light filtered around the seat back behind her. Someone had opened the bus's rear emergency door, and maybe a ceiling hatch as well.

"We'd better get you out of there," a man called congenially. "Everybody hear me?"

Stella lay on her back now against the gravel and the dirt and the side of the bus. She rolled over completely and did a kind of knee-up, arm-up between the seats, which were jammed together closer than they had been before the crash. A feathery, leafy branch somehow got into her mouth and she spit it out, then finished wriggling until she was on her knees.

She had cuts all over, but none of them were bleeding a lot. Stella flailed against the plastic curtain until someone pulled it away with a jingle of hooks.

"Who's in here? LaShawna? You in here?" A man's voice, deep and distinct.

And someone else, "Celia? Hugh Davis? Johnny? Johnny Lee?"

"It's me," Stella said. "I'm here."

Then she heard LaShawna call out. The girl began crying. "My leg is hurt," she wailed.

"We're going to get you, LaShawna. Be brave. Help is coming."

Someone cursed loud and long at someone else.

"You just back off. You stay away from here. This is horrible, but you back off."

"You drove us the fuck off the road!"

"You went into a skid."

"Well, what the hell else could I do? There were cars all over the road. Jesus, we need an ambulance. Call an ambulance."

Stella wondered if perhaps she should just stay where she was for the time being, in the half-dark, and nobody knowing she was there.

Suddenly, someone was pulling on her arm, tugging her out from between the seats and into the space between the top of the seats and the roof of the bus, now a kind of hallway with windows on the floor. It was Will. He crouched and peered at her like a frazzle-haired monkey, his face smeared with blood.

"We can go now," he said.

"Where?" Stella asked.

"It's people coming for us. Humans. They want to rescue us. But we can leave."

"We have to help."

"What can we do?" Will asked.

"We have to *help*."

For a passing moment, she wanted to smear her hand on his face. Her ears felt hot.

Will shook his head and scrambled in a half-hunch to the front of the bus. He looked for a moment as if he were just going to climb out through a window, but then two pairs of arms stretched down, and he glanced back at Stella. A sour look came to his face.

"There's a girl back there; she's okay," he said. "Take care of her, but leave me alone."

Stella sat by the side of the long two-lane highway with her face in her hands. She had banged her head pretty hard in the wreck and now it throbbed. She peeked between her fingers at the adults walking around the bus. About twenty minutes had passed since the crash.

Will lay beside her, hand tossed casually over his eyes as if he were taking a nap. He had ripped his pants and a long scratch showed through. Otherwise, they both seemed to be okay.

Celia and LaShawna and the three other boys were already sitting in the backs of two cars, not the escort cars. Both of the escort cars had run off into a culvert and were pretty banged up—crumpled grilles, steam hissing, trunk lids popped.

She thought she heard the two security guards on the other side of the bus, and possibly the bus driver as well.

Parked by the side of the road about a hundred yards behind were two law enforcement vehicles. She could not see the insignia but their emergency lights were blinking. Why weren't they helping out, getting ready to take the children back to the school?

Would there be an EMAC van coming soon, or an ambulance?

A black man in a rumpled brown suit approached Stella and Will. "The other girls and boys are pretty badly bruised, but they're going to be fine. LaShawna is fine. Her leg is okay, thank God."

Stella peered up at him doubtfully. She did not know who he was.

"I'm John Hamilton," he said. "I'm LaShawna's daddy. We've got to leave here. You have to come with us."

Will sat up, his cheeks almost mahogany from the combination of sun and defiance. "Why?" he said. "Are you taking us to another school?"

"We have to get you to a doctor for checkups. The closest safe place is about fifty miles from here." He pointed back down the road. "Not back to the school. My daughter will never go there again, not while I'm alive."

"What's Sandia?" Stella asked John, on impulse.

"It's some mountains," John said, with a startled expression, and swallowed something that must have been bitter. "Come on, let's get going. I think there's room."

A third car pulled up, and John talked to the driver, a middle-aged woman with large turquoise rings on her fingers and brilliant orange hair. They seemed to know each other.

John came back. He was irritated.

"You'll go with her," he said. "Her name is Jobeth Hayden. She's a mom, too. We thought her daughter might be here, but she isn't."

"You ran the buses off the road?" Stella asked.

"We tried to slow down the lead car and take you off the bus. We thought we could do it safely. I don't know how it happened, but one of their cars spun out and the bus plowed into it and everyone went off the road. Cars all over. We're damned lucky."

Will had retrieved his battered and torn paperback book from the dirt and clutched it in his hand. He peered at the rip in his jeans, and the scratch. Then he stared back down the road at the cars with the emergency lights. "I'll just go by myself."

"No, son," John Hamilton said firmly, and he suddenly seemed very large. "You'll die out here, and you won't hitch any rides because they'll know what you are."

"They'll arrest me," Will said, pointing at the blinking lights.

"No, they won't. They're from New Mexico."

Hamilton did not explain why that was significant. Will stared at Hamilton and his face wrinkled in either anger or frustration.

"We're responsible," Hamilton said quietly. "Please, come with us." Even more quietly, focusing on Will, his voice deep, almost sleepy, Hamilton said again, "Please."

Will stumbled as he took a step, and John helped him to the car with the orange-haired woman, Jobeth.

On the way, they came close to the red Buick that carried Celia, Felice, LaShawna, and two of the boys. LaShawna leaned back in the rear seat, in the shadow of the car roof, eyes closed. Felice sat upright beside her. Celia stuck her head out the window. "What-KUK a ride!" she crowed. A white bandage looped around her head. She had blood on her scalp and in her hair and she clutched a plastic bottle of 7-Up and a sandwich. "I guess no more school, huh?"

Will and Stella got in the car with Jobeth. John told Jobeth where they were going—a ranch. Stella did not catch the name, though it might have been George or Gorge.

"I know," the woman said. "I love there."

Stella was sure the woman did not say "live," she said "love."

Will leaned his head back on the seat and stared at the headliner. Stella took a bottle of water and a bottle of 7-Up from John, and the cars drove back on the road, leaving the wreck of the bus, two guards, and three drivers, all neatly tied and squatting on the shoulder.

The official vehicles turned out to be from the New Mexico State Police, and they spun off in the opposite direction, their lights no longer flashing.

"Won't be more than an hour," Jobeth said, following the other two cars.

"Who are you?" Stella asked.

"I have no idea," Jobeth said lightly. "Haven't for years." She glanced back over the seat at Stella. "You're a pretty one. You're all pretty ones to me. Do you know my daughter? Her name is Bonnie. Bonnie Hayden. I guess she's still at the school; they took her there six months ago. She has natural red hair and her sparks are really prominent. It's her Irish blood, I'm sure."

Will ripped a page out of his paperback and crumpled it, then waggled it under his nose. He grinned at Stella.

32

They've been out hunting, the men, taking along the younger males, those near or beyond puberty; heading up to the high ground to see where there might be some game left after the ash fall. But the ash has covered everything with grit for a hundred miles and the game has moved south, all but the small animals still quivering in their burrows, in their warrens, waiting . . .

And then the men hear the lahar coming, see the pyroclastic cloud that has melted all the snow and ice rippling around the base of the mountain like a dirty gray shawl falling from the black Storm Bear whose claws are lightning . . . or the mountain goddess sitting and spreading her wrap, the edge of the soft skin rushing over the land tens of miles away with a sound like all the buffalo on Earth.

Beneath the wrap, the meltwater has mixed with hot gas and gathers ash and mud and trees, roaring toward where the men stand, pallid and weak with fear.

The chief, with the sharpest eyes, the quickest brain, the strongest arm, the most sons and daughters in this band, yet probably only thirty-five or forty years of age, at the oldest . . . The chief has never encountered anything like the approaching lahar. The ash was bad enough. The distant wall of gray smudge looks as if it might take days to reach them, rolling over and through the distant forests. How could it ever touch where he stands with his sons and hunters, no matter how furious and powerful?

But, just in case, he walks back to be with the women.

Mitch pushed on his knee to get up and started walking toward the camp.

The men lope down the hills, taking the short route from the high ground, puffs of ash rising around their feet as they run, and the chief looks up above the ash cloaking the tiny crew in a choking haze and sees that the cloud has come that much closer in just a few minutes. He trembles, knowing how ignorant he is. Death could be very near.

Mitch strode down into the swale, across the old mudstone and around the whistling patches of brush.

Big old splash coming. Hot breath out of hell unnamed, perhaps un-

thought of then. The chief runs faster as the roar grows louder, the sound bigger even than the biggest stampeding herd in the biggest hunt, the wall of cloud rampaging over the land with a swift but lumbering dignity, like a great bear.

For a moment, the chief pauses and points out that the gray cloud has stopped. They laugh and hoot. The gray cloud is thinning, breaking up. They cannot see the flood beneath.

Then comes the biggest ash fall yet, thick curtains and fat billows, blinding, stinging the eyes and catching in the nose and mouth, gritty between lips and gums, choking. They try to cover their eyes with their hands. Blind, they stumble and fall and shout hunting cries, identity cries, not yet names. The roar begins again, grows louder, rhythmic pounding, screaming of trees, ripping.

Mitch stopped briefly on the upslope of the swale, peering at the weathered layers, the broken, crumbling remains of the ancient lahar. He rubbed his eyes, trying to push back a sliver of light in his vision.

From the top of the crest, he half-slid, half-walked down to the edge of the Spent River, a bluff overlooking the dried-up watercourse. They might have been near the river, waiting to cross, in a straight line between the high ground where Mitch (and the chief) had been a few minutes before, not far from where Mitch stood now, his dead arm at his side, ignoring the tingling there as well as the precessing, aching silver crescent.

He walked along the bluff. His eyes swept the ground a few meters ahead, looking for that weathered-out phalange or even bigger bone or chip of bone not worried over by a coyote or hauled off by a ground squirrel, falling out of its little hollow in the ash, that hard little mold of death.

The roar is loud and growing louder, but the cloud seems to be dissipating. What they cannot see, from where they stand, is the lahar breaking up into long fingers, finding channels already carved and ripped in the land, blowing out the last of its energy, reaching, reaching, but growing weaker. What they cannot see clearly is that this new threat is trying with all of its fading might to kill them.

Perhaps they will live.

They would be on his right, if they were anywhere at all, if they were still here. Their bones might have weathered out and fallen from the bluff centuries ago. He was walking so near the edge that there might be nothing left. The river would have been higher then, its bed not so worn and deep; but the bluff might have been high enough to give them pause . . .

The chief looks northwest. The leading run of the dying lahar roars down the channel. His eyes grow wide, his nostrils flare in rage and disappointment. It is a fuming, curling, leaping torrent of mud and steaming water. It fills his eyes, his brain. It travels faster than they can run. They hunker down and it roars past, below their feet, digging out the embankment. They crawl up the bank to safety, but the lahar vaults up and the spill catches them as they raise their arms. The thick liquid scalds, and the chief hears the others screaming, but only for a moment.

Mitch's breath hitched.

Their women must have died at the same moment, or within seconds, across the Spent River.

The chief falls with his arms over his head. He and all his sons and the other hunters struggle for tenths of seconds against the scalding mud and then must lie still. It covers them, a blanket more than two feet thick, larded with sticks and chunks of log and rocks the size of fists, with bits of dead animals.

As Mitch walked, he grew calmer. Things seemed to fall into place. When the search was on, his mind became a quiet lake.

The land is hot and steaming. Nothing near the river lives that stood above ground. Bushes denuded of their leaves crouch smashed and wilted along the river course. Corpses lie baked and half-buried under gouts of steaming mud. The ground smells like mud and steamed vegetables. It smells like cooked herbs in a meaty stew.

The mud cools.

And then comes the third fall of ash, entombing the remains of the men, the women, and the ravaged land along the Spent River and for miles around.

It was over.

Mitch kept his head down and pressed one eye with a finger, but the pain was coming anyway. Price to be paid.

Rod Taylor pushes the lever forward on the old time machine. The mud hardens under the gray pall of falling ash. Time flies past. The bodies decay within their molds, staining the hard mud. The flesh seeps away and the bones rattle with earthquakes and the mud and stone cracks and fresh water and mud enters, filling the hollow with mud of different density, different composition, holding the bones, finally, still.

The men can rest.

Mitch knew they were still here, somewhere.

He stopped walking and looked to his right, into a step cut into the bluff by hundreds of centuries of erosion. At first he could not see what had attracted his attention; it was hidden by the painful little sliver of light.

The top of the mudstone step was at least six feet above his head. A streak of dark gray capped the step beneath a superficial wig of soil and brush. But his vision tunneled into a bright ball and all he saw was the shiny brown prominence lying horizontally in the stone.

He hardly dared to breathe.

Mitch stooped, arm hanging, propping his knees against the mound of weathered-out clods and pebbles. Reached out with his right finger and brushed along the compacted gray ash and caked mudstone.

The prominence was firm in the hardened layer. It could have been a bone from a deer, a mountain goat, or a bighorn sheep.

But it was not. It was a human shin, a tibia. In this layer, it had to be at least as old as the bones in the camp. He reached down with one hand, sparks flying in his right eye, and felt for the small piece he had seen there, a dark brown talus of bone amongst the rocky talus.

He held it up, turning it until he could see it clearly. It was small, but also from a human. *Homo* at least. He replaced it. Position would be important when they surveyed.

He took a dental pick from his jacket and worked at the hardened mud and ash around the tibia until he was sure, fighting the pain in his cranium for long minutes. Then he sat back and drew up his knees.

He could no longer put it off. The migraine had arrived. He hadn't had one this bad in more than ten years. The dental pick fell from his hand as he curled up on the ground, trying not to moan.

He managed to reach up with one finger and stroke the half-buried length of bone.

"Found you," Mitch said. Then he closed his eyes and felt his own lahar wash over him.

33

Dicken's monitor was filled with comparisons of protein expression in embryonic tissues at different stages of development, looking for the elusive retroviral or transposon trigger that might have crept into a complex of developmental genes, promoting the hymen in human females. Even using prior searches and comparisons—incredibly, he had found some in the literature—it looked as if this would take months or years.

Dr. Jurie had shunted Dicken into the safest and least interesting position at Sandia Pathogenics. Putting him in safe, cold storage until needed.

An odd little dance of utility and security. Jurie was keeping Dicken under his thumb, as it were, just to know where he was and what he was up to, and possibly to pick his brain.

But also to confess? To be caught out?

Dicken would not rule out anything where Aram Jurie was concerned.

The man had passed along a list of rambling, long e-mail messages, cryptic, elusive, and a little too evocative for Dicken's comfort. Jurie might be on to something, Dicken thought, a twisted and crazy but undeniably big insight.

Jurie held the belief—not exactly new—that viruses played a substantial but crude role in nearly every stage of embryonic development. But he had some interesting notions about how they did so:

> *"Genomic viruses want to play in the big game, but as genetic players go, they're simple, constrained, fallen from grace. They can't do the big stuff, so they engage in cryptic little elaborations, and the big game tolerates and then becomes addicted to their subtle plays . . .*
>
> *"Weak in themselves, endogenous viruses may rely on a very different form of apoptosis, programmed cell suicide. ERVs express at certain times and present antigen on the cell surface. The cell is inspected by the agents of the immune system and killed. By coordinating how and which cells present antigen, genomic viruses can participate crudely in sculpting the embryo, or even the growing body after birth. Of course, they work to increase their numbers and their position in the species, in the extended genome. They work by maintaining a feeble but persistent control in the face of a constant and powerful assault by the immune system.*

"And in mammals, they've won. We have surrendered some of the most crucial aspects of our lives to the viruses, just to give our babies time to develop in the womb, rather than in the constraining egg; time to develop more sophisticated nervous systems. A calculated gamble. All our generations are held ransom because of our indebtedness to the viral genes.

"Like getting a loan from the Mafia . . ."

Maggie Flynn knocked on the open door to Dicken's office. "Got a moment?" she asked.

"Not really. Why?" Dicken asked, turning in his rolling chair. Flynn looked flushed and upset.

"Something's come up. Jurie's off the campus. He tells us to sit tight. I don't think we can. We just aren't prepared."

"What is it?"

"We need expert advice," Flynn said. "And you could be the expert."

Dicken stood and stuck his hands in his pants pockets, alert and wary. "What sort of advice?"

"We have a new guest," Flynn said. "Not a monkey." She did not appear at all happy with the prospect.

If Maggie Flynn believed Dicken had Jurie's confidence, who was he to correct her? Flynn's pass could clear them both if his own pass was blocked—he had learned that much yesterday, visiting Presky's monotreme study lab.

Flynn took him outside the building to a small cart and drove him around the five linked warehouses that contained the zoo. Out in the open, away from listening devices, she expressed herself more clearly.

"You've worked with SHEVA kids," Flynn began. "I haven't. We have a tough situation, medically speaking, ethically speaking, and I don't know how to approach it. As the only married female in this block, Turner picked me to provide some moral support, establish a rapport . . . but frankly, I haven't a clue."

"What are you talking about?" Dicken asked.

Flynn stopped the cart, even more nervous. "You don't know?" she asked, her voice rising a notch.

Dicken's mind started to race and he saw he was on the edge of screwing up a golden opportunity. *You've worked with . . . As the only married female . . .*

They're doing it. They've done it. He felt his pulse going up and hoped it did not show.

"Oh," he said, with a fair imitation of casualness. "Virus children."

Flynn bit her lip. "I don't like that phrase." She pushed the cart forward again with the little control stick. "Jurie never worked directly with them. Only with specimens. Neither has Turner, and of course Presky is an animal guy, no bedside manner whatsoever. We thought of you. Turner said that must be why you're here, and why you're being given shit theoretical work—so you can be pulled loose for something like this when the time comes."

"Okay," Dicken said, putting on a mask of professional caution. He pressed his lips together to keep from saying anything revealing or stupid.

"Something's gone wrong at the border, I don't know what. I'm not in that particular loop. Jurie's in Arizona. Turner told me to bring you in before he gets back." Her smile was fleeting and desperate. "The cat's away."

It was an in-house conspiracy after all, and not a very convincing one. Flynn seemed to expect him to say something reassuring and glib. The whole damned lab functioned on a morphine high of glibness, as if to hide the gnawing awareness that what they were doing might someday attract the attention of The Hague.

"God bless the beasts and children," Dicken said. "Let's go."

On the north side of the array of Pathogenics warehouses, a segmented, inflatable silver enclosure perched on a black expanse of parking lot like some huge alien larva. An access tube led from the enclosure into Warehouse Number 5, which contained most of the primate study labs. Dicken noticed two outside compressors and a complicated, freshly assembled sterilization unit on the south end of the sausage.

He didn't realize how big the enclosure was until they were almost upon it. The whole complex was as big as one of the warehouses and covered at least an acre.

They parked the cart and entered Warehouse 5 through the delivery door. Turner met them in a small clinic inside the warehouse—a hospital clinic, obviously equipped for humans and not just for primates. "Glad you could make it, Christopher," he said. "Jurie's dealing with some mess at the border. A bunch of protesters blocked a lab bus, refused to let it enter Arizona. They had help from the local police, apparently. Jurie had to order up another bus at the last minute and route it around the roadblocks."

"No surprise," Flynn said. Dicken glanced between them both. What he saw chilled him. The glibness had completely evaporated. They knew their careers were on the line.

"The preparations have been obvious, but Jurie only told us yesterday," Turner said. Their statements piled together.

"She's a very unhappy girl," Flynn said.

"I'm not sure we should even have her here," Turner said.

"She's pregnant," Flynn said.

"A rape, we're told. Her foster father," Turner said.

"Oh, God, I didn't know it was *rape*," Flynn said, and pressed her knuckles to her cheek. "She's only fourteen."

"They brought her from a school in Arizona," Flynn said. "Jurie calls it *our* school. That's where we've been getting most of our specimens."

"She's pregnant?" Dicken asked, dumbfounded, and then wondered if he had blown his cover.

"That's not generally known even in the clinic," Turner said. "I'd appreciate some discretion."

Dicken let his astonishment come forward. "That's major." His voice cracked. "But she's 52 xx. What about polyploidy?"

"I only know what I see," Turner said grimly. "She's pregnant by her foster father."

"That's absolutely *huge*," Dicken said.

"She arrived at the school a month ago," Turner said. "We discovered her pregnancy when we processed a set of her blood tests. Jurie almost had a heart attack when he got the results from the lab. He seemed elated. He got her transferred to Pathogenics last week without telling the rest of us."

"I was so mad," Flynn said. "I could have clobbered him."

"What else could we do? The school couldn't take care of her, and it's for damn sure no hospital would touch her."

Dicken held up his hand. "Who's working the clinic?" he asked.

"Maggie, Tommy Wrigley—you met Tommy at the party, and Thomas Powers. Some people brought in from California; we don't know them. And, of course, Jurie, on the research side. But he's never even visited the girl."

"What's her condition?"

"She's about three months along. Not doing too well. We think she may have self-induced Shiver," Flynn said.

"That is not confirmed," Turner said angrily. "She's acting as if she has the flu, and that's all it may be. But we're being extra cautious. And this information goes nowhere . . . don't even tell anyone else at Pathogenics."

"But Dr. Dicken would know if it's Shiver, wouldn't he?" Flynn said defensively. "Isn't that why Jurie brought you here?"

"Let's look at the girl," Dicken said.

"Her name is Fremont, Helen Fremont," Flynn said. "She's originally from Nevada. Las Vegas, I think."

"Reno," Turner corrected. Then, his face collapsing in utter misery, his shoulders slumping, he added, "I don't think I can take this much longer. I really don't."

34

BALTIMORE-WASHINGTON

Kaye and Marge Cross sat in the back of the taxi in silence. Kaye looked at the passive neck of the driver below his turban, caught a glimpse of his small grin in the rearview mirror. He was whistling to himself, happy. For him, having a SHEVA granddaughter was no great burden, obviously.

Kaye did not know much about conditions for SHEVA children in Pakistan. Generally, traditional cultures—Muslims, Hindus, Buddhists—had been more accepting of the new children. That was both surprising and humbling.

Cross drummed her fingers on her knee and looked out the window at the highway, passing cars. A long semi rolled past with TRANS-NATIONAL BIRMINGHAM PORK emblazoned in huge red letters on the sides of its two trailers.

"Spent lots of money on *that* one," Cross murmured.

Kaye assumed she was referring to pig tissue transplants. "Where are we going, Marge?" she asked.

"Just driving," Cross said. Her chin bounced up and down, and Kaye could not be sure whether she was nodding or just moving her jaw in time to the truck ruts in the roadway.

"That address is in a residential neighborhood. I know Baltimore and Maryland pretty well," Kaye said. "I assume you aren't kidnapping me."

Cross gave her a weak smile. "Hell, you're paying," she said. "There's some people I think you'll want to meet."

"All right," Kaye said.

"Lars came down pretty hard on Robert."

"Robert's a sanctimonious prick."

Cross shrugged. "Nevertheless, I'm not going to take Lars's advice."

"I didn't think you would," Kaye said. She hated to lose her labs and her researchers, even now. Doing science was her last comfort, her lab the last place she could take refuge and lose herself in work.

"I'm letting you go," Cross said.

To her surprise, the blow did not feel so heavy after all. It was Kaye's turn to nod in time to the cab's rubbery suspension.

"Your work with me is over," Cross said.

"Fine," Kaye said tightly.

"Isn't it?" Cross asked.

"Of course," Kaye said, her heart thumping. *What I have been putting off doing. What I cannot do alone.*

"What more would you do at Americol?"

"Pure research on hormonal activation of retroviral elements in humans," Kaye said, still grasping at the past. "Focus on stress-related signaling systems. Transfer of transcription factors and regulating genes by ERV to somatic cells. Study the viruses as common genetic transport and regulatory systems for the body. Prove that the all-disease model is wrong."

"It's a good area," Cross said. "A little too wild for Americol, but I can make some calls and get you a position elsewhere. Frankly, I don't think you're going to have time."

Kaye lifted her eyebrows and thinned her lips. "If I'm no longer employed by you, how can you know how much time I'll have?"

Cross smiled, but the smile vanished quickly and she frowned out the window. "Robert picked the wrong hammer to hit you with," she said. "Or at least he did it in front of the wrong woman."

"How's that?"

"Twenty-three years ago come August, I was beginning to drum up venture capital for my first company. I was packing my schedule with meetings and heavy-duty lunches." Her expression turned wistful, as if she were recalling an old, wonderful romance. "God dropped in. Bad timing, to say the least. He hit me so hard I had to drive to the Hamptons and hide out in a hotel room for a week. Basically I swooned."

She was avoiding direct eye contact, like a little girl confessing. Kaye leaned forward to see her face more clearly. Kaye had never seen Cross look so vulnerable.

"I can't tell you how scared I was that He was a sign of madness, epilepsy, or worse."

"You thought it was a he?"

Cross nodded. "Doesn't make sense for a couple of strong women, does it? It bothered me a lot, then. But no matter how bothered I was, how scared I was, I never thought about visiting a radiology center. That was brilliant, Kaye. Not cheap, but brilliant."

Kaye glanced at the driver's face in the rearview mirror. He was obviously trying to ignore the words being spoken in the backseat, trying to give them privacy—and not succeeding.

"Love isn't the word, but it's all we have. Love without desire." Cross reached up to wipe her perfectly manicured fingers beneath her eyes. "I've never told anybody. Someone like Robert would have used it against me."

"But it's the truth," Kaye said.

"No, it isn't," Cross said peevishly. "It's a personal experience. It was real to you and to me, but that doesn't get us anywhere in this old, cruel world. That same vision might have compelled someone else to burn old women as witches or kill Englishmen, like Joan of Arc. Cranking up the old Inquisition."

"I don't think so," Kaye said.

"How do you know the butchers and murderers didn't get a message?"

Kaye had to admit that she did not.

Cross said, "I've spent so much of my time trying to forget, just so I could do the work I had to do to get where I wanted to be. Sometimes it was cruel work, stepping on other folks's dreams. And whenever I remembered, it just crushed me again. Because I knew this thing, it, He, would never punish me, no matter what I did or how I misbehaved. Not just forgiveness—*no judgment.* Only love. He can't be real," Cross said. "What He said and what He did doesn't make any sense."

"He felt real to me," Kaye said.

"Did you ever hear what happened to Thomas Aquinas?" Cross asked.

Kaye shook her head.

"The most admired theologian of all. Furiously adept thinker, logical beyond all measure—and pretty hard to read nowadays. But smart, no doubt about it, and a young fellow when he made his mark. Student of Albertus Magnus. Defender of Aristotle in the Church. He wrote big thick tracts. Admired throughout Christendom, and still revered as a thinker to this day. On the morning of December 6, 1273, he was saying Mass in Naples. He was older, about my age. Right in the middle of the sermon, he just stopped speaking, and stared at nothing. Or stared at *everything.* I imagine he must have gawped like a fish." Cross's expression was quizzical, distant.

"He stopped writing, dictating, stopped contributing to the *Summa*, his life's work. And when he was pressed to explain why he had stopped, he said, 'I can do no more; such things have been revealed to me that all I have written seems as straw, and I now await the end of my life.' He died a few months later." Cross snorted. "No wonder Aquinas was brought up short, the poor bastard. I know a hierarchy when I see one. I'm little better than a wriggly worm in a pond compared to what touched me. I wouldn't dare try to tell God how to behave." She smiled. "Yes, dear, I can be humble." Cross patted Kaye's hand. "And that's that. You're fired. You've done all you need to do, for now, at my company."

"What about Jackson?" Kaye asked.

"He's limited, but he's still useful, and there's still important work for him to do. I'll have Lars watch over him."

"Jackson doesn't understand," Kaye said.

"If you mean he's narrowly focused, that's just what I need right now. He'll cross all the *t*'s and dot all the *i*'s, trying to prove he's right. Good for him."

"But he'll get it wrong."

"Then he'll do it thoroughly." Cross was adamant. "Robert's problem was familiar to Aquinas. He called it *ignorantia affectata*, cultivated ignorance."

"God should touch him," Kaye said bitterly, and then flushed in embarrassment, as if that were any kind of punishment.

Cross considered this seriously for a moment. "I'm surprised God touched *me*," she said. "I'd be shocked if He wanted to have anything to do with Robert."

35

Inside the silver tent were eight single wide mobile home trailers, sitting up on blocks on a wrinkled and patched gray plastic floor and surrounded, at a distance of thirty feet, by a circle of transparent plastic panels topped with razor wire. The trailers did not look in the least comfortable or friendly.

Dicken tried to orient himself in the general gloomy light that seeped through the silver tent. They had entered on the western side. North, then, was where a small Emergency Action van was parked, the same van that had presumably brought Helen Fremont from Arizona. South of the mobile homes and the wall of plastic and razor wire, a small maze of tables and lab benches had been set up and stocked with standard medical and lab diagnostic equipment.

A few klieg lights mounted on long steel poles supplemented the dim sunlight.

Dicken saw no one else under the tent.

"We don't have a team in place yet," Flynn said. "She just came down sick this morning."

"Is there a phone connection in the trailer, an intercom, a bullhorn, anything?"

Flynn shook her head. "We're still putting it together."

"Goddamnit, she's alone in there?"

Turner nodded.

"For how long?"

"Since this morning," Flynn said. "I went in and tried to do an exam. She refused, but I took some pictures, and of course, there's the video. We're running tests on the waste line fluid and the air, but the equipment here isn't familiar to me. I didn't trust it, so I took the samples over to the primate lab. They're still being run."

"Does Jurie know she's ill?" Dicken asked.

"We called him," Turner said.

"Did he give any instructions?"

"He said to leave her alone. Let nobody in until we were sure."

"But Maggie went in."

"I had to," Flynn said. "She looked so scared."

"You were in a suit?"

"Of course."

Dicken swung about on his stiff leg and leaned his head to one side, biting his cheek to keep his opinions to himself. He was furious.

Flynn would not meet his eyes. "It's procedure. All tests done under Level 3 conditions."

"Well, we sure as hell follow the goddamned rules, don't we?" Dicken said. "Haven't you at least asked her to come out and have a doctor inspect her?"

"She won't come out," Turner said. "We have video cameras tracking her. She's in the bedroom. She's just lying there."

"Dandy," Dicken said. "What in hell do you want me to do?"

"We have the pictures," Flynn said, and took her data phone from her pocket.

"Show me," Dicken said.

She brought up a succession of five pictures on the phone's screen. Dicken saw a young SHEVA girl with dark brown hair, pale blue eyes with yellow specks, thin features but prominent cheekbones, pale skin. The girl looked like a frightened cat, her eyes searching the unseen corners, refusing even in her misery to be intimidated.

Dicken could tell the girl was exhibiting no obvious signs of Shiver— no lesions on her skinny arms, no scarlet cingulated markings on her neck. A live update chart butted in at the conclusion of the slide show and displayed a temperature of 102.

"Remote temperature sensing?"

Flynn nodded.

"You said her viral titers were high."

"She cut herself getting into the van. They had been instructed not to draw blood, but they sequestered the stain and we took a sample under controlled conditions. That's why the van is still here. She's producing HERV."

"Of course she is. She's pregnant. She doesn't present any of the necessary symptoms," he said. "What makes you think it's Shiver?"

"Dr. Jurie said it might be."

"Jurie isn't here, and you are."

"But she's *pregnant*," Turner said, scowling, as if that explained their concern.

"Have you tested for pseudotype viruses?"

"We're still running the samples," Turner said.

"Anything?"

"Not yet."

"You've had Shiver," Flynn said sullenly. "You should be even more cautious." She looked more angry than distressed now. They were wondering whose side he was on, and he was half inclined to tell them.

"I won't even need a suit," he said contemptuously, and tossed the phone back to Flynn. He walked toward the trailer.

"Hold it," Turner said, his face red. "Go in there without a suit, and you'll stay. We won't—we *can't* let you out."

Dicken turned and bowed, holding out his arms in exasperated placation. There was work to do, a problem to resolve, and anger wasn't helping.

"Then get me a goddamned suit! And a phone or an intercom. She needs to communicate with the outside. She needs to talk with someone. Where are her parents—her mother, I mean?"

"We don't know," Flynn said.

The narrow rooms inside the mobile home were neat and cheerless. Rental-style furniture, upholstered in beige and yellow plaid vinyl, lent them an air of cheap and soulless utility. The girl had brought no personal effects, and had touched none of the stuffed animal toys that lined the shelves in the tiny living room, still in their plastic wrappings.

Dicken wondered how long ago the stuffed animals had been purchased. How long had Jurie been planning to bring SHEVA children into Pathogenics?

A year?

Two dining chairs had been upset beside the dinette. Dicken bent to set them right. The plastic in his suit squeaked. He was already starting to sweat, despite the air conditioner pack. He had long since come to sincerely hate isolation suits.

He looked for other obstructions that might snag the plastic, then moved slowly toward the bedroom at the back of the trailer. He knocked on the frame and peered through the half-open door. The girl lay on her back on the bed, still wearing pedal pushers, blouse, and a denim jacket. The bed's green plastic covers had been tossed aside, and she was staring at the ceiling.

"Hello?"

The girl did not look at him. He could see her skinny chest moving, and her cheeks were ruddy with fever or fear or perhaps despair.

"Helen?" He walked along the narrow space beside the bed and bent over so she could see his face. "My name is Christopher Dicken."

She swung her head to one side. "Go away. I'll make you sick," she said.

"I doubt it, Helen. How do you feel?"

"I hate your suit."

"I don't like it much, either."

"Leave me alone."

Dicken straightened and folded his arms with some difficulty. The suit rustled and squeaked and he felt like one of the plastic-wrapped stuffed animals. "Tell me how you're feeling."

"I want to throw up."

"Have you thrown up?"

"No," she said.

"That's good."

"I keep trying." The girl sat up on the bed. "You should be afraid of me. That's what my mother told me to say to anyone who tries to touch me or kidnap me. She said, 'Use what you have.' "

"You don't make people sick, Helen," Dicken said.

"I wish I could. I want *him* to be sick."

Dicken could not imagine her pain and frustration, and did not feel comfortable probing it out. "I won't say I understand. I don't."

"Stop talking and go away."

"We won't talk about that, okay. But we need to talk about how you're feeling, and I'd like to examine you. I'm a doctor."

"So was *he*," she snapped. She rolled to one side, still not looking at Dicken. Her eyes narrowed. "My muscles hurt. Am I going to die?"

"I don't think so."

"I should die."

"Please don't talk that way. If things are going to get any better, I have to examine you. I promise I won't hurt you or do anything that makes you feel uncomfortable."

"I'm used to them taking blood," the girl said. "They tie us down if we fight." She stared fixedly at his face through the hood. "You sound like you've helped a lot of sick people."

"Quite a few. Some were very, very sick, and they got better."

"And some died."

"Yes," Dicken said. "Some died."

"I don't feel that sick, other than wanting to throw up."

"That might be your baby."

The girl opened her mouth wide and her cheeks went pale. "I'm *pregnant*?" she asked.

Dicken suddenly felt the bottom fall out of his stomach. "They didn't tell you?"

"Oh, my God," the girl said and curled up, facing away from him. "I knew it. I knew it. I could smell something. It was his baby inside of me. Oh, my God." The girl sat up abruptly. "I need to go to the bathroom."

Dicken must have showed his concern even through the hood.

"I'm not going to hurt myself. I have to throw up. Don't look. Don't watch me."

He said, "I'll wait for you in the living room."

She swung her legs out over the side of the bed and stood, then paused, arms held out as if to keep her balance. She stared down at the fake wooden floor. "He used nose plugs and scrubbed me with soap, and then he covered me with cheap perfume. I couldn't make him stop. He said he wanted to learn whether he would ever have grandchildren. But he wasn't even my real father. A baby. Oh, my God."

The girl's face wrinkled up in an expression so complex Dicken could have studied it for hours and not understood. He knew how a chimpanzee must feel, watching humans emote.

"I'm sorry," Dicken said.

"Have you met anyone else like me who was pregnant?" the girl asked, holding, compelling his gaze through the plastic.

"No," Dicken said.

"I'm the first?"

"You're the first in my experience."

"Yeah." She got a panicky look and walked stiffly into the bathroom. Dicken could hear her trying to throw up. He went into the living room. The smell of his sorrow and loathing filled the helmet and there was no way to wipe his eyes or his nose.

When the girl came out, she stopped in the doorway, then sidled through, as if afraid to touch the frame. She held her arms out to her side like wings. Her cheeks were a steady golden brown and the yellow flint-sparks in her eyes seemed even larger and brighter. More than ever, she looked like a cat. She glared at him quizzically. She could see his puffy eyes and wet cheeks through the plastic. "What do you care?" she asked.

Dicken shook his head inside the helmet. "Hard to explain," he said. "I was there at the beginning."

"What does that mean?"

"I'm not sure there's time," he said. "We need to find out why you're sick."

"Explain it to me, and then you can look at me," the girl said.

Dicken wondered how they would react outside if he spent a couple of hours in the trailer. If Jurie should happen to come back . . .

None of that mattered. He had to do something for the girl. She deserved so much more than this.

He pulled up the covering seal and unzipped his helmet, then removed it. It certainly wasn't the worst risk he had ever taken. "I was one of the first to know," he began.

The girl lifted her nose and sniffed. The way her upper lip formed a V was so strangely beautiful that Dicken had to smile.

"Better?" he asked.

"You're not afraid, you're angry," the girl said. "You're angry *for* me."

He nodded.

"Nobody's ever been angry for me. It smells kind of sweet. Sit in the living room. Stay a few feet away, in case I'm dangerous."

They walked into the living room. Dicken sat on a dinette chair and she stood by the couch, arms folded, as if ready to run. "Tell me," she said.

"Can I examine you while I talk? You can keep your clothes on, and I won't stick you with anything. I just need to look and touch."

The girl nodded.

Rumors and half-truths were all she had ever heard. She remained standing for the first few minutes, while Dicken pressed his fingers gently under her jaw, into her armpits, and looked between her fingers and toes.

After a while, she sat on the vinyl couch, listening closely and watching him with those incredible flint-spark eyes.

36

ARIZONA

The three cars split off at a crossroads going through a small desert town. Stella looked through the rear window at the diminishing dot of the car that contained Celia and LaShawna and two of the boys. Then she turned to look at Will, who seemed to have fallen asleep.

JoBeth Hayden had talked about her daughter for the first half hour or so, about how she had been glad Bonnie was not on the bus, being taken to Sandia, yet how disappointing it was not to see her and have her be free.

After a while, Stella had felt her muscles tighten from the aftereffects of the crash, and she had tuned out Jobeth, focusing instead on the pile of crumpled pages that Will had arranged on the seat between them.

Will opened his eyes and leaned forward. "Mrs. Hayden," he said, and ran his tongue over dry lips, avoiding Stella's curious stare.

"Yes. Your name is William, isn't it?"

"Will. I'd like to put these up by you." He dropped some crumpled pages in the middle of the front bench seat.

"That's trash," Jobeth Hayden said disapprovingly.

"I can't keep it back here," Will said.

"I don't see why not."

Stella could not figure out what Will was up to. She rubbed her nose. The front bench seat was in direct sunlight. Will was fever-scenting. She could smell him now, subtle but direct, like cocoa powder and butter. She had never smelled anything exactly like it.

"Can I?" Will asked.

Jobeth Hayden shook her head slowly. Stella saw her eyes in the rearview mirror; she looked confused. "All right," she said.

Stella picked up a crumpled page and smelled it. She drew back, rejecting the urge to frith, and stared at Will resentfully. The paperback was a reservoir. Will had been rubbing the pages behind his ears, storing up scent. She poked him with her finger and flashed a query with her cheeks. He took the paper from her hands.

"We don't want to go to this ranch," Will said to Mrs. Hayden.

"That's where we're going. There's a doctor there. It's a safe place, and they're expecting you."

"I know a better place," Will said. "Could you drive us to California?"

"That's silly," Jobeth Hayden said.

"I've been trying to get there for more than a year now."

"We're going to the ranch, and that's that."

Will dropped another wadded-up page onto the pool of sun on the front seat. Stella could smell Will's particular form of persuasion very clearly now, and however much she fought against it, what he said was beginning to seem reasonable.

Mrs. Hayden continued to drive. Stella wondered if too much persuasion would confuse her and make her drive off the road.

Will cradled his head in his arms. "We're fine. I don't need a doctor./ She's fine, she can still drive."

"We're going to see a doctor in a small town in Arizona, and then we're going straight to the ranch," Mrs. Hayden said.

"It's right across the state line. You have to drive through Nevada, though. Can I see the map?"

Mrs. Hayden was frowning deeply now, and she started to toss back the pieces of crumpled paper. "I don't think that's a good idea," she said. "What are you doing?"

"I just want to see the map," Will said.

"Well, I suppose that's okay, but no more of this trash, please. I thought you children behaved better."

Stella touched Will's arm. "Stop it," she whispered, leaning forward so only he would hear.

Will ignored Stella and tossed the paper again onto the front seat, in the pool of sunshine that warmed it and made it release its scent.

"This is really intolerable," Mrs. Hayden said, but her head straightened and she did not sound angry. She reached over, opened up the glove box, and handed Will an Auto Club map of Arizona and New Mexico. "I don't use them often," she said. "They're pretty old."

Will opened the map and spread it across their knees. His finger followed highways going north and west. Stella leaned into the corner where the seat met the door and folded her arms.

"You'll have to sit up straight, sweetie," Mrs. Hayden told her. "The car has side airbags. It's not safe to slump over."

Stella sat up. Will looked at her. Her back was really hurting now. Calmly, he reached over and touched her hands, her legs, then her back.

"What are you doing back there?" Mrs. Hayden asked, dimly concerned.

Will did not answer, and she did not press the question. His fingers marched lightly up Stella's spine, and she rolled over to let him examine her back.

"You'll be okay," Will said.

"How do you know?" Stella asked.

"You'd smell different if you were bleeding inside, or if something was broken. You're just suffering from a little whiplash, and I don't think there's any nerve damage. I smelled a boy with a broken back once, and he had a sad, awful smell. You smell good."

"I don't like you telling us what to do," Stella said.

"I'll stop once she takes us to California," Will said. He did not seem very confident, and he did not smell sure of himself. This was one nervous young man.

"It's a beautiful day/ I learned a lot in North Carolina," Will doubled. "I'm glad you're here/ That was before they burned our camp."

Stella had never met anyone more adept at persuasion. She wondered whether his talent was natural, or whether he had been taught somewhere.

She also wondered whether they would be in any danger. But Stella was not willing, not yet anyway, to tell Mrs. Hayden her suspicions. She apparently had suspicions of her own. "I'd like to roll down the windows," Mrs. Hayden said. "It's getting stuffy in here."

"It's fine, really," Will said. At the same time, he undered to Stella, "/I need your help. Don't you want to see what we can do?"

Stella shook her head, thinking of Mitch and Kaye, thinking irrationally of the house in Virginia, the last place she had really felt safe, though that had been an illusion.

"Didn't you ever want to run away?" Will asked in a near whisper.

"It really *is* stuffy," Mrs. Hayden said. Will was running out of pages.

"Help me," Will pleaded softly, earnestly.

"What is this place?" Stella asked.

"I think it's in the woods," Will said. "It's hidden, far from the towns. They have animals and grow their own food./ They raise marijuana and sell it to make money to buy stuff."

Marijuana was legal now in most states, but still that sounded dangerous. Stella suddenly felt very cautious. Will looked and smelled scary, with his jumbled hair and cocoa-powder richness, his face that seemed capable of so many expressions. *He's been with others and they've taught him so much. What could they teach me—and what could I add?*

"Would I be able to call my parents?"

"They're not like us/ They'd take you back," Will replied. "We need to be with our own people/ You'll grow and learn who you really are."

Stella felt her stomach knot with confusion and indecision. It was what she had been thinking about in the school. Forming demes was impossible with humans around; they always found ways to interfere. For all she knew, demes were just what children tried on for practice. Soon they would be adults, and what would they do then?

How would they ever find out if humans kept clinging to them?

"It's time to grow up," Will said.

"Why, you're so young," Mrs. Hayden said dreamily. She was driving straight and steadily, but her voice sounded wrong, and Stella knew they had to do something in concert soon or Mrs. Hayden could go one way or the other.

"I'm only fifteen," Stella said. Actually, she had not yet had her fifteenth birthday, but she always added in the time her mother had been pregnant with the first-stage embryo.

"There's supposed to be a man there in his sixties, one of us," Will said.

"That's impossible," Stella said.

"That's what they say. He's from the south, from Georgia. Or maybe Russia. They weren't sure which."

"Do you know where this place is?"

Will tapped his head. "They showed us a map before the camp was burned."

"Is it real?"

Will could not answer this. "I think so./ I want it to be real."

Stella closed her eyes. She could feel the warmth behind her eyelids, the sun passing over her face, the suspended redness, and below that the rising up of all her minds, all the parts of her body that yearned. To be alone with her own kind, making her own way, learning all she needed to learn to survive among people who hated her . . .

That would be an incredible adventure. That would be worth so much danger.

"It's all you've wanted, I know it," Will said.

"How do I know you're not just *persuading* me?" Her cheeks added unconscious quotes to the emphasis on that word, which sounded so wrong, so lacking in nuance, so human.

"Look inside," Will said.

"I *have,*" Stella said, a little wail that brought Mrs. Hayden's head around.

"I'm fine," Stella said, arms folded tightly across her chest. The tires squealed as Mrs. Hayden straightened the car out on the road.

Stella gripped the arm of her seat.

"I'm sweating like a bastard," she told Will with a little giggle.

"So am I," Will said, and smiled crookedly.

There was one last question. "What about sex?" she asked, so quietly Will did not hear and she had to repeat herself.

"Don't you know?" Will said. "Humans can rape us, but we don't rape each other. It just doesn't work that way."

"What if it happens anyway, and we don't know what we're doing, or how to stay out of trouble?"

"I don't know the answer to that," Will said. "Does anybody? But I know one thing. With us, it doesn't happen until it's right. And now it isn't right."

That was honest enough. She could feel her independence returning, and all the answers were the same.

She was strong. She was capable. She knew that.

She focused on fever-scenting for Mrs. Hayden.

"Whoo," Will said, and waved his hand in the air. "You strong, lady."

"I am *woman,*/ I am *strong*," Stella sang softly, and they giggled together. She leaned forward. "Please, would you take us to California?" she asked Mrs. Hayden.

"We'll have to stop for gas. I only brought a little money."

"It'll be enough," Will said.

"Do you need the book?" Stella asked him. It was a yellowed, dog-eared, and now thoroughly reduced paperback called *Spartacus* by Howard Fast.

"Maybe," Will said. "I really don't know."

"Did you learn that in the woods, too?"

Will shook his head. "I made it up myself," he said. "We have to be smart. They were taking us to Sandia. They wanted to kill us all. We have to think for ourselves."

37

The cab dropped off Kaye and Marge Cross at a single-story brick house on a pleasant, slightly weedy street in Randallstown, Maryland. The grass in the front yard stood a foot high and had long since turned straw yellow. A big old Buick Riviera from the last century, covered with rust and half-hearted patches of gray primer, sat up on blocks in the oil-stained driveway.

They walked up the overgrown path to the front porch. Kaye stood on the lower step, unsure where to look or what to expect. Cross punched the doorbell. Somewhere inside the house, electronic chimes played the four opening notes from Beethoven's Fifth. Kaye stared at a plastic tricycle with big white wheels almost lost in the grass beside the porch.

The woman who opened the door was Laura Bloch, from Senator Gianelli's office. She smiled at Kaye and Cross. "Delighted you could be here," she said. "Welcome to the Maryland Advisory Group on National Biological Policy. We're an ad hoc committee, and this is an exploratory meeting."

Kaye looked at Cross, lips downturned in dubious surprise.

"You belong here," Cross told her. "I'm not sure I do."

"Of course you do, Marge," Bloch said. "Come on in, both of you."

They entered and stood in the small foyer opposite the living room, separated by a low wall and a row of turned wooden columns. The inside of the house—brown carpet, cream-colored walls decorated with family pictures, colonial-style maple furniture and a coffee table covered with magazines and a flattop computer—could have been anywhere in the country. Typical middle-class comfort.

In the dining room, seven people sat around a maple table. Kaye was not acquainted with most of them. She did recognize one woman, however, and her face brightened.

Luella Hamilton walked across the living room. They stood apart for a moment, Kaye in her pants suit, Mrs. Hamilton in a long orange and brown caftan. She had put on a lot of weight since she and Kaye had last seen each other, and not much of it from her pregnancy.

"Dear baby Jesus," Mrs. Hamilton let out with a small, wild-eyed laugh. "We were just on the *phone*. You were going to stay put. Marge, what is this all about?"

"You know each other?" Cross asked.

"We sure do," Kaye said. But she did not explain.

"Welcome to the revolution," Luella said, smiling sweetly. "You know Laura. Come meet the others. Quite a high-toned group we have here." She introduced Kaye to the three women and four men seated at the table. Most were in their middle years; the youngest, a woman, appeared to be in her thirties. All were dressed in suits or stylish office work clothes. All looked like Washington insiders to Kaye, who had met plenty. She saw gratefully that they were all wearing name tags.

"Most of these folks come from the offices of key senators and representatives, eyes and ears, not necessarily proxies," Laura Bloch explained. "We won't connect the dots until later. Ladies and gentlemen, Kaye is both a working scientist and a mommy."

"You're the one who discovered SHEVA," said one of the two gray-haired men. Kaye tried to demur, but Bloch shushed her.

"Take credit where it's due, Kaye," Bloch said. "We're presenting a paper to the president within the week. Marge sent us your conclusions about genomic viruses, along with a lot of other papers. We're still digesting them. I'm sure there are lots of questions."

"Wow, I'll say," chuckled a middle-aged man named Kendall Burkett. "Worse than homework."

Kaye remembered Burkett now. They had met at a conference on SHEVA four years ago. He was a fundraiser for legal aid for SHEVA parents.

Luella returned from the kitchen carrying a pitcher of orange juice and a plate of cookies and celery stalks with peanut butter and cream cheese fillings. "I don't know why you folks come here," she told the group. "I'm not much of a cook."

Bloch put her arms around Luella's shoulders. They made quite a contrast. Kaye could tell Luella was six months or more along, although it was only slightly apparent on her ample frame.

"Come sit," said the younger woman. She pointed to an empty chair beside her and smiled. Her name, printed neatly on her tag, was Linda Gale. Kaye knew that name from somewhere.

"It's our second meeting," said Burkett. "We're still getting acquainted."

"Orange juice okay for you, honey?" Luella asked, and Kaye nodded. Luella filled her glass. Kaye felt overwhelmed. She did not know whether to resent Cross for not warning her in advance, or to just hug her, and then hug Luella. Instead, she walked around the table and settled into the seat beside Gale.

"Linda is assistant to the chief of staff," Bloch said.

"At the White House? For the president?" Kaye asked, hopeful as a child looking over a Christmas package.

"The president," Bloch confirmed.

Gale smiled up at Bloch. "Am I famous yet?"

"About time," Luella said, passing around the plate. Gale demurred, saying she had to keep in fighting trim, but the others snatched the cookies and held out glasses for juice.

"It's the legacy thing," Burkett said. "The polls are going fifty-fifty. Net and media are tired of being scaremongers. Marge tells us the scientific community will come out in support of the conclusion that the SHEVA kids won't produce disease. Do you go along with that?"

In politics, even a fragile certainty could move mountains. "I do," Kaye said.

"The president is taking advice from all sectors of the community," Gale said.

"They've had *years*," Kaye said.

"Linda is on our side, Kaye," Bloch said softly.

"Won't be long," Luella said, and nodded, her eyes both angry and knowing. "Mm hmm. Not long now."

"Dr. Rafelson, I have a question about your work," Burkett said. "If I may . . ."

"First things first," Bloch interrupted. "Marge knows already, but Kaye, you have to be absolutely clear on this. Everything said in this room is in the strictest confidence. Nobody will divulge anything to anybody outside this room, whether or not the president chooses to act. Understood?"

Kaye nodded, still in a daze.

"Good. We have some papers to sign, and then Kendall can ask his questions."

Burkett shrugged patiently and chewed on a cookie.

Two phones rang at once—one in the kitchen, which Luella pushed through the swinging door to answer, and Laura Bloch's cell phone in her purse.

Luella clutched an old-fashioned handset on a long cord. "Oh, my God," she said. "Where?" Her eyes met Kaye's. Something crossed between them. Kaye stood and clutched the back of her chair. Her knuckles turned white.

"LaShawna's with them?" Luella asked. Then, once more, "Oh, my God." Her face lit up with joy. "We caught a bus in New Mexico!" she cried. "John says they got our children! They have LaShawna, dear Jesus, John has my sweet, sweet girl."

Laura Bloch finished her call and clacked her phone shut, furious. "The bastards finally did it," she said.

38

"You found them," a voice said, and Mitch opened his eyes to a haze of faces in the shadows. The migraine was not done with him, but at least he could hear and think.

"The doctor says you're going to be okay."

"So glad," Mitch said groggily. He was lying on an air mattress under a tent. The mattress squeaked beneath his shifting weight.

"One of your migraines?"

That was Eileen.

"Yeah." He tried to sit up. Eileen gently pushed him down again on the mattress. Someone gave him a sip of water from a plastic cup.

"You should have told us where you were going," a woman he did not know said disapprovingly.

Eileen interrupted her. "You didn't know *where* you were going, did you?" she asked him. "Just what you wanted to find."

"This whole camp is on the knife edge of anarchy," the other woman said.

"Shut up, Nancy," said Eileen's colleague, what was her name again, Mitch liked her, she seemed smart: something Fitz. Then, it came to him, Connie Fitz, and as if in reward, the pain flowed out of his head like air from a balloon. His skull felt cold. "What did I find?"

"Something," Fitz said admiringly.

"We're taking scans now with the handheld," said Nancy.

"Good," Mitch said. He took a plastic bottle of water from Eileen and swallowed long and hard. He was as dry as a bone; he must have lain out on the rock and dirt for at least an hour. "I'm sorry," he said.

"De nada," Eileen said with a hint of pride.

"It's a tibia, isn't it?" Mitch asked.

"It's more than that," Eileen said. "We don't yet know how much more."

"I found the guys," he said.

The women would not commit.

"Just be happy you didn't die out there," Eileen said.

"It's not that hot," Mitch said.

"You were three feet from the bluff," Eileen said. "You could have fallen."

"They weathered out," Mitch mused, and took another swallow of water. "How many are left, I wonder?"

He peered into the blue light of the tent at the three women: Nancy, a tall, striking woman with long black hair and a stern face; Connie Fitz; Eileen.

The tent flap opened and the light assaulted him, bringing back a stab of pain.

"Sorry," Oliver Merton said. "Just heard about the incident. How's our boy wonder?"

"Explain it to me," Merton said.

Mitch sat alone with Oliver under the sun shade. He sipped a beer; Oliver was working away, or pretending to, on his small slate. He had a tracer cap on one finger and typed on empty air. All the archaeologists from the camp, except for two younger women standing guard at the main site, were at the bluff, leaving Mitch grounded, "to recover," as Eileen put it, but he strongly suspected it was to keep him out of their hair, out of trouble, until it was determined what he had found.

"Explain what?" Mitch asked.

"How you do it. I sense a pattern."

Mitch covered his eyes with his hands. The sunlight was still dazzling.

"You undergo some sort of psychic revelation, enter a trance state, troop off in search of something you've already seen. . . . Is that it?"

"God, no," Mitch said, grimacing. "Nothing like that. Was I showboating, Oliver?" he asked, and did not know himself whether he spoke with satisfaction, pride, or real curiosity as to what Merton thought.

Before Merton could answer, Mitch winced at a spike in his thoughts. His neck hair prickled.

Something's wrong.

"Oh, most definitely," Merton said with a nod and a sly little grin. "Sherlock Holmes, I presume?"

"Holmes was not psychic. You heard them. They still don't know what I found."

"You found a hominid leg bone. All of Eileen's students, searching for two months around this site, haven't found so much as a chip."

"They were making us look bad," Mitch said. "Men in general."

"A camp full of angry women digging out a camp full of abandoned women," Merton said. "Look bad? Right."

"Have there ever been any men here?"

"Beg your pardon?" Merton asked petulantly.

"Working at the camp. Digging."

"Besides me, not a one," Merton admitted, and scowled at the screen on the slate.

"Why is that?" Mitch asked.

"Eileen's gay, you know," Merton said. "She and Connie Fitz . . . very close."

Mitch thought this over for a few seconds but could not connect it right away with reality, his reality. "You're kidding."

Merton tried to cross his heart and hope to die, but got it wrong.

The closest Mitch could come to acknowledging this bit of information was to wonder why Eileen had not introduced her lover to him as such. He said, very slowly, "You could have fooled me."

That's not what's wrong.

"Mr. Daney is amused by it all. He takes quite an anthropological view."

Mitch pulled back from somewhere, an unpleasant place coming closer. "They're not *all* gay, are they?"

"Oh, no. But it *is* a bit of a crazy coincidence. The others appear to be single, to a woman, and not one has shown any interest in me. Funny, how that slants my view of the world."

"Yeah," Mitch said.

"Nancy thinks you're trying to steal their thunder. They're sensitive about that."

"Right."

"It's just you and me, until Mr. Daney gets here," Merton said.

Mitch finished the can of Coors and propped it gently on the wooden arm of the camp chair.

"Shall I crush that for you?" Merton asked with a twinkle. "Just to keep up masculine appearances."

Mitch did not answer. The camp, the bones, his discovery, suddenly meant nothing. His mind was a blank sheet with vague writing starting to appear, as if scrawled by ghosts. He could not read the writing, but he did not like it.

He jerked, and the can fell off the arm of the chair. It struck the gravel with a hollow rattle. "Jesus," he said. He had never had a hypnagogic experience before.

"Something wrong?" Merton asked.

"Eileen was right. Maybe I'm still sick." He pushed up out of the chair. "Can I use your phone?"

"Of course," Merton said.

"Thanks." Mitch sidled awkwardly one step to the left, as if about to lose his balance, perhaps his sanity. "How secure is it?"

"Very," Oliver said, watching him with concern. "Private trunk feed for Mr. Daney."

Mitch did not know whom to trust, whom to turn to. He had never felt more spooked or more helpless in his life.

No ESP, he thought. *Please, let there be no such thing as ESP.*

39

NEW MEXICO

Dicken sat beside Helen Fremont on the couch in the trailer. She was staring at the wall opposite the couch, fever-scenting, he suspected, but he could not tell what she was hoping to accomplish, if anything. The air in the trailer smelled of old cheese and tea bags. He had finished his story ten minutes ago, patiently going back over old history and trying to justify himself as well: his existence, his work, his loathing for the isolation he had felt all these years, buried in his work as if it were another kind of plastic suit, proof against life. There had been silence for several minutes now, and he did not know what to say, much less what would happen to them next.

The girl broke the silence. "Aren't you at all afraid I'll make you sick?" she asked.

"I'm stuck," Dicken said, lifting his hands. "They won't let me out until they can make other arrangements."

"Aren't you afraid?" she repeated.

"No," Dicken said.

"If I wanted to, could I make you sick?"

Dicken shook his head. "I doubt it."

"But if they know that, why keep me here? Why keep any of us away from people?"

"Well, we just don't know what to do or what to believe. We don't understand," he added, speaking softly. "That makes us weak and stupid."

"It's cruel," the girl said. Then, as if she was just coming to believe she was pregnant, "How will they treat my baby?"

The door to the trailer opened. Aram Jurie entered first and was almost immediately flanked by two security men armed with machine pistols. All wore white isolation suits. Even through the plastic cowl, Jurie's pallid face was a pepperball of irritation. "This is stupid," he said as the security men stepped forward. "Are you trying to sabotage everything we've done?"

Dicken stood up from the couch and glanced at the girl, but she did not seem at all surprised or disturbed. *God help us, it's what she knows.* Dicken said, "You're holding this young woman illegally."

Jurie was comically incredulous for a man whose face was normally so placid. "What in God's green Earth were you thinking?"

"You're not an authorized holding facility for children," Dicken continued, warming to his subject. "You illegally transported this girl across state lines."

"She's a threat to public health," Jurie said, suddenly recovering his calm. "And now you've joined her." He waved his hand. "Get him out of here."

The security men seemed unable to decide how to react. "Isn't he safe where he is?" one guard asked, his voice muffled inside the hood.

The girl reached up to Dicken and tightly gripped his arm. "There is no threat," Dicken told Jurie.

"You do not *know* that," Jurie said, staring hard at Dicken, but the comment was more for the benefit of the guards.

"Dr. Jurie has stepped way over the line," Dicken said. "Kidnapping is a tough rap, guys. This is a facility doing contract work under EMAC, which is under the authority of the Department of Health and Human Services. All of them have strict guidelines on human experimentation." *And nobody knows whether those guidelines still apply. But it's the best bluff we have.* "You have no jurisdiction over the girl. We're leaving Sandia. I'm taking her with me."

Jurie shook his head vigorously, making his hood waggle. "Very John Wayne. You got that out very nicely. I'm supposed to growl and play the villain?"

The situation was incredible and tense and fairly funny. "Yeah," Dicken said, abruptly breaking out in a shit-kicking, full-out hayseed grin. He had a tendency to do that when confronted by authority figures. It was one reason why he had spent so much of his life doing fieldwork.

Jurie misinterpreted Dicken's smile. "We have an incredible opportunity here. Why waste it?" Jurie said, wheedling now. "We can solve so many problems, learn so much. What we learn will benefit millions. It could save us all."

"Not this girl. Not any of them." Dicken held out his hand. The girl got to her feet and together, hand in hand, they walked cautiously toward the door.

Jurie blocked their way. "How far do you think you'll get?" he asked, livid behind the cowl.

"Let's find out," Dicken said. Jurie reached out to hold him, but

Dicken's arm snaked up and he grabbed the edge of the faceplate, as if to remind Jurie of their unequal vulnerability. Jurie dropped his hands, Dicken let go, and the man backed off, catching up against a chair and almost falling over.

The security men seemed rooted to the trailer's floor. "Good for you," Dicken murmured. "Hire some lawyers, gentlemen. Time off for good behavior. Mitigating factors in sentencing." Still murmuring legal inanities, he peered through the door of the trailer and saw a cluster of scientific and security staff, including Flynn, Powers, and now Presky, hanging back beyond the open gate in the reinforced acrylic fence. "Let's go, honey," Dicken said, and they stepped out onto the porch.

Behind, he heard a scuffle and swiveled his head to see Jurie, his face contorted, trying to grab a pistol and the security guards doing an awkward little dance keeping their weapons out of his reach.

Scientists with guns, Dicken thought. That really was the living end. Somehow, the absurdity cheered him. He squeezed the girl's hand and marched toward the others standing by the gate.

They did not stop him. Maggie Flynn actually held the gate open. She looked relieved.

40

CALIFORNIA

Stella and Will had left the car after it ran out of gas near a town called Lone Pine. They were in the woods now, but she did not feel any closer to freedom, or to where she wanted to be.

They had left Mrs. Hayden asleep in the car, drained after driving all night and then cutting back and forth across the state routes and freeways and back roads all morning. Will trudged ahead of Stella, carrying two empty plastic bottles.

At noon, the air was cool and hazy. Summer was turning into fall. The pines and larches and oaks seemed to shimmer as breezes blew and clouds raced over the low mountains.

They had seen very few houses along the road, but there were some. Will talked about a place that was in the middle of nowhere, with no humans for tens, if not hundreds, of miles. Stella was too tired to feel discouraged. She knew now they did not belong anywhere or to anyone; they were just lost, inside and out. Her feet hurt. Her back hurt. The discomfort from her period was passing. That was a small blessing, but now she was beginning to wonder who and what Will really was.

He looked more than a little feral with his hair sweaty and sticking straight up at the back where he had leaned against the rear seat in Mrs. Hayden's car. He smelled gamy, angry, and afraid, but Stella knew she did not smell any better.

She wondered what Celia and LaShawna and Felice were up to, what had happened to the drivers trussed up and left by the side of the road.

She had only a dim idea how the map in Will's back pocket correlated with where they were. The road looked like a long black river rolling into the distance, vanishing around a tree-framed curve.

For a moment, she stopped and watched a ground squirrel. It stood on a low flat rock beside the shoulder, hunched and alert, with shiny black eyes, like the Shrooz in her room in Virginia.

She hoped they would end up on a farm and she could be with animals. She got along well with animals.

Will came back. The squirrel fled. "We should keep moving," he said. They trotted clumsily into the trees as two cars rumbled by.

"Maybe we should hitchhike," Stella suggested from behind a pine trunk. She smelled the cloying sweetness of the tree's sap and it reminded her of school. She curled her lip and pushed away from the rough bark.

"If we hitchhike, they'll catch us," Will said. "We're close. I know it."

She followed Will. She could almost imagine a big blue Chevy or a big pickup barreling down the road with Mitch behind the wheel. Mitch and Kaye, together, looking for her.

The next time they heard a car coming, Will ran into the trees but she kept walking. After the car had passed, he caught up with her and gave her a squinch-faced look.

"We're helpless out here," Stella said, squinching back at him, as if that were a reasonable explanation.

"More reason to hide."

"Maybe somebody knows where this place is. If they stop we can ask."

"I'm not very lucky," Will said, his mouth twisting into a line that was not a smile and not quite a smirk. Wry and uncertain. "Are you lucky?" he asked.

"I'm here with you, aren't I?" she asked, deadpan.

Will laughed. He laughed until he started waving his arms and snorting and had to stop to wipe his nose on his sleeve.

"Eeyeew," Stella said.

"Sorry," he said.

Against her better judgment, Stella liked him again.

The next car, Will stuck out his hand, thumb up, and gave his biggest smile. The car flashed by doing at least seventy miles an hour, smoked windows full of blurred faces that did not even look their way.

Will hunched his shoulders as he resumed walking.

They heard the next vehicle twenty minutes later. Stella looked over her shoulder. It was an old Ford minivan, cresting a rise in the two-lane road and laying down a thin cloud of oily white smoke. Neither she nor Will moved back from the road. Their water bottles were empty. It wouldn't be long before they had to turn around and retrace their journey.

The minivan slowed, moved into the opposite lane to avoid them, and passed with a low whoosh. An older man and woman in the front seats peered at them owlishly; the back windows were tinted blue and reflected their own faces.

The minivan pulled over and stopped about two hundred feet down the road.

Stella hiccupped in surprise and crossed her arms. Will stood sideways, like a fencer expecting a strike, and Stella saw his hands shake.

"They don't look mean," Stella said, but she thought of the red truck and Fred Trinket and his mother who had cooked chicken, back in Spotsylvania County.

"We do need a ride," Will admitted.

The minivan backed up slowly and stopped about twenty feet away. The woman leaned her head out of the right side window. Her hair was salt-and-pepper gray and she had a square, strong face and direct eyes. Her arm, elbowing out, was covered with freckles, and her face was heavily wrinkled and pale. Stella saw she had lots of big silver rings on the fingers of her left hand, which rested on her forearm as she looked back at them.

"Are you two virus kids?" the older woman asked.

"Yeah," Will said, hands shaking even harder. He tried to smile. "We escaped."

The older woman thought about that for a moment, pursing her lips. "Are you infectious?"

"I don't think so," Will said, and stuck his hands in the pockets of his jeans.

The older woman turned back to the man in the driver's seat. They shared a glance and reached a silent agreement possible only to a couple who had lived together a very long time. "Need a ride somewhere?" the woman asked.

Will looked at Stella, but all Stella could sniff was the thick fume of oil. The man was at least ten years older than the woman. He had a thin face, bright gray eyes, and a prominent nose, and his hands, on the wheel, were also covered with rings—turquoise and coral and silver, birds and abstract designs.

"Sure," Will said.

The minivan's side door popped and slid open automatically. The interior stank of cigarette smoke and hamburgers and fries.

Stella's nose wrinkled, but the smell of food made her mouth water. They hadn't eaten since the morning of the day before.

"We've been reading about kids like you," the old man said as they climbed in. "Hard times, huh?"

"Yeah," Will said. "Thanks."

PART THREE

SHEVA + 18

"We're in year eighteen of what some have called the Virus Century. The whole world is still running scared, though there are faint and tremulous hints of a political solution.

"Yet the majority of people polled today haven't the faintest idea what a virus is. For most of us, 'They're small and they make us sick' just about says it all.

"Most scientists insist that viruses are genetic pirates, hijacking and killing cells to reproduce: 'Selfish genes with switchblades,' 'Terrorist DNA.' Others say we've got it mostly wrong, that many viruses are genetic messengers, carrying signals between cells in the body and even between you and me: 'Genetic FedEx.'

"The truth probably combines both views. It's a weird old biological ballgame, and most scientists agree we're not even in the second inning."
—*FoxMedia producer pitching a Floodnet* Real Life, Real News *special*; *rejected*

"Who'll buy ad time? It's too scary. What the hell does 'tremulous' mean? I'm tired of all this science shit. Science ruins my day. Let me know if and when the president stays on the pot long enough to get his job done. He's our boy. Maybe if, maybe then, but no promises."
—*Memo from FoxMedia CEO and program executive*

1

Kaye stared into Mrs. Rhine's darkened living room. The furniture had been rearranged in bizarre ways; a couch overturned, covered with a sheet, the bumps of its legs pointing into the air and pillows arranged in a cross on the floor around it; two wooden chairs leaning face-forward against the wall in a corner as if they were being punished.

Small white cardboard boxes covered the coffee table.

Freedman tapped the intercom button. "Carla, we're here. I've brought Kaye Lang Rafelson."

Mrs. Rhine walked briskly through the door, took a chair from a corner, swung it into the center of the room, two yards from the thick window, and sat. She wore plain blue denim coveralls. Gauze covered her arms and hands and most of her face. She wore a kerchief, and it did not look as if she had any hair. The little flesh that showed was red and puffy. Her eyes were intense between the mummy folds of gauze.

"I'll turn my lights down," she said, her voice clear and almost etched over the intercom. "You turn yours up. No need to look at me."

"All right," Freedman said, and brightened the lights in the viewing room.

The lights in Mrs. Rhine's living room darkened until they could see her only in silhouette. "Welcome to my home, Dr. Rafelson," she said.

"I was pleased to get your message," Kaye said.

Freedman folded her arms and stood back.

"Christopher Dicken used to bring flowers," Mrs. Rhine said. Her movements were awkward, jerky. "I can't have flowers now. Once a week I have to go into a little closet and they send a robot in here to scrub everything.

They have to get rid of all the little house-dust things. Fungus and bacteria and such that might grow from old flakes of skin. They can kill me now, if they build up in here."

"I appreciated the letter you sent me."

"The Web is my life, Kaye. If I may call you Kaye."

"Of course."

"I seem to know you, Christopher has spoken of you so often. I don't get too many visitors now. I've forgotten how to react to real people. I type on my clean little keyboard and travel all around the world, but I never go anywhere or touch or see anything, really. I thought I had gotten used to it, but then I just got angry again."

"I can imagine," Kaye said.

"Tell me what you imagine, Kaye," Mrs. Rhine said, head jerking.

"I imagine you feel robbed."

The dark shadow nodded. "My whole family. That's why I wrote to you. When I read what happened to your husband, to your daughter, I thought, she's not just a scientist, or a symbol of a movement, or a celebrity. She's like me. But of course you *can* get them back, someday."

"I am always trying to get back my daughter," Kaye said. "We still search for her."

"I wish I could tell you where she is."

"So do I," Kaye said, swallowing within the hood. The air flow in the stiff isolation suit was not the best.

"Have you read Karl Popper?" Mrs. Rhine asked.

"No, I never have," Kaye said, and arranged a plastic wrinkle around her midriff. She noticed then that the suit was patched with something like duct tape. This distracted her for a moment; she had heard that funding had been cut, but she had not fully realized the implications.

". . . says that a whole group of philosophers and thinkers, including him, regard the self as a social appurtenance," Mrs. Rhine said. "If you are raised away from society, you do not develop a full self. Well, I am losing my self. I feel uncomfortable using the personal pronoun. I would go mad, but I . . . this thing I am . . ." She stopped. "Marian, I need to speak with Kaye privately. At least let me believe nobody is listening or recording us."

"I'll check with the technician." Freedman spoke briefly with the safety technician. She then moved gingerly out of the viewing room, the umbilical coiling behind her. The door closed.

"Why are you here?" Mrs. Rhine asked in a low voice, barely audible.

Kaye could see the reflections in the woman's eyes from the brighter lights behind the glass.

"Because of your message. And because I thought it was time that I meet you."

"You're not here to reassure me that they'll find a cure? Because some people come through here and say that and I hate it."

"No," Kaye said.

"Why, then? Why speak with me? I send e-mail letters to lots of people. I don't think most of them get through. I'm surprised you got yours, actually."

Marian Freedman had made sure of that.

"You wrote that you felt you were getting smarter and more distant," Kaye said, "but you were losing your self." She stared at the shadowy figure in the dark room. The eczema had gotten very bad, so Kaye had been told in the briefing before joining Marian Freedman. "I'd like to hear more," Kaye said.

Suddenly, Mrs. Rhine leaned forward. "I know why you're here," she said, her voice rising.

"Why?" Kaye asked.

"We've both had the virus."

A moment's silence.

"I don't get you," Kaye said softly.

"Ascetics sit on pillars of rock to avoid human touch. They wait for God. They go mad. That is me. I'm Saint Anthony, but the devils are too smart to waste their time gibbering at me. I am already in hell. I don't need them to remind me. I have changed. My brain feels bigger but it's also like a big warehouse filled with empty boxes. I read and try to fill up the boxes. I was so stupid, I was just a breeder, the virus punished me for being stupid, I wanted to live so I took the pig tissue inside of me and that was forbidden, wasn't it? I'm not Jewish but pigs are powerful creatures, very spiritual, don't you think? I am haunted by them. I've read some ghost stories. Horror stories. Very scary, about pigs. I'm talking a mile a minute, I know. Marian listens, the others listen, but it's a chore for them. I scare them, I think. They wonder how long I'll last."

Kaye's stomach was so tense she could taste the acid in her throat. She felt so much for the woman beyond the glass, but could not think of anything to say or do to comfort her. "I'm still listening," she said.

"Good," Mrs. Rhine said. "I just wanted to tell you that I'm going to die soon. I can feel it in my blood. So will you, though maybe not so soon."

Mrs. Rhine stood and walked around the overturned and shrouded couch.

"I have these nightmares. I escape from here somehow and walk around and touch people, trying to help, and I just end up killing everybody. Then, I visit with God . . . and I make Him sick. I kill God. The devil says to Him, 'I told You so.' He's mocking God while's He's dying, and I say, *Good for you*."

"Oh," Kaye said, swallowing. "That isn't the way it is. It isn't going to be that way."

Mrs. Rhine waved her arms at the window. "You can't possibly understand. I'm tired."

Kaye wanted to say more, but could not.

"Go now, Kaye," Carla Rhine insisted.

Kaye sipped a cup of coffee in Marian Freedman's small office. She was crying so hard her shoulders were shaking. She had held back while removing the suit and showering, while taking the elevator, but now, it could not be stopped. "That wasn't good," she managed to say between sobs. "I didn't handle that at all well."

"Nothing we do matters, not for Carla," Freedman said. "I don't know what to say to her, either."

"I hope it won't set her back."

"I doubt it," Freedman said. "She is strong in so many ways. That's part of the cruelty. The others are quiet. They have their habits. They're like hamsters. Forgive me, but it's true. Carla is different."

"She's become sacred," Kaye said, straightening in the plastic chair and taking another Kleenex from the floral box on Freedman's desk. She wiped her eyes and shook her head.

"Not sacred," Freedman insisted, irritated. "Cursed, maybe."

"She says she's dying."

Freedman looked at the far wall. "She's producing new types of retroviruses, very together, elegant little things, not the patchwork monstrosities she used to make. They don't contain any pig genes whatsoever. None of these new viruses are infectious, or even pathogenic, as far as we can tell, but they're really playing hell with her immune system. The other ladies . . . the same."

Marian Freedman focused on Kaye. Kaye studied her dark, drained eyes with a growing sense of dismay.

"Last time Christopher Dicken was through here, he worked with me on some samples," Freedman said. "In less than a year, maybe only a few months, we think all our ladies will start showing symptoms of multiple sclerosis, possibly lupus." Freedman worked her lips, fell silent, but kept looking at Kaye.

"And?" Kaye said.

"He thinks the symptoms have nothing to do with pig-tissue transplants. The ladies may just be accelerated a little. Mrs. Rhine could be the first to experience post-SHEVA syndrome, a side effect of SHEVA pregnancy. It could be pretty bad."

Kaye let that information sink in, but could not find any emotion to attach to it—not after seeing Carla Rhine. "Christopher didn't tell me."

"Well, I can see why."

Kaye deliberately switched her thoughts, a survival tactic at which she had become adept in the last decade. "I'm flying out to California to meet with Mitch. He's still searching for Stella."

"Any signs?" Freedman asked.

"Not yet," Kaye said.

She got up and Freedman held up a special disposal basket marked "Biohazard" to receive her tear-dampened tissue. "Carla might behave very differently tomorrow. She'll probably tell me how glad she is you dropped by. She's just that way."

"I understand," Kaye said.

"No, you don't," Freedman said.

Kaye was in no mood. "Yes, I do," she said firmly.

Freedman studied her for a moment, then gave in with a shrug. "Pardon my bad attitude," she explained. "It's become an epidemic around here."

Kaye boarded a plane in Baltimore within two hours, heading for California, denying the sun its chance to rest. Scents of ice and coffee and orange juice wafted from a beverage cart being pushed down the aisle. As she sat watching a news report on the federal trials of former Emergency Action officials, she clamped her teeth to keep them from chattering. She was not cold; she was afraid.

Nearly all of her life, Kaye had believed that understanding biology, the way life worked, would lead to understanding herself, to enlightenment. Knowing how life worked would explain it all: origins, ends, and everything in between. But the deeper she dug and the more she understood, the less satisfying it seemed, all clever mechanism; wonders, no doubt, enough to mesmerize her for a thousand lifetimes, but really nothing more than an infinitely devious shell.

The shell brought birth and consciousness, but the price was the push-pull of cooperation and competition, partnership and betrayal, success causing another's pain and failure causing your own pain and death, life preying upon life, dragging down victim after victim. Vast slaughters leading to adaptation and more cleverness, temporary advantage; a never-ending process.

Viruses contributed to both birth and disease: genes traveling and talking to each other, speaking the memories and planning the changes, all the marvels and all the failures, but never escaping the push-pull. *Nature is a bitch goddess.*

The sun came through the window opposite and fell brilliant on her face. She closed her eyes. *I should have told Carla what happened to me. Why didn't I tell her?*

Because it's been three years. Fruitless, painful years. And now this.

Carla Rhine had given up on God. Kaye wondered if she had as well.

2

Mitch adjusted his tie in the old, patchy mirror in the dingy motel room. His face looked comical in the reflection, tinted yellow around his left eye, spotted black near his right cheek, a crack separating neck and chin. The mirror told him he was old and worn out and coming apart, but he smiled anyway. He would be seeing his wife for the first time in two weeks, and he was looking forward to spending time alone with her. He did not care about his appearance because he knew Kaye did not care much, either. So he wore the suit, because all his other clothes were dirty and he had not had time to take them down to the little outbuilding and plug dollar coins into the washing machine.

The rumpled queen-sized bed was scattered with half-folded maps and charts and pieces of paper with phone numbers and addresses, an imposing pile of clues that so far had gotten him nowhere. In the last three years of searching across the state, and finally zeroing in on Lone Pine, it seemed no one had seen Stella, no one had seen any youngsters traveling, and most certainly no one had seen any virus children playing hooky from school.

Stella had vanished.

Mitch could locate with stunning insight a cluster of men who had died twenty thousand years ago, but he could not find his seventeen-year-old daughter.

He pinched the tie higher and grimaced, then turned out the bathroom light and went to the door. Just as he opened the door, a young-looking man in a sweatshirt and gray windbreaker, with long blond hair, pulled back a knocking fist.

"Sorry," the man said. "Are you Mitch?"

"Can I help you?"

"The manager says maybe *I* can help *you*." He tapped his nose and winked.

"What's that mean?"

"You don't remember me?"

"No," Mitch said, impatient.

"I deliver hardware and electrical supplies. I can't smell a thing, never have, and I can't taste much, either. They call it anosmia. I don't like the taste of food much, and that's why I stay skinny."

Mitch shrugged, still at a loss.

"You're looking for a girl, right? A Shevite?"

Mitch had never heard that word before. The sound of it—a *right* sound—gave him gooseflesh. He reappraised the thin young man. There *was* something familiar about him.

"I'm the only one my boss, Ralph, will send to deliver supplies, because all the other guys come back confused." He tapped his nose again. "Not me. They can't make me forget to pick up the money. So they pay us, and since I treat them with respect, they pay well, with bonuses. See?"

Mitch nodded. "I'm listening."

"I like them," the young man said. "They're good folks, and I don't want anybody to go up there and make trouble. I mean, what they do is sort of legal now, and it's a big business around here." He peered off into the bright morning sunshine heating up the small asphalt parking lot, the grassy field, and the scattered pines beyond.

"I'm interested in any information," Mitch said, stepping out onto the porch, careful now not to spook the man. "She's my daughter. My wife and I have been looking for her for three years."

"Cool," the man said, shuffling his feet. "I have a little girl myself. I mean, she's with her mother, and we're not married—" He suddenly looked alarmed. "I don't mean she's a virus kid, no, not at all!"

"It's okay," Mitch said. "I'm not prejudiced."

The man looked strangely at Mitch. "Don't you recognize me? I mean, okay, it's been a long time. I thought I remembered you, and now that I see you, it's all as clear as yesterday. Strange, how people come back together, isn't it?"

Mitch made little motions of shoulder and head to show he still wasn't clued in.

"Well, it might not have been you . . . but I'm pretty sure it was, because I saw your wife's picture in the paper a few months later. She's a famous scientist, isn't she?"

"She is," Mitch said. "Look, I'm sorry . . ."

"You picked up some hitchhikers a long time ago. Two girls and a guy. That was me, the guy." He pointed a skinny finger at his own chest. "One of the girls had just lost a baby. They were called Delia and Jayce."

Mitch's face slowly went blank, with both astonishment and memory. He was surprised, but he remembered almost everything, perhaps because it had taken place in another small motel.

"Morgan?" he asked, stooping as if his arms were dragged down by weights.

The man broke into the broadest grin Mitch had seen in months. "Bless you," Morgan said. There were actually tears in his eyes. "Sorry," he said, shuffling his feet and backing off into the sunshine. He wiped his eyes with the backs of his hands. "It's just, after all these years . . . I'm sorry. I'm acting stupid. I am really grateful to you guys."

Mitch reached out to save Morgan from falling off the curb. He pulled Morgan gently back into the shadow, and then, spontaneously, two men who had been through a lot over the years, they hugged. Mitch laughed despite himself. "Goddamnit, Morgan, how are you?"

Morgan accepted the hug but not the profanity. "Hey," he said. "I'm with Jesus now."

"Sorry," Mitch said. "Where's my daughter? What can you tell me? I mean, sounds like you've run into a group of people who don't want to be found." He felt the questions lining up, refusing to be slowed, much less stopped. "SHEVA people. Shevites, is that what you called them? How many? A commune? How did you find out I was looking for my daughter?"

"Like I said, the manager in the motel, he's my girlfriend's uncle. I deliver hardware to the garage he runs up on North Main. He told me. I wondered if it was you. You made some impression on me."

"You want to take me out there, just in case I can't be trusted?"

"I'm pretty sure you can be trusted, but . . . it's hard to find. I'd like to take you there, just in case it is your daughter. I don't know who she is, understand? But if she is out there . . . I'd like to return a favor."

"I understand," Mitch said. "Would you like to take my wife along, too? She's the famous one."

"Is she here?" Morgan asked, preparing to be stunned and shy again.

"She'll be here in a couple of hours. I'm picking her up at the airport in Las Vegas."

"Kaye Lang?"

"That's her."

"Wow!" Morgan said. "I've been watching the Senate hearings, the court stuff. When I'm not working. You know, I saw her on Oprah? That was a long time ago, I was still just a kid. But I really can't promise anything."

"We'll go on faith," Mitch said, happier than he had been in he did not remember how long. "Had some breakfast?"

"Hey, I earn my keep now," Morgan said, straightening and sticking his finger tips into the pockets of his jeans. "I'll buy *you* breakfast. What goes round, comes round."

In the room, Mitch's data phone rang. He half-closed the door as he loped to pick it up from the bed. Mitch pinched open the phone's display door. The call was from Kaye. "Hello, Kaye! Guess—"

"I'm on the plane. What an awful, awful morning. I really need to hold someone," Kaye said. Her image in the little screen looked pale. He could see a high seat back and people sitting behind her. "I need some good news, Mitch."

He held back for a second, hand trembling, knowing how many times there had been false hopes. He did not want to add yet another disappointment.

"Mitch?"

"I'm here. I was just going out the door."

"I just couldn't stand not talking to you. Flight's half full."

"I think we've got something," Mitch said, his voice rough and throat tight around the words. *You know it's right. You know this is it.*

"Is that Dr. Lang? Say 'hi!' " Morgan called brightly from the motel porch outside the door.

"What is it?" Kaye tried to make out Mitch's expression on the little screen. "Is it a detective? Do we have that kind of money left?"

"Just get here safe. I've found an old friend. Or, rather, he's found me."

3

Lake Stannous
NORTHERN CALIFORNIA

The air fell away from the heat of the afternoon. Through the pines Stella Nova could see thunderheads rising in silent, self-involved billows over the White Mountains. The woods were dry and full of the fragrances of lodgepole, spruce, and fir.

She had finished doing her share of the laundry in the big old concrete washhouse near the center of Oldstock. Now she sat on an empty oil drum beside the long lines hung with sun-drenched linens and underwear and some diapers and work clothes, smelling the laundry soap and bleach and steam, sipping a black cherry soda—a rare luxury here, she allowed herself only one a week—and thinking, kicking her feet back and forth, scuffing the concrete slab around the washhouse with her clogs.

From where she sat, she could see the gravel turnaround beside the old abandoned bowling alley, painted gray decades ago, the paint now peeling; three long dark redwood-stained dormitories that used to house seminary students and pilgrims and a few tourists; and up north of that, the fuel cell and solar station that ran the medical center and nursery. Beyond the station and an old fenced-in compound for storing mining equipment stretched a debris field dominated by a small mountain of tailings. The mountain marked the old mine and made that end of the camp a no-man's-land of heavy metals and cyanide. No one walked there unless they had to; sometimes after a heavy rain she could smell the poison in the air, but it wasn't bad enough to make them sick, unless they did something stupid.

In the middle of the last century, humans had mined copper and tin and even some gold at Oldstock, and built a little town—that was where the bowling alley and the seminary buildings had come from. South of town, just off the main road down to the shore of Lake Stannous, you could find weed-grown streets and concrete foundations where houses had once stood, built by Condite Copper Company to house miners' families. In the woods

Stella had come across old refrigerators and washing machines and piles of bottles and bigger junk, abandoned steam and diesel engines like big iron spaceships, squat dark hopper cars, stacks of iron rails orange with rust, and creosote-dipped cross ties glistening with black beads from years in the sun.

Oldstock was a designated Superfund site, located on the north end of Lake Stannous, where fishing was poor, and that combination kept most humans away. But Oldstock was beautiful, and as long as it did not rain too much, the tailings did not wash out into the lake and the village's water was fine. So far, they had been lucky. The weather had been dry for twenty years, ever since Mr. and Mrs. Sakartvelo had bought the place from a Lutheran church group.

Sakartvelo was not their real name. They had been immigrants from the FSU, the Former Soviet Union, the part now called the Republic of Georgia. The name they had adopted was the name of their country the way the natives said it. They had been hiding here for almost twenty years, knowing others would arrive eventually.

Five years ago, the others had started arriving, and the town had slowly come alive once more.

Mr. and Mrs. Sakartvelo were in their sixties. Physically, they were obvious Shevites. They said others like them—not many—went back over two hundred years in Georgia and Armenia and Turkey. Stella Nova saw no reason not to believe them. Mitch had talked about such things.

She closed her eyes and leaned her head back, turning her face like a flower to soak up more sun before it dipped behind the trees. She listened for red-winged blackbirds and jays, mockingbirds and robins. Her cheeks freckled with butterflies of contentment.

A game for the younger kids was Rawshock—freckling up in symmetrical patterns and guessing what they meant. It trained them at cheek flashing. Some came to Oldstock *freckle-dumb,* with no knowledge of how to communicate with their own kind. Slowly, they learned. Stella and others taught the young ones.

The woods had been full of ticks this summer—and deer, as well—but ticks and even mosquitoes did not bother them much. The Sakartvelos taught them how to use fever-scenting to keep biting insects away, and also how to soothe animals—black bears in particular—that they might encounter. The two hundred Shevites in Oldstock were the only inhabitants for ten miles, and the woods were wild.

And of course, the Sakartvelos had taught the children how to keep Oldstock a secret, and trained them in what to do if humans came looking for them.

They had been taught well. No one had ever been taken away, and no one had ever been hurt—by animals or humans. Life had been pretty good, and Stella had started to forget the bad times and even the times with Mitch and Kaye, the good times, though sad. She had started to believe there was a life to live, rooted and real, among her own kind.

Then, Will had gone wrong.

Some still had nightmares of the schools and of living among humans. Stella did not dream about such things. Will had not been so lucky. He had hidden many things from all of them, things he had experienced, that had happened to him.

There were no radios or televisions in Oldstock, no telephones except for a single satellite phone in the main meeting hall, kept locked in a cabinet. It had not been used since Stella and Will had arrived, and probably not for a long time before that.

A breeze made the sheets and diapers flap. Stella wiped sweat from her forehead, got up, and started taking down and folding the dry pieces. She stacked them in a plastic tub and scented the tub by touching the ball of her thumb behind her ear and rubbing the handle.

Randolph—the only Randolph in Oldstock, so she did not know his human last name—came up and sparked a greeting. Randolph was four years younger than Stella, what some called an off-born, not part of the Waves. Those born during the three big Waves were called boomers, she did not know why. They talked with just their faces for a while as they plucked and folded pillowcases and dungarees and diapers. They exchanged pleasantries and imitated the scents of others, a kind of joking gossip that passed the time.

Randolph was being brought into the Blackbird Deme, not Stella's but an offshoot of her group. They could talk openly about deme business, but not about personal affairs within the demes. That required triples, to prevent misunderstanding between the demes: three figures from each deme, engaging in full fever-scenting and sparking and facing. Triples looked like a weird dance to outsiders, but they solved a lot of problems and kept friction way down.

Oldstock had two children from the most recent Wave, foundlings aged two years and twenty-six months respectively. Stella cared for them sometimes in preparation, in training, and enjoyed their wild toddler scenting. Shevite infants raised among their own kind got enthusiastic sometimes and could emit a rank odor like dead skunks, and not from their dirty diapers.

Shevite babies knew how to swear with scent long before they could talk.

Everyone was learning. Fortunately, Mr. and Mrs. Sakartvelo were far from tyrants. They had been sterilized by the Communists in Tbilisi in the 1960s and could not have children of their own. In a strange way, that made them perfect to be everyone's Shevite godparents, their guides in small, cloistered Oldstock.

Randolph finished folding a good share of the laundry and palmed Stella's cheek in a brotherly fashion, with just a hint of the Question that the young males often asked, even of someone in her condition. Even of someone who still had a partner.

Stella responded with a little warning grumble under her throat and a polite chirrup. They smiled and parted, having spoken not a single word. Stella could go for days without speaking, and though sometimes she shouted out loud in her sleep, she could never recall why on waking.

Supper was being served in the refectory for those who had been cutting wood and planing boards starting early that morning. Males and females came out of the fresheners, stalls where they rubbed down with wet towels to take off the sweat—otherwise, most showered less than once a week. Cutting or hiding scent was considered rude. Smelling like heavy labor, however, could also hide scent.

Mr. Sakartvelo had told them, "We're all French, at heart." Stella did not know precisely what he meant. In France, Shevites were employed in perfume factories, they had heard. Maybe that was his meaning.

She felt so ignorant. She was hungry much of the time now, so she stood in line with the workers, hands on her stomach, trying to feel the shape beneath, but there was hardly even a bulge yet. Feeling her stomach made her a little sad. A cup of coffee would help. Caffeine made the day easier. Shevites reacted so strongly to caffeine that coffee and tea and even chocolate were only allowed between the hours of ten and five.

Stella's mind raced all the time even without coffee. Half the time she wanted to cry, the other half just to suck it back and get on with the hours of each day and what they could bring. So much work to do. Months and years could go by and still she could not fit herself in completely. All those years away from her kind . . . Had they handicapped her, made her more human than Shevite?

But there were sweet moments, classes with the younger boomers and especially the babies.

She took her tray from the food line and walked into the refectory, large and quiet, twelve workers off duty, none speaking, gesturing and facing and flashing, pleasant odors of cocoa and yogurt and even jasmine—somebody was being *very* pleasant—mingled together and out of context at this distance, like words pulled out of a conversation and tossed together randomly, the discourse going on at the old wooden tables and benches.

Stella sat by herself, which she did often enough to elicit comments, kindly meant but a little critical. She ate her bowl of canned kidney beans and sprinkled or dribbled in the extra spices and flavorings that Shevites enjoyed, Indian black salt, extracts of broccoli raab and sour anchovy sauce.

Luce Ramone sat down beside her with a bowl of chips. Luce was more talkative than others, and Stella greeted her with a smile that showed some need.

"What, you want a chatty person?" Luce asked. She was a year younger than Stella, from the tail end of the first boomers, small for a Shevite and pale of skin, with thick black hair that tended to bristle. She smelled wonderful, however, and attracted much attention from males hoping to be peripheral to her deme. Stella's deme and Luce's were currently in merger, coalescing but still keeping their bounds. Nobody knew where that might lead, or what it might mean to the domestic anglers, hopeful males and females in either deme.

"I'd love a chatty person," Stella said.

"Hair of the human/ I'm your girl. You're down/ looking stretched."

"I'm thoughtful."

Both were cheek-flashing, but speech over and under was dominant for the time being.

"Joe Siprio, you know him?"

"Will's friend," Stella said.

"He's angling for me. Should I?"

"No way/ too young," Stella said.

"You were angled at my age/ hypocrite."

"Look what happened to me." Not emphasized, but standing alone, no under.

"He's a total cheer-fly," Luce said with a musing glance. "Our bodies like each other."

"What's that got to do with a cat's fart?" Stella asked, irritated. "You're moth. You need to rise to bee." Moth and bee were names for two levels of menarche in the Shevites. Women passed through three stages: the first, moth, receptive to sexual overtures but not to actual intercourse; the second, bee, sexually active but infertile—and this was still a guess, even to the Sakartvelos—to allow more subtle hormonal and pheromonal samplings and communications; and the third, wasp, total fertility, leading to sexual activity with prospects of pregnancy. Shevite females could actually fall back into bee stage if a deme broke up or an angling failed.

Males started puberty at bee and from there went straight to wasp, sometimes within hours.

"Lemon and Lime are old notion about that," Stella added. Lemon and Lime were the fundamentals of the Sakartvelos. "They think you should wait."

"You didn't," Luce said.

"It was different," Stella said, and freckled a warning that she did not like thinking about this, much less talking.

"Lemon and Lime support *you*," Luce said testily.

"They didn't have much choice, did they?"

A ten-year-old male named Burke walked to the end of the table and stood there shyly, hands folded in front of him, rocking on his heels.

"What?" Stella snapped, facing him with cheeks flashing full gold.

Burke backed off. "Lemon and Lime are down at the gate with some others. There's humans down there."

"So?"

"They say they're your parents. Another brought them, the numb-nose delivery guy."

Stella slapped her hands on the table, then drummed them, shaking her head, making the plates rattle. Heads turned in the cafeteria, and two stood in case intervention was the consensus.

Luce pushed back, never having seen her friend this disturbed.

"It's not them," Stella said, and swung her legs around on the bench, then got to her feet. "Not now." She approached Burke, face and pupils ablaze in full accusative query, as if she wanted to punish him.

"The woman smells like you!" Burke wailed, and then others surrounded them and prodded Stella aside with gentle elbow nudges. Touching with angry hands was considered very bad. Burke ran off, crying.

"Go see," Luce suggested, her own color flaring. Nobody was a better persuader than Luce. "If they're not your parents, they'll smoke them out of here and they'll forget everything. If they are your parents, you have to go."

She held out her spit-damp palms, as did others who had formed a circle around the table, but Stella refused them all.

"I don't want to know!" she wailed. "I don't want *them* to know!"

4

Albert V. Bryan United States Courthouse

ALEXANDRIA, VIRGINIA

Senator Laura Bloch greeted Christopher Dicken in the hall outside the courtroom. Dicken was dressed in his usual excuse for business wear, brown tweed jacket and corduroy pants with a wide tie completely out of fashion. Senator Bloch was dressed in a navy blue suit and carried a small briefcase. Behind her stood a younger balding man and a lone, harried-looking middle-aged woman, both wearing suits and carrying their own briefcases.

"She's going to get off," Bloch declared curtly. "She's painting herself as the cop on the beat who protected us all."

Dicken was not much on punishment, and did not look forward to having to testify.

"I wonder what Gianelli would think," Bloch added softly, staring at the benches, the lines of lawyers and witnesses waiting to be allowed into the courtroom to sit and wait until called.

The sound of Mark Augustine's cane was unmistakable. Dicken and Bloch turned to see him making his way down the hall toward the courtroom. He nodded to his attorneys, spoke to them for a few seconds, eyes turning to Dicken, then broke away and stepped gingerly toward them.

"Dr. Augustine," Bloch said, and extended her hand.

"Senator, pleasure to see you." Augustine smiled and shook her hand, but kept his eyes on Dicken. "Sorry duty, eh, Christopher?"

Dicken nodded. "How are you, Mark?"

"Steep learning curve for us all," Augustine said.

Dicken nodded. He felt no triumph, only a hollow sensation of unfinished business.

Augustine pursed his lips and took a folded sheet of paper from his pocket. "Two items of news," he said. "First, I've got Sumner's chief of staff, Stan Parton, on board for a reconciliation joint session. We're going to have a select few children in the House chambers, at the president's invitation. The vice president will be there."

"That's great," Senator Bloch said, her eyes brightening. "Dick would have loved to hear that. When?"

"Could be months. The other news is bad."

The last thing the group wanted was bad news. Bloch sighed and rolled her prominent eyes.

"Let's have it," Dicken said.

"Mrs. Rhine slipped into a coma at six thirty this morning. She died at eleven fifteen."

Dicken felt his breath hitch.

"She had been in pain for years," Augustine said.

"A blessing, really," Bloch said.

Dicken asked where a restroom was on this floor, then excused himself. In the echoing hollowness, he closed the door to a stall. No tears came. He did not even feel numb.

"Funny world," he whispered, and looked up at the ceiling, as if Mrs. Rhine might be listening. "Funny old world. Wherever you are, Carla, I hope it's better."

Then he stepped out of the stall, washed his hands, and returned to stand with Bloch and Augustine outside the courtroom.

Rachel Browning and her attorneys had arrived and now huddled in a tight cluster about twenty feet from Augustine and Bloch. Her face had become deeply lined, pale as if cast in plaster, a death mask. She nodded to the tune of the attorneys' back-and-forth. One stopped to whisper in her ear.

"I'm sorry for her," Dicken said, vulnerable to the point of charity.

"Don't be," Augustine primly advised. "She'd hate that."

The court clerk opened the doors.

"Let's go, gentlemen," Bloch said. She placed her hands on their elbows and escorted them, three abreast, into the courtroom.

5

Mitch held Kaye's hand as a group of more than twenty youths tightened its gyre around them. Morgan had been drawn aside and now stood surrounded by three young men. He held out his hands and smiled nervously, face flushed, windbreaker pulled off one shoulder. He looked surprised.

Several other adolescents and a female in her late seventies were searching Morgan's truck, looking, Mitch guessed, for communications or tracking equipment. They were all quiet and serious.

"We're trying to find a girl named Stella Nova," Kaye repeated. The air was thick with persuasion. Mitch felt woozy and confused already, despite the nose plugs they had manufactured in the motel bathroom out of toilet paper and vanilla-scented lip balm.

An older male, also in his seventies, with ruddy cheeks and an unruly halo of reddish hair shot with gray, came through the gyre and reached to take Mitch's and Kaye's hands in his. He wore a denim jacket with brass buttons. Except for his round face and SHEVA features, he might have been an itinerant farmworker. "There was no need for you to come," he said pressing their hands to his chest.

"We're her parents," Kaye said, eyes pleading. "We've been looking for her for years."

"She isn't here." The old man's cheeks freckled in rapid patterns, unreadable, and his emerald green irises sparkled with yellow and brown. His accent was mild but Mitch could still detect a hint of eastern European. Mitch tried to think clearly, tried to resist the onslaught. Any minute now, he was certain, they would all get back in the truck and drive away, sure they had made a mistake—no matter what Morgan would tell them had happened.

For the first time, Mitch felt frightened, being among his daughter's people.

The old woman stood beside the old man and spoke a stream of over-under in another language.

"Georgian," Kaye said to Mitch. Mitch and Kaye tried to pull their hands back, but the old man was strong and would not release them and

Mitch did not want to start any kind of struggle. They stood in a tight triangle with the old man, who was no longer looking at them, but had focused on the old woman and the adolescents.

"They're your friends!" Morgan shouted, struggling against the clasping arms, his voice breaking with anger and frustration. "I wouldn't bring no enemies here, you know that. She's *famous*! She's been on Oprah!"

The old man let their hands go, but still the gyre of youths, red-headed, strawberry blond, sandy brunette, all colors—Mitch had never seen so many varieties of SHEVA child—stayed close and fever scented the air.

Mitch doubted he would ever enjoy chocolate again.

Kaye stammered a few words of Georgian, then asked the old couple, in English, "When did you come here? Where are you from?"

"Stella!" Mitch shouted at the buildings adjoining the turnaround.

The old man touched his finger to Mitch's lips. Mitch bent his head like a submissive dog and fell silent.

"Please," Kaye pleaded. Mitch supported her as her legs gave way.

"Go home," the old man said.

"Go home," the children said in many voices, over and under, a rising, singing, all-too-convincing and reasonable murmur in the late afternoon warmth.

Mitch saw something from the corner of his eye. He raised his head and stood on tiptoes to look over the crowd. A face he knew, like Kaye's, like his mother's, moved steadily toward the gyre from the direction of the gray buildings. He tried to keep the young woman in sight through the bobbing heads and singing mouths and gold-flecked eyes. She wore a baggy pair of black pants and clogs and a white sleeveless blouse. Her shoulders were narrow, like Kaye's, and her arms were tanned to a reddish bronze, like a statue in a park. Her cheeks formed a butterfly pattern that Mitch recognized instantly, the complicated expression revealing both surprise and uncertainty, and then unwitting greeting.

"She's here!" Mitch said, choking.

Kaye saw Stella and stood up straight and tried to shove her way out of the circle. The youths crowded in to stop her.

Stella stopped outside the gyre, arms crossed, looking this way and that as if she had not found what she had come looking for, or did not want to see it.

Kaye beat at the young people to get free, using no words, just grunts and shrieks.

Stella suddenly dashed forward and grabbed at the members of the gyre.

The old man lifted his hands, the woman did the same, and the gyre dropped back, leaving Kaye and Mitch and Stella at the center of a loose and expanding crowd.

A breeze whispered through the trees and across the gravel turnaround and dispelled the scent. Stella hugged her mother, then reached around Kaye's shoulder and grabbed Mitch's arm and pulled him in, as well.

Other youths arrived, curious, waiting to join in and do whatever was necessary.

"See!" Morgan shouted triumphantly. "Would I shit you? Man, let them be! They're family!"

They said good-bye and thanks to Morgan, and Mitch shook his hand. Morgan was sternly told by the old Shevite man that he was not to return again, ever.

"Hey, it was worth it," Morgan said defiantly. He waved farewell as Stella led Mitch and Kaye to a small meeting room at the back of the old bowling alley.

"They're unhappy that you're here," she said, pulling out chairs around a battered wooden table. She motioned for them to sit. The window at the back of the room was dark; night had fallen. "They don't want us to be found."

"Who are *they*?" Kaye asked, too sharply, but she could not help herself. "Cult leaders? What are their names, Bo and Peep?"

"I don't know what you mean," Stella said.

"They wouldn't talk with me," Kaye said, trying to control her agitation. "Do they hate us so much?"

Stella shook her head, unable to answer for the moment. She could not easily explain how complicated an answer to that question might be.

"I sympathize with all of you," Kaye said. "We both do, Stella. They have a marvelous story, I'm sure of it, but we have been looking for *so* long, we were so afraid!" She pounded the table hard enough to make the floor vibrate and the window rattle.

Mitch placed his hands over hers. "We've both been searching." He watched Stella with alternating expressions of relief and anger.

"I'm sorry," Stella said. "Will and I came here after the bus accident. It was for the best."

"Will?" Mitch asked. "Was he the boy?" John Hamilton had told them about putting Stella and Will in the car with Jobeth Hayden. Hayden had been arrested by state police in Nevada and turned over to the FBI, but she had never been charged with anything.

She had had no idea where the children might have gone. Piles of crumpled paperback pages had been found in her car.

"You saw him in Virginia, in the long building where you found me. Where the girl died," Stella said.

"I don't remember much about him," Mitch said.

"He was my friend," Stella said. She turned to Mitch, examining his face with shy, flicking glances, her own face turning dark and her pupils dropping down to pinpricks. Mitch had never seen his daughter looking so down, so discouraged.

"Was?"

"He's dead."

"How did he die?" Kaye asked.

Stella shook her head and looked away.

"Did he fit in, here?" Kaye asked cautiously.

Stella shook her head once more. "He lived with humans too long. They hurt him. They made him wild. He couldn't fit with any deme, not even mine."

"You've lived with humans," Kaye said softly.

"Not the same."

"Stella, are you pregnant?" Mitch asked, and Kaye jerked as if kicked.

"Yes," Stella said.

Kaye's jaw clenched. Mitch moved his hand to Stella's shoulder. "Will?"

"Yes," Stella said.

Kaye moaned, then wrapped her hands around her mouth and jaw. Stella stared at the window, unwilling to witness her mother's anguish.

"He's the father," Mitch said.

"I went to wasp so quickly," Stella said. "It seemed so right, and he was sweet and gentle, with me, when he was away from the others."

"Did they kill him?" Mitch asked.

Stella shook her head and her cheeks went a lovely shade of sienna, which, Mitch knew, signified a very unlovely emotion: grief. Her cheeks had taken a similar color when they had found Shamus huddled dead in the kudzu, years ago. Lifetimes away. "He stopped eating. Nobody could force him. Nobody would. I don't know why; we can do so much with some who are ill. I stayed with him. We played games. It was his decision. He said he did not fit. He was in such pain, he became so far away."

Kaye laid her head on the table. Mitch saw glints of tears falling from her eyes, darkening the scarred wood.

"He couldn't be with us, and he couldn't be anything he wanted to be away from us. Something was broken inside of him. He knew he would never be right with us or anybody else. Yevgenia and Yuri—our hosts—they tried everything they knew."

"There is so much to learn," Kaye murmured, and turned her head toward her daughter.

"He did not want to live, at the end," Stella said. "We buried him in the woods." She shook her head vigorously. "No more talk about Will."

Kaye got up and stood behind her daughter. "Can we stay for a while?" she asked Stella. "Be with you? Help around here, maybe?"

"I don't know," Stella said.

"Do you want us to stay?" Mitch asked.

Stella stroked Kaye's fingers where they rested on her collarbone. "Yes," she said.

"Are we the first . . . from the old kind of people, to come here, to visit?" Kaye asked.

"No," Stella said. "There are four more. An old man and three old women. They lived at Oldstock when Yevgenia and Yuri bought the place, and they stayed. The man does maintenance and they all work in the cafeteria."

"So it wouldn't be unprecedented. Maybe they can explain some things to us," Kaye suggested.

"I'd like you to be here when the baby comes," Stella said. "That would be good."

Kaye lay her cheek on the crown of Stella's head. "I would be so proud," she said. "Is there a doctor here?"

"Yevgenia and Yuri were doctors in Russia," Stella said. "Mine will be the first baby born here."

"Like mother, like daughter," Mitch said with a hint of his old reluctance. "Pioneers." His wife and Stella ventured smiles.

"You could sing to the baby, like you did to me," Stella said. "You have a good voice, for babies."

"She's right," Kaye said. "What if it's a boy?"

"It is," Stella said. "I can smell him. He smells like Will, inside me."

6

Some said the turning point had come. Kaye was not so sure. After all the years of struggle she could hardly imagine a time of reconstruction, of engagement and change. As she sat with her husband and the three girls in the back of the long passenger van, jouncing along the rutted trails beneath the white glare of Mount Hood, what she felt inside was a kind of frozen patience.

She held her husband's arm and stared between the driver and the Secret Service agent sitting up front. Then she turned to look back at Stella and Celia and LaShawna, and John Hamilton behind them. The girls—young women now—were stiff as dolls, their eyes large. They had watched the landscape change from high arid brush to farms and pear orchards and then to thin forest; saying little, pushed close together on the bench seat. John was looking out the back window at where the long line of vans and cars had been.

He wants to be with Luella, Kaye thought. *He's tired of this fight and he wants to be with his wife. For the next fight.*

No peace. No rest.

Mitch leaned forward to peer through the side window, looking for the first signs of the Spent River and the camp. He had not wanted to return here. "I've given up the dead," he had told Kaye after the visit from Oliver Merton a week ago. "No more dirt and bones for me. Give me the living. They're trouble enough."

Mitch did not like the publicity aspect, nor the connection with William Daney, Eileen Ripper's benefactor at the Spent River dig; it smacked too much of a stunt. None of this junket had appealed to him, and at first Kaye had shared his opinion. Why go forth into the world to help an administration that had come to the table so late, after so much destruction—one of three clueless, terrible administrations in a row?

What good to help the monsters understand? Best to stay in Oldstock, hidden away from everyone and wait for Stella's baby.

But Oldstock was no longer hidden. Morgan had been doing a lot of talking. Reporters were arriving, pilgrims, parents searching for lost children.

It had taken a visit from Senator Bloch to finally persuade Kaye that this was a good idea. Troublesome gifts sometimes came out of left field; it was unwise to ignore them. Or impossible.

Kaye understood that better than most.

The EMAC schools were closing down or being converted to orphanages. Sandia Pathogenics was fighting for its existence and trying to redefine itself. Eileen's Spent River site was about to become an object lesson. The president of the United States wanted it as a symbol for a country trying to come together after a long and awful battle between conscience and fear.

"There are always those who fear the future," Bloch had told Kaye and Mitch. "They fear change, fear being replaced; one thing they do in their fear is kill children. They have to be left completely powerless, or the nastiness will start all over again."

"Either you join in, or you get left behind." Bloch had said. "I think you should go. Fruits of victory. People want to know what Kaye thinks." She had added, "You, too, Mitch."

In the end, it was Stella who had tipped the scales.

"Let's go," she had said in the kitchen of the Oldstock cafeteria, wiping her hands on a dish towel and resting them on her prominent stomach. "I've always wanted to see where Dad worked."

The line of cars and vans crested a rise and descended on the rough road to the dry meander of the ancient river bed. A few of the cars, with lower suspensions, were being left behind.

"There it is," Mitch said. "They've taken off the camouflage." The girls turned their heads to follow his finger. The site had expanded enormously. There were over thirty tents and shelters now on both sides of the old brush-strewn river bed.

Secret Service agents waited for them, checked with the drivers, then flagged them through, diverting the VIP vans to one area and the reporters to another.

The two long vans pulled into a makeshift parking lot marked by crumbling logs and shut off their engines. Senator Bloch waited for them under a white plastic awning. The sun poked through uncertain clouds and illuminated the covered H of the new main dig shelter. Again, linked Quonset huts provided cover. It lay at the end of a fenced pathway leading north.

"Is this where they died?" LaShawna asked.

Secret Service agents opened the van doors. Five photographers, led by a subdued Oliver Merton, surrounded the trucks and snapped pictures and made video. They concentrated on Stella.

Oliver smiled at Mitch and Kaye and stared at Stella with something like reverence. It was a quiet side of Oliver Kaye had never seen before.

"Just a year ago," a reporter was saying into her lapel mike, staring earnestly into a tiny camera mounted on a curved pole poking from her belt, "the sight of a pregnant Shevite female would have caused panic. Now—"

Kaye turned away and refused to listen.

Mitch spotted Eileen Ripper walking along the trail from the big new shelter. He would have recognized her slow, deliberate saunter even had she worn a mask. She did not like this any more than he did, but it was indeed a triumph. A federal circuit court judge had ruled just three months before, after almost twenty years of litigation, that the Five Tribes had no standing—could claim no legitimate relationship to the remains of peoples physically and temporally so far from their own. The Department of the Interior would no longer halt these digs or return any remains found to the complaining tribes.

Thus had ended a long nightmare for North American archaeology.

Strange that Mitch did not feel any sense of victory.

The bones he had found, goaded on by Eileen's challenge, had been just part of the story. He had not, after all, completely understood the motives of the ghosts flitting over the landscape.

Perhaps ghosts also lied to get their own way.

Eileen pushed through the photographers and past Bloch's entourage with hardly a nod. She came straight to Mitch and Kaye, and her eyes lingered for a moment on the girls as she held out her hand to Kaye.

"Welcome," she said with a broad, nervous smile. "And welcome back. Glad you could bring the family."

She set about introducing the others, all moving forward with varying degrees of shyness or confidence or diffidence in front of the cameras.

Mitch was sure this was going to turn out badly.

At the airport, LaShawna and Celia had been glad to see Stella again. Breaking from John Hamilton's protection, LaShawna had grabbed Celia and then Stella and they had all gone off together to the closest women's restroom—a frightening place for them all, even more than the airplane, with the smells of so many humans.

LaShawna had dragged Stella into a stall and whispered fiercely at her,

"What are you doing, girl, going wasp and getting yourself puffed! Was it that boy Will?"

Celia had called through the closed door, "She'll explain later. Let's go! I don't like it in here."

But there had been little time for talk, much less clouding and conveying the full story. The ride in the truck had made them all a little quiet, even with Kaye and Mitch and John along. LaShawna had whispered in Stella's ear, "Your mother looks good."

Stella had pulled back and looked LaShawna full in the face.

"Momma has it," LaShawna had said sadly, dropping her chin to her chest and pulling up her knees, propping them against the seat back. "She's in a wheelchair."

Stella brushed the short hair from her eyes as the wind blew in her face. She stepped down from the truck and blinked at the cameras. Celia and LaShawna seemed to fall in place behind her like ducklings. Being pregnant gave her seniority, she wondered why; it was stupid the way it had happened, stupid losing Will. She had left Oldstock to come here in part to get perspective; she wondered how much longer she would live at the compound.

Without Will, she doubted she would ever find the childish freedom that had once seemed so important. As she smelled and felt the baby inside her, she thought of responsibility and getting things done.

Meeting with a senator and with all these other folks was a start.

The landscape around the dry river bed was somewhere between bleak and pretty and it smelled much like Oldstock though cooler; the trees knew less sun than the trees around Lake Stannous. Quiet, cool pines poked up through gray brush and hard, crusty dirt with broken pieces of purple-black and gray rock overlying.

There was something going on between the woman archaeologist, Eileen, and her father. They were old friends. Something had happened between them along ago; Stella was sure of it. She watched her mother, but Kaye did not seem bothered. In fact, Kaye and Eileen seemed to walk alike and to look around with the same dignified curiosity.

That pleased Stella.

Mitch put an arm around her shoulder. Stella leaned into his embrace and cameras whirred and flashed all around.

"They're *affectionate*," said a male newscaster to unseen eyes. "Isn't that wonderful?"

Mitch gently squeezed Stella. "Never mind," he said in a low voice. "We're going to visit the bones." He sounded as if that would be like entering a church.

And it was. They walked down into the big shelter, following long plywood sheets, and reporters were instructed to turn off their bright lights. A large sunburned man, about thirty years old, in muddy jeans and a sleeveless T-shirt, with dirty forearms and a bandanna around his head, and dental tools and brushes slung on his belt, made the reporters pass through inspection and a shoe scrub. They all donned plastic booties. "Dirt is important here," the man explained, his voice a rich tenor. "We don't want to add anything that doesn't belong."

Eileen broke from a small group of reporters and introduced him. "This is Carlton Fierro," she said. "Carlton the Doorman. We call him that because he can hardly fit through most doors. He's in charge of this dig now."

Stella smiled at Carlton.

"Glad you could make it," he told the girls.

Connie Fitz walked around a sculpted pillar of dirt and hooked arms with Eileen. "We need big boys to protect us when there are reporters around," she said, and winked at Mitch.

Stella did not understand any of this. She focused on Carlton, who was shaking hands with Mitch. "We've got the biggest grouping over here," Carlton said, and led them all along the boards and through a connecting corridor to the second wing of the shelter. They turned right and stood before a wide excavated mesa, sheared off about ten feet below the datum—the level of the surrounding land. Scaffolds had been erected around the mesa and filtered sunlight fell on them all through milky fiberglass sheets.

"Eight at a time," Carlton instructed, "and that includes me." The reporters pushed around him, trying to keep the girls and Kaye in direct view.

He made a path through the crowd for the people Eileen pointed out, holding her hand over their heads and nodding.

"Coming through," Carlton said, and they climbed the aluminum steps. He was the last.

Stella looked down on the excavation. At first, all she saw was a large jumble of dark bones on hard planed dirt, mud, and what looked like old ash. She could smell the dust. Nothing more.

Mitch and Kaye stood across from her, Celia and LaShawna beside her; John Hamilton and Senator Bloch, both very quiet, were catercorner on the scaffold beside Carlton. Oliver Merton was staying out of the way, standing alone in one corner with arms crossed.

Eileen and Connie Fitz and Laura Bloch had also stayed below. It was now Carlton's show.

"There are eight adult females and two children, one male and one female, in this grouping," Carlton said. "A lahar of volcanic gas and mud and water came roaring down this river bed about twenty thousand years ago. They died together, covered with hot mud. One of them dropped a woven grass basket. Its mold is still in that cube of unexcavated mudstone to the right. The woman on top of the group—she's marked with a red plastic square, and her outline is made more clear by the thin strip of blue tape— is taller and more robust; she's *Homo erectus*, a late stage variety similar to *heidelbergensis* but as yet without a scientific designation. She appears to be in her forties, well past child bearing and very old for the time. A grandma type. We think she was protecting the children, and perhaps two other women. The female child and the other females are all *Homo sapiens*, virtually indistinguishable from you and me. The male child is another *Homo erectus*.

"At first, we thought—Connie and Eileen and the pioneers at this site thought, that is; I'm sort of late here—that there were only females, that the males had run off and abandoned them. Later, Mr. Rafelson found the first signs of the males, not far away and across the river. We thought they might have been out hunting and coming back to their females. Well, that may still be the case, but there was a lot more going on. We've since excavated thirteen sites around the Spent River, all within a thousand yards of here. We've found a total of fifty-three whole skeletons and perhaps seventy partials, a bit of femur or skull cap or tooth here and there.

"This was a kind of village, set up in the autumn to take advantage of salmon runs in the river. Family groups made camp along a loose network of trails, waiting for the run to begin. They were caught by the volcanic eruption and frozen in time, for us to find, and to reacquaint ourselves with . . . well, I think of them as old friends. Old teachers, actually."

Stella glanced at Mitch and saw a tear on his cheek.

Carlton paused to gather his thoughts. Celia was transfixed and maybe a little frightened by this big, rough-looking male. Her jaw hung open. LaShawna was frowning in concentration.

"And what they teach us now is pretty simple. They were traveling as equals. Personally, I don't know what they were offering each other. But we've found roughly equal numbers of both species, *erectus* and *sapiens*.

There are children of both species, and males as well. Our first site was anomalous. If I could make a guess . . ."

"He's a lot like you, Mitch," Eileen called from the crowd below the scaffold.

Carlton smiled shyly. "I'd say maybe the *erectus* individuals worked as hunters, using tools made by the *sapiens*. We haven't finished analyzing one of the outermost digs yet, a hunting party, but it looks like some of the *erectus* females served as lead hunters. They carried flint knapping tools and the heavy weapons and some stones that might or might not be hunting charms. That's right. Tall girls with great sniffers leading the brainy boys.

"We're looking for a central butchering ground for game—usually near where the large cutting tools were manufactured. In those days hunters tended to carry big game back to the village and butcher it in a protected area. We aren't sure why—either they hadn't yet thought of carrying the butchering tools with them, or they were trying to avoid attracting large predators.

"The *sapiens* females cooperated in weaving grass and leather and bark and preparing the fish and gathering berries and bugs and such around the camps. We've found beetles and grubs and grass and blackberry seeds in some of the baskets. Everyone had their place. They worked together."

"So should we all," said Senator Bloch, and Stella could see that she, too, was deeply moved.

Stella did not know what to think. The bones were still a tangle, as were her thoughts.

"As we reveal the bones, remove the overburden and brush them clean, we don't know what beliefs they held, twenty thousand years ago," Carlton said softly. "So basically we just respect them with silence, for a while, and gratitude. We get acquainted, as it were. They were not our direct ancestors, of course—we'll probably never find direct ancestors that old. It would be like digging up needles in a mighty sparse and distributed haystack.

"But the people down here, and all around the Spent River, they're still *us*. Nobody owns them. But they're family." Carlton nodded to his own strong convictions.

"Amen," Eileen and Connie Fitz said simultaneously below the scaffold.

Stella saw her father's hands on the rail. His knuckles were white and he was staring directly at her. Stella leaned her head to one side. He moved his lips. She could easily tell what he was saying.

Human.

• •

Eileen and Laura Bloch and Mitch watched as the photographers arranged Kaye and the girls at the base of the mesa, standing in front of the scaffolding. No pictures of the bones were being allowed.

"Rumor has it Kaye met God," Eileen said in a low voice to Mitch. "Is it true?"

"So she tells me."

"That's got to be awkward for a scientist," Eileen said.

"She's doing okay," Mitch said. "She calls it just another kind of inspiration."

Senator Bloch listened to this with a focused pug-dog expression.

"What about you?" Eileen asked.

"I remain blissfully ignorant."

"Kind of a sometime thing, huh?"

Bloch weighed in. "That can't be bad," she mused. "Not for politics. Did she see Jesus?"

Mitch shook his head. "I don't think so. That's not what she says, anyway."

Bloch pouched out her lips. "If there's no Jesus, we best keep it under our hats for now."

"What does God tell her about all of this?" Eileen asked, sweeping her hand over the excavations, the revealed bones.

Mitch scowled. "Not much, probably. It doesn't seem to be that kind of relationship."

"What good is he, then?" Eileen asked petulantly.

Mitch had to look hard to tell if she was joking. She appeared to be, and she lost interest as some photographers came too near a grid square propped against a table and almost knocked it over.

After berating them and resetting the square, she came back and patted Mitch on the shoulder. "Good for Kaye," she said. "Just proves that we're a tough old species. We can survive anything, even God. How about you? Going to come back soon and dig with us?" Eileen asked.

"No," Mitch said. "That's over for me."

"Shame. He was the best," Eileen said to Bloch. "A real natural."

Mitch helped Kaye back into the van. Kaye sat and massaged her calves. Her feet were numb and she had had a difficult time climbing the stairs out of the shelter.

Stella and Celia and LaShawna walked in a tight cluster to the van and climbed in behind her, then sat quietly. John Hamilton and Mitch stood talking as they waited for Bloch to rejoin them.

Kaye could hear her husband and John, but only a scatter of words between whisks of dusty wind.

John was saying, ". . . and bad. They say it's worse with two. Summer in Maryland is going to be tough. She wanted to come here. Just couldn't."

Kaye licked her dry lips and stared forward. Stella placed her hand on Kaye's shoulder and touched her cheek.

"How are you all doing?" Kaye asked abruptly, swiveling around despite the twinges in her thighs and surveying the girls—the young women.

"We're just fine," LaShawna said dreamily. "I wish I knew what this was all about."

"I think-KUK I do," Celia said. "Human politics."

"How are you, dear?" Kaye asked Stella.

"*We're* fine," Stella said, and her cheeks flushed butterfly gold with something like fear, and something like joy.

She gets it, Kaye thought. *What we just saw. She's like her father that way.*

She watched Stella lean back in the seat and put on a distant, thoughtful expression, cheeks paling to beige. Celia and LaShawna sat back with her.

Together, they all folded their arms.

That evening, Stella and Celia and LaShawna sat in their own room in a motel in Portland. Kaye and Mitch and John Hamilton were in other rooms in the same motel; the girls had asked to be together, alone, "To just lie back and revert," Stella had explained.

They had eaten with the others and watched Senator Bloch and Oliver Merton leave in a limo to fly back on a red-eye to Washington, D.C., and now they were relaxing and thinking quietly.

Seeing the bones had bothered Stella. Will was not much more than bones now. All that time, all that life; gone, leaving nothing but scattered rubble. Celia and LaShawna were also quiet at first, absorbed in their own individual thoughts.

They were saddened by the prospect of parting, but they all had things to do at home, loved ones to attend to. Celia was living with the Hamiltons and working with Shevite outreach services in Maryland and had her own life. LaShawna was getting her general education requirements at a local high school and planned on going to a junior college to study nursing. With her father, she took care of her mother, who was not getting around on her own much now, and her baby sister.

So much had changed in a few short months.

Stella sat up from a pile of pillows and made a circling motion with her palm, dipping her head like a bird, and LaShawna seconded. Celia gave a little groan of weary protest but joined them on the bed farthest from the curtained window. They palm-touched and sat in a circle, and Stella felt her cheeks flush and her ears grow warm.

"Who we are," LaShawna sang. "What we are/ who. What we are/ who. Get us in, get us out/ who."

It was a chant that helped them focus; they had done it before at Sable Mountain when the teachers and counselors weren't watching or listening, and especially after a difficult day.

The room filled with their scents. A little something like electricity passed between them and LaShawna started to hum two tunes, two sets of over and under. She was good at that, better than Stella.

The day seemed to melt away and Stella felt her neck and back loosen and they began to remember all the good they had experienced together.

"Lovely. We're in it," LaShawna said, and started to hum again.

"I can-KUK feel the baby," Celia said. "He's so small and quiet. He smells like Will, a little—if I remember, it's been so long."

"He smells like Will," Stella agreed.

"It's so good to be with both of you again," Celia said.

"I had a dream about this, weeks ago," LaShawna said. "I was awake, with my friends, but everything was dark, and I was looking so far down into myself it hurt. I saw something down there. A little glow hidden way at the bottom . . ."

"Like what?" Celia said, squirming in fascination.

"Let me show you," LaShawna said, and squeezed their palms tightly.

Celia bit her lip and closed her eyes. "I'm looking deep."

"Can you see them?" LaShawna whispered. She chanted softly, "If you take away/strip it down/ all the days and years/ all the thoughts . . . Who are we? Umm-hmm. Down there deep in a cave. Get us in, get us out/ Who?"

Stella reached down to where LaShawna was, using her palm-touch for guidance. She actually did see something at the bottom of a long, deep well, three somethings, actually, and then four, the baby within her joining. Like four luminous golden kernels of corn, hidden away at the bottom of four separate tunnels of memory and life.

"What are they?" Celia asked quietly, eyes still closed. Stella closed her own eyes now to see these peculiar things more clearly.

"They're like us, part of us, but way below us," LaShawna said.

"They're so quiet-KUK, like they're asleep. Peaceful."

"The baby's is not much different from ours," Stella observed. "Why is that?"

"Maybe they're the important ones and we're just shadows trapped way up here. We're ghosts to them, maybe. Ummm . . . I'm losing them . . . I can't see them now," LaShawna said, and opened her eyes with a sigh. "That was spooky."

The waking dream ended and left Stella feeling a little woozy. The air in the room had turned cold and they shivered and laughed, then clasped hands tighter, listening to their own heartbeats.

"Spooky," LaShawna said again. "I'm glad you see them, too."

They sat that way for hours, just touching hands and scenting and being quiet together until the dawn came.

7

LAKE STANNOUS

The third snow of the year came in late October, fat flakes slipping down and nodding between the trees and over the dirt and gravel pathways throughout Oldstock. Kaye hurried from her classroom in the overheated school building, clutching a parka over her shoulders. Puffing, her lips and fingers numb, she met Mitch and Luce Ramone on the path to the infirmary—a name Kaye hated, with its emphasis on dysfunction. Mitch wrapped her in his arms and she marched quickly, close to his side, looking up at him with tight lips and large eyes.

"We have the partners and side mothers in the birthing room," Luce said. Most of the children—the Shevites, Kaye corrected—did not speak in doubles, over-under, around them, more out of politeness than any obvious reserve or caution. Slowly, over the last four months, the Shevites had come to trust Kaye and Mitch, and together they had worked out procedures to calm mothers about to give birth. Kaye did not know whether it was mumbo jumbo or a new way of doing things. She was about to find out. Now there were twelve pregnancies in Oldstock and Stella was serving a very important function. *Keep reminding yourself. Be proud. Be coura-geous. Oh, God.*

So much was being learned. So many questions were being answered. *But why my daughter? Why someone who, if she dies, takes me with her, soul if not body?*

The last two months had been the happiest in Kaye's life, and the most tense and awkward.

They gingerly climbed the snowy steps into the old infirmary and down the linoleum-tiled floors, along the plastered hallway lit with dim incandescent bulbs, into the delivery room.

Stella was sitting on the bent and padded bench, puffing and blowing. A rusty gurney covered with a foam mattress and clean white sheets waited for her if she wanted to sleep. She gritted her teeth into a contraction.

Kaye set about arranging the medical instruments, making sure they had been kept in the old autoclave long enough.

"Where did you get these antiques?" she asked Yuri Sakartvelos as he came in, hands held in the air, dripping from the scrub station. Yevgenia smiled at Kaye and her wrinkled cheeks grew golden-green as she slipped the gloves on Yuri's hands.

"Pray they don't have to do anything," Kaye whispered grimly to Mitch.

"Shush," Mitch warned. "They're doctors."

"From *Russia*, Mitch," Kaye responded. "How long since they've done anything but set a broken leg or dress a wound?"

As Mitch caught a catnap, in the twelfth hour of Stella's long delivery—that had not changed much, difficult births for babies with large heads—Kaye stood outside the infirmary and breathed the cold early morning air and watched the snow.

While Kaye taught in the village school, Mitch had helped the Shevites restore a small lumber mill and clear the debris from the old concrete foundations and start putting up new houses for the families.

It was not yet clear what shape those families would take; probably not just father, mother, and children, and on this score the Sakartvelos were as clueless as Kaye and Mitch. There had never been so many Shevites together before; though some said there were larger communities in the East and the South, perhaps in New Jersey or Georgia or Mississippi, lying low.

The young Shevites were designing the homes. They felt uncomfortable when deprived of company for more than a few hours. Large windows Kaye could certainly understand, after so many years in cramped dorms and even cells. But there was no double pane glass available, not yet, and winters in Oldstock could be cold. While the foundations provided some constraint on their imaginations, some of the drawings were looking very odd indeed: bathrooms and toilet facilities without walls—"Why privacy? We know what's happening"—and narrow "scent shafts" connecting adjacent homes. The whole idea of privacy seemed up for grabs.

Kaye's best moments were spent with Stella and Mitch and Stella's deme. Most of the students in Kaye's class were part of Stella's deme. Her curiosity and relative ease with these intruder humans, her parents, seemed to blend over into those closest to her, and that extended family had adopted Kaye and Mitch.

The Sakartvelos, on the other hand, treated Kaye and Mitch civilly enough, but seldom socialized. They seemed a little standoffish even with the others in their community, perhaps because of early trauma and years of living alone, growing middle-aged with little company.

The concept and practice of demes was still growing, but the demes formed thus far made up the most stable of all the social structures and experiments going on in Oldstock, and the oldest. Stella's deme consisted of seven permanent partners—three males and four females—and twelve exchange members.

Deme partners usually did not mate, though they could fall in love— Stella was very definite about that, but not very clear what it entailed. Romantic love was running wild in Oldstock, complete with exchanges of dried fruit, perfumes when available, carved wooden statues, but such infatuations seldom had anything to do with sex.

Sex, it seemed, was too important to be left to the whims of romance. Love, yes, but not this boiling torrent of fickle affection.

In late summer, the paths and woods had sometimes smelled like an explosion in a cocoa factory, mixed with shocking and eye-stinging hints of musk and civet. Couples, all combinations—and sometimes triples—could be seen wrapped in congeries of self-involved, fondling splendor, intertwined, giggling, fever-scenting, persuading—everything but having sex.

At first, Kaye and Mitch had speculated that some of the couples and triples were too young, but soon the sixteen-year-olds were proving them wrong, mating outside the romance, and almost always across demes.

Those who were still prepubescent could become juniors in romantic groups, but such relationships were less demonstrative, more reserved and instructional. Love, and new varieties of passion, it seemed, would find many new uses in Shevite society, and the homes had to reflect these novelties.

Kaye's thoughts darted back to the one thing she did not want to think about, not now. She lifted her eyes to the dark sky. She wanted to be around for her daughter, to be useful to Mitch and to Stella for many years. But the CDC had confirmed that there was indeed a post-SHEVA syndrome. Luella Hamilton had it; so did many others.

The tips of Kaye's fingers and portions of her calves were growing numb as the months passed, her walk less quick, her strength and stamina waning.

She had told nobody at Oldstock, though Mitch knew. Kaye could seldom hide important things from Mitch. Except, of course, for what he did not want to hear.

The caller had touched her just a week ago. A short visit, pleasant but not conclusive; a social call. She had asked if she might be allowed to live to see her grandson born.

As before, no answers.

Inside the delivery room, Stella was surrounded by all the females in her deme. They alternately sang and read stories from old children's books and put their heads together, rubbing their damp palms on hers to calm her and relieve her pain.

Stella leaned back at the last and her eyes seemed to slip up into her head. She gave a long, loud shriek, operatic in its intensity, and the room smelled like saltwater and violets. Everyone moaned together, no signal, just the way it was, would be, moaning in an over-under song of sympathy and greeting.

Stella gave a vigorous wriggle and then a shove, and her son came into the larger world. The moaning softened as the child was examined, and then changed to delighted coos and chuckles.

Yevgenia and Kaye cooperated in lifting the baby onto Stella's stomach. Yevgenia smiled at Kaye. "Now you are truly grandmother," she said.

The afterbirth came. Yuri moved them urgently to one side and caught it in a steel basin lined with a plastic bag. To Kaye's surprise, Yuri insisted on cutting the cord, then wrapping and removing the placenta right away. He cleaned up all the blood with a sponge soaked in bleach, then brought basins of soapy water and insisted the helpers wash their hands.

He bathed Stella solicitously. "It might be dangerous, no touching," Yuri insisted, and left the infirmary with the tissue.

Kaye was beyond analysis or caring. She huddled with her daughter and the females in the deme, and Mitch, and one young male, the stand-in for Will, looking confused and bewildered at this unexpected role.

The infant, wrinkled and small, squirmed slowly in Stella's arms, seeking the breast, then looked up at them all, drawing back his eyelids until it seemed his face was all eyes, wide, mobile, focused. His cheeks flared golden and pink, melanophores shaping at first a series of flower-petal rawshocks. All those in the room, except for Kaye and Mitch, responded to the newborn with the same colors and patterns, flower petals and butterflies, sparks and flares, and the baby saw this and smelled their pleasure and delight. He smiled with saintly ease and reassurance as he took the nipple.

That smile took Kaye's breath away. She squeezed Mitch's hand. Ever the anthropologist, Mitch was watching the deme, the side mothers, all the Shevites in the room, with a quizzical expression.

"Do you have a name yet?" Kaye asked Stella.

Stella shook her head dreamily. "Give us time. Something nice."

Moments later, suckling her son, Stella relaxed and slept. Her cheeks kept showing patterns. Even asleep, the new mother could sign her love.

The infant released his mother's nipple and looked up at Mitch. "Sing," he said.

The deme laughed, and the young man who was standing in for Will, in a burst of emotion, hugged them and shook Mitch's hand. Kaye touched his shoulder and smiled up at him, and Mitch knelt beside the bed and sang the alphabet song, the same he had sung for Stella. *"Ah, beh, say, duh, eh, fuh, guh, huh, kuh, ih, juh, em . . ."*

Mitch's grandson relaxed and took Stella's nipple. His large purple-flecked eyes became heavy-lidded, and then closed. He joined his mother in sleep before Mitch got to *wuh.*

EPILOGUE

Kaye tried to move her lips. Such wonderful thoughts. So simple, so clear. If she could only speak to her husband.

Mitch looked at the lamp on the table, brows knit; he could hear his wife's steady breath and the hum of the medical monitor and little more. When her breath changed its rhythm, he slowly turned his head and saw her lips move. He leaned forward, wondering if she was coming back, but her eyes stared out into space and blinked only once while he watched.

Still, the lips moved. That hurt. Any expectations were painful. Kaye's periods of paralysis had been coming with greater frequency. He leaned forward, hoping with childish hope to see his wife, his woman, return to him, beginning with that small motion. He brought his ear down to her lips and felt the breath against the little hairs on the skin of his lobe. Kaye's breath puffed, worked, to shape a few words.

Mitch could not be sure what he heard, if he heard anything at all. He pulled back to look at Kaye's face and realized she was trying with super-human effort to communicate something she thought was important. The slightest coming together of her brows, stiffening of her cheeks, set of her eyelids, reminded him of earnest conversations years past, when she struggled to convey something not quite within her grasp or authority. That had been his Kaye, always reaching beyond what words could do.

He placed his ear close, almost blocking her lips. He fancied he heard, for a moment, his name, and then,

"Something's . . . going on."

He listened again.

"Something's . . . happening."

Then she lay still. Breath lifted the sheets but her eyes were still. Her face was blank.

She seemed to be listening.

•   •

She felt the love rolling over her in waves, the yearning that was at once so powerful and frightening, the sweetness that lay behind the power. Her death would not come yet, not this minute, not this hour, this she knew, but she was no longer much of this world.

And so she could be embraced and told all.

No fear of addiction now.

Stella brought the baby and sat with them. She wore simple clothes and held the boy in a loose knit wrap, because, she said, he was such a warm-blooded creature, he hardly ever got chilly and fussed if he was covered.

"We've chosen a talking name," Stella said. Then, looking at her mother, she asked Mitch if Kaye could hear them.

"I don't know," Mitch said. His face was so lost. Stella let him hold his grandson and adjusted her mother's covers.

"Nothing's fair, is it?" she asked Kaye softly, leaning over, her cheeks golden. "She looks peaceful. I think she can hear us."

Mitch watched Kaye breathe in and out, slowly, simply.

"What's his name?" he asked.

"We're going to call him Sam," Stella said. "I can't think of anything better. The deme thinks it's good."

Sam was Mitch's father's name. "Not Samuel?"

"Just Sam. He likes the name already. It's strong and short and doesn't interfere with saying other things."

Sam squirmed and wanted to get down. At six months, he was already walking a little, and speaking, of course; but only when he wanted to, which was seldom.

Mitch tried to find a little of Kaye in Sam's features, but there was too much eyebrow. Sam looked too much like Mitch.

"He looks like Will, I think," Stella said. She touched her mother's cheek, gripped her hand. "She has a scent. It's her, but different. I'm not sure I'd recognize her. Can you smell it?"

Mitch shook his head. "Maybe she smells ill," he said darkly.

"No." Stella bowed to sniff her mother from breast to crown. "She smells like smoke from a wood fire, and flowers. We need her to teach us. Mother, you could teach me so much."

Sam walked around the bed, gripping the covers and making sounds of discovery.

Kaye's face did not change expression, but Stella saw the tiny freckles darken under her mother's eyes. Even now, Kaye could show her love.

The memories fall away. We are shaped, but in ways we do not understand. Know that thinking and memory are biology, and biology is what we leave behind. The caller speaks to all of our minds, and they all pray; to all of our minds, from the lowest to the highest, in nature, the caller assures us that there is more, and that is all the caller can do. It is important that each mind be created with absolute freedom of will. That freedom is precious; it enriches and quickens that which the caller loves.

Mind and memory make up the precious rind of the even more precious fruit.

We are sculpted as the embryo is made; we die and cells die that others may take a shape; the shape grows and changes, visible only to the caller; ultimately all must be chipped away, having made their contributions.

The memories fall away. We are shaped. There is no judgment, for in life there is no perfection, only freedom. To succeed or to fail is all the same—it is to be loved.

To die, to fall silent, is not to be forgotten or lost.

Silence is the beacon of past love and painful labor.

Silence is also a signal.

Mitch sat by Kaye as the doctors and nurses came and went. He watched her grow more at ease, if that was possible, while breath still came and heart still beat with a slow, pattering softness.

He finished that night, before he napped off, by kissing her forehead and saying, "Good night, Eve."

Mitch slept in the chair. Quiet filled the room.

The world seemed empty and new.

Silence filled Kaye.

In a dream, Mitch walked over the high rocky mountains, and met a woman on the snows.

Lynnwood, Washington
2002

CAVEATS

Much of the science in this novel is still controversial. Science usually begins with speculation, but must in time be confirmed by research, empirical evidence, and scientific consensus. However, all of the speculations found here are supported, to one degree or another, by research published in texts and in respected scientific journals. I have gone to great pains to solicit scientific criticism and make corrections where experts feel I have strayed over the line.

No doubt errors remain, but they are my responsibility, not the responsibility of the scientists or other helpful readers listed in the acknowledgments.

The theological speculations presented here are also based on empirical evidence, personal and culled from a number of key books. But that evidence is remarkably and uniquely difficult to present scientifically, since it is necessarily anecdotal. That does not make its truth any less apparent to the witnesses; it simply puts this type of life experience in the same category as other human events, such as love, abstract and creative thought, and artistic inspiration.

All of these experiences are personal and anecdotal, yet almost universal; none are easily quantified or understood by current science.

In answer to the obvious questions about evolution, do I support neo-Darwinian randomness or theistic external design? The answer must be neither. Do I support fundamentalist or Creationist views of our origins? I do not.

My view is that life on Earth is constituted of many layers of neural networks, all interacting to solve problems in order to get access to resources and continue to exist. All living things solve problems posed by their environments, and all are adapted to attempt, with reasonable success, to solve such problems. The human mind is just one variety of this natural process, and not necessarily the most subtle or sophisticated. See my novel, *Vitals*.

I also make a distinction between self-aware personality and mind. Human self-awareness is a psycho-social phenomenon resulting from feedback in modeling the behavior of one's neighbors, and, almost coincidentally, modeling one's own behavior to make sure we'll fit into social activities. One offshoot of this ability is the writing of novels.

Self is not an illusion; it's real. But it's not unitary, it's not primary, and it's not always in charge.

It seems apparent that God does not micromanage either human history or nature. Evolutionary freedom is just as important as individual human freedom. Does God interfere at all? Other than my affirming, along with many others, that the presence of something we could call God is made known— a kind of interference, undoubtedly—I do not know.

As Kaye experiences her epiphany, she is made aware that her "caller" is not talking just to her, but to other minds within and around her. Epiphany is not limited to our conscious selves, or even to human beings.

Imagine epiphany that touches our subconscious, our other internal minds—the immune system—or that reaches beyond us to touch a forest, or an ocean . . . or the vast and distributed "minds" of any ecological system.

If the only honest approach to understanding both nature and God is humility, then surely this should help by making us feel humble.

A SHORT BIOLOGICAL PRIMER

Humans are metazoans, that is, we are made up of many cells. In most of our cells there is a *nucleus* that contains the "blueprint" for the entire individual. This blueprint is stored in *DNA,* deoxyribonucleic acid; DNA and its complement of helper proteins and organelles make up the molecular computer that contains the instructions necessary to construct an individual organism.

Proteins are molecular machines that can perform incredibly complicated functions. They are the engines of life; DNA is the template that guides the manufacture of those engines.

DNA in eukaryotic cells is arranged in two interwoven strands—the "double helix"—and packed tightly into a complex structure called chromatin, which is arranged into *chromosomes* in each cell nucleus. With a few exceptions, such as red blood cells and specialized immune cells, the DNA in each cell of the human body is complete and identical. Researchers currently estimate that the human *genome*—the complete collection of genetic instructions—consists of approximately thirty thousand *genes*. Genes are heritable traits; a gene has often been defined as a segment of DNA that contains the code for a protein or proteins. This code can be transcribed to make a strand of RNA, ribonucleic acid; ribosomes then use the RNA to translate the original DNA instructions and synthesize proteins. Some genes perform other functions, such as making the RNA constituents of ribosomes.

Many scientists believe that RNA was the original coding molecule of life, and that DNA is a later elaboration.

While most cells in the body of an individual carry identical DNA, as the person grows and develops, that DNA is expressed in different ways within each cell. This is how identical embryonic cells become different tissues.

When DNA is transcribed to RNA, many lengths of nucleotides that do not code for proteins, called *introns,* are snipped out of the RNA segments. The segments that remain are spliced together; they code for proteins and are called *exons.* On a length of freshly transcribed RNA, these exons can be spliced together in different ways to make different proteins. Thus, a single gene can produce a number of products at different times.

Bacteria are tiny single-celled organisms. Their DNA is not stored in a nucleus but is spread around within the cell. Their genome contains no *introns,* only *exons,* making them very sleek and compact little critters. Bacteria can behave like social organisms; different varieties both cooperate and compete with each other to find and use resources in their environment. In the wild, bacteria frequently come together to create biofilms; you may be familiar with these bacterial "cities" from the slime on spoiled vegetables in your refrigerator. Biofilms can also exist in your intestines, your urinary tract, and on your teeth, where they sometimes cause problems, and specialized ecologies of bacteria protect your skin, your mouth, and other areas of your body. Bacteria are extremely important and though some cause disease, many others are necessary to our existence. Some biologists believe that bacteria lie at the root of all life forms, and that eukaryotic cells—our own cells, for example—derive from ancient colonies of bacteria. In this sense, we may simply be spaceships for bacteria.

Bacteria swap small circular loops of DNA called *plasmids.* Plasmids supplement the bacterial genome and allow them to respond quickly to threats such as antibiotics. Plasmids make up a universal library that bacteria of many different types can use to live more efficiently.

Bacteria and nearly all other organisms can be attacked by *viruses.* Viruses are very small, generally encapsulated bits of DNA or RNA that cannot reproduce by themselves, Instead, they hijack a cell's reproductive machinery to make new viruses. In bacteria, the viruses are called *bacteriophages,* ("eaters of bacteria") or just *phages.* Many phages carry genetic material between bacterial hosts, as do some viruses in animals and plants.

It is possible that viruses originally came from segments of DNA within cells that can move around, both inside and between chromosomes. Viruses are essentially roving segments of genetic material that have learned how to "put on space suits" and leave the cell.

Antibody: molecule that attaches to an antigen, inactivates it, and attracts other defenses to the intruder.

Antibiotics: a large class of substances manufactured by many different kinds of organisms that can kill bacteria. Antibiotics have no effect on viruses.

Antigen: intruding substance or part of an organism that provokes the creation of antibodies as part of an immune response.

Bacteria: prokaryotes, tiny living cells whose genetic material is not enclosed in a nucleus. Bacteria perform important work in nature and are the base of all food chains.

Bacteriophage: see *phage*.

Chromosome: arrangement of tightly packed and coiled DNA. Diploid cells such as body cells in humans have two sets of twenty-two *autosomes* as well as two *sex chromosomes*; haploid cells such as gametes— sperm or ova—have only a single set of chromosomes. The total number of chromosomes varies between apes and humans. Chromosome numbers for so-called ancestral species such as *Homo sapiens neandertalensis* and *Homo erectus* are not known; any DNA extracted from even relatively recent (~20,000 years) fossil specimens is generally limited to mitochondrial DNA. Polyploidy—having extra sets of chromosomes—results in infertile offspring or totally precludes reproduction between organisms and can often define a barrier between species. This should prevent successful mating between SHEVA individuals and older variety humans. Apparently, it does not. This puzzles scientists, and further research is in order.

Cro-Magnon: early variety of modern human, *Homo sapiens sapiens,* from Cro-Magnon in France. *Homo* is the genus, *sapiens* the species, *sapiens* the subspecies.

DNA: Deoxyribonucleic acid, the famous double-helix molecule that codes for the proteins and other elements that help construct the *phenotype* or body structure of an organism.

ERV or endogenous retrovirus: virus that inserts its genetic material into the DNA of a host. The integrated *provirus* lies dormant for a time. ERVs may be quite ancient and fragmentary and no longer capable of producing infectious viruses.

Exogenous virus: virus that does not insert its genes into host DNA on a long-term basis. Some viruses, such as MMTV or mouse mammary tumor virus, seem to be able to choose whether to insert or not insert their genetic code into host DNA. See *ERV*.

Exon: region of DNA that codes for proteins or RNA.

Frithing: also, flehman. Sucking air over the vomeronasal organ to detect pheromones. See *vomeronasal organ*.

Gene: the definition of a gene is changing. A recent text defines a gene as "a segment of DNA or RNA that performs a specific function." More particularly, a gene can be thought of as a segment of DNA that codes for some molecular product, very often one or more proteins or parts of proteins. Besides the nucleotides that code for the protein, the gene also consists of segments that determine how much and what kind of protein is expressed, and when. Genes can produce different combinations of proteins under different stimuli. In a very real sense, a gene is a tiny factory and computer within a much larger factory-computer, the genome.

Genome: sum total of genetic material in an individual organism. In humans, the genome appears to consist of approximately thirty thousand genes—half to one-third the number predicted at the time of the publication of *Darwin's Radio*.

Genotype: the genetic character of an organism or distinctive group of organisms.

Glycome: the total complement of sugars and related compounds in a cell. Sugars can form links with proteins and lipids to make glycoproteins and glycolipids.

Herpes: HSV-1 or -2. Herpes simplex virus types responsible for cold sores and genital herpes. Though herpes viruses are not retroviruses they can lie dormant in nerve cells for years, and often reactivate in response to stress. Chicken pox and its recurrent form, shingles, or herpes zoster, are also related to herpes.

HERV: human endogenous retrovirus. Within our genetic material are many remnants of past infections by retroviruses. Some researchers estimate that as much as one third of our genetic material may consist of old retroviruses. No instance is yet known of these ancient viral genes producing infectious particles (*virions*) that can move from host to host, in *lateral* or *horizontal transmission*. Many HERV do produce viruslike particles within the cells and body, however, and whether these particles serve a function or cause problems is not yet known. All HERV are part of our genome and are transmitted *vertically* when we reproduce, from parent to offspring. Infection of gametes by retroviruses is the best explanation so far for the presence of HERV in our genome. ERV, endogenous retroviruses, are found in many other organisms, as well.

Homo erectus: general classification for fossils of the genus *Homo* dated chronologically and evolutionarily prior to *Homo sapiens*. *Homo erectus* was a very successful human species, surviving for at least a million years. Calling any of these fossils "ancestral" is problematic both scientifically and philosophically, but it's a simple and easily understood description of a complex relationship. There are many interpretations of these relationships in the literature, but growing sophistication in genetics will probably lead to a general shaking out and clarification over the next ten to twenty years.

Immune response (immunity, immunization): the provoking and marshaling of defensive cells within an organism to ward off and destroy pathogens, disease-causing organisms such as viruses or bacteria. Immune response may also identify nonpathogenic cells as foreign, not part of the normal body complement of tissues; transplanted organs cause an immune response and may be rejected. Autoimmune diseases such as multiple sclerosis and various forms of arthritis may occur or reoccur in response to viral activation due to stress. In humans, ERV activation has been suggested as a cause of some autoimmune diseases.

Intron: region of DNA that generally does not code for proteins. In most eukaryotic cells, genes consist of mingled exons and introns. Introns are clipped out of transcribed messenger RNA (mRNA) before it is processed by ribosomes; ribosomes use the code contained in lengths of mRNA to assemble specific proteins out of amino acids. Bacteria lack introns.

Lipids: organic compounds such as fats, oils, waxes, and sterols. Lipids make up many of the structural components of cells, including much of the cell wall or membrane.

Lipome: the total complement of lipids within a cell. Lipids may also form alliances with sugars and proteins (see *glycome* and *proteome*).

Mitochondrion, mitochondria: organelles within cells that process sugars to produce the common fuel for cells, adenosine triphosphate, or ATP. Generally regarded as highly adapted descendants of bacteria that entered host cells billions of years ago. Mitochondria have their own loops of DNA constituting a separate genome within every cell. Mitochondrial DNA, being shorter and simpler, is often the target of choice for fossil analysis.

Modern human: *Homo sapiens sapiens.* Genus *Homo,* species *sapiens,* subspecies *sapiens. Homo sapiens sapiens* could be read as "Man who is wise, who knows." Also, "Man who is discreet, who savors."

Mobile element: movable segment of DNA. *Transposons* can move or have their DNA copied from place to place in a length of DNA using DNA polymerase. *Retrotransposons* contain their own *reverse transcriptase*, which gives them some autonomy within the genome. Mobile elements have been shown by Barbara McClintock and others to generate variety in plants; but some believe these are, more often than not, so-called selfish genes which are duplicated without being useful to the organism. More and more, geneticists have found strong evidence that mobile elements contribute to variation in all genomes and help to regulate both embryonic development and evolution.

Mutation: alteration in a gene or segment of DNA. May be accidental and unproductive or even dangerous; may also be useful, leading to the production of a more efficient protein. Mutations may lead to variation in phenotype, or the physical structure of an organism. Random mutations are usually either neutral or bad for the health of the organism.

Neandertal: *Homo sapiens Neandertalensis.* Possibly ancestral to humans. Modern anthropologists and geneticists are currently engaged in a debate about whether Neandertals are our ancestors, based on evidence of mitochondrial DNA extracted from ancient bones. More than likely, the evidence is confusing because we simply do not yet know how species and subspecies separate and develop.

Pathogen: disease-causing organism. There are many different varieties of pathogen: viruses, bacteria, fungi, protists (formerly known as protozoa), and metazoans such as nematodes.

PERV: Porcine endogenous retrovirus. Ancient retroviruses found in the genome of pigs. See *ERV*.

Phage: a virus that uses bacteria as hosts. Many kinds of phages kill their hosts almost immediately and can be used as antibacterial agents. Most bacteria have at least one and often many phages specific to them. Phages and bacteria are always in a contest to outrun each other, evolutionarily speaking.

Phenotype: the physical structure of an organism or distinctive group of organisms. *Genotype* expressed and developed within an environment determines *phenotype*.

Pheromone: a chemical message produced by one member of a species that influences the physiology and the behavior of another member of the same species. Whether or not this chemical message is consciously detected (smelled), pheromones have the same effect. Mammalian pheromones, in the form of "social odors," that one member of a species is exposed to during interaction with another member of the species, cause changes in hormone levels and in behavior. See *vomeropherin*.

Polyploidy: see *chromosome*.

Protein: genes often code for proteins, which help form and regulate all organisms. Proteins are molecular machines made up of chains of twenty different types of amino acids. Proteins can themselves chain or clump together. Collagen, enzymes, many hormones, keratin, and antibodies are just a few of the different types of proteins.

Proteome, Proteomics: the total complement of proteins within a cell or group of cells, or in an individual organism as a whole. Different tissues will produce different proteins from a standardized set of genes; gene activation in different tissues at different times causes variation in a cell's proteome. Knowing which genes have been activated can be traced through identifying proteins and other gene products. (See *glycome* and *lipidome*.)

Provirus: the genetic code of a virus while it is contained within the DNA of a host.

Radiology: imaging of the interior of a body using radiation, such as X-rays, PET scans (positron emission tomography), MRI (Magnetic resonance imaging), CAT scans (Computerized axial tomography), etc.

Recombination: exchange of genes between or within organisms or viruses. Sexual reproduction is one such exchange; bacteria and viruses can recombine genes in many different ways. Recombination can also be done artificially in a laboratory.

Retrotransposon, retroposon, retrogene: see movable elements.

Retrovirus: RNA-based virus that inserts its code into a host's DNA for later replication. Replication can often be delayed for years. AIDS and other diseases are caused by retroviruses.

RNA: ribonucleic Acid. Intermediate copy of DNA; messenger RNA (mRNA) is used by ribosomes as templates to construct proteins. Many viruses consist of single or doubled strands of RNA, usually transcribed to DNA within the host.

SHEVA: fictional human endogenous retrovirus that can form an infectious virus particle, or *virion*; an infectious HERV. No such HERV is yet known. In *Darwin's Radio* and this novel, SHEVA carries first-order instructions between individuals for a rearrangement of the genome that produces a new variety of human. In effect, SHEVA triggers preexisting genetic "set-asides" that interact in time-proven ways to create a subtly different human phenotype.

Sequencing: determining the sequence of molecules in a polymer such as a protein or nucleic acid; in genetics, discovering the sequence of bases in a gene or a length of DNA or RNA, or in the genome as a whole. Research into the sequence of the entire human genome has made huge strides, but our understanding of the implications of this growing knowledge is in its infancy.

Sex chromosomes: in humans, the X and Y chromosomes. Two X chromosomes results in a female; an X and a Y results in a male. Other species have different types of sex chromosomes.

Shiver: hypothetical activation of dormant endogenous retroviruses in women who have undergone SHEVA pregnancies. Recombination of exogenous and endogenous viral genes may produce new viruses with an unknown pathogenic potential.

Transposon: see *mobile elements*.

Vaccine: a substance that produces an immune response to a disease-causing organism. See *antibody, antigen, immune response.*

Virion: infectious virus particle.

Virus: nonliving but organically active particle capable of entering a cell and commandeering the cell's reproductive capacity to produce more viruses. Viruses consist of DNA or RNA, usually surrounded by a protein coat, or capsid. This capsid may in turn be surrounded by an envelope. There are hundreds of thousands of known viruses, and potentially millions not yet described. See *exogenous virus, ERV.*

Vomeronasal organ (VNO, also known as Jacobson's organ): consisting of two pitlike openings in the roof of the mouth or in the nasal septum, this organ, in non-human mammals, provides a pathway that links pheromones to a hormone response and to sex differences in behavior. "Frithing" is a term used to describe sucking in air over the pit-like entrance to this organ, which is in the roof of the mouth in some animals. Cats can sometimes be observed curling their upper lip when smelling something funky; this is also called the flehman response, usually associated with examination of urine, marking scents, etc. Snakes perform similar sampling by drawing in scents from the air on their flicking tongues. Humans have vomeronasal pits, though they are very small and somewhat difficult to find; they may play a role in mate choice and other behaviors. A 1995 journal article warned plastic surgeons to preserve the human vomeronasal organ during reconstructive surgery, lest damage lead to loss of sexual interest and subsequent litigation.

Vomeropherin: a marketing term for a pheromone detected by the human vomeronasal organ (the same as a mammalian pheromone detected by the mammalian VNO).

Xenotransplant: transplant of nonhuman tissues and organs into humans. Xenotransplants in the past have involved baboon and other ape organs. Most xenotransplant research now focuses on pig tissues and organs. Xenotransplants could be risky because of the existence of latent viruses within the donor tissues. (See *ERV, herpes, PERV.*) The case of Mrs. Carla Rhine described in this novel is unlikely in real life; Mrs. Rhine's maladies come from the unfortunate combination of a relatively rare evolutionary viral event and transplantation. Nevertheless, the possibilities of viral contamination or viral recombination within human recipients of animal tissues is very real, and demands further research.

A concise, elegantly written and conservative view of neo-Darwinian evolutionary theory is available in Richard Dawkins's *River out of Eden: A Darwinian View of Life*, BasicBooks, 1995. Dawkins is one of our best science writers and an excellent whetstone for anyone wishing to challenge institutionalized views of biology and evolution. It is my belief that he is wrong on many points, but he defines the debate in ways few others can.

Published more recently, and going into more detail, Ernst Mayr's summing up of a life's work, *What Evolution Is* (2002, Perseus Books) makes another clear and unyielding statement of the paradigm of modern Darwinism. There will probably be no finer exponents of the old view of Darwinian evolution.

The new view is emerging even as we speak.

Stephen Jay Gould is unfortunately no longer with us. I recommend all of his learned and impassioned books and essays, but in particular the flawed, and for that reason no less fascinating and instructive, *Wonderful Life* (Norton, 1989).

A good bridge to a larger understanding of the turmoil in evolutionary theory is Niles Eldredge's *Reinventing Darwin: The Great Debate at the High Table of Evolutionary Theory*, Wiley, 1995. Eldredge and Gould are currently credited with a particular view of evolutionary leaps known as *punctuated equilibrium*, but the idea can be traced back at least to masters such as Ernst Mayr, and even back to Darwin. Wherever it comes from, punctuated equilibrium was one of the key stimuli to my writing *Darwin's Radio*. Gould and Eldredge should not be blamed for my elaborations, however.

Peter J. Bowler's *The Non-Darwinian Revolution: Reinterpreting a Historical Myth* (1988, Johns Hopkins) is scholarly and entertaining at once.

A fine introduction to genetics is *Dealing with Genes: The Language of*

Heredity by Paul Berg and Maxine Singer, 1992, University Science Books. Though a decade old, its information is still useful and its attitude is forward-looking. It could prepare the reader for the following books.

Lynn Margulis and Dorion Sagan have published an excellent critique of neo-Darwinianism in *Acquiring Genomes: A Theory on the Origins of Species*, 2002, BasicBooks. Margulis is a pioneer in thinking about cooperative and symbiotic systems, and she and her son Dorion make up the single most stimulating popular writing team in modern biology.

More radical still, but just as polite and level-headed as Margulis, is Lynn Caporale, whose *Darwin in the Genome: Molecular Strategies in Biological Evolution* (2003, McGraw-Hill) is a clear and thoughtful examination of how genomics will shape and mutate the debate on evolution.

Lamarck's Signature: How Retrogenes are Changing Darwin's Natural Selection Paradigm, by Edward J. Steele, Robyn A. Lindley, and Robert V. Blanden (1998, Perseus Books) focuses on one possible cause and arbiter of genomic variation.

A key text in modern biology is *Retroviruses*, edited by John M. Coffin, Stephen H. Hughes, and Harold E. Varmus, 1997, Cold Spring Harbor Laboratory Press. Mostly for professionals, this rigorous and pioneering collection of monographs is filled with useful information.

Of particular relevance to my two novels is *Lateral DNA Transfer* by Frederic Bushman, 2002, Cold Spring Harbor Laboratory Press, is an important synopsis of what is currently known about DNA transfer through viruses, transposons, plasmids, etc. I think it is one of the most significant biology books published in the last decade.

James V. Kohl's *The Scent of Eros* (1995; reprinted in a revised edition, 2002, Continuum) is a rich source of information on pheromones, human communication through smell, and the influence of scent on sexuality.

There's a wealth of fine writing on these topics in many other popular science books, textbooks, and magazines. Searching on author names and topics in online bookstores can be a good way to leapfrog through diverse subjects. Which leads us to a very small sampling of Web sites.

Searching on key words in Web engines such as Google ("HERV," "Retrotransposon," "Barbara McClintock," "*Homo erectus*," "Mitochondria," etc.) can lead the curious reader into a combination paradise and mine field of articles peer-reviewed and otherwise, research goals and updates, opinions, and quite a few rants of varying degrees of erudition. Caveats abound—there are dozens if not hundreds of Creationist and other religiously motivated, anti-evolution sites that seem to discuss evolution and genetics with some lucidity, for a while. Generally speaking, the science here is dubious at best.

Nevertheless, searching on Google is how I located excellent articles by Luis P. Villarreal. In particular, I was influenced by Villarreal's "The Viruses That Make Us: A Role For Endogenous Retrovirus In The Evolution Of Placental Species," available on the Web at http://darwin.bio.uci.edu/~faculty/villarreal/new1/erv-placental.html

(Dr. Villarreal, Eric Larsson, and Howard Temin should not, however, be blamed for all the uses their ideas are put to in this novel.)

James V. Kohl's Web site, www.pheromones.com, provides a number of links to articles and other sites that discuss the biology of smell. The Web site of the Molecular Sciences Institute, www.molsci.org, is filled with interesting news and developments. The International Paleopsychology Project, www.paleopsych.org, is a clearing house of fascinating ideas with many links to other Web sites.

Periodically, I will post bibliographical updates on www.gregbear.com, as well as comments from readers about the theoretical underpinnings of the *Darwin* novels.

ACKNOWLEDGMENTS

Special thanks to Mark Minie, Ph.D., and Rose James, Ph.D.; Deirdre V. Lovecky, Ph.D.; Dr. Joseph Miller; Dominic Esposito of the National Cancer Institute; Dr. Elizabeth Kutter; Cleone Hawkinson; Alison Stenger, Ph.D.; David and Diane Clark; Brian W. J. Mahy, Ph.D., Sc.D., director of the Division of Viral and Rickettsial Diseases at the Center for Disease Control; Karl H. Anders, M.D.; Sylvia Anders, M.D.; Howard Bloom and the International Paleopsychology Project; Cynthia Robbins-Roth, Ph.D., James V. Kohl, Oliver Morton, Karen Anderson, Lynn Caporale, and Roger Brent, Ph.D.